By Elliott James

Pax Arcana
Charming
Daring
Fearless

Pax Arcana Short Fiction
Charmed, I'm Sure
Don't Go Chasing Waterfalls
Pushing Luck
Surreal Estate
Dog-Gone
A Load of Bull
Talking Dirty

**And now it was time to pay the piper. I mean sniper.
No, wait...I was...oh, forget it.**

"John?!?" Sig said, then yelled, "GET OUT OF HERE!"

Right, like she had everything under control. As if to disprove that very thought, her words became the drop that burst the dam, and all of the tension and contained violence burst loose.

That's when we found out that we had all greatly underestimated Sig.

That's when the ghosts came out.

Praise for *Charming*

Daring

PAX ARCANA: BOOK 2

ELLIOTT JAMES

www.orbitbooks.net

Orbit
Hachette Book Group
1290 Avenue of the Americas, New York, NY 10104
www.HachetteBookGroup.com

Printed in the United States of America

RRD-C

First edition: September 2014

10 9 8 7 6 5 4 3 2

Orbit is an imprint of Hachette Book Group, Inc. The Orbit name and logo are trademarks of Little, Brown Book Group Limited.

The Hachette Speakers Bureau provides a wide range of authors for speaking events. To find out more, go to www.hachettespeakersbureau.com or call (866) 376-6591.

The publisher is not responsible for websites (or their content) that are not owned by the publisher.

Library of Congress Cataloging-in-Publication Data
James, Elliott.
    Daring : Pax Arcana Book 2 / Elliott James.—First edition.
    pages cm.—(Pax Arcana ; 2)
    ISBN 978-0-316-25340-6 (trade pbk.)—ISBN 978-0-316-25341-3 (ebook)
    I. Title.
    PS3610.A4334D37 2014
    813'.6—dc23

                                                            2013051024

To Marta

*NOW this is the law of the jungle, as old and as true as
    the sky,
And the wolf that shall keep it may prosper, but the
    wolf that shall break it must die.*

*As the creeper that girdles the tree trunk, the law
    runneth forward and back;
For the strength of the pack is the wolf, and the
    strength of the wolf is the pack.*

From "The Law for the Wolves"
by Rudyard Kipling

*Love will find a way through paths where wolves fear
    to prey.*

Lord Byron

PART THE FIRST

*It's My Party and I'll Die
If I Want To*

Prelude

TEN THINGS THAT PEOPLE WHO DIDN'T READ THE FIRST BOOK REALLY OUGHT TO KNOW

I. One day, your father and mother were hugging, and they began to have special feelings. Warm feelings that tingled in their private places. It is likely they weren't wearing any clothes. At any rate, they began to rub against each other like two sticks trying to start a fire, and nine months later, you were born. If this is news to you, please put this book down now. There may well be big bad wolves and evil witches and faeries in the pages that follow, but I promise you, this isn't a children's story.

II. The supernatural is real.

III. You probably don't believe me about point #2 because most of the world is under a spell called the Pax Arcana. This enchantment keeps humans from noticing or accepting any evidence of the supernatural that is not an immediate threat to their survival.

IV. The existence of the Pax Arcana is the real legendary secret guarded by the Knights Templar. Not the Holy Grail, not the secret family tree of Jesus Christ and Mary Magdalene, not the treasure hoard of King Solomon, not a vast political or corporate conspiracy to ruuullllle the world. No, it's the Pax Arcana.

V. Knights are bound to maintain the Pax by a geas, a magical compulsion that passes down from generation to generation like any other family curse. In exchange for being bound, knights enjoy a certain amount of protection against the supernatural; we cannot be compelled, beguiled, or enthralled because we are already compelled, beguiled, and enthralled.

VI. As you might have gathered from that "we," I was once a knight. I was pretty good at it too, until I came down with a mild case of werewolf. Now I'm one of the monsters being hunted.

VII. My name is John Charming. You know all of those stories about guys called Prince Charming who were going around slaying monsters and rescuing maidens and getting magically cursed left and right? That's my family you're reading about, a long line of monster hunters though none of my ancestors were ever actually princes. For that matter, I'm pretty sure that not all of the women they were chasing were actually maidens either.

VIII. I lived on the run and off the grid for a very long time, but while I was hiding in a small southwestern Virginia town called Clayburg, I got caught up in a war between a vampire hive and a small group of monster hunters. Think of the latter as the modern-day equivalent of a mob with torches.

IX. The monster hunters were being led by two psychics: Stanislav Dvornik, an asshat who could see the future, and Sig Norresdotter, a descendant of Valkyries who could see dead people. There was also an Episcopalian priest on mental leave named Molly Newman, an exterminator turned ghost hunter named Chauncy "Choo" Childers, and a cop, Ted Cahill, whose definition of "bad guy" had been considerably expanded in recent years. I got involved because I thought I was rescuing them. In every way that mattered, they rescued me.

X. Sig Norresdotter and I developed feelings for each other. We only spent a short time together, but it was a very intense short time. To give you an idea of how intense, let me add that Stanislav Dvornik didn't like what was happening between me and Sig, and all of this drama was going on in the middle of an ongoing vampire hunt. There was confusion and lots of screaming and hurt feelings all around. Blood was shed, comrades were betrayed, magazine subscriptions got canceled, somebody ate the chicken salad that somebody else left in the fridge, and when the dust settled, Stanislav was dead. So were the vampires, although I suppose in their case they were dead again. Or for real dead this time.

XI. I left Clayburg, but I was worried about Sig and her small band of vigilantes because I didn't know how vigorously the knights who were after me might try to question them. I "left" Clayburg, but I kind of didn't leave Clayburg. I mean, I told everyone I was leaving Clayburg, but I'm very good at skulking. Not sulking. Not stalking. Skulking.

XII. And I know I said this prelude was about ten things, but there's something else you ought to know: I get things wrong sometimes.

~1~

ONCE UPON A TIME BOMB

Once upon a time, Chauncy "Choo" Childers made himself a secret lair. He was a monster hunter who had just helped kill a vampire queen, and there were these trained killers from the Knights Templar sniffing around Clayburg, and Choo thought it might be a good time to hole up some place where he would be hard to find for a while. Choo's new front door was a slab of metal built into the side of an overpass. The overpass used to be near a power plant, but the power plant had moved on a long time ago, so maybe I should call the overpass an overpassed. Or maybe an overpassé. Whatever you call it, the overpass had that feel that dead and deserted places have— even the spray-painted graffiti was faded to the point where it was barely legible, not that it had ever said anything particularly new. I'm here. I'm angry. I'm scared. I'm lonely. Somebody care. What traffic the overpass still got was mostly during commuting hours.

Maybe Choo's new home sounds a little extreme or paranoid, but I don't think you can call Choo extremely paranoid. For one thing, he was an exterminator, and cleaning up abandoned and vermin-infested places was second nature to him. For another, vague pronouns really were out to get him.

THEY arrived at dawn. I know, that's like saying it was a dark and stormy night, but modern-day knights really do like to attack at dawn; it's early enough to ensure few witnesses, and the rising sun discourages nocturnal predators.

The knights approached in two groups of three. One team emerged from the surrounding woods on the east side. Another team exited from a van that pulled up to the west side of the overpass and stopped. It was a pretty good bet that the knights had blocked access farther down the road from both sides, even if all that meant was putting up phony construction or detour signs. It's what I would have done, and these were the bastards who trained me. Or their great-grandfathers were.

The trios walked in loose triangle formations, spread out and advancing at a casual pace that was at odds with the alert purpose in their body language. They thought they had a sniper covering them from the woods, but that was no longer true.

Instead, they had me. Me and an M40A1, an old-school Marine sniper rifle. I was getting a good look at them through its scope while the rifle's original owner slept pacified and zip-tied next to me.

From a purely pragmatic point of view, getting involved probably wasn't a good idea. Choo was only sort of a friend of mine. I liked him but didn't really know him very well. To be honest, I'm not sure that anyone knew Choo very well. Choo had become aware of the existence of the supernatural after trying to exterminate the wrong damned house, and even when not holing up beneath an overpass, Choo lived alone in a house whose basement was full of stockpiled weapons. Choo's house was a reflection of the man himself; normal and friendly enough on the surface but full of secrets that had pointy edges and burned.

Maybe that was why we got along.

In any case, I don't have a lot of friends, and Choo and I had fought together and bled together and watched each other's backs. If that's not a close friendship, it's close enough for me.

Close enough for the Knights Templar too, apparently.

I didn't know the knights' exact motives for being there, but I did know that the rifle I had acquired held silver bullets. Maybe my old brethren just wanted to ask Choo some questions since Choo had spent some time around me. Maybe they wanted to ask those questions forcefully. Maybe they wanted to scare Choo and see if he had any way of contacting me, or threaten him on the off chance that I really was stupid enough to stay in the area. Maybe they wanted to take Choo prisoner and see if I would try to free him, or kill him to see if I would try to avenge him. The problem was, the knights were capable of doing any or all of those things. Their geas only prevents knights from killing supernatural beings without good cause. Normal humans are fair game. Or unfair game, for that matter. Humans are a game without rules.

The knights weren't wearing anything that looked like a standard uniform. They wore light hoodies and thermal shirts and flannel, predominantly in dark colors. Most of them were wearing running shoes and blue jeans, a few of them boots and camouflage clothing. They all wore headgear with brims, either baseball or hunting or painting caps. We were on the outer, more rural rim of Clayburg, and if things went to hell, the knights could scatter and merge into the local population fairly easily.

As soon as they were under the overpass, the knights pulled a variety of weapons out from under their jackets and loose shirts. There would be more sidearms and small blades concealed on their bodies as well. I couldn't see them, but they were there. It was as sure as gravity. As time passing. As the sun.

"You're not fooling anyone, Norresdotter." The knight speaking was on my side of the overpass, and I have very good hearing. He was addressing the lone homeless person sleeping there, a bundle of army surplus clothing.

Sig Norresdotter, also known as the woman I'm carefully avoiding using the word "love" around, emerged from the pile and drew herself up to her full six feet of height and twelve feet of attitude, throwing off an olive green field jacket that was too large for her and pulling off a stocking cap as if it burned. The long shining hair that was her only concession to vanity spilled free. Even in that dim light and from that distance, it looked like liquid gold, like the sun's rays rippling on the surface of a lake, like... oh hell, I really am in a bad way. I don't care; she was a flare of brightness in a gray world. Sig also had a long sword sheathed between her shoulder blades and a SIG Sauer holstered at her hip, though she had been smart enough not to draw them. It was possible there was a spear hidden around somewhere too.

Did I mention that Sig was a Valkyrie?

"I'm not here to fool you, Emil," Sig informed him. "I just don't want to draw attention from anyone else."

It's possible the two of them had some past acquaintance. It's also possible that Emil was living with one or more ghosts, and that the spirit of some being Emil had killed or loved was chatting in Sig's ear at that very moment. That kind of thing happens around Sig a lot. Trust me.

Either way, if Emil was unnerved by Sig's use of his name, he didn't show any sign of it. "And why are you here, Norresdotter?"

"To stop you from harassing Choo, you assjacket," Sig said. A bored *of course* lingered in her tone.

Sig was putting up a good front, but she had been through a

lot recently. She had been held prisoner by an undead sociopath and sedated, and that terrified her in a way that death did not, because Sig had some substance abuse issues in her past. There was also the matter of me killing her former lover, although in my defense, he was a complete douche canoe. Oh, and he tried to kill me first. Creatively.

That kind of stuff doesn't just slide off.

"You must know we are prepared for you, Sig," Emil chided with a tone that was somehow more threatening for being gentle.

"I am a supernatural being and no threat to the Pax," Sig reminded him, leaning against the door to Choo's sanctuary. "Your geas won't let you harm me without good cause, and you're not here for a good cause."

"We don't have to harm you to get you out of our way," Emil said. "Not permanently."

Sig pounded the back of her head against the door as if frustrated, but a moment later she seemed alarmed.

"Choo?" Sig called. Apparently the pounding on the door had been some kind of signal, but nothing was happening and Sig didn't know why.

I knew why.

The answer was lying open on the ground about ten feet away from me. The bastards had opened a witch bottle. The small brown jug was slightly rounded, glazed with salt, and covered with dag runes. The red wax seal had been broken, and the tip of red thread emerging from the open neck of the bottle told me what kind of creature it had contained: a sprite.

In the old days, sprites were bound by cunning folk and used as scouts, spies, and messengers—think Ariel in *The Tempest*. Nowadays, though, sprites are more often used to disable perimeter defenses.

Basically, sprites are tourists from another dimension. It takes a lot of energy for them to condense and pull air molecules together into a physical form here, which is why they usually manifest as tiny winged creatures; that size doesn't take as much energy, and the wings help them get around quickly despite their itsy-bitsy bodies. This is also why sprites disrupt energy transmissions. Sprites can cause security cameras to stop working, cell phones to stop receiving, generators to stutter off, and radio signals to jam. When sent on a specific mission, they can also squeeze into tight cracks and pull wires or snap fan belts or undo nuts and bolts.

Sometimes sprites are referred to as gremlins.

Whatever surprise Choo and Sig had rigged for the knights—and it could have been just about anything from sonics to gases to explosions, because Choo loves his toys—the sprite had made it malfunction.

"My turn," Emil said, and held up a palm. Then he held up his palm some more. Now it was Emil's turn to be nonplussed. He was waiting for sniper fire from my position.

So I gave him some.

I'd had plenty of time to line up and sight, so I took an easy shot at a riot gun. The knight holding it was facing me on the far side of the overpass, and the bullet hit the fat butt of the wooden shotgun stock and tore the weapon out of his grasp.

Nobody in the center of the overpass dove for cover, mainly because there was none. Emil remained where he was, his palm still in the air. Then Emil said, in a voice that was distinctly pleased, "He's here."

Shit, shit, shit, shit. Shitting shitty shittiness. It wasn't that I hadn't expected this. It was that this was exactly what I had expected. Hell, I'd been waiting for this domino to fall since

I first allowed myself to develop some relationships again. Which was shit. Shit, shit, shit.

All I can say is, I'd been lonely past the point of being damaged by it. I'd known the smart moves, told myself I would make them, and instead did the opposite because I had gotten to a point where risking death seemed better than not living.

And now it was time to pay the piper. I mean sniper. No, wait...I was...oh, forget it.

"John?!?" Sig said, then yelled, "GET OUT OF HERE!"

Right, like she had everything under control. As if to disprove that very thought, her words became the drop that burst the dam, and all of the tension and contained violence burst loose.

That's when we found out that we had all greatly underestimated Sig.

That's when the ghosts came out.

❦2❦

THAT'S THE SPIRITS!

Sig is stronger, faster, and tougher than any normal human, but the thing that really makes Sig a Valkyrie is her ability to communicate with the dead.

You know what they say: if she looks like a Valkyrie, bench-presses small cars like a Valkyrie, and developed feelings for you after having conversations with the ghost of your dead lover like a Valkyrie, she's probably a Valkyrie.

Wait. Nobody says that?

Anyhow, consider the nature of ghosts and overpasses. Ghosts are spirits who die unfulfilled or in some particularly traumatic fashion, and people who die under overpasses often do so in unpleasant ways. Homeless people looking for shelter from the weather freeze to death in them, or die from ruptured livers, weak hearts, burst appendixes, thrown clots, or any combination of physical breakdowns that are the accumulation of years of loneliness and desperation. People overdose in over-passes. People are dragged into them to be raped or robbed or set on fire for entertainment. There is a reason that there are so many stories about monsters living under bridges, and it's not just that some of them are true.

Sig had been spending a lot of time in the overpass for the last few days while guarding Choo's back, and apparently she had been talking a lot. You know. To the dead.

Imagine what it must be like to be a ghost, to be lonely and desperate and stuck in the same place for decade after decade after decade after the best and brightest parts of you have moved on, suffering and never fully understanding why or how to make it stop. Hopefully, you have to imagine very hard. But imagine that after all that time, someone finally comes around who can hear you and is willing to listen.

Now imagine someone attacking that person right in front of you.

A knight hiding in the open van tried to shoot Sig with a rifle similar to the one that I was using, only to discover that the rifle was disassembling, falling to the ground in a rain of metal while some helpful soul field-stripped it. He tried to hold on to the stock—not a rational impulse—and it suddenly stopped resisting and slammed into his face.

Another knight, this one holding a souped-up cattle prod capable of knocking out a buffalo, suddenly had the sensation of falling. He wasn't actually falling, mind you. The shadow he was casting on the floor was thickening, rising, moving over him and clinging to him like tar.

A knight with another riot shotgun was simply picked up and tossed aside like a bad idea, hurled through the air, and bounced off a concrete wall in a way that made crunching and snapping sounds.

A knight with a sawed-off shotgun discovered that the barrels of his weapon were unaccountably clogged with ice.

A moment later, he realized that he could not feel any sensation in the hand holding the sawed-off. When he finally managed to violently fling the weapon away from him, it took most of his hand with it.

Sig doesn't control the dead, but she knew the overpass was a hotspot, a breeding ground for paranormal infections that she had been treating for days. And the thing about infections is, as they get better, the bad stuff is pushed closer and closer to the surface, where it can be expelled.

The knight with the katana discovered one of the drawbacks of fighting a western blade; katana have no metal guard to protect their owners' fingers from horizontal strokes—you know, that thin bar that looks like brass knuckles and covers the middle joints of a saber wielder's hand. This is great when a katana wielder wants to put both hands on a hilt in a blindingly fast and devastating sword strike. It is not so good when he or she is facing someone who is faster than they are and waving a heavy long sword around as if it were a fencing foil.

The katana-wielding knight lost half his fingers. The upper halves. His yell was also cut off, and quickly, by an abnormally strong elbow to his jaw.

I really didn't see the rest because a mist was manifesting, a swirling fog that somehow looked cold, although I would be hard-pressed to explain why, since it was rising instead of drifting downward. It just didn't look like a fog that cared a lot about physics. The fog seemed to muffle nearby sounds, but it also seemed to conduct vague and disharmonious noises from some faraway place. I heard laughter, then chanting, then cries. There was definitely a muffled explosion and a lot of yells, but the shouts were from the knights in the overpass, and they sounded a lot more distant than they should have.

Emil was not one of the shouting knights. Emil was walking

calmly out of the tunnel and toward me without looking back, speaking clearly and distinctly.

"That explosion was a wall coming down," Emil explained genially. "Right now, two of us are entering Chauncey Childers's bolt-hole from an adjacent heating duct."

This actually made me smile. My hearing was a lot better than Emil's, and that explosion had been a concussion grenade. Emil's two knights were trying to break into the lair of a man who had a passion for designing weapons and traps, and it wasn't going as well as Emil thought. But any momentary flash of satisfaction I felt was wiped out by his next words.

"There's also a team outside the cabin where your friend Molly Newman is nursing the police detective, Ted Cahill."

Yeah, I know, I've barely mentioned those two. They had gotten into the same fight with a vampire hive that had scarred the rest of us. Ted was either dying or becoming undead, while Molly, the group's priest, was keeping vigil over him.

"And even if you all escape us today, your friends will never be safe again," Emil went on relentlessly. "They might win this battle, but we'll never stop until they're dead, and there are thousands of us. Thousands of us who know how to use explosives and poisons and long-distance weapons. You know that, I think."

I really wanted to shoot this asshole.

"Shoot me if you want," Emil added. "But if you do, your friends start dying. I am offering you a one-time deal. Turn yourself in to me, right now, and we will never bother your friends again unless they do something that violates the Pax. On my honor."

Sig came walking out of the tunnel behind Emil, her sword held in one hand. Her hair was wild but her eyes were focused. She was staring at the small of Emil's back as if she could rip the bones out of it by willpower alone.

Elliott James

Behind Sig, the ghosts began to quiet and the fog slowly dispelled. Even small supernatural manifestations take a lot of energy. That's why temperatures drop and lights flicker when ghosts appear; like sprites, spirits have to absorb energy from the environment in order to pull themselves all the way on to this plane.

Sighting my rifle, I did the only thing I could. I shot Sig on the left side of her skull.

Oh, relax. Silver bullets are softer than normal bullets, and Sig's bones are harder than normal bones. She had recently survived a bullet directly to the back of her head and woke up with nothing more than a migraine to show for it. I was a good enough shot to crease her skull, and even if I wasn't, the bullet wouldn't penetrate, anyhow. Sig didn't heal as fast as I did, but her ability to recuperate was more than human, and I wasn't worried about any permanent brain damage. The bullet's impact did slosh Sig's brain around enough to drop her, though.

I threw the rifle down.

Emil had paused at the sound of the shot, perhaps watching a mental film reel of his life's greatest hits, but after a moment he realized that he was still breathing.

"You've made the right decision," he assured me.

Uh-huh. My right hand shot out into midair and my fingers sank into slippery, translucent flesh. Sprites are very curious, and this one had thought itself safe because it wasn't willing itself to reflect light. It had no way of knowing that my senses were sharp and my reflexes fast. I won't say my heart was pure, but I did have the strength of three men.

The sprite started to ooze between my fingers, and I brought the top of my fist to my mouth and bared my teeth. The slick organic wriggling stopped.

"We need to talk," I growled.

❧ 3 ❧

THERE'S A LOT OF WHAT'S COMING GOING AROUND

Emil walked up to where I had the sniper bound. I had dropped the M40A1 in favor of my own Ruger Blackhawk, and the sprite was making itself visible, flashing around us in a strobe effect. When the little bastards do decide to reflect light, they like to show off.

Up close, Emil looked worn and tough, a hard and rangy man in his fifties with brown hair salted with gray. His skin was leather, his eyes were flint, and his heart was a lump of coal that wasn't becoming a diamond any time soon. He was missing half his left earlobe and the top of his right pinky. "The sniper was always a long shot. No pun intended."

"Just so we're clear," I said, "I'll let you take me in. But that's all. I'm not agreeing to be your prisoner for life. If I get a chance to escape after that, I'll take it. The sprite here has agreed to witness the contract."

Emil gave me a stony look. There are rules among the old races, and if it became known among the supernatural community that knights no longer honored promises of amnesty or truce, the knights' hard lives would become infinitely harder. "You won't get a chance to escape."

"Then you have nothing to lose. Make your offer formally in front of the sprite."

"On my word of honor, no Knights Templar will harm or harass your friends if you come with me now," Emil said softly. "And I swear as the knight who has been officially chosen to bring you in by the Grandmaster of the Order himself, it is within my power to make that promise."

"And the Knights Templar won't hire or encourage or manipulate anyone else into doing it, either," I said firmly. "Or attack other people close to my friends. They are hereby bound to honor the spirit of this agreement as well as the literal meaning of it, and you will report that to your loremaster."

"Agreed," Emil said with a sudden expression that was a smile the same way a tiger is a housecat; they had something in common, but only if you got extremely technical or optimistic.

"And I'll let you take me to your superiors," I said, ignoring the dark flash of amusement in his eyes. "And I won't attempt to escape until after I talk to them, unless someone tries to restrain or kill me."

"That is acceptable," Emil said.

I addressed the sprite tonelessly. "Thank you; you can go now."

The sprite disappeared, and Emil waited for me to make the first move.

"There's one more thing," I said. "Sig has to believe that I took you captive, not the other way around."

Emil remained inscrutable.

"I can't see this working any other way," I continued. "If Sig even thinks I'm trying to give my life for hers, she'll come after both of us."

"She's going to declare war on the Knights Templar," Emil repeated mildly, just so I could hear how stupid that sounded.

"She might."

To his credit, Emil absorbed that thoughtfully. "What exactly are you proposing?"

"I'm going to take you all captive and drive the van out of here," I informed him. "I'll release you after I've talked to Sig and we're safely out of sight."

"I never agreed to that," Emil said, and then he didn't say anything else. It's hard to say anything else when you're lying unconscious on the ground.

～4～

EXIT STAGE WRONG

Do you want to wake her up?" I asked Choo. I had carried Sig back to the overpass and found Choo cautiously inspecting the bodies there. Now we were both looking down at Sig's prone form.

Choo made an *after you* gesture. "You're the one who heals fast."

He had a point, so I kicked the bottom of her boot experimentally.

Choo grinned, maybe for the first time since killing Andrej Dvornik. "I thought you Charming boys woke your women up with a kiss."

"Those are just stories," I observed. "And none of my ancestors had to worry about getting their collarbones broken."

I kicked Sig's boot a little harder and she lunged upward violently, cursing and reaching for the long sword that was no longer in her back sheath.

"You're really not a morning person, are you?" I greeted. I didn't really feel like joking around, but I had to make the effort or Sig would suspect something.

Choo and I had been busy. The van was parked closer, its rear doors open so that Sig could see knights stacked in the back storage compartment like cordwood. We had drugged them with their own tranks and chained them with their own chains, and the tops of the heads of a few others were visibly slumped against the back seat, their owners held in place by gravity and seat belts.

"What happened?" Sig asked.

"The sniper had a backup sniper," I informed her, praying fervently that she wouldn't count the bodies. "I took him out."

Sig smiled faintly at that, then winced when the expression pulled skin tightly over her temple. "You still shouldn't be here."

"I know." I handed her the SIG Sauer she claims to have been named after, though that sounds a little too cool to be true. I've always suspected that Sig's birth name is Dorcas or Hulga or something.

She stood up and took the gun with another grimace. This time, the pain didn't seem to be entirely physical. "We didn't need you today, you know. Choo had my back."

"You don't have to get defensive," I reassured her. "You had them. I'm the one who shot you."

Yeah, like I really said that. The thought did go through me like a colonoscopy, though.

What I actually said was: "The whole reason you're in trouble is because of me."

"You've got to get your head on straight about death," Sig scolded. "Especially since you're around so much of it."

I don't know why that stung. It was nothing but the truth.

"Well, I'm pissed at him," Choo said. "Does that count?"

Sig stared at Choo as if measuring him for a body cast.

Choo ignored her and looked at me instead. "I didn't sign up for this, and I don't want to sleep with you, either. No offense."

"Choo." Sig's voice sounded a little strangled. "John's saved your life at least twice! If you died because of him right now, you'd still be ahead of the game."

Choo didn't like that. "I only needed saving because your last boyfriend went crazy, and that was *because* of John."

That's not really true. I didn't cause Stanislav Dvornik's psychotic break. I exposed it. I could smell "sick animal" coming off that asshole the first time he darkened my door. Choo wasn't really arguing about what he was arguing about, though.

Sig seemed to think so too. "Choo, could John and I have some privacy?"

Choo indicated the scene around us. "Don't look like it."

"Choo." If she had gotten in his face or threatened him, he might have dug in, but she sounded disappointed, and he relented.

"Nothing personal, man," he muttered to me. "Good luck."

"Yeah," I said. "You too."

I watched him go, and when I turned to look at Sig she was closer to me.

Was it crazy that I'd missed her? My whole life, I'd made fun of the idea of love at first sight, and I had fallen for Sig pretty hard, pretty fast. But let's be honest: I had a pretty big emotional void looking for something to fill it.

"Have you been stalking me this whole time?" She wasn't as angry as she was trying to sound. I would have smelled it.

"Not in a pervy way," I said. "Dammit."

Sig had a habit of regarding me steadily. I liked it. We were within arm's reach of each other when she said, "I don't know how to say hi to you."

I knew what she meant. We'd agreed to cool it in the romance department until we got our lives back under control, and that obviously wasn't going too well. But a handshake didn't exactly seem to cover it, either.

So I bent down, took her left hand, and kissed her middle finger lightly. "Hi, Sig."

I didn't let go when I straightened up. My thumb stroked the top of her hand while our fingers interlocked. I always wanted more with her. She was like Chinese food, which might explain why I don't write a lot of love sonnets.

Sig leaned forward and kissed my cheek. "Hi."

My mouth was suddenly dry. "We probably shouldn't take too much time."

"What are you planning?" Sig asked suspiciously.

"Something you won't like," I admitted. "But I guarantee I'm going to get the knights' attention off of you and the others."

"You could try to get help, you know," she said. "There are werewolf packs out there who would probably accept you. Parth says there's a huge one in the Midwest that's already giving the knights the finger. He could get you in touch with it."

Parth was the hacker in Sig's merry little band of monster hunters and also a supernatural being in his own right, a naga. Sig trusted him. I did not.

"The one calling itself a clan?" I asked. "No thanks."

Sig leveled her eyes at me like interrogation lamps. "You will not throw your life away. No beau geste. No kamikaze plans."

She was too smart for my own good.

"Sig…" I began, and she put a finger on my lips with her free hand.

"Shut up. Your life is worth as much as mine. Maybe more. I'm no princess."

I took her left hand and kissed it too, just to be fair. "You're acting like I have a lot of safe choices here."

God, I wanted to kiss her. I think she felt the pull too. At any rate, she pulled me forward slightly and we touched foreheads.

"I know there's a part of you that's ready to die for somebody else because you didn't get a chance with Alison," she said. "I don't want to be something you have to prove to yourself. And I don't like that you're admitting so much, either. Whatever you're hiding must really be stupid."

I didn't like hiding things from Sig. I hadn't from the first moment I'd met her. I'd been up-front with her when it would have been smarter to hold back, trusted her when I barely knew her, and put us both in danger because of it. And I didn't have any excuse for it. She made me selfish, and for some reason that felt like love.

And it had to stop. I have had one true love, and Alison died because she knew me. I had only just started to crawl out from under that weight, and Sig was a large part of the reason why. The idea of having knights kill Sig too was . . . nightmare. Anathema. Poison. Antimatter. There's no word for it.

Unfortunately, even though I'm a Charming, I'm really not all that good at acting noble. I haven't had a lot of practice. I didn't have a speech prepared about it being a far, far, better thing I did than any I had ever done before or whatever. I was scared. I admit it. I usually channel fear into fighting or planning or running or joking. Giving myself up was messing with me. I didn't want to die, but I wasn't going to let anyone else I cared about get killed because of me, and I kind of wished she would just shut the fuck up and let me say my lines.

But I couldn't say any of that.

So instead, I said, "I have to go."

"Don't give me that cowboy crap," she snapped. "I know you have to go! The question is whether or not I'm coming after you."

I almost pointed out that she couldn't come after me if I was dead. Then it occurred to me that maybe she could.

Talk about high maintenance.

"Here." She removed a ring from her pocket and tried it on my right index finger. With a little bit of encouragement, it fit.

I took the ring off and examined it suspiciously. It was plain gold and didn't have any stave runes or markings that I could see. I'd never seen it on Sig's hand before, but if it had any kind of tracking magic or charm on it, the ring wouldn't work because of my geas, anyway.

"That was my father's," Sig said. "I want you to bring it back to me."

"Sig," I protested.

"Knights wear tokens, right?" Sig persisted. "I want you to remember me."

"That's not going to be a problem," I assured her.

"Just wear it, all right?" she said. "Promise."

The gesture seemed a little un-Siggish, but what was I going to say? That the knights were sure to remove the ring when they took me into custody?

"All right," I said reluctantly.

I don't know if I loved her. We had chemistry. Her skin felt like some amalgam of silk and honey and sunlight. I liked her. I wanted her, wanted her so badly that it felt like my body must be glowing with it. I understood some things about her that most people wouldn't get. I know that part of me didn't leave her.

Unfortunately, the rest of me did.

～5～

IT'S NEVER TOO LATE TO PANIC

Emil kept his word and left me unbound while examining the other knights and sending several of them off in the van to get bones set or core temperatures stabilized or body parts sewn back on. The guy really must have had some juice, because the other knights went along with it even though they obviously thought he was insane. The first and last knight who argued got assigned sewer duty in New York for a year.

A lot of things have changed since I was a knight. I doubt sewer duty is one of them.

I rode shotgun next to Emil while knights in two Dodge Chargers escorted us from front and behind. A burly young knight was in the backseat behind us.

"Would you mind getting me some Hershey's kisses out of the glove compartment?" Emil asked casually. "Eight?"

There was a small bag where Emil said it would be, and I counted eight of the candies out. I was trying to maintain my own façade of nerveless cool and appreciated his nonchalance. "Is there something significant about the number eight?"

"I'm not a werewolf," Emil informed me. "Or a young man. I count calories."

I nodded and put the bag back. "You seem pretty confident that I won't break my oath. And you know I care enough about other people to blackmail me with my friends' safety. Does it bother you at all, taking me in to be killed or tortured?"

So much for nonchalance.

The knight in the back stirred restlessly but Emil remained unperturbed. "A little. I've pieced together enough of your movements over the decades to know that you've probably killed more monsters than any knight alive."

From the way the knight's tongue was clicking, he was silently mouthing words that had a lot of "K" sounds. Suck? Fuck? Cock? Dick? Some combination of those words with suffixes and compounds, probably.

"Why did you decapitate Tobias Saunders and nail his head to a church door, by the way?" Emil went on. "Since we're just talking."

So that was the name of the knight who had killed Alison.

"I wasn't thinking too clearly at the time." The words came out strangled. My throat felt thick and my teeth didn't want to separate. "But I was letting you know that I'd had enough. That if you came looking for a monster, you'd find one."

"So it was a warning," Emil said. "Not a declaration of war."

"It was both," I said.

"And see where it got you," the knight in the back muttered, so quietly that I doubt Emil heard him.

"Speak up or shut up, you weak suck," I advised, tilting my head slightly to look over the seat.

"Go ahead and mock me," the knight said fiercely. "Kill me if you can. But at least I'll die with honor. It's too late for you."

I remember when the world was that simple. I miss that world. Or I miss the young boy who believed in it. I think I was three. "That's the advantage of embracing your inner coward," I said. "It's never too late to panic."

"It's easy to mock," he hissed. "Especially when you've perverted everything you ever believed in."

"That's true," I admitted. "What's not easy is getting a lecture on knightly ethics from some weak-ass honorless cowards who only got me to give myself up by threatening to kill innocent people."

The younger knight opened his mouth to hiss something, his face red and his eyes a little insane, but Emil finally intervened.

"Close your mouth, Stuart." Emil's voice was curt and vicious and crackled with authority. "Anger makes you weak and careless. He's playing you like a cheap fiddle."

Stuart backed down immediately.

Yeah, Emil was a problem.

"Well, you've been playing me like a flute," I told him. "So blow me."

Emil remained unflappable. "One of the teams looking for Tobias actually found his head before anyone else did, but when he died, the supernatural protection of his geas died with him. Psychics all over the world were having dreams of a dead knight with his head nailed to a church door by a werewolf."

"You're saying it caused you problems," I said slowly.

Emil shrugged. It was the first time that I could tell his casual pose wasn't real. His knuckles were slightly white on the steering wheel. "Your little gesture became a rallying point for a lot of supernaturals who resent us. You're a symbol of defiance."

No wonder they'd been looking for me so hard for so long.

"So there's not going to be any streamers saying *Welcome Back* when we get to wherever you're taking me?" I asked. "No balloons? No ice cream cake?"

Emil painted that humorless by-the-numbers smile over his face again. "There will be celebrating."

A Dodge Charger passed us slowly on my right, two knights glaring at me through its windows. I waved at them.

∽6∽

THE TRUTH IS A FLAMING SWORD

I don't remember being knocked out, and I don't remember arriving at the wilderness lodge and/or corporate retreat that the knights were using as a stronghold. I don't know if there was some kind of gas in the car that Emil and the knight had been immunized against, or if I picked up some kind of odorless contact poison, or if I was taken out later at some point by a sniper the moment I stepped out of the car.

If that seems strange, you have to consider that a knight's entire existence revolves around concealing events, and Templars were artists with drugs that destroy short-term memory long before Rohypnol became a synonym for date rape. Maybe they tortured me. Maybe I painted half my face blue and gave some impassioned speech about freedom before they shot the shit out of me. Maybe I fought, or escaped and was recaptured. Maybe I killed several people or had long philosophical conversations with a jailor about the meaning of existence.

I just don't know. That part of me is gone. Usually that kind of stuff comes back, because I regenerate damage, including damage to my brain, but the knights had been putting a lot of research into fighting werewolves lately, and they must have found some kind of chemical cocktail with permanent side effects.

All I know for sure is that I awoke druggily, and I know that "druggily" isn't really a word, but that's how I woke up, anyhow. It must have been the drugs.

There was something important, but I couldn't remember it. My secret, my secret, kept so well that even I didn't know what it was.

My vision lurched as it contracted and expanded without any prompting on my part. When I tried to focus, blackness began to close around the edge of my vision, and when I tried to shake my head, I realized that I couldn't feel my ears or my skull, but somehow my brain still felt tight. Everything sounded too loud but far away at the same time, as if I were underwater.

Room. Basement air. Heavy. Still. Chill. Not a basement, a dungeon. I was welded into a steel chair or felt like it. A centaur, except instead of a horse's trunk, my waist ended in four chair legs. A sitaur. Body cold and sweaty at the same time. Not fair, not fair. Seven men sat in padded wooden chairs, their bodies hard whether burly or lean, their skin weathered, their eyes old and cold.

I threw up.

This apparently was not unexpected. I heard Emil's voice, and two guards came and cleaned up my mess. There was still pain, a lot of pain, but someone else was feeling it.

Ever seen one of those old movies where brains have been removed, just floating in a jar of God knows what, pulsing? It felt like that was me, except my body was the jar. I don't know if that makes sense, but it's the closest I can come to describing the effects of whatever they had me on.

Somebody was saying something. Emil again. Wait...who

was Emil? I realized that this Emil someone had been saying something for some time.

I blinked three times, and I didn't wake up in Kansas, but there was a young boy standing in front of me. Where had he come from? For a second I wondered if the kid was me, if this was some dream symbol thing. It was that unreal, but no, it was a real kid holding out a real sword, or at least a white gold hilt that was sticking out of a plain leather sheath. I tried to grab it and realized that I couldn't move my arms.

Just as well. What kind of asshat makes a sword with a white gold hilt? The damn thing would warp in your hand.

Unless it was a magic sword.

Ding ding ding ding ding ding. Pinball lights.

The kid was saying something again, but how the hell did he have Emil's voice? I stared at his mouth, so mesmerized by the way he was making those adult-sounding words without moving his lips that I missed the meaning again.

Something hard slapped the side of my face. Once. Twice. Oh. There were guards behind me and beside me. That wasn't nice. Somehow the slap adjusted my inner ear a bit, even if everything was still too loud.

"...CLAIDEB, ONE OF THE FOUR GREAT TREASURES OF THE TUATHA DE DANAAN." I realized now that Emil was one of the men sitting around me, in the middle. Lean body. Immense dignity. A Grandmaster's signet ring.

Wait. What?

"Hi, Emil," I said, and got another fist-to-face wake-up call. Bam boom, to the moon, Alice. I can name that tune-up.

"THIS SWORD WAS ONE OF THE FOUR FAE ARTIFACTS THAT OUR ANCESTORS SWORE UPON WHEN WE BOUND OURSELVES TO THE FAE'S GEAS. DO YOU UNDERSTAND WHAT THAT MEANS?"

Claideb? Where the hell had I heard that name before?
Someone slapped me again.

What?

Slap. Again.

"DO YOU UNDERSTAND WHAT THAT MEANS?"

"It means that boy is holding the sword of light," a voice said calmly. "Also known as Claiomh Solais. Dyrnwyn. Whitehilt. The flaming blade. The sword of truth."

With a start, I realized that the answering voice was mine.

The voice asking questions became more cautious. "YOU ARE FAMILIAR WITH THE SWORD'S PROPERTIES, THEN?"

"The blade burns, but only in the hands of a righteous man," my voice said. "And if anyone tries to use that sword for evil or selfish purposes, the hilt burns instead of the blade. If a truly evil man holds that sword, the sword remains cold as he catches fire. He lights up like a torch."

Where was this knowledge coming from? I couldn't remember remembering any of this until I heard myself saying it. It was as if the drugs were cutting out the middle man. Me.

"ESSENTIALLY." Emil sounded satisfied now. "NO ONE CAN LIE AND KEEP HOLDING THAT BLADE. AND THE SWORD'S MAGIC IS INTERWOVEN WITH OUR GEAS. ITS MAGIC WORKS EVEN ON KNIGHTS."

I was feeling less disoriented by the second.

"IF WE PLACE THE HILT IN THE PALM OF YOUR HAND, WILL YOU HOLD IT, JOHN CHARMING?"

I took control of a mouth that was too dry and shut it firmly before it could answer, took control of it with a conscious effort at making a conscious effort.

"IF WE PLACE THE HILT IN THE PALM OF YOUR HAND, WILL YOU GRAB IT?"

"Am I...the only one...who finds that sentence...a bit Freudian?" I forced the words out slowly.

There was a stunned silence. That's right. I'm baaaaaack.

This time it wasn't a slap. It was a punch, and I felt the tail end of it. Nothing going down, but a slight aftertaste of oh shit. Slipping and sliding my consciousness through the drugs made me aware of how much my neck hurt. I was pretty sure the rest of my body was soon to follow. Somewhere, a face was tingling, stinging. My face. Stingling.

"Are you really the Grandmaster of the entire order, Emil?" I asked.

He held up a hand, making a stopping motion to someone behind me. "Will you take the sword, John Charming?"

Even as wrecked as I was, I knew that they were only giving me a choice because they had to give me a choice. For some reason, I had to take that sword willingly. I also understood that the choice they were giving me was no choice at all. If I didn't accept that sword, I would be given to the tender mercies of an inquisitor until death looked appealing.

"Sure," I said.

7

ASSFLASHBACKWARDS

I closed my fingers around the hilt and suddenly my mind was like a foot being forced into a sock that was too small for it, a man's mind behind a child's eyes as

The doctor is taping round metal things with wires to my chest. They are cold.

"No one with knight's blood has ever become a vampire or a werewolf after being bitten," Father Dan murmurs from the corner of the room. "The geas just makes us die."

"He wasn't bitten." Turcopolier Boyles doesn't bother to whisper. "His mother was. When she was pregnant with him. Have you ever heard of anything like that before?"

I have been doing well in the PT tests. Too well, maybe, or some knights seem to think so. The harder I work, the more they suspect me. The more they suspect me, the harder I work. Supposedly this new test will tell them if I'm hiding unnatural strength or not. The electricity will make me thrash around and break the straps binding me if I can.

"He never takes that silver cross off. He never changes during a full moon," Father Dan says. "The other pages notice how we treat him differently."

"I've seen his rankings," the turcopolier replies. "If he's not tainted, we're making him stronger."

"With all due respect, your leadership"—Father Dan doesn't sound particularly respectful—"you sound like a Crusader."

"You shouldn't say that name as if the Crusaders are a curse," the turcopolier reprimands sharply. "There are worse things to be than true believers."

He is looking directly at me when he says this.

I nearly bite my tongue in half when the electricity surges through my body.

"Maybe you're feeling sorry for yourselves, but let me tell you a secret." Preceptor Rivera is the youngest instructor at the orphanage, crippled by a werewolf prowling in Nazi trenches three years earlier. He shot his own leg off at the knee before the werewolf's bite could infect him, and the smashed face and cane and wooden leg give him an air of mystery and terror.

Preceptor Rivera savors his secret as if it is a fine cigar before sharing it. "Most orphans aren't valued. They're raised by drunks and perverts and failures. Evil men take the money meant to feed and clothe them. Then those same men sell the children to factories or mines or farms or worse."

We are hanging on his words. Literally. We are upside down like bats in a cave, suspended from the ceiling by leather straps wrapped around our ankles, our arms bound to our chests in straitjackets.

I am eight years old.

"I know you miss your parents," Preceptor Rivera goes on. "Even those of you who never knew them. But you have something that most orphans don't have, something that a lot of Americans don't have right now. A purpose."

We all know where he is going with this. It's his favorite speech, how the Templars send their best teachers to the orphanages, not their worst, because it's a chance to train warriors from childhood without distractions or temptations. How we will have a huge advantage over other squires if we advance and go on to one of the private Catholic schools where those of the proper bloodline are trained for knighthood in earnest. His wooden leg seems to drive his point home as it thumps on the concrete floor.

"Preceptor Rivera is stumping for the order," An Rong whispers behind me, and I smile until several foolish boys around us gasp and giggle. Preceptor Rivera begins to move our way remarkably fast.

I like An Rong even if he does have a big mouth. Rong, pronounced "Wrong." He is possibly the only student in the orphanage with a worse name than mine. Ethnicity doesn't really matter among knights the way it does in the "normal" world. There are blacks and Latinos and Asians and Native Americans in the orphanage, though pages of Eastern descent are more common in our chapter, with its emphasis on martial arts and meditation. The only thing most knights care about is if you're human or not.

Unfortunately, some of them think I'm not.

I am tensing and relaxing my muscles, taking in breaths that are as deep as I can make them, using the slack created as I exhale to bunch my hands into fists beneath the straitjacket when I find myself staring at Preceptor Rivera's navel.

"You think I'm some kind of joke, Mr. Charming?"

"Sir, I…" An begins to say, but Preceptor Rivera barks at him to be quiet. I know then, as sure as I know anything, that Preceptor Rivera doesn't want An to confess. He knows I wasn't the one who whispered. When he looks at me, he sees a small shadow of the thing that makes him wake up screaming in the middle of the night.

"I asked you a question, Charming," Preceptor Rivera reminds me. "You think I'M some kind of amusing freak?"

I don't like the way he put the emphasis on "I'M."

"You're half right," I say before I can stop myself.

Preceptor Rivera doesn't ask which half. He drives the cane into my stomach.

The soil is too hard and cold to dig my fingers into. I want to pull up dirt to blind him or rocks to hit him with, but all I do is make my fingers bleed. Don Cooper is driving my face into the ground until it feels like my teeth are going to break, but I can't move my head. My arm is twisted behind my back and his knee is on my neck and he outweighs me by a hundred pounds. He is seven years older than me, separated by the gulf of puberty.

In theory, the geas should keep him from killing me, but we can act impulsively and pay for it later. And Don Cooper is an idiot. Accidents happen.

"Say it!" he demands. "Say it!"

If he breaks my neck, I will never be able to get him back for this.

"I'M A WOLFBITCH!" I scream between mashed lips. "I'M A WOLFBITCH!"

Confanonier Jaworowski is sitting at a table in the common room, a massive block of muscle reading a book called A Tree Grows in Brooklyn. *It surprises me. Not that he's reading—the confanonier is always trying to get us to read. He says that knights need to learn to park their brain someplace fun or their heads become snake pits. What surprises me is that he's not reading one of his history books or detective novels.*

He sees me staring at the book. The confanonier sees everything. He is an active field knight and only here for a year while he recovers from some kind of shoulder injury.

"It's a piece of schmaltz," he says. "But it has some good parts

in it. Like the part I'm reading now. These children in a school have head lice, and they get their heads shaved and have kerosene rubbed in their scalp in front of all the other children, and they get laughed at. But then a few months later, other kids get lice and have to get the kerosene treatment, and the same kids who were laughed at sit back and laugh at the new kids."

He waggles the book as if weighing it. "The author says that the children didn't learn any compassion from their suffering, and therefore their suffering was wasted. I like that."

I have a feeling that this isn't a random comment, but I remain silent. The confanonier didn't ask me here to talk about a book.

The confanonier sighs. "When Nailer comes for you, remember that he broke his right leg a few years ago. He puts his weight on his left foot when he shouldn't. Feint to distract him and go for his left knee or ankle. You'll slow him down and open him up like a Christmas present."

Tom Nailer is an older kid, a big-shouldered, blockheaded boy who's as dumb as a stump. He gets embarrassed in our lore class a lot, and he takes the fact that I don't as a personal affront.

The confanonier taps his head. "You need to learn to get inside here. The kinds of things we fight, knowing what they're going to do in advance is the only way to move faster than them. You need to figure out what buttons to push to make them react in ways that you can predict. That's how you control the outcome."

Why is he telling me this? "What about all that stuff about school kids and lice and being nice?"

The confanonier turns a page of his book idly. "Nailer is too fucking stupid to worry about what you're going to be like four years from now. You're not."

We train with knives in a meat locker, staying in constant motion to keep our blood flowing, releasing breath in steaming hisses. The *things we are training to hunt will always be bigger and faster than we are, and in close quarters there is no better equalizer than a knife. Fast and devastating both physically and psychologically, a knife can stab or sever or slow. In the hands of someone who doesn't hesitate, there is virtually no real defense against a knife except distance or a faster offense. That is the foundation the knights are trying to build, even more than technique—they want to eliminate hesitation.*

We practice our knife attacks on corpses hung from hooks.

The knights have to let us out sometimes. They want us to be able to function in the world, not emerge from the order's training like aliens from another planet. Sometimes they take us out on field trips. Sometimes they send us out on errands or missions or scavenger hunts, alone or in teams, chaperoned or unescorted, to practice picking pockets or springing locks or burning down abandoned buildings or spying on a specific person without being noticed. Other times they send us out alone without money or food to fend for ourselves for days. Most of the pages are quick to develop strategies or contacts or bundles on the outside.

Some of the pages try to run away and are forced to come back by the geas, furious and ashamed and frightened, hounded by nightmares and migraines. Some of them get arrested and discover that many of the Boston police are of the blood, men who washed out of squire training and became coppers so that they could continue to be useful to the order. These boys are quietly returned to the orphanage in failure and shame. Some are discovered in clinics or hospitals, not all of them suffering physical injuries. It is rumored that some had heart attacks or went into comas choking on their own words, trying to tell the outside world about the Pax Arcana.

Some of the pages turn up dead. Some simply go missing and are never seen again.

Me, I spend a lot of time hiding out at the movies, particularly the comedies. The fights in the adventure films are too silly to take seriously, and the musicals are just bizarre, but the comedies... not taking them seriously is the whole point. Murders, monsters, mobsters, poverty, war... no subject is too dark to deal with by making fun of it. The Marx brothers are my favorite, though the theaters don't replay them as much as they used to, and the Cary Grant and Spencer Tracy and Katharine Hepburn and Crosby and Hope films are always good too.

I sit in the dark mesmerized, mouthing the lines silently.

Father Dan turns on the lights, and I blink. The dummy I have been dancing around and punching has squeakers buried beneath the padding in places where vital organs and nerve clusters would be located, and I have been making a lot of noise hitting them fast and repeatedly, working on my night fighting.

"Why aren't you making the floorboards creak?" I ask.

He laughs and begins to adjust his weight from foot to foot, making the wooden slats beneath him squeal. Is there a special way of walking, or has he really memorized which parts of the floor make noise?

There's always too much to learn. Not just fighting but poisons and first aid and tracking and alarm systems and languages and lore and lipreading. We are probably the only place in the world that has a class that is simply called "Fire."

"Why aren't you sleeping, John?"

When I picture God, I see God as rueful, concerned, caring, but ultimately committed to letting us work out our problems or not, even if he'd like to step in. I picture God as Father Dan.

"I'm afraid I won't be me when I wake up," I say.

It is true, Father Frank's talks about demons taking men over have been the most frightening thing I have ever heard. It is a fear

I don't know how to fight. The harder I try not to think about it, the more I panic when I think about it anyhow. What if my geas has been compromised by the circumstances of my birth?

"I thought it might be something like that." Father Dan sounds sad. "Do you know what I think about our immortal souls, John?"

I don't.

"If our souls are immortal, that doesn't just mean they will live forever. That means they have lived forever. And there's only one thing that's lived forever, and that's God."

I turn around to see Father Dan tapping his chest. "We've all got a little piece of God inside us, and nobody can take that away. We can be tricked into believing we've lost it. We can try to give it up, or even rent it out. We can try to destroy it. But nobody can take our souls if we don't want them to. Can you feel the truth of that, Johnny?"

And the thing is, I can.

"Our souls are our own," he reiterates. "And don't you forget it, buster."

Preceptor Akers and two knights that I don't recognize lead me to a large concrete room in the hidden basement level. I walk into a series of cages, literally. Ten feet away from me is the door to a jail cell. The bars are thick and three inches apart.

In the adjoining cage is a tall, muscular man covered in tattoos. He is trying to push himself through the bars; his right hand is reaching past them, stretching and straining toward me. His right shoulder is mostly through the bars, but his head and his breastbone are wedged. That doesn't stop him from pushing until screams of pain are torn from his bloody mouth. His eyes are wide and bulging, and saliva drips over his jaw.

Every page has a knife ceremony specifically designed for him, and this is my test. This is the obstacle I have to get past to become a squire.

"What is it?" I ask, dead-voiced. Somehow I doubt other pages are facing anything quite this dangerous.

Preceptor Akers hands me my knife. "A cunning man tried to create a cauldron of rebirth. This is what happened." There is a certain satisfaction beneath Preceptor Aker's tone that does not seem appropriate. "It is physically human, but it has no soul. Look at it."

I do. There is nothing remotely redeeming in those eyes. They are not even animal. Animals are not obscene.

"That is the opposite of creation that you are looking at," Preceptor Akers continues. "That is death and pain on legs. It has no conscience, no joy, no desire other than to..." He trails off because my knife is embedded in the thing's forehead.

I walk across the room, past two wordless knights, and reach through the bars to yank the hilt of my knife from cracked bone. The twitching spasm on the floor doesn't mind.

"You were supposed to wait until we released it!" Preceptor Akers says angrily.

"You trained me better than that, sir." I resume a formal waiting stance.

The compliment disarms Preceptor Akers more effectively than disrespect would have. He is a vain man, and it is a point that he does not want to argue in front of the other knights. You have to learn to get inside your opponents' heads, find the buttons to push that will let you predict their reactions and control the outcome.

I learned more from Confanonier Jaworski in one year than I've learned from Preceptor Akers in five.

I never do find out what my grade is. But I become a squire.

An Rong dies during his knife ceremony.

"That bird you were with had a nice little wazoo. Did you get yourself a poke ride? Or was she all show and no go?" Stephan *smirks. I don't like Stephan, and he doesn't like me. He is only sitting next to me on the bus and pretending to be friendly while I read a copy of* That Hideous Strength, *so that he can get some of the information that he loves to use against other squires.*

There is a nearby Catholic school where our female counterparts learn how to attract strong, healthy mates and indoctrinate them if they aren't knights or support them if they are. The young women research lore and learn how to administer first aid and keep separate account books and cook healthy meals and mend clothing and make false identification and take care of weapons and raise warriors.

Being bred like prize stallions is an important part of being a knight. The mortality rate is high, and we are encouraged to marry and start having many children young. We are being given some free time to fraternize, and there are even special classes with both sexes commuting between schools. Even I participate. Me, who was given a vasectomy two years ago. Just in case.

I had liked the girl, Connie. We had danced, and then walked, and she had guided me to an empty classroom whose lock was easy to pick, and we had kissed. Once. That was all, just talked and kissed. It was our first dance, and no one had known me at her school. I understand, without even having to think about it, that boys from my school have been talking to girls from her school, and the next time I see Connie, it will be different. I am a Charming, but it is my coach that will turn into a pumpkin.

Still, I like the girl. I don't like Stephan.

But I have to live with Stephan, and I am so tired of being an outcast.

"You writing a book or something? Go flog your log." It is the right thing to say, but I say it with a knowing smirk. His smirk. A coward's way of being a shit.

*   *   *

The lights go off while I am cleaning the gym floor. Four of them come for me, several of them large, almost eighteen. Rob's older brother, Kevin, no doubt, and two of his cronies. The smaller shadow hanging behind is probably Rob. They are all carrying escrima sticks.

I have committed the sin of being ranked number one in my class again.

"You really think I'm number two, oddball?" Rob had sneered.

"I think you came out of your momma's butthole," I'd replied. "Or did you mean some other kind of number two?"

Several younger squires doomed me by snickering.

"Cut the gas," a voice hisses. "Let's pound this clown!"

Kevin's friends begin to flank him, and I kick the large bucket at my feet over violently so that the soapy water spills out and flows beneath their feet.

The mop I have been dipping in the mop bucket isn't a mop—it's a staff. They try to react quickly, but the floor is soapy and slippery, and unlike me, they don't have thin chains wrapped around their shoes to keep them from sliding. The faster they try to move, the more off-balance they become.

I am number one in my class for a reason.

I keep beating them past the point where it is necessary. I want them to have to visit the infirmary with transparent stories and humiliating injuries, broken jaws and knees and arms and ankles and collarbones. I want everyone to know what they tried to do. I want everyone to know what happened to them.

It really must be extended self-defense. My geas never even twinges.

Susan is five foot ten, almost an inch taller than me, and she is built wide. Wide head, wide shoulders, wide hips, wide mouth, pretty and in proportion, but on a large scale. She will never be slim, though there is little in the way of excess flesh on her. Her hair is long and brown and frames her face like stage curtains. Her lipstick is a bright garish red that draws attention to her generous lips. Somehow, her skirt seems shorter than the other girls', although it is a regulation uniform.

Susan is almost my female counterpart. She is very vocal about women being capable of being knights, and adept at bringing up cases of female pirate captains and Hindu noblewomen who fought in war and Celtic warrior maids. According to Susan, there has never been a war where dead soldiers weren't discovered to be women in disguise while bodies were being looted or removed from the field. She contends that Spenser's character Britomart, the female knight in disguise in The Faerie Queene, *would never have been written in that time period if there weren't commonly known real-life precedents.*

There are rumors that she is a dike.

Susan removes a cigarette from her purse and lights it. "So what is it that you wanted to show me?"

We have broken into the atrium beyond our gym. I figured out the blind spots in the cameras a year ago, and you can actually reach wiring to the pressure-sensitive alarms in the floor from a hole in the wall in the boys' bathroom one floor down.

"Come here." I motion.

I am not sure why she agreed to come, but there is something about her smirk that makes me instantly hard. Fortunately, it is dark. I shine a flashlight on a large wooden plaque with panels where names on slats can be entered and removed. The plaque lists school bests in various athletic events, distances and times and consecutive wins, many of them breaking Olympic records. Almost half of the names are Charming. Eric Charming. Luke Charming. Alan Charming. And mine too, there among the others.

"Wow," Susan says softly.

"If I didn't set any records, they'd say I was a disappointment," I say. "When I do, they think I'm some kind of freak."

She offers me a puff of the cigarette, but when I take it, I walk over and stub it out in a nearby water fountain.

"Hey," she says, still softly.

"The guards don't have regular patrol patterns," I explain. "Do you really want cigarette smell in the air if we have to hide?"

It is two in the morning.

"Where would we hide?" Susan says, looking around.

I don't even have to think about it. "With the rolled-up wrestling mats. They're right past that door over there."

"Is it true that they made you get a vasectomy when you were a kid?" Susan asks. The question throws me off guard. I didn't know that was common knowledge. With all of the rumors about her, she of all people must know how much emphasis knights place on breeding. My inability to have children is as shameful and humiliating as if I had been neutered. I will never be husband material.

"Yes," I say hotly.

Susan shakes her head slowly, then smiles. It is an odd, self-mocking smile, although I don't understand why.

"What?!?" I demand angrily, still embarrassed and raw.

She begins to unbutton her shirt. "Stop talking."

It might be the best advice anyone has ever given me.

"You oughta like this, Charming," Geoffrey smirks. "She's a regular sleeping beauty."

The woman is beautiful and naked and unconscious, and somehow Geoffrey and his friends have snuck her into the dormitory.

"Enchanted sleep," Geoffrey gloats. "We found her counting sheep in the cellar of a cunning man. We're taking her to the medical ward. Eventually."

All of the boys are breathing heavily. There is something dense and dark and ugly in the air, something animal. My cheeks are flushed with shame and something else, and I'm breathing heavily.

I don't say anything. I walk over to where the fire alarm is. Every room in the dormitory has one.

"What are you doing?" Geoffrey calls.

I pull the alarm.

"You cats grew up in the same orphanage? That's wild." My partner, Nick Arbiter, has a gleam in his eye. Nick is an older guy, almost forty and a father of six, and he has taken an almost paternal interest in me. Part of this is because his last partner died badly, and he and Nick were close. It's also because I am good at what we do, and I make keeping Nick alive a priority. Nick and his wife both appreciate that, and being around their family has been emotionally rewarding and devastating at the same time. But I don't talk about my childhood much.

"I realize that you're going through a midlife crisis, Nick," I reply without looking up from the Heinlein novel I am reading. "But God as my witness, you use the word 'groovy' and I'm going to punch you."

Nick ignores me and addresses our pilot. "So what was John like as a tyke?"

Don Cooper is flying the bush plane. He works as a pilot for a commuter service that the Knights own outright. He was never knighted, but he still functions as a lay servant, providing transport and supplies. Our flight isn't being documented, and neither is the cargo in a plastic tarp in the back.

Don flicks an uneasy glance my way. "I really don't remember."

I could say a lot of things. Don was a bully, and I often dreamed of finding Don somewhere alone when we weren't separated by the gulf of puberty and one hundred pounds, but he washed out of *training before I was ready. It would be easy to say the words that would lead to a little private discussion on the side of the airfield when we land.*

I waited a long time for a fair fight with Don Cooper.

But it wouldn't be a fair fight now. Don is a coward. He picked on smaller kids to try to conceal or deny the fear that was gnawing at his guts constantly, but he froze in the field a year later when a hag killed his mentor in front of him. I am taller than Don now, in much better shape, have more training, and have many times faced down the reality of death that paralyzed him.

If I fight him now, I will be the bully. There will be no satisfaction in it. Violence without necessity is wrong. I can't help wanting it, but I can help doing it. As long as I have control, I know the monster hasn't gotten in. Or gotten out.

"We were just stupid kids." I turn a page.

The malaria I caught hunting draugr in a bayou is a fevered delirium. I sweat, dear God, I sweat, and I ache. Our chapter has a clinic in the slums, and I recover in a back room there. Nick or his wife visit me every day, and the odd thing is that even though they look worried, it is also impossible to mistake a look of relief in their eyes.

I am normal after all. Werewolves don't almost die of malaria. Even the doctors and nurses, Catholics of the blood who run this facility as an excuse to administer to wounded knights without the necessity of forms or police reports, treat me differently than any of the people who constantly examined me while I was growing up.

I don't tell them that I can hear things from the streets beyond the clinic that I shouldn't be able to hear, or that the smells in the clinic are almost unendurable. There is a man in the room beyond who has an infected wound that the nurses haven't caught yet. Beneath the scent of liniment and mint, I can tell the doctor has been drinking.

Apparently, something inside me has woken up in order to keep my body alive.

The sound of muffled screams and the smell of burning flesh wake me, and I come to under a pile of bodies in the bomb shelter. Nick's empty eyes are staring at me from a blood-covered face. I shift and see the skinwalker with his back turned to me, standing some three yards away in his natural form, a wiry male with all of his hair shaved off. His naked body is covered in symbols and sigils made out of fresh blood. The suit he made out of our quartermaster's skin is carefully laid out on the floor by his feet like a set of Sunday clothes.

Turcopolier Crockett is the one screaming through a gag, and in a moment I see why.

The skinwalker is cooking the turcopolier's right foot in a portable camp stove, doing some kind of dance around the flames while he chants in a language I don't know.

Skinwalkers have the ability to assume another person's form. The neutral ones can do this by looking in a person's eyes and claim their gift comes from the Great Spirit, but the evil ones learned to duplicate the power through unnatural means. They mimic another creature's form only after eating that being's flesh and making a suit out of that being's skin, a suit that they wear like a pelt. This skinwalker obviously plans to make a new suit out of the turcopolier. Perhaps it is working its way up the Knights Templar's chain of command.

From a purely tactical viewpoint, that probably saves my life.

The most dangerous thing about the evil skinwalkers is that their magical disguises are also a kind of armor. The skin suits redistribute energy down their length and into the fourth dimension, where they are anchored, like a chain that conducts electricity and disperses it into the ground. The magical disguises work that way with all energy: heat, impact, whatever.

But the skinwalker isn't wearing one of his magical skin suits now.

I erupt from beneath the bodies of my brothers. The skinwalker is moving at the normal human speed that I have left behind, and I break his neck with a forearm hammer before he has half turned around.

The skinwalker collapses, and I stare at Turcopolier Crockett. He lays there bound, broken-limbed, and bleeding.

He saw me take a shotgun blast to the stomach. He has seen too much.

"Do it," the turcopolier rasps around his gag. "And to hell with you."

I unstrap my belt and begin to make a tourniquet around his right leg. "I'm not that kind of monster," I tell him.

At least I will have a head start.

The yukshee is staring upward at me, caught in the bottom of what used to be a large well. The well is thirty feet deep, the stone sides slick with the oil that I poured down it. It took me the better part of a night to move the stone remains of the well and cover the pit with a thin sheet and dirt.

"I had to kill him," she claims, and then says some things I don't understand. I came to India hoping to learn meditation techniques that might help me contain some of my stronger…instincts…a few months ago. My Hindi is still pretty basic, but I catch the word prana *in there, a term for life force, and something about making love and a man looking old.*

Yukshee are Indian succubi, parasites that drain life energy through sexual contact.

"And Akhil Marar?" I ask. "You had to kill him too?"

That silences her for a moment. Akhil was four villages and twelve days ago.

I wordlessly pick up a torch whose original source was a holy fire outside a Hindu temple. I used that sacred flame to light a candle five days ago, and I have kept that fire alive in one form or another ever since, transferring it from candles to lamps to fireplaces to torches.

"Don't kill me like this," she pleads. "Not with fire!"

I drop the torch with her begging still in my ears, stand there while the pleas change to screams.

Christmas Eves are always hard, even in non-Christian countries, where it's treated more like a kind of Valentine's Day and people still go to work and school. I'm in a Japanese movie theater. Clint Eastwood is staring down mercilessly at some punk who is begging for his life. I don't know why I thought this would be less depressing than paying for a geisha. There are three other people in the theater with me, and I'm pretty sure one of them is dead. I think the other two are knights.

I like being a fry cook. I don't have a hard time getting enough to eat without anyone noticing, and the manager is never around to mess with me too much on the night shift.

I have long stretches of quiet where I can read, and busy periods where I don't have time to think. Both are good with me.

The only problem is the nurse.

Alison isn't my normal type. But there's something about her. Her face is open and her eyes are warm and her smile is a small sun. She cusses like a sailor, but she never says anything mean.

I can't stop thinking about her. Alison comes to the diner at least three times a night, before her shifts, during her shifts, after her shifts, and she says it's because she's a coffee addict and I make great coffee, and I do, but it's more than that.

We're both readers. She brings books to the diner, and I always have a book nearby, and pretty soon we have a two-person book

*club going. She has this way of starting conversations that makes
me actually talk to her. Sometimes she needs to unload about a
patient who is making her sad or a hospital administrator who's
making her angry, and I'm a good listener.*

*I think this is what falling in love might be like. It is a bad idea.
It is a terrible idea.*

*But there's a persistent little voice that keeps whispering. It's
been over a decade since I've even seen a knight, and I really think
he believed that I died in that fire. Most of the knights I grew up
with are dead, and with the vampire war, the Order has more
important things on its plate than a quasi-werewolf who never
messes with anyone unless he's messed with. More than ten years,
almost fifteen. They might not even think of me at all anymore.*

Every time the door opens, I check to see if it's her.

"Witness protection?" Alison asks gently. "Are you AWOL? A
recovering drug addict? What's your story, Wyatt? I deal with a lot
of survivors. I know you've seen bad things."

*She has no idea. I try to talk and the words choke in my throat.
I don't know if it's the geas or wanting something this much. It feels
like I'm tearing something out of my brain when I plunge my forearm on the side of the hot grill, something with roots.*

"WYATT?!?"

*I lift my arm, holding the burn up where she can see it. It goes
from second to third degree in front of her eyes.*

"My name is John." *My voice is hoarse.* "Run."

*Alison's eyes are wide, her lips parted. She starts to drop her cup
and I reach out and close my hand around her shaking fingers.*

One reflexive gesture, and everything turns on it.

"This is the dumbest-ass movie I've ever seen." *This is an exaggera-
tion, but not by much.* "When's the damn boat going to sink?"

"Hush." We are half sitting and half lying on her couch.

"Look at that woman's hands and forearms," I say. "That's no pampered upper-class aristocrat. That actress has done real work. She could snap Kate Winslet's neck like a chicken's."

"Ooh, analyze the actors' muscle tone and body language. I love that." It is possible that Alison is being a tad sarcastic.

I kiss Alison's upper cheekbone where her head is propped against my shoulder and adjust my arm beneath her breasts.

"I love you," I say, and my eyes get hot and wet and my throat tightens up and my chest feels like a furnace kicking into gear.

I would have sworn it wasn't possible for Alison to nestle any farther into me, but she finds a way. She pretends not to notice that I am shaking, and eventually I stop.

Her spinal column runs beneath her skin like a ley line, and I trace its length with my lips, the heat of her thighs cradled in my palms, the warm rich musk of her filling the room.

She tries to twist away as I lower my focus, and she says something about a big ass.

"Hush." I take the top of her right buttock in my teeth, the bounty and the beauty of it, and nibble gently. My hands slide inward slightly.

"God," she breathes. "Where did you come from?"

"A bad dream," I whisper.

I'm actually watching Alison's car when it explodes. It's a habit of mine. Philadelphia is dangerous, and I always watch through the window when she leaves, sweep the street with my eyes for any sign of potential predators.

She is just running to get some pantyhose to replace the ones she tore. We are going to her sister's, and Alison always gets a little nervous when we're going to see her sister.

And her car explodes.

For one moment, I don't feel anything. It's as if the entire universe has stopped. There is nothing except me and this moment, and I know that I'm going to feel something in a second, something worse than anything I've ever felt in my entire life. I'm standing in front of a tidal wave of emotion, and I have one thought before it hits, one clear, rational thought from the part of me that always knew I didn't have a right to be happy, that's been waiting for something like this... one moment before the guilt and horror and hate and despair crash over me and tear me loose from my moorings. It's a selfish thought, not really about Alison at all.

Don't become a monster.

I find the knight on a roof with a sniper rifle. He figured my back would be to him when I left the building to go to Alison's car. But I didn't go to Alison's car. She's dead. He is still watching the street when I come up on him from behind.

I kill him quickly before I can do all of the things I know how to do that would kill him slowly.

It's the best I can do.

Two weeks blind. It is the damned geas, and it might be the only thing that keeps me alive. I lie there, anonymous, in the psych ward of a hospital that doesn't want to spend a lot of money on tests for a nameless man with no obvious injuries or insurance. I got a trucker to drive me here by telling him my brother worked at this hospital, in this city. It is one place the knights would never think to look; in fact, they have probably taken the people who normally check hospitals for signs of paranormal attacks off of their posts to look for me elsewhere.

Why would someone who heals fast and can't afford to be examined too closely go to a hospital?

For two weeks, I lie there and think of ways to locate and kill knights, until the hate begins to fade into self-loathing and then apathy. Until I realize that the knight was working alone, that he must have been some kind of misfit or sociopath who hunted by himself because he didn't work well with others. If he had reported finding me, the knights would have sent a strike team.

I was supposed to be his trophy. Maybe his redemption.

I lie there, and my sight doesn't come back until I admit to myself that the person who really killed Alison was me.

The cabin is a hole. I haven't bothered to keep it up. Haven't bothered to keep myself up, either. My beard is wild and unkempt. My fingernails are long and have black streaks where dirt has become embedded underneath them. I haven't taken off the clothes I'm wearing for at least a week. I am a cliché. I can spend hours trying to work up enough energy to make a meal, then lie down to build up enough energy to make the next one. My life, if you can call it that, is timeless inertia. I spend most of my time not feeling anything at all except a vague, omnipresent weight that pushes me down into my bed. It is a kind of relief.

I am cutting down a tree for firewood when the woods go quiet. A scent from an errant breeze washes over me, a smell of decay, corrupt and fetid. I pause, holding the axe loosely by my side, and wait. I don't have to wait for long.

He is a relatively new wendigo. He still has on a jacket from his previous life, though he lost his boots and pants as his body became gaunt, ravaged by eternal hunger and an increased metabolism rate. Black hair has grown unchecked to the point where it is almost fur, smeared with pus from weeping sores, and his fingernails are gnarled yellow claws.

Probably some nature enthusiast or grad student or romantic who got lost in the wilds of Alaska with a friend. Starving, he must have resorted to betrayal and murder at some point, maybe killing a companion for the remaining rations before finally resorting to cannibalism. Continuing to starve but not die, slowly going insane from hunger and self-loathing and directionless rage. It is the traditional way wendigos are born.

I consider letting it kill me. Are we really so different, it and I? But when it lunges, I move, all instinct and muscle memory. A feint, a blow to its jaw with the blunt side of the axe, and then I am cutting its left foot out from under it literally and figuratively, bringing my axe down on its thrashing mass again and again, screaming louder than it is, feelings that I have trapped inside me boiling out like lava.

It is not the wendigo I am trying to kill. It is myself, or the weak, useless, half-dead thing I have become.

Later, with trembling hands, I find a wallet in its jacket pocket. At some point it was named Trevor Barnes.

I usually channel fear into fighting or planning or running or joking. Giving myself up was messing with me. I didn't want to die, but I wasn't going to let anyone else I cared about get killed because of me, and I kind of wished she would just shut the fuck up and let me say my lines.

... the world caught fire. I understood instantly that not all of the legends about the sword were complete. If flames didn't lick over me, they still burned through me. Fire roared in my veins, incinerating the drugs in my bloodstream, melting and fusing my broken bones, cauterizing my maimed and bleeding flesh. White light filled my brain, and if I could have inclined my head, I would have.

I'm sorry, I thought, not sure who I was thinking it to. I was so tired.

The thought seemed to go on forever. I was still thinking it when I realized that I was alive. The white light wasn't coming from behind my eyes anymore... it was coming through their lids from in front of me.

I opened my eyes and saw that the blade of the sword was ablaze with white fire, held upright in my hand without seeming to weigh anything, anything at all, the hilt cool in my palm.

Every pair of eyes was transfixed on that blade, but gradually those eyes moved disbelievingly from the sword to me.

"Don't look at me," I told them. "I'm as surprised as anyone."

∾8∾

GO DIRECTLY TO HELL. DO NOT PASS GO. DO NOT COLLECT TWO HUNDRED DOLLARS.

Are you the leader of the werewolves who have been attacking us?"

Now that I was no longer feeling the effects of the drug or recent injuries, the inability to arch my spine was starting to get to me. My butt hurt, my back hurt, and my neck hurt, but the sword was still in my hand, still burning brightly. Holding it wasn't uncomfortable at all.

"No," I said.

Emil remained quiet while the six knights who were apparently each a Knights Commander hit me with a barrage of questions. They were all older than most Knights Templar ever get, all bearing marks of damage: missing limbs and scarred flesh and slight misalignments of the shoulders or spines. I was referring to them mentally as Fire-face, Tex, Stinky, Stumpy, Itchy, and Twitchy.

"Do you know who the leader of the werewolf clan is?"

"No."

"Have you had any interaction with any werewolf packs or clans?"

"No."

"Have you trained any werewolves to fight?"

"No."

The room was becoming colder somehow, and not in terms of room temperature.

"Did you kill a knight in Foster Falls by literally ripping his arm off and beating him to death with it?"

"..."

"You think that's funny?"

"I...don't know how to answer that. I don't think this sword I'm holding does well with complex truths. No. And yes, sort of. And definitely not."

"Did you kill a knight in Madison by disemboweling him?"

"No."

The litany continued on in this mode for some time, and that was without them repeating questions the way interrogators would during a normal sweat session. There had apparently been a fairly impressive number of unsolved deaths caused by werewolves in the last few decades.

Finally, Emil cleared his throat. Apparently Templar higher-ups didn't use Robert's Rules of Order. "Gentlemen, it's dangerous for this many of us to be gathered in one physical location for too long."

"You're the one who brought us here, Lamplighter," Fire-face accused. Even if half his face hadn't been ravaged by fire, I still might have called him Fire-face just because of how red the other half was.

"Would you have believed what happened here today if you

had seen it on a computer screen, Thomas?" Emil's voice had that same gentle quality he had used with Sig.

"I'm having a hard time believing it now," Twitchy drawled in an accent that was pure Texas. He was completely bald and apparently suffering from some kind of nerve disorder that made the right corner of his mouth spasm periodically. I think he was trying to defuse tension.

Even back when I was a knight, decades ago, the Templars had split into different sects. There were the Crusaders, the hardcore religious order. The Swords of Solomon, the knights who believed that using magic to fight magic made sense. There were the Heretics, knights who were openly atheist or agnostic, and the Pragmatics—sometimes called Rat Runners because lab coats and rats and mazes were all tied together back then—knights who believed that scientific study was the best way to level the playing field. My own order had been called the Monks, or sometimes, less respectfully, the Monkeys or the Pajama Party. We had embraced the path of the warrior monk, focusing on martial arts and meditation. There had even been some knights who wanted to work peacefully in the supernatural world, though they had been marginalized and were called Bug Huggers.

There were probably new names and nicknames now.

In any normal order of things, the different factions would have broken off or killed each other, but knights were shackled to the Order and each other by a geas and a common enemy. It was like those lines from the poem "The Equilibrists" by John Crowe Ransom: *At length I saw these lovers fully were come / Into their torture of equilibrium; / Dreadfully had forsworn each other and yet / They were bound each to each, and they did not forget.*

"Brothers, it is time we held a vote," Emil said.

Fire-face stood up in his chair and leveled an index finger at me. He had thick, meaty hands and a voice clogged with outrage and contempt. Here was a man who had by God had enough. "YOU CAN'T TRUST THIS FREAK! WE NEED TO BE DRAWING LINES, NOT BLURRING THEM!"

"We're all familiar with your viewpoint, Thomas." Emil's voice was still mild. "You've expressed it many times. Now you can express it with your vote."

"IT TOOK US HALF A CENTURY TO CAPTURE THIS THING! WE CAN'T LET IT GO!"

"You didn't capture him, Thomas. I did," Emil chided.

Something clicked. Emil hadn't just gone along on that expedition because he had some kind of complex about leading from the front or taking risks. He had been garnering political capital. No matter what else had changed in the Order, I couldn't believe that competence and courage in the field didn't speak. There was some kind of power struggle going on behind the scenes here that I wasn't privy to.

Emil continued. "And we wouldn't be letting a prisoner go; we would be firing a heat-seeking missile. At an enemy who is currently winning."

Thomas started to say something else and Emil interrupted. "On your territory."

That last observation didn't do much to calm Fire-face down. "I WON'T ALLOW IT!"

Suddenly, the tension in the room took on a different... what? Vibration? Tautness? Density? The body language of every man I could see changed. Facial muscles stilled. Shoulders squared. Feet shifted weight. Palms subtly angled downward. Sweat took on a tang of apprehension.

"Perhaps you should take the sword from the prisoner's

hand, then, Brother Thomas," Emil said reasonably. "If you are so sure of the purity of your motives."

There was an appalled silence.

"I'm serious," Emil said, though I don't think anyone in that room thought he was being lighthearted or frivolous. "Take Claideb, and if its blade bursts into flames, I will step down as the Grandmaster of the Knights Templar. This offer is real and binding by the consent of all the witnesses here. By all means, Thomas, save us from ourselves."

Fire-face was poleaxed. His eyes uncontrollably flickered toward the blade in my hand, and they were filled with lust and horror. Seeing that naked glance among men who prided themselves on their powers of observation and control, I realized that this moment had been engineered. Emil wanted Brother Thomas taken down a peg. It might even be that my capture was the least important item on Emil's agenda. I was the excuse needed to bring the Sword of Truth to this place, to this man, in front of these witnesses. And Fire-face had fallen into the trap.

Fire-face was never going to take the Grandmaster's offer. One look at Fire-face's left eye, wide open and terrified among all that burned dead flesh, told me that much. Even if he was confident of his virtue, Fire-face was afraid of fire, and Emil knew it. But when word got out among the knights that Brother Thomas had refused to hold the Sword of Truth as the price of becoming Grandmaster, his reputation would be as irreparably damaged as his face.

Fire-face tried to bluster his way out. He glared past my shoulder and quoted Matthew 4:7, the passage where the devil tempted Christ to throw himself off a mountain so that angels would catch him. "It hath been written. *Thou shalt not tempt the Lord thy God.* Even a grandmaster should consider that."

"Oh, I do." Emil made a motion to a guard beside me. "Brothers, let us vote."

A hypodermic needle was plunged into my left arm.

∾∾

I woke up in a windowless room that smelled like disinfectant. The wall behind me was stone, and I was manacled to it by thick cuffs around my ankles and wrists. There was some kind of metal collar around my neck too, though it wasn't bound to anything. I was in a basement. A deep basement. The quality of the air told me that much.

Emil was facing me, straddling a chair turned backward. It is the way that knights sit when they are in a hostile environment. The back of the chair protects the soft, vulnerable organs in their torso, and the chair is braced so that the knight can push off of it quickly, even pick it up as a weapon. He was flanked by four guards decked in armor, and by armor I mean Kevlar bodysuits with some kind of black space-age plastic plates woven in to the outfit over their nerve clusters and vital organs.

"Wow, the soundproofing in here is really impressive," I croaked. "I can't hear anything past the walls."

Emil's face didn't change. "Bad things happen here."

"Ah." I cleared my throat. Whatever drugs they were using on me gave me cottonmouth. "So, what's up with this collar around my neck? Are the Templars taking slaves now?"

"We're all slaves, John," he observed. "But that device monitors body temperature. If you start to heat up, it will shock you and keep shocking you until you stop or fall unconscious."

A werewolf's body temperature is a degree or two warmer than most under normal circumstances, but it really goes up when he or she starts to change into a wolf. It's all the molecular agitation and increased metabolic activity.

He wasn't lighting a cigarette with a blowtorch or anything like that. Emil just watched me, which is a kind of interrogation technique all its own when the other party has reason to be nervous. I didn't try to wait him out, though. "How did the vote go? And what was it about exactly?"

He didn't answer directly. "Did you notice a pattern about the werewolf attacks they kept asking you about two days ago?"

Two days?

"They were mostly in the Midwest," I said. "And centered around Wisconsin. Illinois. Montana. Ohio. Minnesota."

He nodded approvingly. "Someone was setting up separate werewolf packs that were too small to attract attention individually. Whoever this person is, he or she did it over a long period of time so we wouldn't notice."

"But some knights did," I said. "Hence all the death-by-werewolves. How could you not notice that?"

"We did notice it. We thought it was you." Emil's face was sour. "We thought you were going on a killing spree after what happened to your woman."

I didn't know what to say to that.

"Whoever this leader is, they even helped us reach that conclusion by occasionally decapitating knights and leaving their heads nailed to doors."

I shook my head, though I didn't have a lot of range of motion. I don't know if it was an admiring or despairing gesture. "That was clever."

"Yes." Emil's tone was flat. "Whoever this werewolf leader is, they're very clever. When he or she was ready to move, the leader pulled all of the packs together into a clan. It was like tightening a noose around our necks."

I tried to stretch my neck and shoulders, with limited success.

"You must have figured out it wasn't me after you found me in Alaska. Why haven't you identified this leader yet?"

"We haven't been able to infiltrate the werewolf clan." Raw and recent emotional wounds began to show in Emil's voice, bleeding frustration. "For one thing, this has been occurring in Brother Thomas's territory, and as you might have gathered, he's a blowhard and an idiot. His response to unrest is to terrify the werewolves he *can* identify, which just causes more of them to go into hiding and creates more unrest and more werewolves willing to go to war against us. This job requires a scalpel, and he's trying to use a baseball bat."

He wouldn't be telling me all of this if he didn't think I needed to know it. He was briefing me on a mission.

"For another, the Clan can literally smell anyone who's not a werewolf from half a mile away," Emil continued. "We've tried blackmailing real werewolves into spying for us, but the clan can smell emotions and hear heartbeats and pulses. Do you understand?"

I understood. "Knights can't get near them, beings without our training can't lie to them, and technological surveillance won't work in gatherings where there's a huge concentration of magic or magical beings. Basically, you're screwed."

Emil's smile was without mirth. "But you...a real werewolf with a monk's training, bound by the geas to eliminate threats to the Pax..."

"Are you offering me amnesty?" I asked.

"I can't do that." He sounded genuinely regretful. "I can offer to release you into Clan territory without torturing or killing you if you vow to identify and kill the werewolf leader. I can promise you that we won't be diverting massive resources into hunting you down any longer if you do kill him or her..."

"But I would still have to hide," I clarified. "You're talking about some kind of unofficial *Don't Ask, Don't Kill* policy."

"That's the best I can do," he said. "A grandmaster isn't a dictator, John, or at least a good one isn't. The test of the sword and humiliating Thomas were the only things that convinced the others to go along with this much, and that's because they expect you to die anyhow."

"But I'm no threat to the Order," I protested. "I'm still bound by the geas just like you are."

"Just by existing, you're a threat to the Order," Emil countered. "Most of the monsters we deal with live longer and are faster and stronger than us. Some of them are better people than we are. But we don't envy them. We hunt them. We don't befriend them. We hate them. We don't experiment or compromise or bargain, because we are afraid for our souls. Do you understand? Our task is impossible without boundaries. You cross too many lines."

I didn't answer. "How did you know the sword would blaze for me?"

He shrugged. "Even if it didn't, the sword works as a polygraph. But I did everything I could to stack the odds in your favor. Those drugs you were on disconnected you from anxiety or guilt. You were starved for three days. I maneuvered you into sacrificing yourself for others. I gave you a chance to keep your vow even when you didn't have to when I left you unbound in the Jeep. I got you to discuss your sins frankly."

"You're saying you put me through some sort of purification ritual." I wasn't sure if I admired the scope of his machinations or just wanted to kill him. I started mentally ticking stages off in my head: Fasting. Acceptance. Sacrifice. Confession. And what had happened right before the sword blazed? I had been sorry. Repentance.

"So, you were using them to manipulate me," I said. "And you're using me to manipulate them. All because you came up with this plan to set me against this werewolf leader...when, exactly?"

"Years ago in Alaska," he said calmly. "When I realized that you couldn't possibly be the Clan leader."

Right. The werewolf leader had used me to trick Emil. Emil wanted to use me to trick the werewolf leader. There was an element of pride and competition somewhere in that decision. I was a pawn in some chess match between two adversaries who used living people as playing pieces. I sure as hell wasn't a knight.

"Here's the problem, Emil," I said. "I'm not promising to kill anyone on your say-so. I'll agree to check things out, but for all I know, this werewolf leader is some kind of King Arthur or Robin Hood or Tecumseh, and you guys are wearing the black hats."

"That's not good enough," Emil said ruefully, and the bastard took a sip from a glass of water. I didn't ask for any. "I want your promise, John."

"Because you know my oath means something to me," I croaked.

"Yes."

If my mouth hadn't been so dry, I would have spit. "You can't have it."

"Grow up." Emil sounded irritated. "You're acting as if you have a choice. I almost like you, John, and I sure as hell respect your capacity for causing chaos. But I've sacrificed men I liked a lot more for less reason. I've lost my own flesh and blood to the wolves as far as that goes, a brother and a niece, in fact. Don't think I won't send a man named Brother Gerard in here to persuade you less respectfully if I have to."

"Go to hell."

∾9∾

FOUR-LIMBED IS FORE-ARMED

The guard Emil left behind didn't talk to me, though I tried a variety of strategies to engage him in conversation. He just stood there with a transparent round shield made of some space-age bulletproof plastic strapped on his back and an AN-94 rifle loosely pointed in my direction. I wouldn't have minded so much if the damn thing hadn't had a grenade launcher attachment. There wasn't much time, so I didn't take too long to decide that I wasn't going to get anything useful out of him.

"I'm ready now," I said.

I wasn't talking to the guard.

The sprite from the overpass began putting on a light show, changing colors and smacking straight into the guard's face and bouncing off, sprinkling disruptive magical energy around like fairy dust. The lights in the room flickered, and the guard automatically took one hand off of his rifle and drew a silver steel knife from a forearm sheath, slashing outward and narrowly missing the sprite. It took him precious extra seconds to realize that if the lights were experiencing weird power fluctuations, the collar monitoring and inhibiting my body's changes might be malfunctioning too.

I was already changing into a wolf by then.

Look, when I made an agreement with the sprite in the overpass, I didn't just ask it to witness my contract with Emil. The sprite was my Plan B, and as soon as I'd knocked Emil unconscious, I ate it.

Well, okay, I swallowed it. Sprites aren't human. They don't need to breathe, because they're mostly condensed air molecules, and they don't think like humans, either. Whatever dimension they're from, they don't experience Time and Space the same way we do—if they thought of small enclosed places and the passage of time as a form of torture, they'd go insane from confinement when bound into witch bottles.

Believe me, I didn't enjoy putting that sprite in my stomach, but I knew it was the only way to get the sprite past the protective wards and sigils and magical detection devices that were sure to be layered around whatever location the knights took me to.

When I threw up the first time in the interrogation room? I was releasing the sprite.

And now I was releasing the wolf.

I remember knowing, absolutely knowing with every cell in my body, that the only way the geas would allow me to change to a wolf would be if I resolved not to kill the guard.

I remember thrashing around violently in my manacles, scraping skin off of limbs that healed as fast as they peeled, gagging and choking as the collar slid about. I remember feeling like my entire body had a migraine, my eyes getting hot as my vision went red, thousands of coarse hairs poking needle-like through my skin. I remember howling while I dropped to four feet and scrambled at speeds that no human could attain.

I remember lunging upward awkwardly from a strange angle with my neck muscles and biting the guard's hand while he was trying to drive his silver steel knife through my eye and into my brain.

The first time I changed, I didn't remember anything afterward. Maybe I was making progress. Maybe I was one step closer to hell.

My next memory is of crouching over the guard's unconscious body, his right arm ending in a bleeding stump where fangs had peeled back the end sleeve of his armor and bitten through his wrist.

I removed his armor as fast as I could, then drove his knife into his elbow joint several times, pulling and sawing tendons until I'd amputated his lower arm. There were bandages and cords in some of the armor pouches, and I managed a tourniquet and a field dressing fairly quickly. There was a chance I'd kept whatever was in my bite from spreading up his bloodstream, and a chance that he wouldn't die from shock or blood loss.

I would have done the same even without the geas. It wasn't logical. I was ready to kill anyone I had to, but not if I didn't have to.

Mercy is a luxury. And I take my luxuries where I can find them.

∼10∼

I SAID I WAS READY TO DIE. I DIDN'T SAY I WAS READY TO DIE QUIETLY.

Stay alive and get out of here," I told the sprite. "I still need you to be a witness to Emil's oath."

I opened the door to the cell at normal speed and shot the pair of visible guards in the back of their heads while the sprite flitted around their eyes. They were wearing bulletproof helmets along with their Kevlar field suits, but it was still an AN-94. And it was still their heads.

Maybe they woke up with headaches later, or maybe they died, or maybe they had spasms or stutters or twitches or more serious mental impairments for the rest of their lives. Maybe they would have aneurysms twenty years later. Head trauma is like a box of blood clots. You never know what you're going to get.

A knight on my left tossed a flash-bang grenade my way, timed to go off directly in front of the door, but I used the AN-94's butt to smack the grenade back with faster-than-human reflexes. I bit down on a pressure switch inside my helmet that activated foam inserts over my ears, and I still heard the bang and saw too much bright light through my closed eyelids.

Bullets glanced off my ribs at an angle as I darted back into the doorway while a knight on my right fired for my center mass. Partially blind, I fired a concussion grenade in a bank shot off the far wall. I was assuming that the guard was in a parallel position to the one on my left, and that must have been close to the truth. He was torn off of his feet like a small child being yanked by one extremely angry mother.

The remaining guard on the left tried to lunge across to the far wall, firing his own AN-94 into the doorway. Unfortunately for him, I was no longer in the doorway, a fact that he couldn't see or hear because he had been blinded by the flash-bang grenade, and his automatic fire was deafening.

I couldn't really see or hear him very well either, and we almost passed each other in the hallway with guns blazing. We both started to swivel, but I was faster and actually felt our rifle barrels smash into each other like foils crossing in a fencing match. I fired a two-round burst into his chest.

He went down, and I drove my rifle butt into something that made him stop moving.

I didn't think the bullets had broken any of my ribs, though a few were sore as hell. My vision was clearing but spotty and my ears were ringing, and the floor was shaking again, big-time. A large group was coming down the hall on my right, out of sight but approaching the corner. I caromed another concussion grenade off the far wall and around the corner just to make them slow down.

It worked.

I've worked a lot of construction jobs while roaming around looking for work that pays under the table, and corners usually have two big, solid blocks forming an angle that anchors the drywall. That part of the corner facing me would be bulletproof. But basement walls often have furring strips behind the plaster in front of the corners, vertical supports evenly spaced apart that leave a lot of interior space behind the plaster.

So I charged the wall next to me, firing my rifle into it to identify the open spaces. I smashed through the plaster beside a furring strip and found myself tearing the plastic tray off of a Xerox machine while charging through a small storeroom of some kind. Bizarrely, the room held ordinary office supplies. Their very normalcy seemed out of place, somehow.

I kept charging the far wall, headed toward a little space beside a shelf rack. This time, I bounced painfully off a furring strip and erupted through drywall on the other side. Suddenly, I was in the middle of a pack of knights in a hallway. The lights were flickering, the sprite's work, and I shoulder-charged one of the knights off of his feet and started swinging the butt of my rifle at helmets superhumanly fast while they couldn't fire without the risk of hitting each other. Those few seconds were a disorienting nightmare, but when they were over, I was the only one standing. My left arm was throbbing where it had caught a rifle butt, and the top of my right shoulder was sore where a bullet had grazed the top of it, but there were four knights on the floor.

There was a narrow stairwell in front of me, and I went up it fast, using a crack of light under the door as a guide. As I neared the top, I jumped up, pushed one foot off the stairway railing, and propelled myself into the air above the door. Spreading my legs out, I braced the flats of my feet against the wall so that I was suspended above the door when automatic fire tore through it from the other side. What was left of the door was flung open and two rifle barrels and a shaft of light burst through.

There were a lot of things wrong with that picture. The arms holding the rifles weren't in armor, for one, and the weapons were different. They were rifles I'd never seen before, LWRC PSD rifles that fired a heavier armor-piercing round, actually, although I didn't find that out until later. I was already dropping before I realized that these men weren't knights. They smelled like wolves.

I didn't have time to ask questions, because even if these men didn't have knight training, they had some training, and jacked-up reflexes to boot. I fell half between them and half on them, and the next thing I knew, my own weapon was flying out of my hand and a stronger-than-normal elbow was shoving me backward through the air. I grabbed out with my suddenly free hands and seized the straps of their Kevlar vests, pulling them with me.

It probably would have looked cartoonlike to an observer: three men rolling over and ricocheting off of each other in a superhumanly fast frenzy of lashing limbs and dropping weapons and curses as they tumbled down a stairway.

I managed to drive the stiff side of a hand into a throat and crushed a larynx, then tumbled another man over me with my knees while we were rolling. For a moment, he managed to slow our roll with his hands on the stairwell walls, and I grabbed a Taurus 44 Tracker out of his side holster and shot him in the face. He went limp, and as soon as he stopped bracing us, I began sliding painfully down the stairs on my back, holding him on top of me and using his body as extra protection down the last few stairs.

The Taurus wasn't firing silver bullets. He would be fine after he woke up in an hour or so with the mother of all headaches.

The other one had stopped tumbling a few stairs above us and was sitting upright and clutching his throat, trying to force breath down into his lungs and making frantic pecking motions with his chin. I shot him in the head too, and then shot the new guy who was standing at the top of the stairs above him with another PSD rifle. I knocked him out of the doorway with several rounds into his torso.

"WAIT!!!" a voice screamed from the top of the stairs. "JUST WAIT A MINUTE, DAMMIT! YOU'RE HIM, AREN'T YOU?!? YOU'RE JOHN CHARMING."

"What if I am?" I said cautiously. I didn't raise my voice. Why bother? These were werewolves.

"I THINK I'LL GO HOME AND CHOP MY DICK OFF!" the voice yelled.

This was a safe phrase that Sig and I had worked out before going down into a vampire lair. I had taken it from an old George Carlin routine where the comedian was trying to come up with a combination of words that had never before been spoken in the English language.

The phrase was a way for Sig and me to let the other know that everything was okay and that we weren't being held under any kind of duress.

Whoever these guys were, Sig was either with them or had sent them.

That's how I met the wolf clan.

PART THE SECOND

*You Make Me Feel Like a
Natural Wolfman*

∾11∾

DEAR JOHN

My escape from the wilderness retreat the Templars were using as a stronghold is a series of blurred impressions: the sounds of scattered fighting before sonics went off somewhere and someone began flossing my skull with barbed wire. Running through a hallway just in front of a spreading gas cloud, the sweet smell of wolfsbane stinging at the root of my nostrils and causing my nose to bleed. Stepping over bodies in a darkened common area, running around the hood of a garbage truck that had rammed through double wooden front doors, and then, open morning air, a gravel parking lot where a truck was running over cars, presumably the knights' cars, a Nissan pulling up to us driven by a black-haired man with a single large eyebrow and a thick moustache, piling in with two other men and taking off.

I don't know where the sprite went. We weren't close and had been a little too close at the same time.

As soon as we were out of the range of the sonics and skidding too fast around the bends of a gravel road, the short red-haired guy in the shotgun seat began dialing on a cell phone. He was swollen with muscle, and when he twisted his head to address the backseat, his neck bulged with cords and tendons. "We're the Clan. We're here to rescue you. Gabriel, explain what's what to our guest."

The werewolf next to me, another short guy, though this one was wiry, looked like a full-blooded Native American or indigenous Mexican. He never took his eyes off the rear window while he talked. His nose had bled a little too. "Hi. I'm Gabriel. We're the Clan. We're here to rescue you."

There was a massive Hardee's bag full of wrappers and napkins jammed between the front seats, and I removed a napkin from it and began wiping my nose. "How did you get that code phrase?"

"I don't know," Gabriel said tersely.

"Let me clarify," I said. "If I think you harmed the person you got it from, I will kill every one of you right now and go back there and start killing your friends."

It was only then that he noticed the high-powered rifle that I'd taken off one the wolves I'd knocked out. It was pointed at his head.

"Hold on," Muscles the Leprechaun said from the front seat. I don't know if he was talking to the phone or me, but he withdrew a letter from somewhere, unfolded it, and passed it over the seat. I only glanced at it. I didn't know what her handwriting looked like, but it smelled like Sig.

The first two words were "Dear John."

Great.

The second line was "Don't kill the men you're with unless you have to. I've made a deal with them."

I only had one hand free, so I shoved the letter into a pouch in my armor. It was a page long and I didn't have time.

Muscles was having a tense discussion. Normally, I would

have been able to hear whoever was on the other line, but the car was making a lot of noise on the roads.

"It's a clusterfuck! There were a lot more knights there then we were expecting. We took them by surprise, but they were holding us off when we left. Maybe doing better than that. Our reinforcements from the woods never showed up."

There were more knights than they expected because the Grandmaster of the whole order was there, but I didn't share that information. I didn't know anything about these people.

"..."

"Yeah, we got him. He's fine. He was loose when we got there. He damaged two of us pretty badly, and there was a hallway full of dead knights behind him."

Probably not dead, or not most of them, anyway. Again, I didn't overshare.

"..."

"I don't know. He was about to start shooting us before I gave him the letter."

"..."

"Yeah."

"..."

"They probably have reinforcements coming. You can send them, but I don't know. Are you ready to turn the raid into a small-scale war?"

"..."

"No, I haven't seen them."

"..."

"Jesus! Well, what do you expect? We're werewolves, not weremonkeys. Do you want us to go get them?"

"..."

"He's dead."

"..."

"All right."

The Nissan suddenly braked at the side of a mountain road, and Muscles put the phone away with a quick "We gotta go."

Gabriel opened his side door and got out, urging me to hurry up after him, and the black-haired driver took off again as soon as I closed the door behind me. I followed the other two into the woods.

It was early morning, a soft bluish gray light outlining the trees, the ground beneath our feet slightly softened by the water that was still evaporating into the dense air around us. A beautiful sight. It was as if the world wasn't paying any attention to our bullshit.

"I'm Robert. We've got a Jeep parked on a logging trail near here," Muscles told me. "Are you ready for a short hike?"

"It would be better if we ran," I said.

Muscles nodded abruptly. "Let's go."

We loped through mountains and forest at a speed that no humans could maintain, falling into an easy pattern that felt natural. It was affirming in a way, bond-forming even, feeling them around me without looking, knowing I didn't have to hold back or explain anything. We were still edgy and wary when we arrived at a Jeep that a tall black man had parked next to a river, but there was a tangible difference, an almost-reluctant acknowledgment that we had achieved a shared purpose.

We took care of a few details fast: the black man was named Devonte. Muscles didn't want to tell me where we were going until he was sure we'd gotten free and clear. Nobody was sure if more werewolves than knights had been killed in the raid, etc. Nobody pulled a weapon on me after we filed into the Jeep, and I slowly unfolded Sig's letter. The ride was jolting and I had to pause frequently while reading, but I didn't really notice.

DARING

Dear John,

Don't kill the men you're with unless you have to. I made a deal with them.

I guess you want to know how I found you. That ring I gave you didn't really belong to my family. It belonged to a woman named Suzanne who committed suicide after her husband died, and Suzanne's spirit will follow that ring anywhere. I used her in a way that I'm not really proud of, but I know you lied to me. I don't want to be the person you give your life for. I don't want to be some point you make to yourself, or an excuse for you to finally quit and feel justified at the same time. Sorry.

You don't know how badly I want to bust in there and kill those knights so that I can kick your stupid ass myself, but I can't do it alone, so Parth contacted someone who could. The wolf clan... don't call them a pack, they hate that for some reason... won't let me come with them, but once they heard about you, they agreed to rescue you. It's not free, though. You have to go through some kind of thing. They won't really explain it to me, but it sounds like a cross between a cult initiation and fraternity hazing and basic training.

I think you should join them. You and I are in an impossible situation and we're working against each other and not telling each other everything, and that's not good. Neither of us wants to feel responsible for anything bad happening to the other, and we're both too wounded or guilty or god knows what to work well together.

My sponsor has been telling me about this phenomenon called New Relationship Energy. It's about chemistry and hormones and what we think is love at first sight, and sometimes people who barely know each other at all can think they've found the love of their life, especially if they're lonely and...fuck it. You're smart enough to know what I'm trying to say.

And you've never been with your own kind before, and you need that. Do you know what I would give to find a group of Valkyries to take me in? But really, the Clan can protect you in ways that I can't. I know, you're the man and you want to protect me. Go to hell, John Charming. I just got out of one fucked-up relationship with a man who was pretending to protect me from our world, but the truth is, he was just using that as an excuse to be who he was because he was afraid to be anything else. I had to take care of him in every way that really mattered. He was keeping me in the same place, and I don't want to be in the same place anymore. I want to grow up. If I aged normally, I'd almost be middle aged. I should have grown up a long time ago.

I don't know if I'm an addictive personality or not, but my mother set that example for me, and I'm back in that place I don't want to be. I know doing anything to escape my head right now is a bad idea, but part of me doesn't care and that scares me. I'm hanging on by my finger-nails here. I don't know what's right, and I can't be in a place where I'm worried about some man, and I don't know what's going to happen to him and I don't have any control over it. I have feelings for you, very strong feelings, but that's why you're not good for me right now. I'm sorry, but that's the way it is. Knowing that you were away and safe somewhere would be good for me, and it wouldn't be bad for you either, obviously, so if you really care about either one of us, why don't you just do that?

Okay, some jerk with a uni-brow is telling me to hurry up. And I know you're reading this letter first too, moron, and yes, I'm talking about you, uni-brow. And you'd better show this letter to John after you read it, because he won't cooperate with you if you don't. And if I ever see you again, good luck keeping all of your teeth. Or fangs. Whatever.

Sorry, John. I can't be any more confused and scared than I already am right now. I need to focus on the things that I have some control over. I think I said that already. I hope you can understand that. I do care about you and want you to be good, but I also know that's a long way away for you. Me too. I need some peace for a while and your life is chaos. I don't know if you look for it or if it looks for you, and I don't know how to end this letter. There's no time, and I shouldn't say what I want to say, and I don't want to say what I have to say. Heal. Survive. Even if you have to forget about me to do it. I am going to try to do the same.

Sig.

I read the letter several times. It didn't change. The Jeep abruptly skidded to a halt and Muscles turned around as far as his seat belt would allow. His face bore the distinct scars and burns of a lot of wrestling mats, and he looked a little agitated. "We need some air."

Devonte started to protest, but Muscles repeated himself with a crisp snap in his voice. "We need some air."

It was a good call. There was already a lot of adrenaline and testosterone in the atmosphere, and rage was pouring through my skin and filling up the crowded confines of that Jeep. My escorts left the doors of the Jeep open and fanned out into a wide triangle around me. I didn't bother trying to meditate, and I didn't scream up at the sky or kick the Jeep into scrap.

I just stepped out, sat on dry mud and leaves, and braced the stock of my rifle on the ground. Just sat there and thought about different ways to kill them all if they tried anything.

It calmed me.

I read Sig's letter one more time, searing the words into my memory, then burned the letter, literally, with a lighter from an armor pouch. It wasn't some big dramatic symbolic gesture. I just didn't want to leave behind any tangible proof that Sig had anything to do with the attack on the knights. Emil had given a witnessed oath that the knights would leave her alone if left alone, and it turned out he had more than enough authority to make that stick.

I understood what she'd written. All that stuff about simplifying her life, focusing on what she had control over, the mention of a sponsor. Sig had obviously been going to some AA meetings, and that was a good thing.

It was a great thing.

Yippee.

Muscles got back on his phone and talked to somebody else about who died and who didn't and gave the person on the other end of the line an estimation of my size. When he was done, he walked over to me and squatted down about ten feet away. He had good balance in spite of being top-heavy, and his small, thick hands had done a lot of fighting. He didn't smell like fear, but he was respectfully lowering his elevation so that he wouldn't seem aggressive or dominant, keeping his ego out of it. That's why he was the leader.

"You realize that you didn't actually save me," I told him. "I was freeing myself when you found me."

"I suppose you could argue that," he agreed carefully with an accent from somewhere down Pennsylvania way. "But we lost a lot of people on your account, and we did it because your woman asked us to. She promised us you'd go through our training camp."

The supernatural world takes promises very seriously.

"Balls. You would have gone anyway," I asserted rudely. "You saw a chance to take out some higher-ups in the Knights Templar and you took it."

He took a deep breath, released it. "Like I said, I'm not going to argue. I just lost some friends getting your ungrateful ass out of there, and arguing wouldn't be good for either of us. Your woman promised us you'd come along. If she lied about that, you can leave, but we'll have to visit her and renegotiate. We can't have people thinking they can use us."

For a brief, ugly moment, I got a surge of black satisfaction at the thought of Sig having to deal with a large, hostile werewolf paramilitary group while living her peaceful, controlled life. I'm not proud of it, but I had that moment.

On the other hand, it was a moment because it didn't last.

"You're telling me that if I want to protect the woman who's rejected me for trying to protect her without asking, I'm going to have to keep a promise that she made for me without asking in order to protect me."

He tried to untangle that sentence for a second and then gave up. "If you say so."

"I need a few days to take care of some things," I told him. "I'll come join you after that. And this time I'll be the one who gives you my word."

He didn't pretend to think about it. "No. You're coming with us or not. You have to decide now."

"You might want to step away and shut up again for a minute," I advised.

He smelled what was coming off of me and did.

So, yeah, that happened.

~12~

I THINK I CLAN I THINK I CLAN

One of the primary terms of the Pax Arcana is that monsters whose condition is contagious can't target specific humans for political or martial gain. A vampire can't start changing politicians into vampires in order to gather power, for example, and a small-scale war erupted between vampires and knights when heat-seekers started doing just that around the turn of the millennium. Along the same lines, a werewolf who wants to form a strong pack can't start tracking and biting ex–special forces members.

So when I eventually wound up in a national forest reserve and met a werewolf who was a forest ranger, I was a little disturbed by the coincidence. We were neck-deep in the Chequamegon-Nicolet National Forest of Wisconsin at this point. And just for the record, I was never interrogated, branded, tattooed, paddled, or taught any passwords or Latin chants by anybody in hooded robes. The worst thing I had to go through was some greasy fried chicken at a gas stop that served food out of grimy glass-covered bins, and a rest stop bathroom that hadn't been cleaned in the history of ever. I'm not prissy, but when you have an enhanced sense of smell, you notice these things.

The forest ranger was a lean and rangy werewolf who didn't have his defenses up the way the rest of us did, and he introduced himself by name, Lee Jacobs. Lee gave me one of the backpacks lying at his feet. The others shouldered backpacks of their own, and Lee then led us on a twenty-mile hike.

I wanted to know if the pack had intentionally targeted Lee and turned him into a werewolf because his job made him useful to them, but I was surrounded by alpha types itching to establish dominance on their own territory and my status was unclear, so I decided to be subtle.

"Hey, Lee," I asked. "Did the pack intentionally target you and turn you into a werewolf because you'd be useful to them?"

"Who cares?" Lee answered.

"No," said Gabriel, the only one there who seemed to understand the full ramifications of what I was asking. "We didn't."

"Okay," I said. "Is Gabriel your real name, by the way? Are you Native American or Latino or what?"

He didn't seem offended. "My mother was Chippewa. At least, my sister always says so. We grew up in a Catholic orphanage."

I wondered how old Gabriel really was, though I didn't ask. That question is as rude in the supernatural world as it is in the mundane one, though for different reasons. But the kind of situation he was describing with Native Americans and Catholic orphanages used to be a lot more common when I was a youngster.

After we'd walked in silence for a time, I ventured some more questions. "So, what is this place I'm going to, anyway? Is it a cult? Basic training? Obedience school? Is there a swimming pool and a weight room? Will I get clean towels?"

"Yeah, it's a werewolf spa." Lee snickered.

Gabriel took me seriously. "Phase one is more like one of those mental health retreats that Bobos go to in order to stop being Bobos."

"Bobos?" I asked.

"Bourgeoisie types who want to be spiritual or artsy while keeping their high incomes," Gabriel said helpfully. "You meet a lot of them when you're one of the People. Yuppie hippies."

"The point is," Muscles said impatiently. "We don't train newcomers to fight until we know they're stable and loyal."

"Not that you knights seem to care if we act responsible or not," Gabriel added.

I could have called Gabriel on including me with the knights, but like Muscles had said, these men had lost friends recently. There was real grief in their grimness, and restraint too, and *that* I respected. Respected it all the way to a heavily wooded area where a werewolf had been killed recently. I could smell the body though I couldn't see it.

Three males and one female, all werewolves, were waiting for us. Their leader was a small, trim Asian man, and his status would have been obvious even if my escorts hadn't stepped aside to let him inspect the small bags of flour and sugar and salt in their backpacks. The alpha had big glasses and long, thick black hair tied in a ponytail, and the machete slung over his shoulder reeked of disinfectant.

He and Muscles conferred.

The other three wolves and I were left looking at each other. The female, an attractive woman who, like Gabriel, could have been Native American or Latino, was staring at me a little more openly than the others, and not in a flirtatious way. She was athletic-looking, with short brown hair so dark that it was almost black, and a face of planed mahogany. Her body wasn't slender or long or big-breasted like a model's; it was solid and small-breasted. She was firm and strong-looking and had pleasing features and a dense, musky scent.

Her eyes widened as Muscles described our lodge escape to the Asian man—they were standing a polite distance away, but that's all it was: politeness. We could all hear everything.

"Welcome to the pack," she said quietly.

Not quietly enough. The Asian man left my escorts and came over to address me. "We do not call ourselves a pack. We call ourselves a Clan to emphasize our humanity. We are fully sentient beings, and we are here by choice as much as by instinct."

Wow.

"I'm not here by choice or instinct," I informed him.

He absorbed my comment seriously, turned it over in his head a few times, and decided that he needed more data. "You are welcome here nonetheless. My name is Chai Song, and I am the leader of this paw."

"Paw?" I repeated. "As in daddy?"

"The Clan is our father," he agreed. I wondered if the Clan was as patriarchal as that sounded, or if he just thought of it in those terms because his name was Hmong. "But that is not why we call ourselves a paw."

I went along with it. "So why do you?"

Chai held up his hand and flexed all five fingers. "These camps are for new or young wolves, and we are organized in groups of five, like digits on a paw."

Or like sleeper cells or strike teams. If any of us were captured by knights, we couldn't tell much about the organization as a whole.

"How does the word *paw* emphasize our humanity?" I wondered.

Chai's eyes narrowed. It was pretty obvious that I wasn't going to be his favorite. "We are also set apart. This place is not about denying what we are. It is about recognizing our dualities and rejecting the boundaries that are illusions. It is about embracing our nature. All of it."

I wasn't sure if I was supposed to applaud or howl, so I just nodded.

"We do not allow stimulants of any kind here," Chai went on. "Not coffee or chocolate or cocaine derivatives or types of speed. You may not get your paw mates to do your share of the chores or harass them sexually. You may not leave the perimeter that I will walk you around. You may not carry any weapons other than the knife I will give you, not until we have accepted you into the Clan. You do not have to join us, but if we determine that you are unable or unwilling to control yourself and that your behavior represents a threat to the Clan's continued stability, we will kill you. Do you understand?"

"There's no coffee?" I repeated blankly.

By this time, Chai had collected enough information to conclude, almost correctly, that I was being sarcastic. "Let's have an opening exercise. Each one of us will introduce ourselves, but instead of identifying ourselves with nouns the way Americans are trained to do, we will give our name and one adjective describing ourselves. Not our former occupations. Not where we are from or how much money we made. Not a hobby or our religion. An adjective."

He looked over at the woman. "Mayte, why don't you start us off?"

She was biting her lip, but she complied. "I am Mayte Reyes, and I am amused."

The next one to speak was a young, baby-faced blond kid

who had lost a lot of weight fast, and recently too. Becoming a werewolf burns a lot of calories, and this kid looked kind of soft and silly, sheathed in loose skin that hadn't had time to reabsorb or slough off or contract or do whatever the hell it is that leftover loose skin does. "Jelly, and I'm hungry."

I nodded politely.

The third person to speak up was a muscular young male, probably the early- to mid-twenty-year-old that he looked like. He had a lot of tattoos and shaggy black hair and fairly vibrated in place. He wore his cargo pants and long-sleeved thermal shirt with a calculated air of casual insolence that I might have believed if I couldn't smell how angry and scared he was. "Cory. Cory Davis. I'm frustrated."

After a moment he glanced at Mayte and added, "Sexually too."

Mayte rolled her eyes.

Cory wanted to continue but Chai indicated me, and Cory shut up immediately.

"I'm John Charming," I said, ignoring the awkward silence that followed this. "Huggable."

"Sarcasm is for those who are afraid to embrace life," Chai said softly.

"Then I just told you something about myself," I pointed out.

He bowed his head slightly. "Chai Song. Welcoming."

Is that something you can just declare? I didn't feel very welcomed.

"Seriously?" I asked.

"Seriously." Chai held his palms out. He could have been going for a Buddha pose or giving me an air hug despite my penchant for irony. "It is tough love around here, but it is love. We want what is best for everyone."

The other three were suspiciously silent.

"Why don't you show John around and explain how we do things," Chai told Mayte. "John and I can talk privately later."

There wasn't a lot to show me. My new community had one tent, but apparently that tent was being used to store meat, not to sleep in. I smelled blood and bear and salt coming from it, anyway. The tent was near a dead campfire too, and I guess the tent's screens and smoke would help keep insects from laying eggs in the meat. The tent was going to have to be cleaned a lot or burned at some point, though.

Two tarps had been strung over a handmade log platform to make a roof and a floor. Three other vertically hung tarps made crude walls. There were still air mattresses that hadn't been deflated on the platform and Mylar sleeping bags. Presumably, the tarp I'd brought would fill the hole where one had been removed.

"Chai keeps encouraging us to sleep in a big group huddle for warmth," Mayte observed. "I'm not spiritually enlightened enough yet."

"Even with Cory being so respectful about boundaries?" I asked.

She laughed. "Even with."

It was near the fire site that I found the source of the death stink. A body was bundled up in a tarp and set on a handmade travois. Gabriel and Lee came by and didn't say good-bye or good luck; just picked up the travois between them and left.

"Why didn't you just bury the body somewhere out in the woods?" I wondered.

"Really?" Mayte asked. "That's your first question? Not who he was or how he died or why?"

I shrugged. "There are lots of reasons I can think of for killing a werewolf. I can't think of many for keeping its dead, stinking body around."

She thought that was amusing for some reason. "I don't know, but I've only been...you know...for a few weeks. Maybe the Clan has some kind of special burial ceremony."

"So who was he?" I asked. "How did he die? Why?"

She barked a short laugh. "He was the last guy who gave Chai a hard time."

I whistled softly. "That really is tough love."

"Well, he did try to rape me," Mayte said. "And escape. And then he attacked Chai. I guess we run on a three-strikes program here."

"You don't seems too upset about the attempted rape."

Mayte lowered her chin. It's an instinctive thing people do when they're trying to protect themselves, covering their throat, and often a useful poker tell. "I'm trying not to get upset about anything. Too many strong feelings around here already. And anyway, Chai didn't stop him. I did."

"Ex-cop or ex-military?" I asked.

She laughed again. "Both. I was an MP in the army."

"And you do some kind of unarmed combat that involves lots of punching." I could tell by her hands.

"Tim wouldn't have been much of a threat, anyway. He was a wreck. He was going through meth withdrawal on top of..." Mayte hesitated, then curled her fingers so that they looked like claws and made a big dramatic snarl face. "You know."

I smiled a little grimly. "I know."

Mayte's answering smile was lopsided. "Tim couldn't handle it all. So Chai cut his head off with that machete of his."

Yep. That would do it, all right.

"Is everyone here newly turned?" I asked.

"Werewolves don't turn," Mayte mock-lectured me. The slight accent and soft voice she affected sounded exactly like Chai, and her face took on his air of intent seriousness. "To *turn* implies opposition. Vampires *turn* from life to death. Werewolves *change* into something new and exciting. We are not monsters. We are butterflies."

I was supposed to laugh, but I couldn't. "Chai actually said that?"

"He did," Mayte affirmed. "He says a caterpillar is frightened while it's changing. It feels closed in by this thing that's bigger than it is, and it's thrashing around, trying to get free, and has no idea what's going on. But it's on the way to becoming something beautiful. I like the idea of being a butterfly."

Sure she did. A carnivorous butterfly that grew claws and fangs and had territorial instincts and fight-or-flight instincts out the ass.

My stomach growled, and Mayte slapped my abdominal muscles with the flat back of her hand in a friendly fashion. "It's almost lunchtime."

"Bear stew?" I ventured.

Mayte chuckled. "There are other things to eat, too. Fish and birds and rabbit and deer and cross-country skiers."

I didn't say anything, and after an awkward moment, she relented. "You know the skier thing was a joke, right?"

I smiled and she added, "It's not even winter yet."

I liked Mayte, and as soon as I realized that, I had a Sig spasm. Ever seen those movies where an actor or actress gets their body hair removed by waxing? The attendant just rips off a patch with this sudden sharp tearing sound and holds up a fur-covered adhesive strip while the person on screen gasps and whimpers? When I thought about Sig, it felt like my heart had just gotten waxed.

Mayte didn't notice, or if she did, she didn't care. She went ahead and elaborated on some of the rules Chai hadn't spelled out. All weapons, tools, and eating utensils were communal property except for our knives. Newcomers that we were, we weren't encouraged to change into wolves to hunt. At the same time, only designated hunters were allowed to use crossbows, and only on big game. We killed small game by using our speed, and senses, although I might be allowed to help Chai set snares and fishing lines since no one else knew how. All kills were shared.

Members of the group rotated responsibilities. One day I might be in charge of sanitation, another hunting, water gathering, food preparation, sentry duty, wood collecting, or foraging.

"That doesn't sound too bad," I said judiciously.

"Maybe to you. I never set foot in the woods before any of this. Now I'm supposed to know how to do all this survival stuff just because I'm a..." Mayte hesitated again. I wondered if she'd ever actually called herself a werewolf out loud. In any case, her next words either changed the subject or continued it obliquely. "That meth addict I was talking about? I kind of know how Tim felt."

I stayed silent to encourage her to continue.

"It's not all bad, this wolf thing," Mayte confessed. "It's just everything is more intense. There's a reason so many people try to dull their senses, you know? With alcohol or drugs or television or whatever."

"I know what you mean," I agreed, and I did. It seems like half the time people are doing stupid things to artificially put themselves to sleep, and half the time they're doing stupid things to artificially wake themselves up.

"I feel like a power line." Mayte made a *bzzzzz* noise and vibrated as if she were being electrocuted to demonstrate. "Sometimes it's kind of cool, but other times it's too much stuff to deal with all at the same time."

I pulled my arms in and stuck my hands out awkwardly high, next to my shoulders, then flapped them frantically like tiny wings fluttering to lift my obviously too-heavy body. "Butterfly, Mayte. Butterfly."

She laughed and smacked my shoulder with greater-than-human strength.

It reminded me of Sig.

∾13∾

OCTOPUPPY

So, wait, the knights wanted you to infiltrate us?" Mayte hadn't been an investigator for the military police, but she still had a tendency to turn our group sessions into interrogations. I didn't mind. In fact, I was finding Mayte increasingly attractive.

Sig had told me to get lost and heal. Maybe I should just bury myself in somebody else. Penis-first.

No, a small hermetically sealed group of emotionally charged people dealing with becoming werewolves was not a good place for recreational distraction sex, and I was too old for that sort of dumbfuckery anyhow. Not too old for the hurt impulse though.

"Yes. The Order wanted me to spy on you," I said. Usually, these sessions were brief little sit-downs where us newbies gave Chai something he called emotional weather updates—if we were having a good day, we might say that we were sunny, for example. "Stormy" usually meant angry, "Foggy" was confused, and references to rain and clouds usually indicated some kind of sadness. Sometimes, the emotional weather reports turned into long sweat sessions where one person talked and everyone else got to make observations or ask questions.

I was currently on the spot because I had made the mistake of joking about my internal weather update. I had said that I was cloudy with a slight chance of crippling self-doubt. Chai had decided my comment was worth exploring. Chai was a very literal and serious werewolf, which sort of sounds like the first sentence of a children's story, but I can't help that.

We were all sitting around a campfire, perched on benches made out of fallen trees that we'd pruned and dragged into the site. I liked the land but didn't much like the wind or the cold.

"And the Clan just let you in?" Jelly asked.

It was unusual for Jelly to actually listen or participate. He had been a low-level meth dealer, had in fact been the drug connection for the late Tim, which was also how he'd wound up getting bitten. Jelly wasn't very bright or energetic, and I had a feeling that becoming a meth dealer hadn't been a decision that Jelly had made so much as the result of a long string of decisions that he had avoided.

"The Clan didn't *let* me join," I told him. "They insisted I join."

"So how do we know you're not pulling some kind of James Bond bullshit and spying on us?" Cory demanded. Cory was full of restless energy, an extreme sports type, or at least he had been before he and several friends stumbled across a pack of wolves while looking for a good place in the middle of nowhere to go rock climbing.

"Ask Chai," I said.

"You're all letting John deflect you," Chai chided. "He's very good at avoidance strategies, and he brought up the knights because every time he mentions them, you start asking him questions about them instead of him."

It was true. My paw mates were new to the supernatural world, and the existence of the Knights Templar fascinated and frightened them.

"Yes, but if John is here to spy on us, wouldn't that be causing him stress?" Mayte asked disingenuously.

I dug my pocketknife out of my pants and spoke into it like it was a microphone. "They're on to me. Code Purple. I repeat, Code Purple."

"Just saying." Mayte smiled cheerfully.

"If I'm a spy, this Clan is the worst evil organization ever," I said. "James Bond never had to sit around a campfire talking about his feelings."

"I think you're missing the point," Chai said, still calmly. "If you were a spy, you would be the bad guy. The Knights would be the evil organization."

"So what would that make you?" I asked. "Chai Bond? James Song?"

"Leave Chai alone," Mayte admonished, but she had a twinkle in her eye. The human mind can adjust to just about anything, and the shock of seeing Chai cut off a man's head had begun wearing off with my paw mates somewhat. Chai was always composed and determinedly logical.

"What is causing your stress, John?" Chai repeated quietly. His voice was still clinical and cool, but I could hear the faintest suggestion of cracks forming in the ice. He might be some kind of guru or sensei, but Chai was still a werewolf whose authority was being challenged in front of other wolves.

I considered pushing Chai a little more just to see what would happen. There were all sorts of ways to play with the idea of a werewolf therapist being James Bond. *Live and Let Cry.* No wait, would *Live and Let It All Out* be better? *Live and Let Chai? Full Moonraker. The Spy Who Emotionally Displaced Needs onto Me. Dr. Noooooarrrhgggh!*

But I let it go.

"I don't know, Chai," I said. "Maybe I'm upset because I spent my whole life being raised by a brotherhood that wouldn't accept me and wouldn't let me go, and now I've been kidnapped by another so-called family with the same attitude. Maybe I'm frustrated because the knights who I grew up with could never trust me because I was a werewolf, and you werewolves will never be able to really trust me because I was a knight."

Chai started to say something, but I overrode him. "Or maybe I'm upset because it doesn't make any sense but my fucking heart feels like it's fucking broken whether it makes any fucking sense or not, even if all I've lost is a potential for something real, and instead of talking to the one fucking person on this planet who I actually want to talk to, I'm stuck here collecting fucking splinters in my ass and getting grilled about my fucking feelings by a bunch of people I don't know and don't trust and don't really give a damn about, if you want God's honest truth."

Something had loosened in my chest. Blood was rushing through my face and emotions were breaking through my voice. "Or maybe I'm upset because your Clan wants to use me. You want to kill me to show that knights aren't invincible, or recruit me to show that werewolves are better than knights, or study me to see if you can figure out something about knights that will help you kill them more efficiently, and I get that, I really do. Hell, I might even do the same. But you don't care about me, and I'm fine with that, but I wish you'd stop pretending because this touchy-feely new age stuff is bullshit! I'm not falling for it, and I really wish we could just skip all this and get to the part where you screw me over and the killing starts, but apparently that isn't happening anytime soon."

Nobody said anything.

Then Chai began to clap. One by one, the others joined in, like they were extras in the climactic scene of a romantic comedy.

"Fuck you all," I told them.

∾14∾

YOGA DO, WE MUST

We were doing Qigong at sunrise, our breath misting and sparkling in the sporadic shafts of light that pierced the canopy of trees as if angels had been firing arrows through them. Our hands and ears cold, we moved until sweat began to condense on our warming skin, until our muscles loosened and our focus sharpened.

In some ways, Qigong is combat-oriented. It's kind of like the concept of that first Karate Kid movie where Pat Morita has Ralph Macchio practicing martial arts movements by cleaning things in spiraling block patterns over and over. You know, "wax on...wax off"–type movements whose repetition lays a foundation for martial arts to build upon later. Cool concept, even if the execution in that movie was complete shit.

"Strengthen your spine, Mayte."

Chai's tendency to always single people out by name annoyed me. Specific commentary requires more commentary, and it can create competition. I imagined pulling energy out of the ground through my feet.

"Keep your face soft and expressionless, Cory."

Chai's own face wasn't soft and expressionless. It looked slightly pained. Sometimes, these abnormal growths called fistulas form in the rectum. Chai looked like he had a fistula.

I'm not ruling out the possibility that the fistula was me.

"Breathe into the movement, Jelly."

That's right. Breathe. I took a deep, cleansing breath and tried to follow it all the way down into my center, though my legs, my feet, into the ground.

"Try to be more fluid, Jelly."

Fluid. I imagined gravity flowing off of me. Invisible balloons pulling my arms up into the air.

"You're all thinking about what you're doing too much; relax."

Oh, for God's sake. I had a sudden picture of Chai standing above us on an elevated platform, yelling down at us through a megaphone: "DISCOVER EQUANMITY, TRANQUILITY, AND STILLNESS, DAMMIT!!!"

I stepped out of horse stance without asking and began silently walking among the others, adjusting Cory's hips and shoulders, stepping on the tops of Jelly's feet to force them off their heels. My touch made them a little uncomfortable, but they didn't challenge it, and Cory gave me a terse nod.

Mayte didn't seem to mind my touch at all. In fact, she somehow leaned the small of her back into my palm even while allowing me to smooth her spine out, consciously or unconsciously.

A lot of Americans find another's touch uncomfortable. I think our society tends to either sexualize physical contact or isolate it, maybe because we're bombarded with sexual imagery so constantly that we're either hypersensitized or desensitized. Maybe because physical contact forces people to be aware of their own bodies, and Americans are taught to ignore their bodies. I'm not an America-basher, by the way—every country has its own cultural strengths and weaknesses and weirdness. I will say that as far as I know, only in English are the words "self" and "conscious" put together to mean something bad.

My efforts had at least one positive effect. They shut Chai up for a few minutes, until he said, "John, why don't you model Bow Stance to Shoot the Hawk for us?"

I stared at him. I was okay one on one, but being the direct focus of a group was where my own hang-ups came in, and Chai knew it. Was Chai trying to help me grow or put me in my place? Was he saying "I think you're ready" or "You think it's so easy, you try being an instructor, smart-ass"? Did he even know?

I planted my feet, squaring my shoulders and settling my weight. Then I pulled energy up from the ground with my breath, into my groin, where it drew my tailbone in. The energy, imaginary or not, flowed up my spine, straightening it. I swiveled my hips until I was facing Chai and pointed my left foot at him though this was a knight variation, centered my knee and my chin on him as well. My hands were drawing up to my chest in the same motion, and I inhaled while my hands went out, as if breathing in were creating a vacuum between Chai and me that was pulling the hands onward. When I drew the bow with my right hand, I exhaled, then inhaled on the release.

I had forgotten everyone else by this point, even Chai, though a part of me was focusing on him intently. I reversed the movement and slid my right foot forward, let myself empty so that the universe could come in, an ocean pouring through my body, shaping my movements.

There have been times when that feeling of connection has been the only thing that's kept me sane. Assuming I am.

Mayte's voice snapped me out of it. "You are so full of shit."

I didn't halt my movements. "Could you be more specific?"

"All the attitude. The whole bitter act," Mayte sort of elaborated. "But when you do this stuff, it's like watching a poem written by God."

"God is fine," I said as I released another arrow toward Chai. "It's the rest of us I have a problem with."

～15～

INTROSPECTION FOR DUMMIES

One-on-one sessions with Chai were in a glade far enough away from the camp that there was actually some degree of privacy. A portable CD player played some kind of new age stuff that sounded like aborigine instruments being used to help a woman imitate Enya. At any rate, there was definitely a bull-roarer and a didgeridoo in there somewhere.

I think the music was meant to mask the sounds of our conversation from eavesdroppers. Either that or just drive them away.

"We need a smokeless fire for daytime cooking," I told Chai.

I was a lousy patient, if that's what I was. I won't deny it. I was using my solo session to try to convince Chai to address the camp cooking issues. The Clan had a strict policy about not lighting fires during the day, because it didn't want to leave any smoke trails floating above the tree line. It was a major pain in the ass, because we had to do everything involving fire use after sunset, including cleaning and sterilizing.

As it turned out, Chai knew full well what a Dakota smokeless fire pit was though he didn't call it that himself; Chai hadn't told me a lot about his life, but it was clear that he'd spent a lot of it outside and knew something about concealing trails and scents and minimizing noise and disposing waste. You can't spend days on end with somebody in an outdoor setting and not pick up on stuff like that.

"Bernard's orders about not cooking during the day were very clear," Chai responded. I still hadn't met the mysterious leader of the Clan, but whenever Chai dropped the B word, it was like he had discovered one of the ten thousand names of God. If names weren't capitalized, this Bernard's would have been anyhow.

"If this is about avoiding detection, smokeless fire pits are actually better than burning fires at night," I argued. "Knights have access to aerial spotters and satellites."

I felt a slight internal wrench when I offered this information. Geez. I mean, Geas.

To his credit, Chai thought about it. I wondered what the penalty for error had been when he was growing up, or where he'd grown up, or how he'd wound up in the middle of a Wisconsin-based werewolf clan.

Unexpectedly, Chai's façade cracked a little. He sighed, and it was like watching an accordion fold. "This is the problem with being both the head of a paw and its counselor. I'm triggering your authority issues left and right."

"Personnel shortage problems?" I guessed.

His face froze. "That's clan information."

I waited.

Chai sighed again. "My point was, you are not the only one caught between a rock and a hard place, John."

I waited.

"I'll make you a deal," Chai said. "I'll get you permission to build a wind funnel fire. But you need to teach Jelly and Cory how to make them as well."

I grimaced. "It would be more efficient if we just did it ourselves."

"It's not about the making," Chai said patiently. "It's about the teaching."

"So why exclude Mayte?" I wondered.

He shook his head. "You are less guarded around females than males. Have you noticed that?"

I thought about it. "Most of my issues come from growing up among hostile males. Women get under my defenses easier. And I like the way they smell."

Thankfully, Chai didn't take this opportunity to explore my lack of a mother figure. "This is for Cory and Jelly too. You can help teach them self-discipline. I can only teach them other-discipline."

He smiled sadly. "I limited myself to that role when I had to kill Timothy in front of them."

"Does that happen a lot? You having to kill..." I trailed off. What were we? Recruits? Students? Patients? Cult members? Chai might say we were family, but could you really say that just because we were all werewolves?

"How much is a lot?" Chai sounded tired. "It happens more than it should. But the Clan saves far more werewolf lives than it takes. How long do you think Jelly and Cory would last without supervision or guidance?"

"Not long," I admitted.

"The knights don't have any programs for teaching new werewolves to adapt." A rare growl entered Chai's voice. "They expect us to figure it out or die. But giving werewolves time and space to work things out among peers causes far less disruptions to their precious Pax than waiting for eruptions and eliminating them."

"Large groups are harder to conceal than individuals," I said cautiously. Chai didn't open up much, and I didn't want him to stop.

Chai disagreed, and not all that politely. "The answer is control, and werewolves have social instincts. It's the most powerful control mechanism for moderating our behavior there is, but the same knights who want us to control ourselves do everything in their power to isolate us."

That actually made sense.

"It must be difficult," I probed. "Having to kill someone after spending so much time trying to understand them."

"Of course it is." Chai smiled but not really. "Everything I know about martial arts, I learned as a by-product of meditation. I had weak lungs as a child. I learned Chinese boxing because someone told my family that its breathing techniques would help clear and strengthen my lungs. And it did. But I always wanted to be a healer."

He looked at me wryly. "I suspect that we are opposites in that respect. Everything you know about meditation, you learned as a by-product of learning how to kill people."

I didn't confirm or deny that. "So it's doubly hard for you to kill someone you've tried to understand."

Chai waved that off. "That's hard for anyone. It's why knights don't want to understand us."

"It's why I don't want to get to know you too well," I admitted. "I'd like to believe that this isn't all going to end in blood somehow. But I don't."

Suddenly, Chai became so intense that he seemed to freeze time. It was as if he were absorbing gravity and light, becoming the center of the glade. "That is when it is most important."

He didn't explain what "it" was.

He didn't have to. "Who did you lose, Chai?"

He smiled that sad smile again. "Work with Cory and Jelly."

∿

"What I really want is some itos," Jelly said, and those normally dull and lifeless brown eyes of his contained a low guttering flicker of pure lust. "Doritos, Fritos, Tostitos; give me any kind of ito as long as I can dip it in some cheese. Nacho cheese."

Food was really the only thing that Jelly talked about without prompting, at least with any frequency or passion. We hadn't killed any boars, and he had just finished a five-minute treatise on bacon.

"Well, there's Danny DeVito." I was smacking and packing dirt around the edge of the pit Jelly was digging. "I guess you can eat him."

Jelly lowered his shovel and looked around as if trying to spot the actor. It was the closest thing to a joke I'd seen from him.

Cory grunted and cupped his testicles. "How about my big burrito?"

Jelly didn't bother to respond directly. "How about some coquitos with a little sausalito?"

"Sausalito is a city in California," I pointed out. "You're a werewolf, not Godzilla."

"I'll bet he could do it," Cory muttered.

"Make your exit point slope more." I walked over to demonstrate. The trickiest part about building a Dakota smokeless fire pit is not collapsing the ventilation tunnel. Basically, you build a pit, then build a sideways hole with a sloping exit out from the bottom of that pit. The idea isn't to channel the smoke out—the hole draws wind in and fans the flames of the fire, keeping them so hot that they burn the fuel bits that usually produce emissions. "You can't make the hole vertical, Cory."

"The hell I can't," he snickered.

I didn't even know what that meant, and I still wanted to smack him. One thing I'd discovered in the last hour was that hanging around two idiots who healed fast gave me lots of Three Stooges–style impulses.

Cory continued his theme. "Just don't get any ideas about eating Mayte. I saw her first." He stuck out his tongue and waggled it suggestively. Suddenly there was an underlying hostility and tension in the air. He was pretending to make a joke, but he was giving me a real warning.

Ignoring Cory really wasn't working. I planted the tip of my spade in the ground and leaned on the handle. "You need to adjust your attitude about Mayte."

I was going to elaborate on how we were a bunch of people in a volatile state who were crammed into a small space and that emotions were running high and sexuality was one hell of a spark when it came to making drama explode even under normal circumstances—I really was. But Cory responded by jumping out of the furrow he was digging and strutting up to me as if ready to start something, holding his collapsible trench shovel at his side and shaking it up and down. I casually swung the spade in my hand like a golf club and dislocated his left kneecap. Cory dropped his trench shovel and fell to the ground howling.

"Was there something you wanted to say to me, Cory?" I asked mildly.

"Fuck you!" he yelled, then tried to regain his feet before collapsing into a half-fetal position and yelling again.

"Yeah, healing fast isn't really going to help you here," I said sympathetically. "Nothing is broken or ripped. Your kneecap is just locked out of place."

Cory tried to grab his knee and straighten it then, but screamed and thrashed backward almost immediately.

I crouched down. "The thing is, Cory, I like Mayte. When you talk about her that way, it hurts my feelings."

"Fuck you!" he screamed again.

"Jelly?" I spoke slowly and clearly. "Would you hold Cory's arms against his sides and brace him? I'm going to fix his knee."

It took a little awkward negotiating after that, but once I had Cory's knee firmly locked, anything resembling a fight went out of him. I torqued his leg sharply to the right with my weight pressing downward, and he screamed as his kneecap snapped back into place.

I stood back up and waited for Cory to quiet down. Even with a werewolf's healing, I had a little bit of time before he would be moving quickly on that leg again. "So what's with all the sex talk, Cory? Are you a perv or something? You one of those guys who goes into porn theaters in a trench coat?"

"Fuck you!" he gasped again.

"I'm being serious," I said. "Nobody thinks you're funny. You're sure as hell not turning Mayte on. You ought to be able to smell that. What's going on with you?"

Cory got so red that he looked like a sunburn victim. Jelly smirked, but fortunately he was still behind Cory when he did it. Cory struck me as the kind of guy who would try to shunt embarrassment away by humiliating somebody weaker.

"I...look, it's my body, all right?" Cory said. "This is messed up! Before all this happened, I was running six miles every day over rooftops! I was climbing stuff and lifting weights and doing things, you know? And now I've got all this energy and I'm not doing anything at all, and I'm not doing anything else to take the edge off, either! It's driving me crazy!"

I did kind of know what he meant. My normal exercise routines had been disrupted too.

"No real exercise, no sex, no television, no drinking, no

smoking, no video games!" Cory went on, tears starting to stream down his cheeks. "My friends are dead, man! The only one I've got left got put in some other group and I can't even talk to him! Who knows what my family thinks. And I'm goinna die if I don't go along with it? What the hell?!?"

I'd forgotten that Cory was in a group of people who were attacked by wolves. He never talked about it during Chai's sessions. Some people's sex drives get amped way up when they see death firsthand. It's a real thing, like an alarm has gone off and their sperm are trying to jump out of a burning building.

Cory pleaded, "Why can't we just take a day and go running on some rocks?!? Burn off some energy!"

Something clicked. For whatever reason, Cory's lifestyle had been arranged to avoid having to focus on his feelings. Now he was being forced to isolate his feelings and examine them at the same time that he had more intense feelings than he'd ever had before, and all his coping mechanisms were gone.

A thought about getting him a copy of *Introspection for Dummies* flashed through my mind like a passing subway train, but I didn't let it out of my mouth.

"Maybe you and I can spar a little," I offered. "I need to burn off energy, too. Hell, you're more relaxed now, aren't you?"

Cory actually laughed. He looked away and mumbled an invitation to oral sex under his breath, but he laughed.

"We're not supposed to do stuff like that until we become a claw," Jelly objected.

Becoming a claw was the next step in a paw's evolution. It was where clan members began receiving military training.

I stared at Jelly, thinking about what Cory had just told me. If Jelly had been a comfort eater before becoming a werewolf, maybe that explained his food obsession too. It had to be frustrating. Here he was, hungrier than he'd ever been, able to eat massive quantities without gaining weight for the first time in his life, and he couldn't get near a cheesecake or a stack of waffles or a plate of French fries.

"People die from overdoses," I told them. I hadn't meant for it to be a cryptic statement, but they both looked at me blankly.

"So?" Cory demanded.

"They die from eating too much too." I looked at Jelly. "Or drinking too much. They get so addicted to texting, they do it while they're driving. They get so addicted to endorphin rushes that they get heart attacks from pushing their bodies too hard. Do you understand what I'm saying?"

Cory made a short *tchht* sound. "Man, I hardly ever understand what you're saying."

"If you were free to do whatever you wanted, you'd get yourselves killed right now," I said. "I don't know how it would play out, but you would. If you didn't kill yourselves outright, you'd draw attention to yourselves, and then somebody like me would come along to quietly take you out."

"I thought the Clan was supposed to be bullshit," Jelly observed.

I didn't have an answer for that.

∾16∾

ME AND MY SHADOW SELF

We all have a shadow self."

For this exercise, Chai had made us take down two of our tarps and rehang them to make a wall on the edge of a clearing. We were standing across from the side of the wall that was facing the sun, staring at our reasonably undistorted shadows. I couldn't decide if this was an effective visualization tool or a lot of work for a steaming pile of horseshit.

Mayte waved at her shadow tentatively. Hi there. Cory gave his the finger. Jelly had his hands shoved in his pockets as he stared at his shadow sullenly. I used my hands to make a bouncing shadow bunny.

Chai, on the other hand, studied us, and I realized that this was the real point of the exercise, not for us to visualize our shadow selves in a physical metaphor, but for Chai to observe our body language as we did so. Mayte was friendly and hopeful. Cory was self-destructive. Jelly was passive. I was using humor as a defense mechanism. It was a cute trick.

"Face your dark side," Cory intoned dramatically, and then dropped into a fighting stance. Despite my attempts to erase some of his bad habits, he still extended his lead foot too far and angled his elbows dramatically away from his center of gravity. It was better to look good than to fight good.

"Your shadow self is not evil, Cory." Chai's voice held a mild reprimand. "That is a common Western misconception. The shadow self is just the part of ourselves that we are afraid of. Someone society considers bad might have a shadow self that is gentle or compassionate."

Chai made air quotes around the word *bad*. "A *bad* person might push caring feelings down because they make that person feel weak or vulnerable."

"But that's not common," I observed with some air quotes of my own. "*Bad* is whatever most people in a society *aren't* doing. Otherwise, we'd call it something else."

Chai didn't appreciate the contribution, but he went with it. "That is true. Most shadow selves are aggressive or selfish or sexual. The feelings their owners were taught to feel guilty about and repress as children. But these qualities are not inherently evil. They are necessary, in moderation."

I eyed my shadow. For me more than the others, my shadow self would be the wolf. The rest of the paw hadn't grown up believing that werewolves existed or fearing that they might be one. "So when we change into wolves..."

"The wolf doesn't repress anything," Chai said firmly. "The wolf doesn't care about man law. The wolf cares only about what it really feels. This is why our shadow selves tend to come out when we transform, and this is why so many people think lycanthropy is a disease or a type of demon possession. Have you heard anything I've said, Jelly?"

"I don't get it," Jelly said, his face closed off. He said it with the certainty and ease of long practice, a kind of smugness, even. That had probably been Jelly's mantra all through the high school he hadn't graduated from. He had probably sat there blank-faced and bored and inert and insolent and repeated, "I don't get it," whenever any teacher asked him anything, until the teacher either gave up and answered the question for him or moved on to some other student who was demanding attention.

"What are you afraid of, Jelly?" Chai said softly, stepping closer.

"I don't know," Jelly said, not even pretending to think about it.

Chai stepped up into Jelly's personal space. "Really? I know. I know exactly what you're afraid of."

Suddenly, Jelly remembered seeing Chai cut off a man's head. His eyes opened all the way. His spine stiffened.

"You are afraid of sudden, unpredictable violence," Chai said softly, almost like a lover but definitely not.

Jelly was squirting fear out of his pores now.

"Do you know how I know this, Jelly?" Chai asked, his voice still silk.

Jelly didn't say anything. I'm not sure he could.

Chai walked around him then, circling like a shark. "Because I want to beat the shit out of you right now just to get your attention. You are acting in a way that makes me want to do it."

Chai leaned in from behind and whispered in Jelly's ear. "Fear makes people behave in a way that makes their fears come true."

"But you're saying there are werewolves who really do become gentle and meek when they transform under a full moon?" Mayte was upset about something, and I don't think it was the way Chai was sweating Jelly.

"Yes." Chai's face was unreadable, though his scent was full of adrenaline and his heartbeat was accelerated. "Which do you think becomes a legend, the werewolf who quietly hunts rabbits and squirrel and deer and runs through forests, or the one who takes out its repressed rage on that annoying neighbor or ex-lover?"

"I have to pee." Mayte abruptly walked off smelling like sadness and fury and shame.

There was a story there that she hadn't shared with the rest of us yet. Maybe Chai knew it.

"So it's that simple?" I demanded. "The werewolf becomes the impulses that we've been shoving down?"

Chai sighed. "Of course not. Mostly, the werewolf is simply complete. But for some, the ones who have been violently repressing a part of themselves to unhealthy extremes and denying emotional needs, the feelings that haven't been getting to express themselves will take center stage. They might refuse to step off. There is more than one kind of hunger."

I stared at my shadow.

Chai noticed. "What are you afraid of, John?"

"Becoming the kind of monsters I hunt," I admitted.

"Then that's the part of yourself you need to accept."

I glared at him. "You want me to become a monster so that I won't become a monster? That's helpful."

"What I'm trying to tell you is that you won't *become* anything." Chai stared into my eyes. "You need to make peace with the monster you already are."

∾17∾

OPEN THE DOOR AND LET ME IN

The sun had set, and we were sitting, kneeling, getting up, pacing, cursing, sweating, grunting while Chai droned on about letting energy move through us in a monotone that was supposed to be soothing or hypnotic. To be fair, maybe his voice was both of those things. Maybe Chai's voice was exactly what we needed, just not enough of whatever that was, a drop of water for people who were on fire.

Cory had been the first one to take off his clothes, doing so without any embarrassment or fuss. Sig had teased me about how frequently I seemed to wind up being naked, but under a full moon, the compulsion is real. Perhaps it is the way our flesh burns as our molecular rate speeds up, or perhaps it is our bodies anticipating change and not wanting to be confined. Jelly slid out of his overlarge britches grublike, pale and pissing himself. I forced myself to stand and remove my garments methodically, and if my movements were abrupt and jerky, I still managed to fold my clothes.

Mayte positioned herself behind Chai. She was fumbling

with her own clothes, her hands trembling violently. Cory was staring at Mayte hungrily.

Jelly was huddled in a fetal position whimpering, his head clutched between his forearms while his fingers scrabbled mindlessly at his back like the legs of large hairless spiders. Those same fingers had grown thick gnarled nails, and his skin was parting beneath them, bleeding and reknitting in a frantic cycle.

Butterflies, I thought.

I could barely make sense of Chai's droning. Normally, I would be running right now. Running and running and running through endless stretches of forest. I had to do something. Anything. I tilted my head up at the sky and howled. Answering howls sounded from the woods around us.

Okay, maybe not *anything*. How many paws and claws were out there in the forest reserve, anyhow?

The howls seemed to tilt some kind of balance. Chai shifted into a wolf almost seamlessly. He fell forward as a man, his face contorted in something that might have been pain or ecstasy, but it was a wolf whose paws hit the ground. Cory changed more violently, his back arching upward, his fingers flexing and unflexing while his jaw contorted, his body hair elongating and thickening. The two of them were diametrically faced off against each other.

Cory was screaming. Jelly and Mayte weren't making any sounds at all, but I couldn't make myself look at them. I was on my hands and knees, staring at my fists as they clenched tighter and tighter, driving my fingers into my palms and my knuckles into dirt and leaves and twigs and small chips of rock.

I wasn't changing.

I expected to change. I needed to change. But the geas doesn't allow any outside magic to get behind the steering wheel of my psyche unless it's the only way for me to survive, and the geas wasn't letting me go.

I was relieved and horrified at the same time.

Relieved because I didn't really want to change into anything against my will.

Horrified because I was a naked and kneeling man surrounded by wolves.

Talk about socially awkward.

Other wolves began to slink silently into the periphery of my vision from all sides. I don't know if they were responding to my howl or if our paw had been their destination all along. They crept through dark and moonlight in seamless ripples of fur and shadow, unhurried, unworried, but not without purpose.

A good twenty feet back, I saw the leader. I don't know how I knew he was the leader. Body language, scent, position... some wolf knowledge buried in my brain before I was even self-aware. The wolf was large and dark and still, though not motionless. It was not sitting on its haunches, but there was something relaxed in the set of its shoulders, in the way it was putting weight on its forelegs. Looking at that unnatural poise and pose, I knew though I don't know how to articulate how I knew, that the mind of a satisfied man was in that wolf's body. On a full moon.

It was an impressive display of control. I saw it and wanted it.

The wolves behind me moved closest first. I knew this game. I pretended to whirl on them, then spun around to kick aside a wolf that had jumped at me from the opposite direction. Another tried to bait and switch, darted in from an alternate side to draw my attention, but I feinted it into a retreat as well, then spun on my real attacker. A third wolf warily joined the circle around me. Eventually, one of them would get in close enough to tear my back or get jaws on my throat or sever an Achilles tendon.

They would wear me down. I would be pulled down beneath a wave of teeth and claws, torn into so many wet shreds of flesh and sprays of bodily fluid that there would be no possibility of ever healing again.

They weren't giving me a choice. The man had to die for the wolf to survive.

I opened my mouth to scream. The wolf snarled out through it.

~18~

NOT BY THE HAIR ON MY CHINNY CHIN CHIN

I woke up on the forest floor, surrounded by the smell of frying bacon and a nimbus of dried blood splatter and shed fur. A lot of the blood and fur were mine. Other than being slightly cold, my body wasn't in any kind of pain, though. Neither was my mind. I felt calm and relaxed.

There was only one other person in the campsite next to me, a tall and heavily muscled fellow with a trim brown beard. He was clad in jeans and green flannel, crouched next to a campfire where the bacon was frying on a large pan set on a foldable grill. The top of the grill was wrapped in aluminum foil to provide a flat surface, and peanut butter sandwiches were toasting on its outer edges. A stack of paper plates and two cartons of eggs were on the ground next to it.

The man proceeded to place strips of bacon on paper plates, breaking the eggs and frying them directly in the bacon grease left over in the pan, methodically stopping to remove and replace the peanut butter sandwiches as he did so. I'd never had a toasted peanut butter sandwich before, but they smelled good.

My clothes had been placed on the ground next to me, still folded. I got up and unhurriedly began to put them on.

"You've been sleeping for almost two days," the man observed. "That's a sign that you're not fully integrated."

Was that why I was so relaxed? No, the calm and peace I felt was odd under the circumstances, but that didn't particularly alarm me, either.

"It looks like I was in a hell of a fight," I commented, gesturing at the signs of struggle.

"You were," the man agreed pleasantly. "It took a long time for you to submit."

"Submit?" I repeated softly.

"As a wolf." Now that I could see his face, I saw that it was pockmarked around the edges of the beard, ravaged by something harsher than acne. His head was square, his nose blunt and broad, his eyes a dark hazel green. He was an ugly man, but some people refuse to be uncharismatic despite their looks. "You finally joined us rather than be torn apart. Sit."

Submit, my ass. I buttoned my jeans. "If that's a dog command, you'd better be ready for round two."

He laughed. "It's an invitation."

I sat. It made it easier to pull on my socks and shoes.

He shoveled some eggs on to a plate full of bacon and passed me a fork to go with them. "Try the toasted peanut butter. It's good."

I was starving. Who cared if it was good or not? We ate quietly for a time.

"Is it normal for the wolf leader to give food to someone he considers a subordinate?" I eventually asked.

He chewed over his response, literally and figuratively. "This is a human ceremony, host to guest. We came to terms as wolves, but like I said, you're not fully integrated yet. Now I'm trying to reach the part of you that you think of as a man."

"How do you think of it?" I was challenging him, but I was also genuinely curious.

"I don't really make a distinction between wolf and human anymore. It's all one to me."

"Why am I getting breakfast in bed?" I asked. "You're not going to tell me we made out, are you?"

He smiled. "I am courting you in a way, but not that way. I made breakfast for the rest of your paw while you were sleeping."

"What do you want from me?"

"I want you to help me make peace with the knights."

I chuckled, then put my plate on the ground when the chortles kept coming and growing until I convulsed with laughter. It had been a tense couple of decades.

"I just...tried that...for myself." I gasped between gales. "The knights told me...told me...to kill you."

He smiled and offered me his hand. "Bernard. Bernard Wright. That's Wright with a W."

My laughter died down, and I gave him a pretty good stare. Both the man and his hand remained unshaken.

"John," I said. "John Charming."

"That's a hell of a name," he observed, taking his hand back.

"I didn't choose it," I said. "It chose me."

"I made Bernard Wright up," he confessed, then laughed. "My mate says I just like being *right* all the time, so I had it legally changed to Bernard B. Wright."

I didn't ask for his real name. In my world, you don't. "I had a friend named Rong once. R-O-N-G. If he was here, you could be Wright and Rong."

He chuckled. "Whereas you and I can be Wright and Charming. How often does *that* combination happen?"

I didn't laugh. Instead, I clarified. "You want me to follow you."

"Yes," he said with no trace of awkwardness or apology.

"Would I get my own parking space?" I wondered. "Full dental?"

He laughed again. Well, he could afford to. The woods around us were teeming with his disciples. "Being in the Clan is like that line from Shakespeare. It is a wind that blows over flowers, both giving and taking."

The line was from *Twelfth Night*, and it was actually about giving and "stealing." And what the wind gave and stole from flowers was odor. The language is a little disturbing because we normally think of flowers as having aromas or scents or fragrances, not odor. The language from that scene describes beautiful things with ugly words because the character is afraid and emotionally conflicted. Orsino wants love, but he knows how easy and dangerous it is to give yourself to attractive things you want but don't truly understand.

What? I've lived a long time and lived it alone, mostly, and I like to read, and I like Shakespeare. Fuck off.

"Why should I follow you?" I demanded.

"Because you need to belong to something larger than yourself. Everyone does."

"Not good enough," I said quietly.

"Then how about because we're the good guys?"

"Everybody thinks they're the good guys."

He nodded as much to himself as to me. "Let's start over. You seem like a man who likes to study history, yes?"

"I know my way around an epoch," I said guardedly.

"Then you know that before the Nazis started putting Jews

in concentration camps, they made all these rules that set the Jews apart but at the same time kept them from organizing or being powerful. Jews couldn't hold any kind of political office. Jews couldn't join the military. Jews couldn't assemble in large groups. Jews had to wear yellow stars. And so on."

I remained silent.

"Now look at the rules that the Knights Templar have laid down for supernatural beings. They won't let us run for public office. They won't let us join the military. They won't let us assemble in large groups. They keep obsessive records of who we are and where we live, but they don't want us to do anything that might reveal our true nature."

"That's cute, but there are some big differences between knights and Nazis too," I argued. "For one thing, the knights didn't lay down those rules. They didn't even ask for their jobs. And the same geas that makes knights monitor supernaturals also keeps them from harming any magical beings who are staying below the radar. Knights could never try to commit genocide or put beings in concentration camps."

He wasn't impressed. "So knights can only be sadists and murderers to people who don't follow their rules. Comforting."

"Every word I just said is fact, not opinion," I said. "I don't care whether you find them comforting or not. You don't have to tell me that there are bad knights or that they do bad things, but some of the rules knights enforce are good for everyone. How long do you think it would take some bastard offshoot of a djinn to blow his or her cover if they were allowed to become pro athletes in front of millions of viewers? And would it be ethical if they did? Military schedules are strictly enforced... how is a werewolf supposed to keep his or her existence a secret if they're in a barracks or a trench with other soldiers when a full moon comes around, or if they grow back limbs that get blown off? Not to mention that this planet is already struggling with a massive overpopulation problem...how much worse would it be if the numbers of beings who live for thousands of years just kept multiplying and multiplying unchecked? And what do you think would happen to us supernatural beings if our existence did become known? Say what you want, but some rich asshat would have us on a dissecting table trying to figure out how to become immortal, or some general who wanted to make better soldiers. And scientists could experiment on our regenerating bodies for a long, long time."

Yeah, I know that was a hell of speech, but this was something I'd thought about a lot. And I hadn't even gone into the possibility of whole new levels of race discrimination and holy wars.

"That all might be true," he said. "But part of the reason it is true is that knights have kept the supernatural community in a state of stasis for centuries. We're in the exact same boat we were in eight hundred years ago. We're not protected by the Pax any longer. We're confined by it."

"That's not the knights' fault," I defended. "It was the Fae who made the Pax Arcana."

"And the Fae are all about staying the same and preserving the status quo," Bernard answered. "That's why they had to leave. Humans need to change and adapt in order to survive, both as individuals and societies, and we are humans, John. Do you doubt that?"

"And what do you want to change?"

"The Pax Arcana is starting to break down, and we can't be isolated and easy to pick off when it does." Bernard's eyes were agleam. "We need to have lawyers. We need to have PR specialists and media consultants and friends in law enforcement. We need safe houses and emergency funds and false identification papers. We need to have a plan, and we can't do that unless we're organized and able to communicate, and the knights won't allow that. They see any large group of werewolves as an organized conspiracy and a threat."

"So you began conspiring to organize in secret," I noted. "And now you're a threat to them."

His smile was rueful. "That's how it works."

Yeah, life is full of irony. "You killed a lot of knights who stumbled onto warning signs of what you were up to."

"I killed them before they could kill me or mine." He smiled again, but this time there wasn't anything good-natured about it. "This is about the survival of our kind, and not just our physical survival, either. It's our identity at stake. Our soul. We're wolves. We were never meant to be herded like sheep."

"But you said you wanted me to make peace with the knights," I reminded him. "Not war."

"Don't you want to live in peace with the knights, John Charming?" he asked softly.

I didn't answer.

"And how is that working out for you?"

That was a little too close to a nerve cluster. "You just attacked a lodge where there were a lot of important knights. They're going to retaliate, and hard."

Bernard held his palms out in a way that both included me and indicated a lack of options. "Their leaders have been trying to identify and kill me for years. Let them have a taste of what that's like. And you're werewolf business."

I didn't know what to say to that. A rush of pride, gratitude, panic, and angry denial washed over me. Sig. I forced myself to focus. "So where do things stand now?"

"The knights have been assassinating, imprisoning, and torturing us." Bernard's voice was no longer relaxed. "And yes, we have been doing the same to them. I have told them to get out of Wisconsin. All of them. Their families. Their informants."

"To go with that Jewish comparison, you're trying to create a werewolf Israel in the middle of the United States," I commented.

"Suppose I am?" he growled.

"How's that working out for you?"

He didn't like that a bit.

"The difference between you and me," Bernard snapped, "is that I have people I care about and who care about me. I can't just run away and hide and pout."

My throat was tight. "Can I?"

He regarded me skeptically. "Do you really want to leave?"

"I need to have a choice," I said.

He stood up then. "You're fighting for a choice. I'm fighting for a chance."

I remained crouched down. It wasn't an animal dominance thing. I still had food on my plate. "I'm here. Not killing anyone. Doing the initiation thing and keeping a promise someone else made to you. Right now, that's the best you're going to get."

"You've been fighting your wolf for a long time, John." Bernard's tone and body language had a strange nuance, almost parental. "Forget peace with the knights for a minute. If you're ever going to have peace with yourself, you need to start listening to the wolf. That part of yourself has needs, and you've been starving it for a long time."

"I didn't have a choice." I picked my plate up again and resumed eating. "That's why I need one now."

Bernard walked off. He wasn't being rude or angry. He wasn't saying good-bye. We were done for the moment. Not too long ago, it would have freaked me out that I understood all of that without a word being uttered. I would have weighed and sifted and questioned that understanding suspiciously, trying to figure out what dark shadowy region of my brain the knowledge lurked in.

Now, I kind of liked the idea of being among people who just understood certain things.

～19～

PACK MENTALITY

You know, I used to watch that television show *Survivor*," Cory said. "This camp is nothing like that."

I had thought that Cory would be more relaxed after the full moon, but he was worse than he'd been before he started making progress. Chai probably knew why. I didn't.

"In *Survivor*, they just showed people sitting around a campfire roasting animals on a stick," Cory continued. He was trying to grouse, not growl, but frustration was building in his voice and sweat. "Wilderness movies are like that too. They make it look easy."

"Wild animals sometimes have flukes or worms," I observed. We were in the process of cutting half a dozen snowshoe hares into very small chunks and dropping them in a boiling pot of water. Boiling meat really doesn't take too much of the flavor out, and most of the paw still tended to burn meat over a live flame, leave it charred on the outside and raw on the inside.

"Besides, it's too early to start complaining," I added. "Next time we get some large game, I'll show you how to use intestinal casings to make sausage."

Cory cursed and Mayte smiled at me wryly while Cory's head was bent down over his task. *Ah*, her look seemed to say. *Male bonding.*

Sig spasm. It was getting really annoying, the way Sig itched at my soul. I had tried to banish Sig from my thoughts, make up my mind once and for all that Sig and I were never going to happen and get over it. Then at least maybe whatever was going or not going on with us would stop worrying at me so that I could concentrate on little things like staying alive.

Wait. Cory had said something. "What?"

Mayte gave me a different kind of look. The tension coming off Cory had suddenly amped up.

"I said, why don't you just fuck her." Cory's teeth were gritted and he was glaring at Mayte. His hands were tight around his knife and he wanted to hit something. "She wants you to. You want to. Just fuck her."

I should have had some moment where I realized that this was part of what was eating at Cory, or at least the part he felt comfortable blaming. He was a young male and hadn't been good at processing emotions before he became a werewolf, and now he had somehow convinced himself that he was in love with Mayte on top of everything else he was going through, or maybe as a way to deal with it. Or maybe he really cared about her. What did I know? I should have gained some kind of empathy or insight.

Instead, I kicked the pot over and sent boiling water scalding over Cory's shin. He screamed and tried to leap back but I held him in place by spearing my knife through the radial nerve in his right wrist.

The knife Cory had been holding fell to the ground.

Cory had improved as a fighter over our last few sparring sessions. He managed to tear my knife out of my hand with his body weight, but when he tried to move his left hand over to grab the hilt sticking out of the back of his wrist, I followed him in and swiveled, pulled the outside of his wrist with one hand, and broke his elbow with a forearm hammer from my other.

Cory screamed again, turned and tried to use the right arm that had a useless knife sticking out of it, but I went with the motion again, whirling inside his reach, dropping and using my weight to tear him off his feet, to turn him, to bring his own momentum and weight on top of mine and throw his back down on my knee.

His spine broke with a loud snap. So did I. My personality fractured into two completely different sets of reactions and drives, and I dropped Cory to the ground, paralyzed between a desire to step back and a desire to step on his throat.

All that sparring with Cory…he knew what I could do and he was still talking smack. Daring me to do something he couldn't stop, and why? Mayte? Hopeless. Two seconds and he was already belly up and exposing his throat. Had he been bitten by a wolf or a bunny? I bent down slightly and pulled my knife free. "You shouldn't be worried about what Mayte or I do, Cory." My voice was a growl. "The only thing you should be asking is what *you* can do. Nobody can

What the hell was happening here? I don't use violence unless I have to. That's one of my rules, my warning flags. Did the fact that Cory would heal quickly or that talking wasn't getting through to him really excuse this? I couldn't control Cory. The only person I could control was me. I had never hurt anyone who was so much weaker than me and who wasn't actively threatening me or someone else. Cory's long-term chances might have just gone up because of what I'd done, but regardless of save you here but you. So stop arguing and start listening and figure out how to do that."

the intent, the act itself was that of a sadist or a bully. This wasn't who or what I wanted to be.

Cory's eyes were bulging and the sounds coming from him were gasping whimpers.

"This is what it means to be a lone wolf, Cory," I said. "I've been one my whole long life, and trust me, you only have two choices if you want to survive here. Get a lot smarter and tougher fast, or join the Clan with all your heart and soul."

I heard those words being spoken by my voice and wondered where they were coming from.

It takes a lot to make me throw up, but the sight of Cory's body beneath me came close. This wasn't me. This wasn't me. I had stepped over one of the boundaries I'd set up to make sure I never became evil, and I hadn't even thought about it. I'd sworn to kill myself if I found myself doing things I had no control over, and here I was, standing over a burned and broken boy with no real training who hadn't attacked me directly.

"Pick up that meat and start another fire when you're done healing," Mayte told Cory, and she tapped me on the arm. I let her lead me away from where Cory was twitching and sobbing on the ground.

∽20∽

MAYTE HARI

What the hell was that?" I demanded once we were out of Cory's hearing range, which took a while. My voice was shaking.

"That was you trying to help Cory." Mayte didn't turn around. I wasn't sure where she was going, and it occurred to me that I might not want to follow her. We were somewhere on the outer fringes of the paw's territory, and I was so emotionally unsettled and caught up in my own head that I hadn't noticed when Mayte started smelling like lust. Also, while my thoughts were churning and whirling, I suddenly realized that my eyes were staring at her ass. It was a nice ass, heart-shaped and strong and firmly curved.

My god, we were in the middle of a mating ritual. Cory had just challenged me for Mayte, and I had put him down. She was my prize. My mind was hurtling down a dark road, and very old and primal instincts were trying to grab the steering wheel.

I gritted my teeth. "It might help Cory. But that wasn't *me*."

Mayte made a dismissive noise and smacked an overreaching tendril of bush out of the way. "Maybe it was your shadow self."

"I need to be alone." I didn't stop walking, though.

Mayte reached her hands under her shirt while she continued to stride forward. "That's the last thing you need."

What was she doing? I mean, I knew what she was doing, but why was she doing it? "Mayte, stop. I need to think."

"That's also the last thing you need."

I wasn't sure you could have two last things, but Mayte's hands emerged from under her shirt and flung her bra backward in my direction. I caught it wordlessly and stopped. We were in a copse, a relatively clear opening surrounded by trees with low-hanging branches and weeds with delusions of grandeur.

Mayte turned around as if completing a dance move and peeled her shirt off in one continuous motion.

"Dear *Penthouse*," I said a little hoarsely, "I never thought this would happen to me..."

Mayte's only response was to kick off her shoes, toss me her shirt, and begin unbuttoning her pants. She was brown and strong-looking, with athletic, smooth shoulders, small, firm breasts, and a sweet curve to her hips. Her eyes were a deep, rich hazelnut green and her cheeks and jaw were round.

Her panties were faded, soft-looking, and faintly pink.

"Mayte," I said while she rolled her jeans down over hips that were moving in a slow sinuous sway. "This isn't you. This isn't us."

"You think too much," she said.

"This is some kind of pack instinct." My voice sounded like it was scraping against a cheese grater. "Just like what I did with Cory."

She squatted down and pulled her panties over her knees in a businesslike fashion. "We're a clan. Not a pack. And you have too many hang-ups."

I growled. "This isn't some sex-is-evil thing. I like sex. Consenting adults. Honesty. Individual responsibility. I get all that. But I am not doing this. Not when I just hurt a kid and something that's not me is trying to make me do it. Not when you're not you."

"This is me. I miss someone too." Mayte finished stepping out of her panties with uncharacteristic daintiness. "I maybe miss him more than you miss whoever it is you keep thinking about. But you know what? I was missing him before any of this happened. Love sucks and you can't control life. You can't control other people, either. You just have to take whatever you get and be grateful."

I suddenly couldn't form words. She wasn't wrong.

"I like you," Mayte continued. "You like me. It's time we screwed our brains out until we're not so sad anymore."

She looked at my crotch then, boldly. "Your body knows it."

"Yeah. See you." I turned around and ran. Flat-out ran. It was possibly the most undignified, embarrassing thing I've ever done, and I've never been what you might call a smooth master of decorum. But I did it. Hurtled through the woods, pulling in softball-sized gulps of air, and counting on my longer legs and shod feet to get me away from her. Five more seconds and I was going to be cradling those smooth brown ostrich egg buttocks in my hand, pulling her tongue into my mouth, pressing her breasts against me and feeling those erect nipples...

I ran.

It was one reaction she wasn't ready for. It took more than a few moments for Mayte to yell my name, and when she did it was almost a question. A question I had no intention of answering.

Not like this. I wasn't doing anything major while I was freaking out, not until I knew what the hell was going on with me. I wasn't. Dammit, I wasn't.

I was still running when I encountered Bernard and two other werewolves, one of them Uni-brow, the guy who had driven me away from the lodge. More LWRC rifles were in their hands as they waited motionlessly. Bernard was kneeling and pointing the automatic rifle at me, though he quickly shifted his aim slightly to the side when he saw who I was. The other two werewolves were standing behind him and didn't do me the same courtesy.

"Who's after you?" Bernard hissed.

I halted. "You can put the rifle down. It's not that kind of threat."

"Then what kind of threat is it?" But he lowered the rifle until it was pointed at the ground.

I heard Mayte call my name in the distance. We all heard her call my name.

"A woman," I admitted. I could feel my face, blushing furiously. "I'm shy."

Some expression twitched across Bernard's face before he got it under control. Then another. His guards didn't have quite as much self-control.

I ground my teeth. What had happened with Cory was still too fresh in my mind for me to see the humor. "Go ahead and laugh."

Instead, Bernard rose and grinned, the smile frozen because his mouth was stretched as wide as it could go. "I don't know if this makes you the dumbest man I've ever met or the smartest. But don't tell my mate I said that."

It was only then that I realized the significance of the bulletproof vests they were all wearing, the KA-BAR knives sheathed at their sides, the HK45 sidearms, and the camouflage fatigues.

"Who's chasing *you*?" I asked.

The smiles went off all their faces then, blown out like candles.

"Let's wait for Mayte," Bernard said. She was audibly getting closer. "I was coming to get her too."

"Because she used to be an MP," I said.

In answer, he removed his rucksack and took a thick belt from it. The belt was threaded through the holster of a Beretta M9, a canteen, and a sheath holding a silver steel knife. The silver steel knife that had been sheathed in the armor I'd stolen from the Templars. A werewolf killer. "Here. Your expertise is needed elsewhere."

"Knights?" I picked up the belt. I wasn't sure what I'd say if the answer was yes.

He shook his head. "We don't know what it is. That's why we need you."

∾21∾

FURRENSICS

Are you insane?" I was addressing Bernard Wright, but I was looking at Nikolai "The Saw" Sokolov, a man who had been a professional heavyweight fighter a decade earlier. He had never been a world champion, but he'd fought for the title once, and anyone who followed boxing would know him.

Nikolai had grown some thick black hair over the skull he used to keep bald and had shaved off his old hybrid trident moustache-and-goatee arrangement, but he was still recognizably "The Saw." Six foot five tends to stand out, and the scar tissue he'd gained before becoming a werewolf had never healed. His face looked like one big callus.

I really was furious. Famous people are supposed to be off-limits to supernatural predators. Do you have any idea how much grief Elvis caused before a knight finally put him down years after his official obituary? He generated so much attention that the public actually started creating Elvis tulpas—walking, talking Elvis duplicates that were manifestations of concentrated psychic energy from some kind of group dream mind. The knights only got the whole situation under control by coming up with the concept of Elvis impersonators.

Bernard winced as if passing a gas bubble. "Crazy or not, I had nothing to do with Nikolai. Some young, dumb, full-of-come werewolf wanted to test his abilities out and jumped Nikolai outside his gym. As fast and strong as a lycanthrope is, Nikolai was still giving the kid a beatdown, and the idiot panicked and changed and bit Nikolai. I just took Nikolai in."

We had driven to an area where the woods were much thicker, the cover of trees so dense that a few hours after sunrise, it almost looked like evening. The pungent, bittersweet stench of burning marijuana clung to the air, trapped in a hazy limbo between leaves and ground. I pulled my arms out of the sleeves of my T-shirt, then tugged the collar of it over my nose and tied the sleeves behind my neck so that I had a mask and air filter of sorts. What I was smelling wasn't the aftereffect of someone's recreational use. Entire fields of dope had been burned in the area recently.

Nikolai, for his part, grunted while suspicion and hostility trickled off of him. "I told Bernard he was crazy when I heard about you too."

We weren't the only three people there, even if it seemed like it at the moment. There was a crew of firefighters made up entirely of werewolves running about, which showed a degree of foresight on Bernard's part that I found a little disturbing. Lee was also on scene, whatever his capacity in the Forest Service, and I kept catching glimpses and whiffs of at least four other werewolves out in the woods around us, presumably on guard detail. I also spotted Gabriel, Muscles, and Uni-brow, three of my escorts from the Templar safe house. Or unsafe house. They were standing near a body where Mayte had joined them, all heavily armed and wearing Kevlar vests.

"Nikolai is my left hand," Bernard informed me.

"Is that the one you jerk off with?" I asked.

Nikolai considered hitting me, and unlike most people he probably could have, but Bernard defused the moment by laughing ruefully. "Nikolai is my backup. He takes care of things behind the scenes while people are watching my right hand."

"Who's your right hand?" I asked diffidently.

"My mate." Bernard didn't gaze off into the distance dreamily when he said that, and I didn't hear any lutes or harps. "Catherine."

"I can see where you would be great at operating behind the scenes without being noticed," I observed to Nikolai. "You're so indistinct and easy to overlook."

Nikolai smiled. It was a remarkably unfriendly expression. Nikolai was at least four inches taller than me and outweighed me by somewhere between seventy and a hundred pounds, not much of it fat.

"Nikolai wants to beat you into a coma and rip your head off," Bernard announced casually. "He thinks you're here to gather information on the Clan and assassinate me. It's time to show Nikolai why you're valuable. Something has killed one of the Clan. I want you to take a look at the scene."

"Grace will be here this evening," Nikolai reminded him.

"Grace is one of us and a coroner," Bernard explained to me. "She's been busy lately."

I was tired of listening to them argue while pretending to talk to me. "Okay." Making Bernard follow me wasn't exactly werewolf protocol, but I walked off toward the body.

"Give me the word," Nikolai breathed to Bernard. He knew I could hear him.

"Shush," Bernard murmured, which meant they were old

friends or more than friends. A hard man who is a leader among tough guys doesn't tell another tough guy "Shush" unless they're close. He says "Be quiet" or some cruder variation of it, ranging anywhere from "Shut up" to "Don't open your mouth unless you want me to put my dick in it."

Hey, I don't make the rules.

The dead werewolf was stiff and posed in a state that was half man and half wolf, which was crazy yet somehow true. When a werewolf dies, it reverts to its human form, period. Not semicolon, period. But this werewolf was caught in a hybrid state, naked and randomly covered in thick tufts of fur, its nose and mouth not quite a muzzle, claws emerging from human-looking hands instead of fingernails. One of its human ears was visible and slightly pointed, and its human teeth were a little too long. The man-wolf was frozen, a sculpture of agony. It had actually clenched its fists so tight that it had driven its claws through its own palms. Oddly enough, those hands were covered with black ash, though the body was some distance away from where crop fields had been burned. It had a massive wound in its stomach and a hole where its heart had been torn out of its chest. The top of its skull was crushed and gray matter was splattered over the ground. Someone had literally beaten its brains out.

Removing either the heart or the brain from a werewolf will kill it. The heart needs the brain to command it to keep pumping blood. The brain needs blood from the heart to keep sending out commands for the werewolf's body to regenerate. Neither organ regenerates fast enough to keep the other from shutting down if either is completely and violently removed.

Oddly enough, the sight of the body calmed me down. I could sense old coping mechanisms and defenses sliding over me like a second skin now that I was back on familiar territory. It was a relief, feeling unfeeling, and I stuck my right hand into the dead thing's stomach wound and probed. "I'm guessing we've crossed the border into the Chequamegon park reserve?"

"Does that matter?" Bernard asked curiously.

"I'm not sure," I admitted. All of the land around us had been ancient Native American hunting territory at some point, but names have power.

"No, it doesn't matter," Nikolai muttered. "Not if a spy among us managed to send some kind of signal to the knights about where we are."

"The knights had nothing to do with this." My tone was clinical as I examined the padded areas between the man-wolf's finger/toes. "They'll only have the element of surprise once. They wouldn't waste it on a lone guard. When they come, it will either be a massive attack on everyone or a surgical strike to take out Bernard."

"When they come?" Bernard asked. "Not if?"

"I call it the way I see it," I said. "And speaking of how I see things, I didn't realize I was hanging out with drug dealers."

Bernard's air of sangfroid frayed a little. Is that called sang-frayed? "We have a lot of side operations that generate income off the grid. It takes money to buy military-grade weapons, and it can't be money that the IRS can track, either."

I was still absorbing that when Bernard returned to the subject at hand. "What do *you* think we're dealing with here?"

"A bakaak." I pronounced the word "beh-kuck" but that might not be right. I've never heard the word said out loud by a native Ojibwe speaker.

There was an uncomfortable silence all around.

I ran through some other names from some other Native American languages I didn't know. "Baykok? Pekak? Baguck?

You know, undead Native American hunters? Skeleton-looking things? Invisible flesh but their bones are still visible? Any of this buzzing your apartments?"

Even Gabriel looked blank. I guess they hadn't told him a lot of Native American legends in his Catholic orphanage.

"Enlighten us," Bernard suggested dryly.

I wiped my hand on the dead werewolf's shirt and tried. "According to legends, bakaak are undead Native Americans who became obsessed with hunting. As far as I know, it's not spelled out, but there's at least an implication that bakaaks started hunting men for sport. They definitely murdered among their own tribe at some point. It might be that becoming a bakaak was a divine punishment. It might be that bakaaks are men who became so caught up in the hunt that they only walked the spirit paths halfway—then turned around and came back to this earth to keep hunting."

"Hunting what?" Bernard asked softly.

"Anything challenging or dangerous," I said. "A bakaak wouldn't bother with a random hiker, but it might hunt an armed werewolf who had violated its territory."

Uni-brow interrupted. "How do we know you're not talking out of your ass?"

"Bakaaks use a paralyzing poison on their arrows, kind of a like a spider's venom." I indicated the body at our feet. "Then they eat their victims while they're still conscious. That's why your crop guard is still half wolf. The paralyzing toxin is slowing his body's change."

"I don't see any arrow wounds," Nikolai said grimly.

"It shot him here, then used a knife to enlarge the wound." I indicated the gaping wound in the stomach. "Among a lot of Native American tribes, the liver was the prize that belonged to the successful hunter. Lots of vitamins. This man's liver is missing, and when I stuck my hand in to check, the tip of my index finger went numb."

I held up the finger in question. "There must have been a trace of the paralyzing poison left in some kind of hollow or bone."

"Is that all?" Bernard asked curiously.

What? That wasn't enough?

"No, that's not all," I said evenly. "Do you smell anything? This thing used something with an ammonia base, probably some kind of distilled urine, to destroy scent molecules. You see any tracks? It swept the ground and burned it to mess with our infravision. This thing was expecting werewolves. That should tell you this is a badass hunter even if you don't know what a bakaak is."

I began pointing to the scene. "And see the way the guard's brains are splattered? In all the stories I've ever heard, a bakaak's hand-to-hand weapon is a war club. Bakaaks hunt at night, and this happened last night."

"Yeah, but..." Uni-brow began.

I held up a thin shred of translucent membrane to silence him, then passed it to Bernard, who took it carefully. "And I found this between your guard's knuckles. It probably got wedged there when its digits were closer together and matted with fur."

"Invisible skin," Bernard said softly.

"That's why the bakaak hunts at night," I noted. "They don't dissolve in the sun like vampires, but transparent skin doesn't protect against sunburn, and their eyes don't see as well in the day."

"But it could attack during the day if it wanted to?" Bernard asked.

"That's what knight lore says," I told him. "In an area like this with thick tree cover? I wouldn't bet my life on the bakaak not coming out to play early."

Bernard's eyes narrowed. "You think it's coming back?"

I nodded. "See how it poured black ash all over your guard's hands? That's a message. One of the associations of the name *bakaak* is to *pound black ash*."

Mayte jumped in. "You just said it did all those things to hide itself. Why would it leave a message?"

Were they really this slow? "Would any of you have gotten that? The clue was meant for another hunter. This is the bakaak's way of saying *game on*."

But Bernard wasn't interested in the bakaak, at least not for the moment. "Can all knights do this?"

"Do what?" I wasn't being a smart-ass. I was in my hyperfocus mode, and the question wasn't specific enough.

"You just put all that together in less than a minute with no lab equipment, no clues from your werewolf senses, and no Internet searches," Bernard pointed out. "You took one look at that body and identified the killer, its motive, and its probable next move, like some kind of Sherlock Holmes, except those stories make him look brilliant, and you make it look like anyone who read the right Wikipedia article could have figured it out. I'm standing here feeling stupid, and I'm not stupid. Can all knights do what you just did?"

"Probably not as fast," I admitted.

"And you think this is supposed to make me feel better?!?" Nikolai was confronting Bernard. He had moved so that he was back in Bernard's field of vision while keeping me at an angle. "If I was a knight, this dude is *exactly* who I would send to spy on us!"

"Uh, could you maybe wait and talk about whether or not to kill me later?" I asked. "We're on the bakaak's hunting ground, and this thing is serious."

"How serious?" Bernard asked.

I gestured at the body at our feet. "The black ash is a sign. It's werewolf season."

∾22∾

TESTING, TESTING. IS THIS THING ON?

At my insistence, we moved to the middle of the burned fields. There was a lot I didn't know about bakaaks: I didn't know if they had enhanced hearing, for example, or if it was possible that one could have learned English. I didn't know if their hunting magic included scrying spells. What I did know was that I felt safer with a lot of wide-open space and daylight surrounding me on all sides.

Nikolai did not. "We're exposed out here."

"We'll hear any arrows traveling through this much open air in time to react," I assured him.

"What if this things has upgraded to sniper rifles and high-explosive rounds?"

Then we were fucked anyway, but rather than say that, I settled for: "A bakaak is all about its hunting traditions. That's in its magical DNA...what drives it and how it came to be."

"So what do we do?" Bernard challenged. "In your expert opinion."

"We leave the Chequamegon reserve," I told him. "Now."

"You want us to run?" Uni-brow demanded. "Why? Is this thing female or something?"

Half the group didn't get it. Bernard smiled faintly and Mayte snorted, not necessarily amused. For my part, I made a mental note to have a little discussion with Uni-brow at the earliest future point where we could afford to waste time on such things. But to be fair, testosterone was pretty thick in the air and nobody was too happy about my suggestion.

"What's your plan?" Bernard asked curiously.

"I want to get some detailed survey maps," I said. "Whatever else this thing is, it's still an unclean spirit that hunts on land, and that means it can't cross running water."

Nikolai started to say something, but I overrode him. "But it's going to want to be near a river because I guarantee you that it's gathering wolfsbane, and lots of it. It will also want to be near a cave. Not only does this thing hide from the sun, it's the ancient spirit of an obsessive Native American hunter, so there's a good chance it's going to want to do some hunting magic. That includes painting pictures on cave walls."

I was past the part I'd already worked out and thinking aloud by this point. "The damned thing won't want to be between bends of a river, because that would put running water around it on three out of four sides, and that would make it easier to pen in. So it's going to make its base of operations near an outer curve of a river, somewhere near cave complexes. It won't want to be in any lower elevations or near too many wide stretches of open land, either. Get me a detailed map and I'll narrow our target area as we travel."

"Travel how?" Bernard asked.

"The best way to go would be by kayak or canoe during the day. Did any of you ever read *The Song of Hiawatha*?"

Everyone just looked at me. Gabriel's snort sounded a lot like Mayte's.

"Look, traveling on water would keep us in open sunlight," I said, trying not to adopt a this-is-basic-arithmetic-so-please-don't-make-me-explain-it-to-you-again attitude. I wasn't used to hunting by committee. "And it would limit the bakaak's area of attack to one side of the river. The bakaak wouldn't be able to lay traps in the water, and we could anchor our food and supplies in the boats where it couldn't destroy them or poison them easily."

"Anything else?" Bernard's tone was dry, but I took him literally.

"It's supposed to be freakishly fast, so shotguns with wide-dispersal would be good. Some homemade Molotov cocktails made out of holy water put through a moonshine still would be good too. And this thing uses infravision, so magnesium flares might blind it. From what I saw at the knight compound, I assume you can get your hands on those things."

"The holy water moonshine thing is kind of weird, but we can get the rest of it fast." It was Muscles who agreed, over-developed forearms crossed over his overdeveloped chest.

"This is all horse shit!" Nikolai interrupted. "We can't just leave! Devonte expects to find us here."

Devonte? The guy who had driven the Jeep when I escaped the knights?

Then Nikolai shut his mouth abruptly—the way people do when they just revealed more than they meant to and are hoping nobody will notice.

"Nikolai." Just the name, but Bernard packed a world of meaning in it. Friendship. Suspicion. Resignation. Warning. Regret. Anger. Understanding.

"I sent Devonte's claw out to track this thing down," Nikolai said sullenly.

Oh, hell.

"And you didn't tell me." Now there was no nuance in Bernard's voice, no tone, no inflection, but that lack was just as significant as any excess of emotion.

"I send people out on stuff all the time." Nikolai sounded like a child caught in a misdeed. A six-foot-five child with smoldering brown eyes and muscle definition and hands that made fists the size of grapefruit. "You weren't here."

"And you didn't tell me this first thing when I got here." Bernard sighed. "Did you think it wasn't important?"

Nikolai fell back on the first defense of noncoms and subordinates everywhere. He shut up.

"Did you do this because you wanted to prove to me that we don't need John?" It sounded like a question, but it really wasn't. "Let the knight put on a dog and pony show, and then prove that we have our own way of doing things and they work just fine?"

"We do." Nikolai gave me a dead-eyed look.

Bernard wasn't having any of it. He got in Nikolai's face and didn't seem to care how the Saw's eyes fluttered or how his muscles tensed. "So you want to undermine what I'm trying to do? Do you want to kill me and take my place, Nikolai? Is that what this is about?"

Nikolai started to say something, but Bernard didn't give him time to respond. "Because your new reign is off to a brilliant start! YOU JUST SENT FIVE OF OUR PEOPLE AFTER GOD KNOWS WHAT ON ITS OWN FUCKING TERRITORY WITH NO PLAN OR BACKUP OR WAY TO COMMUNICATE WITH US! OR MAYBE YOU DIDN'T NOTICE THAT OUR CELL PHONES AREN'T WORKING AROUND HERE?!?"

By the end of the sentence, Bernard's face was red, and spittle was flying out his mouth. His eyes were just this side of sane, and his skin was leaking KILL KILL KILL, and he was pretty sure that he could do it.

Just how physically dangerous was this man?

In any case, Nikolai backed down. It had to be some kind of wolf group instinct just like the thing that had led me to attack Cory. I don't think Nikolai was afraid of Bernard physically, exactly, but he was afraid of something. Maybe of losing Bernard's respect? His love? The Clan?

Bernard turned on me. "And *you*. QUIT PLAYING WITH THAT KNIFE!"

My hand *was* on my knife. When had that happened?

I forced my hand to release my knife handle with a deep breath that was a mistake. There was still a lot of aggression in the air. "What do you want?"

"I still need your expertise, *monster hunter*," Bernard snarled. "How much danger is Devonte's fist in?"

I looked at Nikolai. No games. "Are they coming back before dark?"

Nikolai shook his head. He was trembling, and it wasn't fear. He managed one word. "No."

"When did you send them?"

He looked at his watch, the old-fashioned wind-up kind that work during supernatural energy surges. "Six hours ago."

I focused on Bernard. "Then it depends. If the bakaak stays underground or goes back to some spirit world during the day, we might have time to find them. If it's prepared to attack in daytime, your people are probably already dead."

"Five werewolves? It's that dangerous?" Bernard asked quietly.

"It's not the bakaak's physical capabilities that make it dangerous," I said. "It was an expert hunter before it ever became a monster, and it's had a long time to work on its skill set. How long have you been growing dope here?"

Bernard looked at Muscles's back. "Robert?"

Muscles grunted. "Lafayette finally got too hot about five years ago."

Lafayette? Where had I heard... oh, right. All of those beasts of Bray Road stories were from around that part of Wisconsin.

"This thing studied your operation and made preparations before it struck," I said. "I promise you that. It's ready for werewolves to come after it. It *wants* werewolves to come after it. That's why I want to come back over the river. If we try to track it directly, we're going to have to travel through traps and ambush points."

Bernard weighed that and the choice presented him: go after some damnable thing half-cocked and endanger even more of his people, or abandon five of his people who might already be dead anyhow so that the rest of his clan could take a less-dangerous approach.

"This paralyzing poison it uses, it works on werewolves." He was talking to himself.

"Yes," I said.

"And you said it uses ancient shamanistic magic," he mused. "Like the kind that made the first were-beings. So it might have other tricks that affect us."

"That's a theory," I said carefully. "But this thing is definitely as strong as we are, and probably faster. In some stories there are lines about bakaaks flying through forests, but I'm pretty sure that's just a metaphor for how quickly they move and the fact that they like to hide up in trees."

"We're going after them," he decided. "And you're going to lead the way."

Say what?

"You want to rush into a trap, that's your business," I informed him. "I'll hunt this thing alone, or I'll follow along with your group, but don't ask me to lead if I can't lead my way. You're trying to put a fire out by throwing bodies on top of it."

"The Clan needs you," Bernard said gravely. "But the Clan also has to trust you. The only way this works is if you lead us, and from the front."

I was suddenly reminded of Emil and the lengths he had gone to in order to make the knights accept me as their living weapon. Again, I had this sudden image of me on a board between two men playing chess.

"Politics and PR make bad battle strategies." I indicated Unibrow with a twitch of my head. "You want to *make* somebody *volunteer*, make him."

"Mayte?" Bernard called instead. "I want you to take point."

Wait...what?

She didn't argue, though several of the males turned or stiffened and generally looked like they wanted to protest. Gabriel's head shot up alertly, his eyes hot, and Muscles started to raise his hand like he was in a classroom. But they remained silent when they saw Bernard's face.

Mayte was carrying some kind of custom-made long-distance handgun I'd never seen before, one with a scope. She had a machete sheathed on her back too, and a frag grenade on her belt. "Where can I pick up this Devonte's scent?"

"What are you doing?" I asked Bernard. "She has less experience as a werewolf than anybody here, and she was an MP, not a tracker."

He answered Mayte's question instead of mine. "Nikolai can take you to the starting point."

I got it then.

"You asked what you were doing here," I told Mayte. "This is it. You're here to give him leverage over me."

Mayte's shrug was sad and hurt and angry. She didn't much give a damn about what I said, or thought, or thought I said, or said I thought. "Is it working?"

How badly had I hurt her pride?

"No," I said. I don't know if I was answering Mayte's question or protesting it.

Mayte shrugged again. "Bernard's my leader. It's his job to make use of me."

The Clan blew me off then, just started preparing and left me standing there. Bernard called out and sent a couple of people off with Lee to fill in claw leaders about what was going on. Some guy came back with a jerryjug of water and some protein bars while other people stepped aside to relieve themselves and others cinched or tied or buttoned things. Most of them had M9s.

Nikolai started to walk, nodding at Mayte to follow him.

"You know, just because my name is Charming doesn't mean I have some kind of damsel-in-distress complex!" I called after them.

They kept ignoring me. Mayte was making her own choice, and it wasn't my job to save her from it. That impulse was sexist or something. That kind of thinking had lost me Sig. Might have lost me Sig. Probably lost me Sig.

Sig. Even if I had idealized her, even if she didn't want me around, I had told her I would come back to her if I could and find out if there was anything real between us. My word used to mean something.

Shit shit shit.

I stalked forward, snatching the Kevlar vest out of Mayte's hands while she was still in the process of readying it and walking past her. "Fine."

"Where are you going?" Mayte called after me.

"Devonte started looking at the place where the fire began,"

I snapped over my shoulder. "You don't even know that, and you're going to lead a hunting party?"

"I..." Mayte gave up and showed me her teeth. She wasn't smiling; Bernard was.

"Don't get too happy there, Sparky," I advised him, turning back to the front. "If you really want me to become a true believer, you just lost a lot of ground."

"No, I haven't." His voice was calm behind me. "You respect results and pragmatism."

And the truly damnable thing was, I think he was right.

~23~

IT'S NOT A SLAUGHTERHOUSE, IT'S A SLAUGHTERHOME

The forest reserve was hundreds of miles by hundreds of miles, and it was dusk when we found two more clan members in that bizarre half state between men and wolves. They were impaled on a barricade of slim wooden pikes that smelled faintly of the bakaak's paralyzing poison and wolfsbane. The pit they had fallen into wasn't your typical steep drop; it had opened up into an increasingly sharp decline with loose gravel leading toward long stakes slanted at an angle, their ends sharpened and scorched by fire. The hairy half-human bodies looked like discarded puppets, their limbs held up and splayed at unnatural angles.

Off in the distance, perhaps a half mile away, the screaming that had led us here continued. It was one voice, which meant the rest of the claw was dead. More, the voice wasn't able to form words and it wasn't muffled. Someone's tongue had been removed so that his garbled shrieks would draw us in without being able to give us any specific warnings.

It was working.

If we had all been knights, the prisoner could have timed screams in Morse code. If we had all been knights, we could have done something complicated and counterintuitive and set up skirmishers. If we had all been knights, I could have told the rest of them to ignore the screams of their brother and wait while I proceeded cautiously and carefully alone, and I would have known that I would be obeyed.

But we weren't knights, so we went forward the way we'd discussed en route, in a firing-team wedge, four teams in a roughly diamond-shaped formation. One team of two was front and center and slightly ahead of the others. Two teams of two were on the left and right flanks respectively, slightly behind. The reserve force was farthest back to reinforce or take advantage of any openings as necessary. All of us had combat training of some kind, and we moved together instinctively, kept track of each other with our enhanced senses and maybe a little bit of something else, some bond that verged on telepathic if it didn't outright spill over into that territory.

The bakaak had indeed been busy for days, perhaps weeks or months, before ever attacking the first guard. The air was full of a confusing screen of disgusting smells, rotting entrails hanging from tree limbs like Christmas ornaments, fetid river mud smeared on trunks, the lingering trace of burned animal oils and dead carcasses that had been dragged over the ground multiple times in different directions. I suppose it was possible to use our sense of smell to get our bearings, but it was impossible to do it quickly, and we needed to move quickly.

I bounded in six-foot running leaps that put me near narrow trees, close enough that I could grab on if I went down a pit but not directly beside the trunks. I was holding my Kevlar vest on my left hand like a shield instead of wearing it, my hand looped through the armholes. Mayte was trailing me.

I didn't have a weapon in my right hand yet. I wanted that hand free to grab at anything that lashed out or dropped down.

Maybe thirty feet to my right, I could see another dead clan member who had triggered two traps in a combination I'd never seen before. Some kind of twitch snare had yanked him upside down and off his feet, which wouldn't have held him long, but apparently the sliding rope of the twitch snare had then released the kind of pig-spear trap that is meant to kill boars or bears. A large pike had pinned him upside down to a nearby tree, and the smell of wolfsbane was in the air.

I was having a hard time putting my emotions aside, and I think it's because they weren't all my emotions. These were my family, something was saying, or many somethings. It felt like there were a lot of feelings combined into one huge pressure that was swelling against my conscious mind like water against a dam. This was my territory! This was my home!

On the far left, Uni-brow went down into a pit. Several hides had been sewn together, then set across a hole and covered with loose dirt and pebbles and twigs and small clumps of dung to confuse his sense of smell. He went down and tried to grab on to the ground around him, but there was no ground, just shifting hide pulled down by his own weight. Uni-brow's efforts ceased when he was impaled on sharp stakes coated with paralyzing venom.

But that wasn't the end of it.

Slowed, stiffening, Uni-brow was helpless as the rest of the trap fell into place. The edges of the hide were anchored by bladders full of distilled alcohol. When Uni-brow's weight pulled the hides abruptly down, the bladders were pulled in after him, bursting and soaking him in flammable liquid. A burning arrow, the source of the smoke smell, ignited the entire area. Uni-brow's claw mate tried to stop and grab the edges of the hide then, tilting his head back as he strained upward, and an arrow went through his nasal passages and into his brain.

I didn't even know their names.

What I did know was that the bakaak was firing from an elevated point somewhere west of my location. I was heading toward an embankment of sheer stone, perhaps forty feet high with no end in sight, and I could picture the rest of the battle—if you could call it that—unfolding in my mind's eye. The sloping incline that we would find somewhere far to our right, no doubt larded with pitfalls and deadfalls and snares and barricades designed to slow us down while the bakaak waited to pick off the brave fool who would inevitably try to sneak up on its vantage point by climbing the rock face stealthily.

Perhaps the bakaak would retreat to its next fallback position then, some narrow underground passage where we could only approach it one at a time, or a chasm with some makeshift bridge that it could disable behind it, or some patch of woods that it could set ablaze to cover its retreat until it was ready to attack again.

I looked around for some way to alter the equation, scanning the tree line with a vague idea of finding a tall tree that might just get close enough to the top of the cliff face for a werewolf to jump across, and that's when I saw it—a narrow dead tree some sixty feet in height that was almost ready to collapse, perceptibly leaning and made of wood that was bare of bark and dried out and gray.

I sprinted past the tree and then skidded to a halt. It was possible. It might have even been possible if I was only human. I ran straight back at the tree and saw Mayte coming to a halt behind me, stopping to stare at me openmouthed. At the last moment, I pivoted and pointed my foot and turned my hip and aimed my butt cheek at the nexus point I wanted to hit, the juncture next to a hollow hole in the trunk, and I let my momentum drive all of my body weight into a sidekick that shattered that rotted surface. Chunks of brittle wood went flying with a sharp crack like a rifle going off, and I rebounded backward some little ways but managed to stay on my feet and charged the tree again.

I hammered another kick into the tree, and then another, pivoting rapidly, left foot, right foot, wood spewing from the opening I'd made as if the tree were spitting out crumbs, and then its top-heavy frame began to lean forward even more with the sound of a hundred envelopes being ripped open at once. The weight bearing down on the thinned base snapped it and the entire tree toppled forward. Its new base thundered into the ground and the top fell against the cliff at a diagonal angle, almost reaching the apex.

I leaped on to the sloping tree trunk and began to run up its length. It was a steep angle but climbable. A slight hiss, and I moved the Kevlar vest I was holding like a shield upward. An arrow thumped into it. The arrow stung my forearm, hot and sharp, but it didn't penetrate the bulletproof material.

I kept running into a section where the branches were negotiable next to the trunk but extended out into smaller and thicker networks, providing me cover even while they slowed me down. Another arrow cracked into a branch right in front of me.

To my right, a fairly thick branch jutted upward, and I saw a chance and took it, running up the branch and leaping for a ledge on the embankment and making it, moving around a small outcrop of rock on the cliff face while another arrow shattered on stone behind me. There was a rock jutting a few feet before and above me, and I didn't try to grab it; I leaped upward as far as I could and used it as a foot brace and then jumped again and then I was rolling over the top of the embankment.

I just had time to unsheathe my knife and gain my feet when another hiss made me turn my head just fast enough to make an arrow tear out my left earlobe instead of anchoring in the side of my neck. Then the bakaak burst through the undergrowth and we were in closing distance.

God, I missed my katana.

It really was faster than me, just like legends said, and I'm not used to fighting things that are faster than me. Stronger than me, yes, often, but not faster. I couldn't see much of it; it was shorter than I was and covered in pelts and a greasy layer of animal fats and charcoal that had been melted into paste. Only its eyes were plainly visible, two smoldering red dots in shadow.

We halted then, circling each other while it told me its name and who it had been in its previous life, speaking of its motivations and hatreds and dreams. The bakaak just happened to speak contemporary English, and it bragged of its plans for the werewolf clan and taunted me with my inability to prevent them.

Okay, all of that was a lie. The bakaak didn't say a damn thing, it just tore my left eye out with the end of the bow, using its length like a staff. It was so fast that I couldn't stop it, though the knife that I tried to block it with did belatedly slash the bowstring a microsecond later. This actually saved my life, because I was staggering back and the bakaak was already beginning a move that would have strung another arrow and fired it through my face at point-blank range. It wasted a second realizing that the bowstring was cut, and I grazed the side of its knee with a short kick instead of breaking it squarely like I'd hoped.

Damn, the thing was fast!

The bakaak dropped the arrow in its right hand so that it could reach for its war club, but the bow in its left swung and caught my foot on my now-blinded side, pulling me off balance. I fell next to its foot and my knife pounded all the way through the bakaak's soft felt boot and anchored into the hard soil beneath it.

Flit through the forest like some darkest nightmare now, you bastard.

The bakaak freed the war club from its side before I cleared my gun, and it smacked the weapon out of my hand with a whistling swing that broke several of my fingers, and then wolves were bearing the bakaak backward and down, one, two, three of them.

They must have followed me up the tree ladder I'd made. As fast and skilled as it was, the bakaak didn't last long after that.

Mayte came and pulled me away from the carnage, hooking her hands under my arms. That was fine, but then Mayte started to suck on my wounded ear, spitting blood out intermittently. I tried to tell Mayte to quit it, but the words came out garbled because the left side of my face was dead, which might have been a blessing because that eye was missing and it probably would have hurt like a bitch otherwise. She tried to say something back, but her lips and tongue had gone numb. We both started to laugh, strange-sounding hoots that were maybe a little hysterical.

Mayte collapsed down beside me, and we lay there on the ground with our heads close together and listened to the sound of tearing flesh in the background.

❧24❧

PLEASE DON'T SQUEEZE
THE CHARMING.

Oh, hell." I was looking through a pair of binoculars though I could just as well have been using a telescope. My left eye was still bandaged. Regrowing an entire eye was turning out to be a real pain in the...socket. The orb ached and itched and apparently didn't grow a protective lens until the last stage.

"What is it? Do you recognize those guys?" Mayte was sitting next to me on a boulder overlooking our base camp. Bernard had sent us out on picket duty so that we could work out the awkwardness between us. The cynical part of me noted that he couldn't keep using her well-being as leverage otherwise.

We were east of a rock face that we were pretty sure hid the bakaak's lair. Cell phones had started working again, and several high-riding Jeeps with thick tires had arrived, transporting goods and clan members. Mayte and several others were going back to our paw in one of them. I was not.

I handed her the field glasses. "Look at the guy with the walking stick. I'll bet you a hundred to one he's the expert Bernard's been waiting for."

The man she was looking at had waist-length brown hair that was totally impractical for any kind of fight, and even from a distance, it had a kind of greasy sheen. He was short and gaunt and hollow-cheeked despite the light beard, and he was wearing a dark T-shirt and combat boots that I doubted had ever seen combat. More tellingly, he carried a thorny walking stick made out of stained black hawthorn, and runes and sigils were carved in it. A large golden icon that looked like a T with elephantiasis dangled from his neck.

"Jesus," Mayte said.

"Probably not." I took the binoculars back from her. "That's a Tau cross he's wearing. Although the actual crucifixes Romans used often looked more—"

Mayte's head dropped as she pretended to fall asleep.

"Fine," I grumbled.

Mayte's head popped up again. "So, what's your problem with him? Other than his fashion sense."

"He's a cunning man," I said.

Her brow furrowed. "How can you tell?"

"No, I mean he's a..." I hesitated. "Cunning folk is an old term. I guess you'd call him a wizard, but knights don't like to use that word because it comes with too many misconceptions. But cunning folk study magic. And this one is a werewolf."

"Why is that so bad?"

I went back to observing him. "Because cunning folk go around poking magic hornets' nests with sticks, and werewolves don't age much. Trust me, the last thing this world needs is a cunning man with a lot of extra time on his hands. It's why liches are so dangerous."

"Like Lord Voldemort," she said pensively.

I would have made fun of her, but I love those damn books.

"No wonder Gabriel is so jumpy." Mayte laughed. "He was already freaking out."

"I noticed that," I admitted. "What's up?"

"Gabriel and his sister grew up in a Catholic orphanage. He's an all-around atheist now. God or the Great Spirit, it doesn't make much difference to him." Mayte shook her head. I don't know if she was condemning Catholic orphanages or Gabriel. "Being around all of this spirit stuff is getting to him."

"How do you know all this?"

She stared at me. "Gabriel's sister is Bernard's mate. We've been with these people for three days. How do you *not* know all of this?"

"Nobody's going to tell me anything personal with Nikolai hanging around giving me the stinkeye," I grumbled.

Her lips made a raspberry. "Maybe you're just not good at small talk."

"Maybe," I admitted. "I sure as hell didn't find whatever water cooler you've been hanging around."

The fact that she was pretty and surrounded by males probably didn't hurt, either.

Mayte let it go. "The way I hear it, Gabriel's sister really got into exploring her heritage. She joined an Anishinaabe werewolf pack and became like an adopted daughter to their leader, Ben Lafontaine. That's why Bernard courted her."

This was getting interesting. "Big Ben didn't trust the white man with the forked tongue?"

Mayte gave me a look that was considering being irritated. "Maybe you ought to be respectful. We're on Native American land with pissed-off spirits running around."

"Good point," I acknowledged. "So this Catherine sealed a contract or something? She and Bernard got married for political reasons?"

Her look became something that twitched between fond and scornful and sad. "Most women don't find their Prince Charming, you know."

"Lucky for them," I muttered. She was starting to smell like arousal again, and I was starting to respond to it.

"I just get the impression that Bernard wouldn't volunteer to lead a dangerous mission so that his mate wouldn't have to." She stared into my eyes. "Most men wouldn't do that for a woman unless they wanted to sleep with her. But you don't want to sleep with me, do you?"

I cleared my throat. "No."

She put a palm flat on my chest, flexed her fingers around the muscle there. "Yes, you do. But you don't *want to* want to sleep with me. What's that about?"

"Look, I've kind of been through an emotional roller coaster lately," I said. "And there's a woman I need to see. I think she just tossed me out of her life, but I need more time or I need to see her before I move on. Something. I can't explain why."

Mayte sounded amused. "I'm not asking for your class ring."

I smiled wryly. "That's good. My school didn't encourage us to wear things that identified where we came from."

She ignored this and adjusted her position so that she could regard me steadily. "And sex can be healing, you know? It doesn't have to mess everything up."

"Look." I fumbled for the right words. "If we get free and clear of this place and I have time to talk to a woman you don't know, and grieve, and get my head on straight, and know for sure you're not out of your head with a second set of instincts you never asked for, then maybe at some point—"

"I guess we ought to go back." Mayte made to stand up and I put a hand on her wrist.

"Wait…"

She shook my hand off. "If you tell me you just want to be friends, I'm going to shoot you in the balls."

"Good to know sex wouldn't have made things complicated." I made to get up and she lunged into me and tried to knock me flat again. I flipped and pinned her from habit.

"You're right. I'm not being fair," Mayte breathed into my mouth.

What the hell? She was still learning how to deal with some high-octane feral emotions, but what the hell? She wrapped her legs around my waist. There was a look in her eyes as old and wild as time.

"You're making this difficult," I panted.

She gripped me with her legs and arched her back, forcing her pelvis against mine until the bulge in my pants pressed into her. I could feel the heat of her through the fabric of my jeans, and the pressure got tighter. "You mean I'm making it hard."

I released her and pushed her knees apart with my elbows. "Did Bernard tell you to do this?"

"What?!?" She scrambled out from under me, crab-walking.

"Something's not right here," I said, groping for anger and confusion and truth to force the lust back. "I don't know what it is, but something's off. I'm not wrong about that."

She stood up then, angrily smacking dust off of her pants. "Are you calling me a whore?"

"Are you going to keep answering my question with a question?" I rose to my feet too.

Mayte got a little too close, but then, boundaries weren't exactly her thing. "I'm not used to having to work this hard for a guy. Maybe I'm not very good at it. But if I'd known you were a paranoid jackass, I wouldn't have tried."

"Well, now you know." I turned and started walking back.

Mayte caught up with me. We trudged silently side by side

for a time, both radiating anger, but gradually the tension started to wear off a little until she finally spoke again. "So, are you really in love with this woman?"

What was I supposed to say? That Sig had briefly carried the spark of a woman whom I'd loved and who had died, and that part of me had sensed it and responded way out of proportion? That Sig was the one who had broken through all the walls I'd put up and hid behind, and maybe she had assumed an almost mythical status in my imagination because of that?

I hesitated. "I barely know her. But whatever I am, I'm not over it yet."

"So what's your plan?" Mayte wondered.

"I have no plan," I admitted. "I'm just trying to survive until I figure out what the hell is going on and what I should do about it."

"I understand," Mayte said gravely. "You're a fool."

I stayed quiet. What was I going to say? She was right.

~25~

WOLVESRUNTOGETHERJOHN

The cunning man...or maybe I should say cunning were-wolf...smelled like rosemary and hemlock. Seriously. He was sweating in the noon sun and it wasn't very warm outside. His sweat smelled clean, but his pupils weren't dilating normally and his heart was beating fast even for a werewolf. I wondered if he'd just taken some kind of stimulant.

"Phoenix," he said gravely, offering his hand.

Phoenix? What kind of tool calls himself Phoenix?

"Is that your first or last name?" I took his hand and shook it.

"It's just my name." His voice was strangely low and reedy at the same time. I think he intentionally pitched his words from deep in his chest because his voice was naturally nasal and he didn't like it. "Phoenix. And you are..."

"Unicorn," I said. Being horny makes me grumpy.

Gabriel tried to cover a startled laugh, and Phoenix gave me a dirty look.

I relented even though he was a cunning werewolf. The expression on his face had real hate in it, but real hurt too. "Sorry. I'm John Charming."

Phoenix didn't have a light touch with sarcasm. "Yeah, because that name's not strange at all."

"Truth," I admitted.

Bernard came back from seeing the Jeeps off and easily picked a large rucksack off the ground with one hand. I looked at him and maybe managed to keep my tone neutral. "So why is Phoenix here?"

He clapped Phoenix on the shoulder. "You said that this bakaak's lair would have hunting magic. Phoenix is the Clan's magic expert."

"So, you didn't kill Nikolai because he was famous," I summarized. "You didn't kill me because I'm a knight. And you didn't kill this guy because he's a cunning man. Hell, Bernard, don't you have *any* standards?"

Nikolai was behind me, the way he usually was when Bernard was around, and he actually chuckled. Phoenix glared. Gabriel twisted his mouth. Bernard laughed delightedly. "You sound like Groucho Marx. He didn't want to join any club that would have someone like him as a member."

Yeah, I remembered.

We said some boring and obvious things and then proceeded to climb up the rock face.

"I'll stay down here and rearguard," Gabriel called from behind us.

"I don't think so, brother of mine," Bernard said sternly. "If there's any lingering Native American presences, you might be the only one here they wouldn't object to."

"I don't believe in any Great Spirit," Gabriel said irritably. "And I don't want to have anything to do with any other kind. That's why I'm here with you palefaces, remember?"

"We all do what we have to do for the Clan," Bernard growled. "Hell, man, I even married your sister."

Gabriel unexpectedly grinned. It made him look young for real, not just physically. "Well, if you put it that way..."

We didn't need any mountain-climbing gear, at least not yet. There was a path of sorts, though it was steep and winding, and the bakaak hadn't bothered to mask its scent. Almost any animal but us would run away from its smell, anyhow.

We followed the path to a crevasse concealed by a dust-covered hide. It blended with the rock face almost perfectly.

"Let me perform a cleansing ritual." Phoenix started to walk forward, and I put a hand on his shoulder.

"Let's clear those rocks up there first," I said dryly, pointing up toward several boulders that were positioned like billiard balls.

"What rocks?" Phoenix squinched his brow dramatically. I guess he was looking for giant bowling-ball rocks that were directly overhead.

"Trust me, that's a deadfall trap," I said. "Even if it's a natural one."

Phoenix looked around some more, again overdoing every gesture. "If it's a trap, where's the trigger?"

"I don't know." I was already walking away. "That's why we should go up there from the side and clear the boulders."

Phoenix made a rude noise, but Bernard was shaking his head and the others were already following me as I made my way west out of the avalanche line. They all still had fresh memories of the kind of traps a bakaak was capable of.

"This is why John's here," Bernard told Phoenix. "You'll get your turn."

Cunning werewolves. Maybe I should have just moved to the side and kept my mouth shut.

∽∾

The bakaak was shooting an arrow into a creature I'd never seen before. It was a huge humanoid a bit like a wendigo but less hairy, gaunter, and longer-limbed. The target was trapped in some kind of quicksand or swamp. Was it possible that it was a hidebehind? I looked at the cave painting a little more closely; I'd seen a hidebehind's bones once, but I'd never seen a picture of a living one. The creature was casting a shadow in the wrong direction—was that a clue?

"You've been studying these paintings ever since we got here." This from one of the people who had accompanied Phoenix, a short, middle-aged-looking bleached blonde with low bangs. She was supposed to take pictures of everything we found, but her camera wasn't working. I was mentally referring to her as Photoshop; I'm not sure why. Photoshop gestured at the paintings on the cold gray cavern walls around us, none of which showed dogs playing poker. "Do you know something I don't?"

"I know you're going to have to get a very old camera if you want to take any pictures here," I said. An undead thing had resided where we were standing, maybe even passed back into our world from this very location. The shadows seemed a little darker for it, bottomless and baneful. The walls were suffering from some kind of electromagnetic hangover. "I'm talking about the kind that uses copper plates instead of film."

"Why don't I just get out a stone tablet and a chisel?" she muttered.

We were in a large, roughly oval cave low lit by a large bonfire. The flames took a little bit of the chill off my skin, at least the chill that was temperature-related. Unholy has its own vibe, and the place gave me a serious case of the creeps.

"What's so interesting about the pictures?" Nikolai was

helping Bernard tend the bonfire and generally not saying much. He was still processing the death of the men he'd sent out to track the bakaak, and the memory wasn't going down easily.

"These paintings tell stories about how to hunt supernatural beings." I took a sip of hot chocolate from the red mug I was holding. One of the advantages of hanging with Bernard was that we ate and drank a lot better than my paw had. The hot chocolate wasn't great, but it wasn't that weak, watery stuff that most campsites wind up drinking, either. "If there's something useful to learn, I want to know it."

"I don't see stories." Photoshop gave up and shoved her camera down in her purse in disgust. "I see scenes from stories, maybe."

"Then you're not looking closely enough. Come over here." I pointed to the most recent painting, which showed the bakaak smashing a werewolf's brains out with a war club. Unlike most of the paintings in the cave, this one was still fresh enough that I could smell the wild onion skins and walnuts and pokeberries that the pigments had been extracted from.

"Check out those blazing footprints walking toward the Clan sentry." I pointed them out. "We assumed the bakaak burned your crops after it attacked, but these indicate that it burned the crops first, so that the smell would conceal it while the blaze drew your sentry forward. And see how the moon is positioned and how specific the stars are? It tells the time of the attack."

"How did it have time to come back here and paint this?" Nikolai wondered.

"It didn't paint this *after* the attack," I said a little impatiently. "It painted it *before*. That's how hunting magic works. It's a way of giving the universe a little nudge, encouraging it to make possibilities work out a certain way."

"What's with the bobcat-shaped cloud?" Photoshop wondered.

"See how the rain looks like it's coming from the bobcat's crotch?" I indicated the drops. "We know it wasn't raining that night, but rain cleans and conceals tracks. It's a metaphor. I think the compound the bakaak came up with to break down scent molecules was distilled from urine it took out of a bobcat's bladder."

"WHAT?!?" Phoenix's voice came from farther down a cave passage. "Hold it! Wait!"

The cave passage he was traversing wasn't precisely convenient. A larger man would have had to squeeze through at least one tight patch, then another that forced him to crouch down as he ascended or descended. We could see the light of the lamp Phoenix was carrying bobbing while he climbed.

Phoenix rushed into the chamber and urgently grabbed me by the upper arm, his eyes wild. Definitely on stimulants. He was looking right at me, but he might as well have been looking at a chair or a doorknob. "Have you found any more paintings that have clues about how the bakaak makes things?"

For some reason, Bernard's primary interest was the paralyzing poison that could even affect werewolves. The cave den Phoenix had just been in had a ceramic pot with remnants of the stuff in it. His assistant, either a botanist or a chemist or both, was still down there.

I ignored Phoenix and addressed Bernard. "Are you sure you want to try to duplicate that poison, Bernard? If it affects werewolves, wouldn't it be better to destroy it?"

Phoenix ignored the fact that I was ignoring him. "You can't destroy knowledge!"

Which pretty much summed up the reason why knights and cunning folk hate each other right there. Knights spend their entire lives getting rid of magical evidence, and cunning folk spend their entire lives trying to piece it back together and document it.

"I can try." I indicated the cave paintings with a head shake. "It was messing around with this kind of magic that created werewolves in the first place."

The amusement in Bernard's voice was eloquent. "And that's such a bad thing? If I weren't a werewolf, I'd have died of old age by now. Instead, I'm trying to help good people not think of themselves as monsters and contemplating making a s'mores."

"Maybe you should write a self-help book," I noted dryly. *"For Better or Curse."*

I would say that Nikolai scowled, but it would be more accurate to say that his expression didn't change. Bernard chuckled, though.

"Even if all that stuff you said is true, we're talking black magic, and nothing good ever comes from messing with black magic," I continued. "Have you noticed that every time somebody stumbles across one of the components of the original werewolf spell, it's almost always toxic or lethal?"

Phoenix rolled his eyes, and I could tell he was about to go off on some tangent about how no magic was white or black, but Photoshop interrupted him. "What are you talking about?"

"The reason wolfsbane works against us like a normal poison is because it was a component of whatever spell created us way back before written history," I said. "There's probably some ingredient in this paralyzing poison that was part of that spell too."

"The paralyzing poison has other applications, John," Bernard said patiently.

"Like what?" I demanded. "Anesthesia? I'd rather take the pain. Or are you looking for more efficient ways to subdue our own kind?"

"It would be nice to be able to subdue out-of-control were-wolves without ripping them to shreds," Bernard said gravely. "But that's not what this is about. The poison slowed poor Kenneth's change. What if the drug could be developed to keep people from changing until a full moon was over?"

Whoa. I gave that some serious thought. "You mean, were-wolves wouldn't have to change into wolves?"

"No, John, I *like* that we change into wolves," Bernard said patiently. "But what if we could keep our pregnant women from changing until they came to term? Or keep children from changing until they were old enough to handle it without dying? I'm tired of being an evolutionary dead end."

I was speechless. It's a fact of life that a werewolf fetus dies during the first full moon. The fetal sac can't handle all the tearing and shifting. The idea of werewolf children? It took a few moments to even wrap my brain around the possibility.

"I want children," Bernard said. "And I want a world where I could raise them safely."

"That's a nice dream," I admitted. "But history is full of people who went down dark paths, thinking they could accomplish good things with bad magic. Hell, look at the people who rediscovered how to create werewolves back at the turn of the seventeenth century."

In the late 1590s, there was a werewolf epidemic in France, kicking off thousands, maybe tens of thousands of werewolf trials. A lot of it was caused by the rediscovery of the potion or salve that created the first werewolf. There was probably more to it than that...chants and gestures and symbolic times and places and crap...but a lot of serial-killing werewolves like Pierre Bourget and Michel Verdun were caught with a mysterious ointment. It became the catalyst for a new wave of inquisitions.

"I am looking at them." Bernard stood up by the fire and stretched. "The Gandillons were a werewolf *family*. They had sons and daughters."

"A family of cannibals and human sacrificers," I pointed out, giving Phoenix a not-so-subtle look. "Werewolf cunning folk."

"You're missing the point." Bernard walked over to where Phoenix and I were squaring off. "I'm not arguing that there have never been bad werewolves. That would be like saying there have never been bad humans. That's all we are, John. Humans with bells and whistles."

"I'm not missing the point," I assured him. "I'm disagreeing with it."

"You've been studying these walls, trying to learn from them for the past twenty-four hours," Bernard pointed out. "How is that any different from what Phoenix is doing?"

"..." Damn. That was a good point.

"We're really not that different, you and I," Bernard continued. "I've probably killed more werewolves who went insane or were just bad people to begin with than you have. It's why I'm working so hard to change the world that creates werewolves like that. I don't like killing. Do you?"

"No," I admitted. "But none of this changes the fact that I'm standing in a seriously messed-up place that smells like death and crazy while you talk about werewolf Lamaze classes."

"You need to start showing some respect," Nikolai said ominously from his place by the fire.

"He's allowed to question me, Nikolai." Bernard seemed amused. "You do it all the time."

Nikolai didn't take his eyes off of me. "I earned it."

Nikolai started to add something else, but Bernard spoke first: "You and Nikolai don't have to be friends, John."

"Oh, I think we do," I said earnestly. "I think this is the start of one of history's great bromances. I just get that vibe."

"You and Phoenix don't have to be friends." Bernard continued undeterred. "You and I don't even have to be friends, although I hope we are becoming so. But you told me you'd give your clan initiation an honest effort. Is your word good or not?"

I didn't get a chance to not know how to respond to that, because Phoenix interrupted. I'm not sure he'd actually been listening for anything but a pause where he could jump in. "Keep looking over these paintings for clues! I didn't know knights could think abstractly. Keep it up and I might even consider making you my apprentice. Show you that wizards aren't so bad."

He was serious.

Bernard anticipated the smart-ass response forming in my mouth and said my name like a warning. "John."

I waved him off. "I got it. I'll keep working on my bakaak merit badge."

"Good man." Bernard clapped me on the shoulder even while he was looking significantly at Nikolai. "The Clan needs you."

"Bernard," I said, suddenly tired. "I'm the last thing your clan needs."

That got his complete attention. "Why?"

I gestured at Nikolai. "He's right. Even if I agree with everything you're doing, as long as I'm being driven by a geas, I'll always be a ticking time bomb. If you do something that I think is seriously threatening the Pax Arcana, I'll start getting compulsions to stop you."

"Exactly," Nikolai growled. "And that's the best-case scenario."

"Your clan and I had a good thing going for a long time," I

persisted. "I was distracting the knights on the left. You were distracting the knights on the right. We didn't even know each other, and we were dividing their focus. Just let me go, and we can go back to helping each other like that."

"Except," Nikolai stated grimly, "you might wind up getting captured and telling the knights everything you've figured out about us. And I had a problem with that even before you started solving murder mysteries and going all Da Vinci code on cave walls."

So, it was coming down to blood after all.

Bernard smelled that reaction and put his hands on my shoulders. "Stop it! You're a wolf! That's stronger than any geas."

I stilled. All of me. Inside. Outside. My soul held its breath. "What do you mean?"

He smiled. "I know you've felt it. That's why you were running from Mayte that day. You've gotten so used to fighting your wolf impulses that they freak you out."

"What's going on with me?" I asked hoarsely.

Phoenix laughed. It wasn't a nice laugh, and Bernard shut him down with a look so intense that it practically had sound effects. "Why haven't you tried to kill Nikolai, John?"

Nikolai growled.

"Because you said he was an accident," I said slowly. "And he's clan."

Bernard grinned. "And why aren't you trying to destroy the Clan?"

I was having a hard time forming words. "Because I'm not sure the Clan is bad for the Pax. I think maybe the knights are the ones threatening the Pax in this case and don't even know it."

Bernard laughed delightedly and slapped my shoulders, looking at Nikolai with a *See? I told you so!* kind of look. "The strange feelings that you've been feeling are just race memories. Phoenix is right; you've been dealing with them your whole life. They're just amplified among others of your own kind."

I nodded slowly.

"Wolves are meant to run together, John," Bernard said firmly.

"Yeah," I said. "But not like candle wax."

Bernard chuckled and released my shoulders. "God, you're stubborn. Who's going to make me laugh if you leave us when your initiation is over?"

"I tell one hell of a knock-knock joke," Nikolai suggested from his place by the fire.

I smiled while I thought, *A man's soul is his own, and you'd better not forget it, buster.*

~26~

ASHES, ASHES, WE ALL FALL DOWN

There were three different curtains or walls made out of animal hide staggered between the entranceway and the lair, and I was meditating between the first two when the birds told me something was wrong. Flocks were calling out to each other as they flew overhead in the night, and a lot of those calls belonged to birds who were not nocturnal. I sat there listening, then turned and called out a warning.

After a brief explanation, Muscles went out to join Gabriel on patrol and Phoenix's crew began gathering their work. Bernard and Nikolai formed a command center of sorts.

Bernard located a spot outside where cell phones worked, but he couldn't reach anyone in the training grounds. He could reach people in a sixty-mile radius surrounding them, but none of the paws he'd scattered throughout the forest reserve were responding.

Nikolai came and stood near me at the cave entrance while Bernard talked to someone in Woodruff. "Knights?"

I hesitated. "Probably."

A vein pulsed in his temple. "You said that they wouldn't move unless it was a massive attack or a surgical strike to take out Bernard."

"Or both," I said.

Nikolai cursed and Bernard came back to join us. We went back inside the cave.

There was a vehicle hidden about two miles away from the cave, and Nikolai and Bernard began to discuss how to proceed—argue, really, with Nikolai maneuvering to make Bernard's safety the main priority. The rest of us rounded up weapons and gear.

Gabriel came running in while Bernard and Nikolai were still hammering out the details. It was one of the first times he'd been in the cave since we'd moved in. "The forest animals are stampeding!"

"What?!?" Phoenix blurted. "How big a force are the knights sending?"

I heard the sounds of an engine and went back through the grid of hides so that I could look up at the sky. I couldn't distinguish the colors, but a fixed-wing aircraft was briefly silhouetted against the moon as it flew north overhead.

Muscles joined me and peered upward. "That's an air tanker. A firefighting plane."

I didn't ask him how he knew about planes. Why weren't there any werewolves among those stampeding forest animals?

I knew then. Knew it in that part of me that is always waiting for the next disaster. My paw was dead. Mayte. Chai. Jelly. Cory. But some knowledge you don't accept, and some you can't accept. Some you have to verify anyway. You have to.

"Bernard?" I didn't have to ask loudly or stop looking at the sky. Something in my voice made everyone within forty feet stop talking.

"What?" His voice came from within the cave, beyond the hides. He didn't have to respond loudly, either.

"I know you can't reach your firefighters right now," I said. "But you need to call someone who can track down where they were when their cell phones stopped working."

∽

We picked up another claw that was heading toward Bernard's base camp and took them with us, then found the first and last member of Bernard's werewolf firefighting unit a little over an hour later. The fire was closer now—we were actually traveling in its wake at the moment—and the air was full of smoke and ash and had a biting taint that stung in our lungs. The woods were black, and burned trunks and stumps still fed guttering flames.

The firefighter had been winged with a shotgun shell full of silver shot, and he had only gotten away by crawling through flames. His wounds weren't healing.

"Where are the paws, Steve?" Bernard asked, crouching down. Steve's face had been the least burned part of him when we removed his mask, but his face was still cooked. He was lying on the ground and no one wanted to move him.

Steve's lungs had been toasted, and his scraping sucks of breath hurt in my ears. "They were dressed like us. Like fire-fighters. But they weren't."

He was talking about a knight strike team, sweepers.

"We'll find them," Bernard promised, but I doubted it was a promise he could keep. "Where are the paws?"

"They didn't make it," Steve rasped. "No way."

"How is that possible?" Bernard had control. I couldn't hear a quiver in his voice.

"There were two fires," Steve gasped. "Real pro jobs. A large one. It was...north...fast. With the wind. Smaller one moving to meet it. The bigger one made a vacuum. Pulled the small one in. The campsites were caught between them. Real pro jobs."

"The paws," Bernard repeated grimly.

"Between them," Steve said. "The fires. The paws."

Complete immolation is an effective way to kill werewolves. It is how villages used to execute us in the Middle Ages.

"And the planes," Steve gasped. "Some weren't dropping flame retardant."

"What were they dropping, Steve?" Bernard asked gently.

"Gas crystals. We got caught in it. Two of us died. Switched to oxygen tanks."

Wolfsbane. I could catch the faintest whiff of it in the air. The kind of weaponized wolfsbane they'd used at the lodge. Gas clouds of the stuff.

ᏏᏏᎧ

We found the first remains about half an hour later, and it was a miracle we found it that quickly. We couldn't track the bones by smell and ash was everywhere and our infravision was useless.

"We have to go," Bernard growled.

He was right. The smell of wolfsbane was stronger and the air was getting hotter, as if maybe the fire had shifted again. The sight of planes overhead was becoming more frequent and we could hear men yelling in the distance.

My paw was dead. I would never find the bodies. But my paw was dead.

There was no real reason to feel like I was standing on that rooftop in Philadelphia again, to feel choking fury and grief. Mayte wasn't Alison. Chai...who I had started to respect and like...wasn't An Rong. What was it Chai had tried to make me understand? Something about how important it is to get to know people when life is fragile.

I understood him now.

The paws hadn't been killers, at least not yet. They hadn't asked for any of this. They were just innocent, messed-up people trying to get their act together like anybody else. The knights had done this because Bernard had attacked the lodge, and Bernard had attacked the lodge because of me, and everything was all tangled up and somebody had to cut the knot in half with a sword.

Emil had tried to make me the knights' slave. Bernard had offered me a choice.

"All right." The words vibrated painfully in my chest. My head was bent low, my hands fists that I couldn't unclench.

Bernard was there in an instant, his voice a growl even if the words were recognizable. "What is it?"

I tried to say it and couldn't. Swallowed and moved my jaw and finally bit the empty air as if an invisible gag were in my mouth. It seemed to help.

"I'll join your clan," I croaked.

PART THE THIRD

Mission Impolitic

~27~

FLASHASSFORWARD

I was sitting on the couch in Eileen Williams's living room when she came out of the shower. She was forty-three years old and looked at least ten years younger, auburn-haired and fit despite being a mother of four. She took one look at me and gave a startled scream before dashing for the bedroom down the hall where she and her husband kept a shotgun in the closet, flashes of buttock visible under the white towel she was wearing.

As soon as she reached her bedroom, she screamed again.

A moment later, she backed into the hallway, her face drained of blood. Nikolai was walking behind her. Eileen moved silently into the living room while Nikolai remained in the hallway.

"Have a seat, Eileen." Eileen took long showers, and I took a sip of the coffee I had made while waiting for her to finish. Eileen or her husband apparently liked to grind gourmet coffee at the local grocery store and buy it in plain paper bags. It was okay.

Eileen was remarkably composed under the circumstances.

White-faced and trembling but keeping it together. "May I get dressed first?"

"Nikolai will let you put on a bathrobe," I said. "But that's all."

She wasn't in any immediate danger, at least not from me, but it was good that she felt vulnerable. I wanted her to take what I was about to say seriously.

Eileen hesitated, then went back into her bedroom, followed by Nikolai. A few moments later, she came back with a creamy green bathrobe wrapped tightly around her. She sat in an armchair adjacent to me rather than across from me, reaching underneath her bottom to adjust her robe before crossing her legs. They were good legs, but I observed them with clinical detachment.

We were in a comfortable living room, brick outer walls with a big fireplace and one of those insulated heated floors that are not uncommon in Wisconsin. The living room furniture was oak with over-thick cushions. There was a sword hanging on the wall that looked ornamental and wasn't, and there were a lot of sandstone pictures on the walls from Okinawa. The big coffee table that dominated the room had eleven frameless photographs lying flat on it. Eileen glanced at them and then looked away. She was crying but not sobbing. "You're one of them, aren't you?"

"I'm a werewolf, yes." I didn't offer her coffee, but only because I knew she wouldn't drink anything I gave her.

She gripped the armrests of her chair as if to keep from floating out of it. "Are you going to kill me?"

I smiled sadly. This was how my pregnant mother had gotten the werewolf bite that eventually created me and killed her. Werewolves had tracked my father to his home and found her there. In a way, I had come full circle.

Life can be cruel and strange.

"I will die defending you if anyone tries," I promised her. "But you need to get your kids out of school and leave Wisconsin as soon as we're done talking."

She swallowed. "What about my husband?"

I shook my head. "We warned the knights to get out of Wisconsin. The deadline was up months ago. He should have listened."

Eileen tried to talk, then started over. Her voice was unsteady. "My husband isn't a knight."

I knew that, actually. It takes five to seven personnel to support one combat soldier in the US military, and it's not that much different for knights. Most people aren't emotionally or physically cut out to be warriors, and a lot of people who are born under the geas support the Templars by becoming citizens with useful careers—and not just military, law enforcement, or political careers either, although the Templars have a lot of those types. I'm talking doctors, nurses, dentists, lawyers, accountants, plastic surgeons, computer programmers, engineers, journalists, pilots, mechanics, PR specialists, small business owners, scientists, merchants, and so on. And that doesn't even include the people who help the Templars because they were woken up from the Pax by some kind of tragedy or trauma.

The Clan was having a lot of success destabilizing the knights in Milwaukee by going after the Templars' infrastructure, their spotters, informants, hosts, suppliers, intermediaries, and civil servants. False modesty aside, I was a large part of the reason for that. Identifying those people was my idea, and I had the knack. Finding knights who came in and out of town without a fixed location was difficult. Locating lay servants with mortgages and families and civic ties and local histories was less so.

And one lay servant inevitably led to others. Community was a double-edged sword. If those of the blood only hung out with normal civilians, their children would become soft. Instead, their young children went to the same dojos and played sports for the same leagues in preparation for page and squire training. Their families went to the same churches. It was how we had found the Williamses.

"He may have washed out of knight training, but your husband has been using his position at airport terminal security to target werewolves," I said. "His dog has been specifically trained to spot our kind and signal him."

Her anger came to surface then. "Is he dead?"

I gave her a measuring stare. "If you really want to free him, you can give me useful information in exchange. In my experience, wives almost always know more than their husbands think they do."

She pressed her front teeth into her bottom lip so tightly that there was some danger of drawing blood. "You asshole."

"That's probably true," I agreed. "But not because of what I'm doing here. See those pictures on the table?"

Eileen didn't look at them.

"Those are people who were abducted after your husband tagged them for the knights. It took us a while to figure out how the knights were identifying them. Three of them tried to spy on us because the knights threatened their normal human families. We found four of them with their hearts stuffed into their mouths because the knights wanted us to find them. Four of them are still missing. There are probably more we don't know about."

Eileen didn't say anything.

I took another sip of the coffee. "Unlike your husband, I don't target innocents. You and your children are in no danger from me. If you don't want to give me information, don't."

There was a yellow legal pad and a pencil on the edge of the table. Eileen stared at it.

"The thing is," I said, "we don't want this war the knights are trying to start with us. We really don't. The knights and the Clan are going to wind up destroying each other. If I knew of another way to get the Order to back off, I'd try it. I really would."

"This won't stop them," Eileen said tonelessly.

"It'll stop one of them," I answered.

"You're John Charming." Her expression was suddenly filled with distaste. "The traitor."

"The knights cast me out, hunted me, and killed an innocent woman that I loved before I ever said boo." There was an edge to my voice that could have cut diamonds. "And now they're calling me a traitor?"

Her eyes did not fill with sympathy or understanding.

I got up to leave. "This is a waste of time. For what it's worth, your husband will die quickly and with dignity."

"Wait!" She grabbed for the legal pad then. "Just wait."

I sat back down, and she began scribbling on the legal pad. A few minutes later, I heard a gunshot off in the distance. Then another. They were silenced shots, fired through a suppressor, but Nikolai and I had enhanced hearing. Eileen paused when Nikolai's cell phone rang. He listened expressionlessly, then hung up the phone. "It's done."

I got up to leave. "You can put the pad down, Eileen. You don't have to stall us any longer."

The pad fell to the floor. She didn't seem to notice, her expression alarmed. "What are you talking about?"

"We just took out the strike team moving through the woods behind your house," I informed her. I didn't know how she'd signaled them, but I had been pretty confident that the

Williamses would have some kind of emergency protocol. Maybe there was a transmitter hidden in the closet where she'd gotten the bathrobe, or maybe she had managed to hit a hidden button somewhere, or maybe they had surveillance devices in their house that were activated by a keyword.

She wasn't speechless for long. "What about my husband?"

"I told you we'd give you your husband back if you gave us anything useful, and you did," I told her. "He'll be at the train station in time for the 3:15 to Chicago. Get your kids and get the hell out of Wisconsin."

∾28∾

DON'T BITE THE CLAW THAT FEEDS YOU

We need to talk." Nikolai was driving, which I actually found reassuring. I liked it when those canned hams he called hands were occupied.

"Really?" I was messing with the radio dials to see what kind of music Nikolai liked. I'd been expecting metal or rap, but he liked country. "You didn't just come along because you wanted to hang out?"

I'd made that "Besties" bracelet for nothing.

"Quit clowning around," Nikolai said irritably.

Easy for him to say. I had just lured twelve knights into a wooded area where forty-five pissed-off lycanthropes were waiting for them in wolf form, and in spite of everything, that didn't go down easily. On top of that, I had just made myself a threatening presence in the home of a woman, and that bothered me. And Nikolai was sitting next to me, sweating aggression.

"Bernard wants you to become an administrator," Nikolai said without preamble.

I looked at him as if he'd just said, "Hobbadoogawgaw ixnay on the brillo creamay in the pumpkin hammock."

"Me," I finally said, pointing both thumbs at my shoulders. "Administrator."

"Yes."

There was a paper lying on the front seat between us. I picked it up and began looking through it.

"What are you doing?"

"I'm looking for any articles about hell freezing over," I said conversationally.

Nikolai's mouth tightened. "Look at the front page instead."

I did. There was another article about the Butcher of Abalmar, the nation's latest serial killer. This one was particularly noteworthy because he or she focused on children.

"Bernard says we need you in Abalmar."

"Does it strike you as sad," I asked idly while I read, "that there have been so many serial killers called 'The Butcher' that we have to designate them by location now?"

Nikolai didn't respond.

It was a disturbing article. I hadn't had a lot of time to keep up on national news lately, and I missed it. Before the Clan, I'd had a lot of free time in between hunting and running over the decades, and I missed reading for fun and live music and learning to cook things and researching and hiking and even napping. Now I was living in a house with two other members of my claw, and it was strange. I didn't miss being lonely, but sometimes I missed being alone. I didn't miss hearing about serial killers, though. This one was killing young females and removing their entrails and leaving their bodies behind. Which was bad enough, but what was really freaking everyone out was that the killer seemed to be able to enter and leave heavily populated areas unseen.

"I'll go," I said. "But let me go in alone as a hunter. Forget this administrator nonsense."

Nikolai sidestepped the whole administrator question for the moment. Not a good sign. "You'll take Gabriel and the rest of your claw with you."

Putting Gabriel and me together had been one of Bernard's strokes of genius. Gabriel was a bit of a problem for the Clan because while his sister was Bernard's mate, Gabriel tended to get in trouble. Gabriel didn't always think before he spoke. But Nikolai trusted him, so Gabriel was the perfect choice to keep an eye on me, and I was well suited for keeping Gabriel out of sight and in line. His bluntness didn't bother me, and I didn't give a crap about his social or political connections.

Nikolai glanced sideways so that he could eye me balefully. "So you agree this killer is a supernatural?"

I put the paper down. "A lot of serial killers remove organs for trophies or food."

Nikolai gave me an impatient look. "But?"

"There's a kind of magic called anthropomancy that uses the entrails of young females to try to divine the future." I sighed. I didn't like thinking about it. "It's one of the reasons witches in the stories so often prey on children. That and the whole virgin sacrifice thing. And that kind of magic would be strongest now, during harvest season. It sounds like the killer is misusing the Pax Arcana to conceal its movements too. Odds are this butcher is one of the cunning folk."

Nikolai grimaced. He was wearing dark jeans and a gray hoodie, which had turned out to be a mistake. There were dried bloodstains on the jacket that he was having a hard time getting out. He ran a hand through his hair, and even that casual gesture made his jacket tight. "Bernard wants you to make this go away so the knights will stop flooding Abalmar."

I shrugged. "Good. But you really want me being some kind of supervisor for the area?"

"I want you to be on another continent." Nikolai's glare wasn't pro forma. "Maybe you're not working for the enemy, but you're too soft. And you encourage it in Bernard too. We should have killed that woman in there. And her children that are going to grow up hunting our friends."

"I have rules," I admitted. "But it's not about winning the knights over. If we can convince them that we're no threat to the Pax, their geas might force them to come to terms in spite of themselves. And killing people indiscriminately would make us a threat to the Pax."

It wasn't much of a chance, but it was something. When you're trapped in a burning house, there's no harm spitting.

"Whatever." Nikolai dismissed my twaddle with a curt jerk of his chin. "We need Abalmar. It's not as big as Green Bay, but it's close, and it's right in the middle of a lot of supply routes. Lots of meat-packing plants and military warehouses there."

"Again, what's that got to do with me taking charge?" I asked.

Nikolai looked like he'd swallowed a grenade. "Bernard is grooming you for bigger things."

"I don't want bigger things," I said.

"I don't like it, either," Nikolai assured me. "The problem is, Bernard wants it. And maybe you haven't noticed, but Bernard has a way of getting what he wants."

"So, how's the current leader in Abalmar going to like it when I come in and start moving the furniture around?"

Nikolai gave me an I'm-getting-to-that-fool kind of look. "That's part of why Bernard wants you to go. Matthew only respects tough. He's a good soldier, but he's not a good manager. He's running the tribe there like a biker gang, and it's not working. He's been given multiple warnings and nothing is changing."

I thought I understood the subtext.

"I'm a hunter," I informed him. "Not an assassin."

The look Nikolai gave me then was enigmatic. "We'll see."

Nikolai gave me a few more logistics details and then let me out at "Jesse's Garage," though the original Jesse had died of colon cancer two owners ago. The newest owner was a clan member, and the operation was small enough that he'd been able to train up all the help he needed from werewolf stock. It was a useful place for turning captured or stolen vehicles into untraceable rides.

My claw was spread out all over the two repair bays.

Space had been cleared on a table so that Gabriel could lie on it, though the surface wasn't particularly sanitary. He had a bottle of Tennessee sipping whiskey but he wasn't sipping it; he was slugging it down while Paul picked silver shot out of Gabriel's right thigh with a pair of needle-nose pliers. Gray-haired and fit, Paul had been a field medic for his Navy SEAL unit before leaving the service to work at a veteran's hospital. It was there that he had been bitten by a freaked-out veteran who was "convinced" that he was becoming a werewolf.

Paul was chuckling to himself.

"What's so damned funny?" Gabriel demanded irritably.

"I just remembered—the only reason I became a doctor was because I couldn't get into veterinary school." Paul's chuckles became outright laughter.

Paul had a weird sense of humor.

One of the vans had a missing windshield, and another had a small hole centered right over the driver's seat. I looked over at Tula and she smiled tightly. Tula had been in the Finnish military and only quit after they refused to let her go to sniper school. It was their loss; she was a hell of a shot, and I had no doubt that she was the one who had taken out the drivers. Brown-haired, busty, and attractive in a stocky way, she was lovingly reassembling her newly oiled rifle, a TRG-42. Apparently, it was a popular weapon in the Finnish military, or had been when Tula was a part of it.

Virgil came up to me and Nikolai as if he'd been waiting to pounce. "They're hiding out somewhere near a brewery." Bald, round-shouldered, and brown-skinned, Virgil had been a member of the Milwaukee police force for fifteen years before heading up some kind of special task force. I forget the task force's name because it was called something other than what it was in order to get some kind of federal funding. Basically, Virgil had specialized in youth relations and tracking down runaways among gangs and pimp stables and homeless communities. And, eventually, a werewolf pack.

Virgil knew Milwaukee better than any other member of the Clan. He could tell you where you'd just come from within a block just by taking a sniff.

"There's something weird about these vans too," he said. "They're old but they're in practically new condition. But they still have that mothball smell, and the tires are old even if they aren't worn down."

"The knights probably use them for risky operations and then keep them in storage for long periods of time," I said.

"That's what I'm thinking," Virgil confirmed. "I'm going to talk to some people I know about abandoned warehouses around the breweries."

"It could be the knights own a storage silo park around that area too," I said thoughtfully. "That's one of their favorite dodges—buy an entire storage facility and then rent the silos out to individual knights and their families so that the knights will have a secure storage area and the Templars will have a legit paper trail for the IRS."

Virgil cursed. "A place like that will probably be a weapons depot."

"Yeah," I agreed. "But that's not our concern any longer."

They all heard me. They were werewolves.

I had no illusions about my claw. Nikolai had handpicked them to keep an eye on me. Gabriel was from Bernard's inner circle even if he was in exile. Virgil was a detective who could monitor me. Paul was ex–special forces if he had to take me on up close. Tula was a markswoman who could take me out from a distance. But they were mine all the same.

∾29∾

SHUT UP WHEN YOU'RE TALKING TO ME

There was something stark and desolate about Abalmar. I liked Wisconsin in general—in some ways, it reminded me of Alaska, both the place and the people. But Abalmar had a bit of a Rust Belt vibe going on. Of course, my perceptions might have been influenced by the fact that I was coming there to hunt a supernatural serial killer, but we passed several abandoned sites whose function looked vaguely industrial and agricultural while we were driving through the outskirts of the city.

"Somebody ought to pay some local artists to prettify places like this," I said. We were passing a big machine whose white paint was peeling and whose function was uncertain. It seemed to be some kind of mobile vertical conveyer belt.

"Artists," Vigil snorted from the backseat. Tula was driving our Ford Escort. I'd wanted to sit behind the steering wheel, but Tula claimed to get motion sick if she couldn't drive. I'd never heard of a werewolf getting motion sick before, but if she was lying, she was doing a good job of it, and I respected that.

Virgil elaborated. "The kinds you're talking about would papier-mâché giant penises over everything."

"What kinds do you think John is talking about?" Tula wondered. Something about her question suggested that Finland apparently had a lot more respect for artists and government subsidies than Virgil did. She only got that tone when there was a "Stupid Americans" subtext running beneath her words.

"The kind that take grant money from the government," Virgil said. "They feel ashamed of taking money from Big Brother, so they go out of their way to be controversial. So they can tell their friends they're sticking it to the Man instead of being bought off."

"Biting the Man that feeds them," I mused. "You're thinking of someone specific." There was too much bitterness in his voice.

"A couple that turned their art studio into a foster home," Virgil admitted. "Professional leeches and child neglecters."

"That doesn't mean you have to stereotype," Tula chided. "That would be like me saying all cops are grouches who hate artists just because I know one."

"I don't hate artists," Virgil said. "I've just met a lot of cop-hating parasites who hid behind that term."

Tula turned up the music. I forgot what it was as soon as I heard it. Some generic Auto-Tuned dance babble, but it served its purpose and ended the conversation. When the song was over, she turned the radio down and addressed me. "Are you sure you don't want us to go with you?"

"I'm sure," I said curtly. "Come get me in an hour and a half."

"Should we bring a hearse?" Tula wondered.

I was about to test Matthew Bradley's security. A werewolf

209

from the Abalmar tribe had been killed just that morning, found with a silver bullet in her head, and it hadn't been Matthew who had informed Bernard about it. The information had come from another werewolf in Matthew's organization, or his disorganization. I wanted to get a good look at Matthew's operation without warning him I was coming.

"Look," I said, "Nikolai says this group runs on testosterone. If they catch me, I'll praise them. If they don't catch me, I'll put them on guard in a way that they need to be put on guard."

"And if they kill you, I get my ass chewed by Bernard," Virgil grumbled. "And I take ass-chewings a lot more seriously now that they're not just a figure of speech."

"I think you just want to play ninja," Tula added, but she wasn't trying to argue me out of anything. Tula liked trouble. She had come to America specifically because she had heard that a group of werewolves was taking on the knights there. "You could let Paul do this."

"There's some alpha male posturing involved," I admitted. If Matthew's inner circle was as big a bunch of swaggering assholes as Nikolai said, they were going to challenge me anyway. Better to take them off balance and get it over with fast, on my terms. "I want to establish my credentials."

"So that's how you're going to introduce yourself?" Tula made her voice raspy. "I'm Batman."

"See, ideally, you two would realize I wasn't in the car at this point," I said. "And Virgil would ask how I did that. But I don't know how to open a car door quietly."

Virgil chuckled. "I'll pretend not to see you leave if it'll get your ass out of here."

"Just for that, I'm leaving Tula in charge." I got out of the car, but I could still hear them talking after I closed the door and hit the woods on the side of the road.

I couldn't decide if making a firing range the Abalmar tribe's de facto headquarters was inspired or idiotic. "Fire on the Hole" was miles outside of the city, and it said something about this Matthew Bradley that the tribe's seat of power wasn't accessible. On the other hand, clan members had a legitimate reason for keeping weapons around, there was plenty of surrounding land for werewolves to roam around as therapy or security, and everyone in the Abalmar tribe could get practice with firearms.

Still, if I was a knight and wanted to attack the place, I wouldn't have a hard time getting a gun inside the perimeter. I would just pretend to be a paying customer. So, maybe it was a good thing Matthew didn't seem to have many.

I was in sight of the place when I first caught the smell of cigarette smoke. Dumb. It not only made the sentry easy to locate, but having a nicotine stick fired up right under his nostrils made it harder for him to scent me. Deciding to wait and watch for a while, it didn't take me long to figure out that the sentry was stationary and not taking his job very seriously.

I couldn't move around the other side, not with werewolves and the wind the way it was, but grass was tall on the fringes of the surrounding tree lines, and when I scanned the area with my field glasses, I could see a patch on the opposite side of the firing range where waist-high stalks had been crushed down recently. Another sentry, most likely, posted on the opposite side. The land in back of the firing range had been cleared for at least two thousand yards for outside distance shooting, and if there was anyone that far back, I was content to leave them be.

There were three large trash cans parked outside a side door, and I could smell that they weren't empty. If I could reach them, they would hide me from the sentry with the cigarette, conceal me from both his eyes and nose. I waited. Soon I heard a car with loud music blaring out of the windows pulling up the driveway. It was my other claw member, Paul.

Paul had been scoping the area out with a long-range rifle. Now he was providing some noise cover and drawing eyes his way. If he saw any of signs of trouble, he would try to help me. If not, he would turn around as if he'd gotten lost and drive off again.

I moved. It was five seconds from the edge of the woods, but I didn't rush. Quick, darting movements in someone's peripheral vision actually attract people's attention more than slow and casual motions. Besides, if the sentry saw me dashing for the door, he'd level his rifle immediately. If he saw me walking confidently, he would take a few seconds to try to identify me and figure out who I was and how I belonged there.

I made it to the trash cans. The cigarette sucker was probably staring at Paul's car, which was now halted in the driveway while Paul looked at a map.

I couldn't hear anyone on the other side of the door, and the lock would have been easy to pick if it weren't for the weird side angle I was coming from and the fact that I had to time my efforts in sync with the target-shooting going on inside. But I slid the door open as a gun went off, and the door didn't have loud, creaking hinges and the music from Paul's radio was still providing some cover. I slipped into a break room.

There was a storeroom with a keypad, but it was dark and werewolves see in infrared. Something shifted in my optic nerves while I stared, and then the world went red and I could tell which buttons had been punched by the heat impressions on the keys. I could even tell which number had been punched first and which last by the intensity of the thermal impressions, though the middle ones were harder to distinguish, and that made it easy to figure out the code, though again I had to time the beeps with gunfire from the back of the building.

From there, it was easy to make my way to the opposite door between the storeroom and the front lobby, where a group was having an animated discussion. The voices became more distinct as Paul's car drove off.

"Hell, how do we know it was a knight, Matthew?" A deep gravelly voice.

"You can't just make a silver bullet, Brett." Nikolai had said that Matthew had been an army engineer. "They won't cycle through a chamber properly unless they're near perfect, and silver is temperamental."

"What, you mean the Lone Ranger wasn't real?" This voice was kind of high-pitched. Not shrill or squeaky, but high.

Matthew spat into some kind of bottle or jar. "You'd need custom-made bullet molds, furnaces that were programmed down to the decimal point, timing charts, and motherfucking *insane* control conditions to keep impurities out. I'm telling you, boys, nobody but knights make industrial-grade silver bullets. They've got secret facilities."

"You said you had some." The voice sounded suspicious.

I could hear Matthew slide a magazine out of a gun. "What I've got is a lead missile with a silver payload. I just drill the open notch in a hollow-point a little deeper, melt down some silver, pour it in, and bam! One werewolf to go. Cheap and sexy. Just like I like it."

"But...why are *you* carrying silver bullets around?" That was from someone who didn't sound very bright. If I wasn't mistaking the sounds, the speaker was playing checkers with someone else.

There was an awkward silence.

"Hold on." A voice that was deep but somehow suggested youth. Real youth. I could tell that the speaker was intervening to take some of the attention off of his friend. "If it takes a factory, how did they make silver bullets back before they had factories?"

Matthew clapped his hands. "Boone, back in the old days, you could shove just about anything down a big-bored musket. You coulda probably tamped down the silverware with some gunpowder, and boom! Thar she blows! Nowadays, we have precision weapons."

If running Matthew's pack was just a question of knowing something about guns, the guy would be a lock.

Matthew's voice went grave again. "That's why it was a knight that killed Sharon."

"What about a werewolf knight?" Brett asked.

I could tell from Matthew's tone that he was smiling one of those smiles that aren't real. His voice had an amused edge. "Why would this Charming character kill Sharon?"

"Maybe he wants to make you look bad so Bernard will give him your place," Brett suggested. "Doesn't it seem weird, him coming here and Sharon dying on the same day?"

Okay, enough of that. I opened the door. "Yeah, because everything was going great before I came along."

Brett, Matthew, and I were the only ones behind the service counter. Brett was a big sandy-haired lunk with a big moustache and a baseball cap, a lumbering six-foot-six mook who had never heard of manscaping. Matthew was a curly-haired brownish blond who was about my height and gaunt but muscular. A wiry blond youth with shoulder-length hair was sitting at the counter, and a huge, burly brown-haired man was playing checkers with a muscular black-haired youth whose genes had gone through an ethnic blender set on high. The latter could have been Native American or Latino or Caucasian or Hawaiian or Asian or some combination of all of those things.

Everybody had at least one item of clothing that had come out of an army surplus store.

"SHIT!" the wiry blond yelped. Brett turned and took a step closer to me, a confused look on his face. Matthew slapped the clip back into his handgun and aimed it at me, but he half lowered the weapon when he realized that I was unarmed and standing motionless. The two checkers players turned their bodies to face me but otherwise remained still.

"Hi, I'm John Charming," I said. "I wanted to see how tight your security was."

Nobody said anything.

"It's not," I added helpfully. "Tight, I mean."

"What the hell are you doing?" Matthew's voice was low and taut.

"My job," I assured him. "Bernard wants me to whip this tribe into shape."

"By disrespecting me in my own house?"

"It's only disrespect because I got this far," I pointed out. "If you'd stopped me, I'd be respecting the hell out of you right now. But you've got a sentry out there who's smoking and texting. You've got trash cans right next to your side entrance, and you're not wiping down your keypads."

The big one, Brett, muttered, "He's trying to make you look bad, just like I said."

I smiled without really smiling. "And you have a right-hand man who's giving you bad advice because he wants your job. He's trying to get you to take me out so Bernard will take you out, and he'll have an open field."

"Shut your damn hole before I shut it for you," Brett growled.

"Don't be like that, Brett. You're a hoot," I said. "Watching you try to be a smooth manipulator is like watching a moose do ballet. What did you do, read *Machiavelli for Dummies?* Or do you just like Godfather movies?"

Brett yelled something that wasn't a word and came for me.

If he'd used his height and reach to keep me at a distance while he threw punches, he might have given me a hard time, but I guess Brett liked to rely on his fast healing and weight to take smaller, more skilled fighters to the ground. I bobbed under Brett's first lunging swing and came up strong with two rapid palm-heel strikes that he ran straight into. The first one broke one of Brett's ribs. The second one drove that rib through a lung. I was aiming for his heart, but that hardly ever happens. Too much muscle and bone in the way.

I stepped aside as momentum made Brett stumble past me. He took another halting step while clutching his chest. I imagine he had a horrified expression on his face, but I didn't really see it. He sank to one knee, wheezing, and I stepped behind him, got one arm along his jaw while I grabbed his temple with one hand and his chin with the other, and snapped his neck by turning my whole body.

"So, anyway, I was with Nikolai when your tribe member was killed this morning," I said conversationally while Brett collapsed. "And Nikolai wants to know why he had to hear about it from somebody else."

By this time, the wiry blond also had a gun on me. Matthew still had his gun at half-mast, but the mention of Nikolai calmed him down considerably. He smiled crookedly. "I had this dumb-ass idea that maybe I could handle my own damn problems."

"Yeah, well, I'm mostly here to find the Butcher of Abalmar," I said. "The sooner that's done, the sooner I'm out of your hair."

Matthew indicated the spot where Brett was gagging and gurgling. "Ah... is he all right?"

"He'll mend," I assured him. "Trust me, if it were that easy to kill a werewolf, nobody would need silver bullets."

"That's good, then." Matthew re-holstered his Beretta. "And you're wrong about Brett wanting my job. He's been giving me bad advice my whole life."

I shrugged. "If you say so."

"I do," Matthew stated firmly. "Hey, maybe you should try to break into this place every day until you can't do it anymore."

Subtext: he wanted a chance to shoot my ass without getting in trouble for it.

"Good idea," I said. "But I don't want anyone thinking it's some kind of drill if knights come calling."

"I'll talk to Lester and Sam," he said grimly.

"So, the werewolf that was killed this morning was a real estate agent, right? Did your tribe acquire a lot of property through her?"

Matthew raised an eyebrow. "A couple of us. How did you find out about it so fast?"

"Somebody named Stacy reported it to Bernard," I said.

Matthew got a sour look on his face. "Stacy wants to run the tribe like a PTA meeting. That bitch acts like she does all the work and I'm just a deadbeat, but as soon as things get rough, she finds a hole to hide in until I take care of it. Then she acts like it's my fault that things get out of hand at all. She's handy with all the paperwork and shit, but I'm getting tired of her attitude."

"You say she wants to run the tribe like a PTA meeting," I repeated. "How do you want to run it?"

"This is the Wild West, brother. We're off the grid," Matthew said. "We can't call the cops. There's no werewolf congress. You want to make committees to talk about taking werewolf censuses and collecting werewolf dues and making werewolf budgets, that's all good, but when it gets down to the bone, we're a gang or a cartel."

"Even cartels have accountants," I pointed out. "Property managers. Lawyers. Investors. Real estate agents."

"Yeah, but they don't mouth off about their bosses," Matthew said. "If I was as bad as Stacy makes out, I would have gotten violent with her by now."

"Okay," I said, not agreeing or disagreeing. "But the real estate angle worries me. This Sharon probably knew a lot more about who's who and who's where than your average tribe member, and from what I understand, this Stacy is out there right now, contacting people who bought property through Sharon and relocating them."

"Like I said," Matthew said tightly, "she's useful."

"Do you know what codependence is?" I asked.

Matthew quirked his lips. "If I say yes, will you get off my ass?"

"No. It's when two people use each other to avoid things they don't want to deal with, and they resent the hell out of each other the whole time," I said. "It sounds like you and this Stacy are codependent, but I'm not a marriage counselor. Have you considered offering Stacy protection right now?"

"Yeah, I considered it," Matthew said. "And then I remembered that Stacy never gives me any credit when I step in and help her out. This time, she can come here and admit she needs help."

"What, you don't feel appreciated?" I held my arms open. "You want a hug?"

Matthew smiled a mean smile. "Fuck you. Bernard wants me to get my people in line. I'm getting my people in line."

In other words, Stacy could either stop being a problem, or the knights could remove Matthew's problem for him.

I wanted to ream him out and give him direct orders, but again, we were in front of his men, and I wasn't ready to give up on Matthew. He had handled my intrusion pretty well, and it seemed to me there was still hope for the man. Not a lot of hope, maybe. Kind of a starving, weak, and beaten hope. But hope is like fire. Sometimes it can turn into something big fast if you can just keep a little bit of it alive.

Besides, I didn't know enough to know who would take Matthew's place. If it was Brett, God help the Abalmar tribe.

"After a knight attack is not the time to go on strike," I managed. "It makes it look like this Stacy is protecting your people while you're doing nothing. If she dies, she won't be an example. She'll be a martyr. If this is about power, order Stacy to tell you who needs protecting and where to send your soldiers. Tell her you're sending men to keep an eye on her whether she likes it or not. Be the man she says you're not."

He rubbed his jaw thoughtfully. He kind of liked the sound of that, even if he didn't like the source.

"You can't sit around waiting for her to do what you want her to do," I pressed. "That keeps you on the sideline in the middle of the game. You have to be the quarterback."

That's right. I was using sports metaphors.

"Large and in charge," Matthew muttered.

"Exactly," I agreed, and tried not to look like I'd just thrown up in my mouth a little bit.

God, working on my people skills sucked.

∽30∾

THIS LITTLE PIG WENT TO MARKET

There's probably something ironic about werewolves gathering in the back of a Piggly Wiggly, but it worked for us. This particular grocery store was open twenty-four hours a day, and the entire night crew was made up of clan members, or members of their normal human families who were in the know, including the cleaning service that came in independently to do the floors. God help anyone who came in and tried to rob the place at 3 a.m.

"We've identified six hot zones just by having people drive around with their cell phones on continually." Stacy was an intensely private woman, stocky and pale-skinned and radiating a kind of quiet authority. She had no combat capabilities and no interest in gaining them, and I could see how Matthew had fallen into a trap. After knowing her for a week, I was completely dependent on her. Administration and delegation and management aren't my thing.

They actually weren't Stacy's thing, either—or at least, no more than they are for any elementary school teacher. She had taught third graders B.C. (Before Clan)—but I would never have guessed she wasn't some kind of career civic leader. Matthew was scarier and kept people in line, but Stacy kept the trains running on time, so to speak. She didn't have an official title.

"How come people haven't noticed?" I wondered.

"Most of the zones aren't places where people live or work." Stacy dipped four potato chips at a time in some kind of salsa. I've probably mentioned this before, but werewolves love to eat, which was another advantage to meeting in a grocery store. The plastic-topped table we were sitting around was loaded with bear claws and cheese balls and crackers and salami wedges and assorted nuts and steaming beverages. "They're just-passing-through kinds of places. Except for one."

I was actually looking at the exception on the map she had given me. "This is excellent work, Stacy. Thank you."

I meant it. It would have taken me a month to make that map, walking boundaries and recording times on my own, and Stacy had gotten it done in a few days. Whoever we were chasing was using some kind of Turn Away ward to perform their ritual dissections. The Abalmar Butcher wasn't just invoking the Pax—the butcher was making people avoid specific locations for hours at a time without even manifesting an obvious threat. One alley in particular had been a thoroughfare, and cars had driven by the alley without even thinking about turning into it. People who lived above the alley hadn't heard any screams. A store security camera facing the alley had gone on the fritz two hours before Caitlin Akers even went missing, and stayed that way for another four.

In other words, someone skilled in apotropaic magic had been making some serious preparations.

"What is this map about?" Barbara Ann asked. She was sitting across me, sort of pretty but overly made up. Her black hair had been tightly confined by a stylist and her body was tightly confined by clothes that were too small for her. Barbara Ann liked to ask questions about what everyone else was doing so that she could explain how it was her idea later.

"It's about putting yourself in the place of your opponent," I said. "This killer is probably doing some heavy-duty magical activity in the area."

"How do you know that?" Barbara Ann demanded.

"These girls are being used in multiple divination ceremonies." I was being patient, but only because being impatient wouldn't have gained me anything. "Someone who uses magic has big plans, and they're trying to reverse-figure something out by trying different things and seeing how their experiments impact the future."

Barbara Ann's face stayed blank.

"They also know that people like me are looking for them," I said. "They can't afford to draw attention from nosy neighbors or passing motorists or door-to-door missionaries or neighborhood watches."

Stacy cut to the chase. "John thinks they've set up one of their wards around their base. And the ward interferes with cell phone reception. I've had people driving around with their cell phones on, recording times and places where the cell phones went dead."

Barbara Ann started to say something else but I cut her off, addressing Stacy again. "Can you tell your people to look out for the smell of dillweed too? It's really strong and bitter, and I caught traces of it at all of the crime scenes."

Stacy scrunched her brows. "Can I get some from a local store to let them smell it?"

"I don't know," I said. "But if you can, it would be worth it to get a look at those stores' invoices."

I glanced over at Carl, whose age was hard to assess. He was eighteen years old when he became a werewolf, was twenty-six now, still looked fifteen, and dressed like he was fifty. His conservative suits and sweater-vests were always immaculately groomed. Like Stacy, he was a steadfast noncombatant and somewhat of an outcast because of it. "Hey, Carl, can I see the map you made of the places where the bodies were found?"

"You could, but…" Carl held up whatever the latest electronic notebook was called and shrugged helplessly.

Clan policy was that members change back and forth from wolves to humans before any meetings so that the magically charged atmosphere would keep anyone from remotely turning cell phones and computers into surveillance devices. But Carl was from Generation Text and was having a hard time adjusting to a world where technology wasn't a constant. It was like I'd asked him not to rely too much on oxygen.

"Here." Stacy had already dug through her notes and found a printout.

"Marry me," I said. "We'll have agendas and raise a bunch of issues together."

She laughed. "No, thanks."

"Then would you marry Carl?"

"I don't plan on marrying anyone in the Clan." The humor went out of Stacy's eyes. "I shouldn't have to."

After a moment, I tilted my chin to let her know I got it. From what I'd seen, all the primary leaders in the Clan were male, and women became secondary leaders by mating with them, whether this actually qualified them to lead or not. Barbara Ann was only at the meeting because she had achieved status by marrying Brett, Matthew's childhood friend and second-in-command. I could have told her to go away, but Matthew was acting more like he was the sheriff and I was a visiting FBI agent than like I was the new man in charge, and I was okay with that attitude until I knew more.

If Brett really was ambitious and looking for ways to get Matthew to fail so that he could take over—and I still believed this to be the case, despite Matthew's assurances—then I was willing to bet that Barbara Ann was the reason for Brett's designs. She seemed like the type who would play Lady Macbeth to a macho but easily manipulated husband.

The Clan was kind of feudalistic in structure, come to think of it.

"Thanks again, Stacy." I marked the hot zone Stacy had identified on the abduction map, and it pretty much confirmed what I'd visualized. The suburban area where cell phones consistently didn't work was in the middle of the places where people had gone missing. Not directly in the center, and not forming a magical symbol or anything as far as I could see, but in the middle nonetheless.

"Why are we focusing on this mess?" Barbara Ann tended to sulk when she wasn't the center of attention. "Aren't we in the middle of a war?"

"If you're thinking of some scenario where all the werewolves and all the knights meet on a big battlefield and go at it and kill each other in one big fight, then no." I took the opportunity to grab a thick, soft pretzel. "We're more like two groups spread out and knife-fighting in the dark."

"That's why we should be making alliances with other magical beings against the knights," Barbara Ann snapped. "Not attacking them!"

"That's an opinion," I said carefully. "What's a fact is that I am not allying myself with something that kills young girls and removes their entrails for some kind of ceremony."

Barbara Ann started to respond angrily, and Stacy said,

quietly, "Me either." Barbara Ann paused. Stacy didn't say things like that.

"Or me," Carl chipped in.

Barbara Ann lost whatever momentum she was trying to build up. "I wasn't saying we should all become serial killers!"

It was moments like this that kept me in the Clan. "Let's talk about all of the werewolves pouring into Wisconsin."

"Let's not." Stacy laughed. "Please? I'd like to get home in a few hours."

"Where are we?" I insisted.

"We're getting new arrivals every week," Stacy said. "And those are people who are already werewolves. That doesn't count the new werewolves that some of them are creating when they get here."

"Give me a new werewolf any day." Carl was munching on a bear claw. "We're getting entire packs and families who are more loyal to each other than us."

"Even them I can handle," Stacy groused. "The lone wolves are the worst. You can't tell the old-timers anything. They think they're here to fight a war, but none of them want to follow orders."

"Some of the new arrivals are being blackmailed to spy on us by the knights," I said. "We've seen a lot of that in Milwaukee."

"But that's the whole problem!" Stacy elaborated. "We don't have the resources to handle this. If we take the time we need to check them out, the new wolves are running around unsupervised. If we try to house them and feed them and hide them and train them while we vet them, we create a big honking target again, and where's the money going to come from?"

The subtext here was that Matthew didn't want to deal with any of this. Matthew was like the slob who lives with a woman but won't help clean the house and doesn't like being nagged about it. Stacy was the housewife who was getting increasingly unhappy and passive-aggressive.

"I'll tell you what we need to do." Barbara Ann jumped in again. "We need to start turning more civil administrators into werewolves. More police officers too. And some wealthy people while we're at it..."

"Eight out of ten people bitten by werewolves don't survive their first full moon, Barbara Ann," I reminded her. "You're talking murder."

"Ten out of ten people don't survive life!" Barbara Ann had a gleam in her eye when she said this. "Anyone would risk it all if they had a one-in-five chance of living for centuries."

Just as a way of highlighting how messed up life is, Barbara Ann was a hospital administrator. I don't know if that's a comment on hospitals, administrators, or Barbara Ann.

"I think people will notice if we start killing four politicians or cops every time we want to recruit one," I pointed out. "Or killing one multimillionaire, much less four."

"So we cast our net wide," Barbara Ann said. "They don't all have to be locals."

I gestured around the room and tried again. "Look around. There are four of you here with me. According to you, I should kill all four of you if it would make the next person to come along useful. And that's assuming millionaires would automatically give up all their money to the Clan just because they became werewolves in the first place. Once people caught on to what we were doing, we'd be just as likely to make new enemies as new friends."

"Spoilsport," Gabriel said from where he was sitting in the corner.

"What if all four of us were going to die if you didn't make some hard choices anyway?" Barbara Ann's voice was getting shriller.

I swallowed a particularly chewy lump of pretzel. "I don't know, Barbara Ann. But you just got my vote for person-I'd-least-want-to-be-stranded-in-a-life-boat-with."

Barbara Ann scowled. "I thought knights were supposed to be hard-asses."

"I kill dangerous monsters who threaten the Pax, Barbara Ann." My voice and manner were pleasant. "If I ever decide you're one, you won't survive the experience."

Her mouth opened and Gabriel interrupted. "I've seen him when he gets like this. You'd be better off quitting now."

Calculation washed over Barbara Ann's face and receded like a wave over a beach shore. Whether she believed me or not, she didn't want to get into it with the brother of Bernard's mate.

Stacy intervened. "I've been thinking about getting someone in the Clan to start a homeless shelter. From what I understand, we'd have some discretion about who we let in as long as we kept our beds filled, and our people could run off anyone who wasn't a werewolf quickly. It would be tax-free, and we could house and feed a lot of people cheap and off the grid while Matthew trains and vets them. Plus, we wouldn't have to worry about making a profit for the IRS."

Carl hesitated before making the transition. "Even if that weren't crazy, it would still cost a lot of money we don't have."

"I actually have some discretionary funds that I don't think I'm going to have to use now." I wrote a number on Stacy's notepad. "I think it's a good idea. Do you think this would get you started?"

Stacy looked at the figure and her mouth tightened. Was she angry that I had that kind of money at my disposal while she was begging for scraps, or was her mind already thinking about how much work would be involved? "It would help."

"At the very least, it's worth looking into," I said. "You could get donations from werewolves with jobs too, and volunteers to work on construction and such. You keep complaining that we're not enough of a community here."

"Earl Dylan would probably head it for you," Carl said thoughtfully, getting on board. "He keeps making noise about wanting a religious service for werewolves. I'll bet he'd help if he got a chance to offer an optional service. He'd probably be good at getting donations from businesses and churches too."

I looked at Carl. "I don't like the idea of taking money that might go to actual homeless people, personally. But Earl is a good idea."

Stacy's expression became contemplative. "I'll start asking around if you'll stop threatening to kill people."

I looked at Barbara Ann and smiled grimly. "I was just making a point."

Barbara Ann flushed. Her voice shook with shame and fury. "Do you have a task for me, master?"

"No," I said.

Barbara Ann abruptly stood up and walked out of the room. She didn't stalk. She was retaining dignity. I nodded at Gabriel, and he quietly unsheathed a knife and slipped out of the room after her.

Okay, no, I didn't. And no, he didn't. Dammit.

Stacy waited until Barbara Ann was out of hearing. It took a while.

"That was kind of gratifying, but you need to stop making points that way if you want me to work with you," Stacy said darkly. "We get enough of that from Matthew."

"I do want to work with you," I told her. "I need your help, and you're great. But it's way too easy to talk about killing people when you're not the one who has to do it or see it up close."

"You seem to talk about it easily enough." Stacy's lips were tight.

"Maybe that's why it's a sensitive subject." I tapped the map. "I'm about to try to kill someone for real. I worry that it's getting too easy for me."

Stacy held my eyes, then nodded quietly. "I believe that. You've been a nice surprise for the most part."

"Listening to some coward who will never take any risks..." I shook my head, unable to find the right words and unable to quit trying. "I mean, yeah, right now, Barbara Ann is a blowhard, but tapping into anger and fear is an easy way to get power. I'm old enough to remember when we imprisoned Japanese-American citizens during World War II, and the Jim Crow laws, and Hiroshima, and the McCarthy hearings. This stuff isn't just theoretical to me."

"You've convinced me." Carl made a pistol out of his hand and acted like he was sighting down his index finger at me. "The next time somebody shoots their mouth off, I'm going to shoot their mouth off."

Carl was a bit of a smart-ass. I liked him.

I laughed reluctantly and held up my hands in surrender. "Fine. But listening to some sociopath go on about killing people just because they're not like us...I didn't sign up for that."

Gabriel spoke up unexpectedly. "That's easy for you to say. But as the only one here who grew up as a conquered people? Personally, I'd rather be on the winning side than the right one this time."

I didn't have anything profound to say to that.

~31~

HERE GOES THE NEIGHBORHOOD

It's a good thing it's raining and nighttime," Virgil commented from the shotgun seat. "I bet they don't see too many big black men riding around looking at houses around here."

Abalmar's black population came in around four percent.

"Who do you think they'd call first?" Virgil wondered. "The police or their real estate agent?"

I glanced over at him. Virgil was wide, not tall, dressed in a black all-weather coat made out of some fuzzy felt material. It went down to his shins and wouldn't have been inappropriate in a church. "You're kidding, right?"

"What?" We were speaking over the throaty roar of the car heater and the intermittent squeaks of the windshield wipers and the patter of rain and a satellite radio station that neither of us was paying much attention to.

"Virgil, just because you're not a cop anymore doesn't mean you're not a cop," I explained patiently. "You radiate it."

It was true. Virgil was an island of calm and authority. Anyone who saw us would assume we were cops. I was even wearing a suit to bolster that effect. "I asked you along to make me look respectable."

He wasn't sure if he liked that or was offended by it. "You want the people we're looking for to think cops are checking out their neighborhood?"

"The people we're looking for aren't afraid of cops," I said grimly, and gestured at a house a street over. "What do you think of that place?"

Virgil glanced over. "Which one?"

"What do you mean, which one?" The house was on the edge of the building division, with a backdrop of scraggly woods that were maybe a quarter of a mile wide and a mile long, standing in the middle of a long stretch of marshy ground that looked like Mother Nature had pissed on it. The building was a huge two-story affair with what was probably a big-ass attic to boot. It was belching thick black smoke literally darker than the night. The yellow paint should have been cheery, set off by green shutters and sills, but when I looked at that place, I shuddered. The lights coming from the windows were dull orange and didn't fill the rooms so much as make the shadows back off a little.

"What do you mean, what do I mean?" Virgil was a tad surly. "There's more than one house. That's why they call it a neighborhood."

"The one that doesn't have any electric lights on." I pointed straight at the house and grabbed the steering wheel, guiding Virgil on to a small inlet street that would put us in the right direction. "That's candle- or torchlight coming through the windows."

Magic must have been messing up technology in the house constantly.

"It is?" Virgil had already gone back to looking at the house directly beside him.

Any Turn Away ward protecting an area that size that strongly 24-7 was powerful magic. I wasn't affected because of my geas, but police officers or census-bureau types canvassing the area would probably skip over the house without even realizing that they were doing it. Neighbors probably wouldn't be able to describe the occupants if they tried.

The house was at the end of a large cul-de-sac, in the middle of a big, round, slightly elevated slope. The water table must have made it awkward for contractors to build beside the house, or some family had held on to land for a long time. There was a lot of empty space on either side of the place.

More interestingly, the mailbox wasn't in front of the house. It was right next to the nearest neighbor's, some one hundred feet away. As soon as we got near the mailbox, the satellite radio went off the air and started crackling and hissing. Virgil stopped the car. His mind seemed to be wandering.

We were at the boundary of the magical hot zone: they'd had to put the mailbox outside the radius effect or the postman would have overlooked it. The faint scent of dillweed came through the heater.

I didn't say "Got you" softly or anything like that. There might be beings with enhanced senses around.

But I thought it.

～32～

JUGGLING CHAINSAWS

I have a lead on the Butcher," I told Matthew. "I'm going to need to focus on it for a few days."

I was still working on the worrying-about-other-people-while-on-a-hunt thing.

We were in the back room of a music store in the Abalmar Grande, a shopping mall that was struggling not to get sucked down the economic black hole left behind by the impact of Internet shopping. The manager was one of Matthew's tribe. There was a lot of background music with a heavy beat to discourage listening devices that measured vibrations in the air, and enough people around us to discourage any open raids by knight teams.

Matthew took a cautious sip of the bad food-court coffee that we were drinking from Styrofoam cups. "I know what you said about the Butcher being a child killer and all, but you're here to help us too, right? We've got knights running around killing our own."

Four new arrivals, a small werewolf pack from Maine, had been found slaughtered in their RV. The wife of the leader had found them after she had gone out to get supplies. The RV had been full of blood and bullet holes.

We had managed to get rid of the bodies, but we hadn't managed to stop the fear and anger rippling outward from their discovery like earthquake tremors.

"I've got a plan for drawing the knight strike teams out of hiding." Actually, calling it a plan was a bit generous. I had the beginnings of an idea. "But I need to nail down the Butcher to put it into effect."

"And I could use some help circling my wagons," Matthew said. "I admit it."

"I'm putting Virgil on the RV," I said. "And I'm putting Paul on that MRE distributor who's trying to jack up prices. And I'm giving you Gabriel if you need any extra hands. But Matthew, you're going to have to protect Stacy and Carl."

Matthew's eyes narrowed and his voice went taut. "I have to protect all of my people on my territory. Even you, John."

Cute.

"I can't keep being the middleman between you and your noncombatants," I said. "Think of Stacy like your sergeant. Do you know what happens to officers who can't work with their sergeants?"

Matthew worked his jaw. "That woman ain't no sergeant."

"It's called a metaphor, dumb-ass," I said.

Actually, I didn't say that. My soul said it. My brain blew fuses while somewhere way down in my mental cellars, my id shook its fists up at my ego and screamed it. But my mouth didn't say it.

"This thing between you and Stacy is a problem," I managed. "You seem to think that being a leader means that she has to be the one to fix it."

"Why do I get the feeling that you're not all that worried about *me* being a target?" Matthew asked bitterly.

"I know you can take care of yourself," I said. "You need to prove that you can take care of someone else."

∽33∽

FOOLS RUSSIAN...I MEAN, RUSH IN

There were six people living in that scary-ass house, three men and three women, but from what I could tell, the only one who regularly left it during the day was Greg Apraxin, the husband of the house's registered owner, Mila Apraxin. It was Greg who fetched the mail, bought groceries and household sundries, delivered and received dry cleaning, visited greenhouses, picked up the occasional takeout meals, and took a laptop to various eateries that offered a wireless carrier. Much of his online activity seemed to consist of buying and selling stocks.

Was it possible that young women had been killed in divination ceremonies just so that someone could invest in the stock market wisely? I put a pin in that one. Well, more like a knife, actually. I put a very sharp knife in that one.

Greg didn't smell of dillweed. If he had, I might have killed him then and there. In fact, Greg smelled of a subtle and no-doubt-expensive aftershave. He was a handsome man, reaching middle age and using good tailoring to hide his expanding waistline and a beard to hide his incipient double chin. His tailor-made suits were cream-colored or white, his shirts a soft yellow or light blue, and he always wore suits, though he didn't have an official day job as far I could tell.

Greg was popular with waiters and waitresses and clerks. He had a sunny smile and chatted and twinkled and laughed frequently and tipped well.

Knowing what I knew, his act seemed obscene. Tula and I followed him in shifts, only letting each other nap while everyone in the Apraxin household was on site.

Another man left the house at night. I didn't know his name, but this individual was extremely fit and well trained. He was dressed all in black, though not in some Hollywood version of a burglar outfit, and he moved through the unlit yards of the surrounding neighborhood like a ghost. I'm not sure I would have been able to tail him if I hadn't had the ability to follow his scent trail.

I never got closer to him than three hundred feet.

The man was clearly making security rounds, checking neighborhood houses for any signs of unusual activity, occasionally even climbing on rooftops and lying down on sloped surfaces beneath outcroppings. Maybe checking to see if anyone was following him, maybe looking for good sniper positions.

The third man in the house never left it. He was a small old fellow, though his movements seemed spry enough. I saw him only through windows.

As for the three women, they occasionally left the house during the day to do landscaping. One of them was old and gray; one of them was dark-haired, middle-aged, and beautiful; and one of them was young and fair. At night, they traveled down to the sparse woods behind their home unescorted, wearing nothing but bikini-style sash wraps against the cold and damp.

I don't know if they were magically protected against the cold somehow or if they were just that hard-core.

It made sense that the men didn't participate in these ceremonies. Russian male and female witches, vedmak and vedma, don't work well together. The men in the household were clearly servants, not peers.

There was something odd about some of the trees in those woods too. I took some pictures of them via a telephoto lens and asked Tula to see what she could find out about them. As it turned out, Tula didn't have to ask anyone.

"They are Russian olive trees."

"I thought olives only grew..." I began.

"They are not real olives," Tula said impatiently. "The...I guess you would call them fruit...just sort of look like them."

"So those trees were transplanted here?" I said thoughtfully.

"I would guess so." Tula's broad face scrunched in on itself. "Does that matter?"

"I don't know," I said. "Do you know anything about Russian witches and sacred groves?"

Tula tried. "Don't witch covens have to have thirteen members?"

"That's just a superstition." And it was. Judas was the thirteenth person at the Last Supper. Satanists or some wannabe witches might care about that kind of thing, but not the real thing, and certainly not vedma. They predated Christianity in Russia.

Tula walked off. "Let me know when it's time to kill someone."

Her comment about the number of witches got me thinking, though. There is a very specific and powerful type of Russian coven that gathers in threes. I was beginning to suspect that I was dealing with a Baba Yaga.

Not the Baba Yaga in the popular children stories—the evil old witch who rode around on a broom and lived in a house that walked around on stilt legs. I mean the Baba Yaga of the older stories; the Baba Yaga who was never one witch but three. Baba Yaga wasn't their name, it was their title, though a lot of people get confused about that because they called each other sister.

And in all of the old stories, Baba Yaga had a penchant for abducting children.

∾

The next morning, I followed Greg Apraxin into a coffee shop. It was the closest I'd gotten to him physically. I was dressed in a suit just like he was, though mine was darker, and also carrying a laptop. When his coffee was almost empty, I walked into an alcove outside the restrooms and took out a cell phone that Carl had given me and pretended to text into it.

As soon as Greg left to get another cup of coffee, I walked to his table and sat down, taking pictures with the cell phone I was pretending to stare absently at. I got a shot of his screen and the transparent stickers with product information that were still on the corners beneath his keyboard. It only took a few seconds.

Greg still hadn't turned around when I got up. I proceeded as if I were taking in my surroundings for the first time and acted abashed.

"Sat down at the wrong table," I explained shamefacedly to the two neighboring women who were watching me. Then I held up my cell phone. "Damn things eat brains."

They laughed good-naturedly and agreed, and I went back to my own table and laptop and resumed reading up on the half-remembered stories that had made me suspect I was dealing with a Baba Yaga in the first place.

In a lot of the old fables, the Baba Yaga has three male servants called horsemen. Keep in mind that in those days, in that time, "horsemen" could mean anything from cavalry officer to chauffeur to groom to valet to messenger. One of the Baba Yaga's horsemen was called Day and dressed brightly. Another was called Night and dressed in black. And the third was called Sun and dressed in red colors.

I thought about that. If the three women were the real power in that house, then Greg Apraxin could be considered their day servant. He was the public face of the household, a pleasant and sociable man who interacted with the public and did their day-to-day errands.

The man who was sneaking out among their neighborhood at night could be considered their night servant. He moved like a man with martial training and probably did the things that the vedma wished kept secret, unsavory acts of darkness.

But what function did that old man who never left the house serve? What the hell would a Sun Horseman do? And if the stories were just allegories about nature and had no relation to real Russian witches or how some of them organized or operated at all, where was the horseman called Moon?

I stood up while I was thinking about it. Greg Apraxin had taken his coat off while he was typing, and I still had to get a look at what was in his wallet.

∾34∾

SOMEBODY'S BEEN PEEING
IN MY BED

So, you need my help with a computer problem." Carl had a
laptop open on the small table in his breakfast nook, but he was
turned away from it. He seemed to find it amusing that I had
come to him with a technological problem after the crap I'd
been giving him about his social media addictions. I was leaning against his kitchen island, surrounded by red coffee mugs
and a wide variety of cooking utensils that dangled from the
ceiling.

"You think I contradict myself?" I slightly paraphrased.
"Very well, I contradict myself."

Carl stared at me blankly, apparently not a Whitman fan.
Well, neither was I, actually.

"I am large," I said. "I contain multitudes."

"Good for you," Carl told me. "What do you want?"

Fine. "This Greg Apraxin guy uses a laptop at coffee shops
and libraries and community colleges," I said. "I need to know
if you can hack into his computer remotely. I have all kinds
of product numbers off his laptop and website addresses and

a list of some of the wireless servers he's used and the times he used them and numbers from a debit card and one of his credit cards."

Carl began to take me seriously. "You do?"

"John here is a jerk of all trades," Paul called from Carl's den. His six-foot-two frame was half in and half over an armchair while he watched a golf game on ESPN. You don't often see a werewolf with gray hair—the hearts of most people over forty can't take the stress of the first change—but Paul had been a fit fifty when he was bitten by a werewolf. I'm pretty sure Paul's job was to kill me on command, but other than that, we got along well. He liked to read about history and spar. Having grown up in Virginia Beach, he also thought tossing a Frisbee around was the perfect form of meditation, and I could see his point.

"He picks pockets," Paul added. "So keep one hand on your wallet."

The thick blue bathrobe Carl was wearing was open to show a T-shirt and red flannel pajama bottoms. He was sitting on a pull-out bench and drinking a beer with the steak and eggs he'd made for breakfast, which surprised me a little. "This doesn't sound like you just want information."

I removed a sheet of paper wrapped around a credit card from my back pocket. "If you can copy files from his computer without his knowing it, that would be gravy, but mostly I want you to order this item from a store in Poughkeepsie using this stolen credit card. There's a PO box that I want it sent to on there too."

Carl unfolded the paper gingerly and examined the card. "Why not just use this Greg person's credit card if you've got the numbers and you're trying to frame him?"

"Because Apraxin wouldn't," I said. "If I make it too easy, the knights will never bite."

Carl carefully unfolded the paper and looked at it. "What is this thing I'm supposed to order?"

"It's a kind of Etruscan crucible," I said. "Trust me, it will send up some flags. Can you do this or not?"

"Bhoot-nee ka! How far have you fallen, John Charming?!?"

No one moved. The voice had come from Carl's laptop.

"Parth?" I asked cautiously.

A window suddenly enlarged and engulfed Carl's laptop screen. It was in fact Parth, one of the immortal serpent beings called naga from Hindu mythology who can assume human form. Parth had used his however many untold centuries to evolve into a software mogul. He had also somehow become a friend of Sig's in the process. "Hello, John. Are you seriously going to entrust a task of this magnitude to this infant?"

"Not anymore," I admitted, doing my best to pull off the unflappable thing. "How long have you been monitoring Carl?"

I only saw half of the dismissive wave on Carl's computer screen. "A year, give or take a month."

Carl smelled scared. Well, he should. He'd been lecturing me on how paranoid I was about technology since I got here, and he installed firewalls for a lot of the local clan members. Still, I wasn't going to tear into Carl in front of an outsider, so I just gestured for him to move. He did so hurriedly. Paul had come around the kitchen island by this point and looked as if he wanted to draw his gun and shoot the laptop.

I sat down at the bench. "A year? I haven't been in the Clan that long."

"Not everything is about you, John," Parth said smugly. "I like to stay informed. You know that."

I showed him what would have been my fangs if I'd been a wolf. "Yes, I do know that. Are you offering to help me, Parth?"

"Why, yes, I suppose I am."

"Carl, make me some more coffee." Not all slaps to the face are physical. "Why should I trust you, Parth? The first time we met, you attacked me and wanted me to be your science experiment."

"Are you still obsessing over that?" Parth acted astonished, and maybe he was. He was extremely intelligent, but life wasn't something that Parth took personally.

"I hold grudges," I admitted. "Why should I trust you, Parth?"

"That's complicated." Parth wasn't in his house in Clayburg, Virginia. He was outside and somewhere sunny. "I do enjoy talking to you, John, but that conversation could take some time."

"Highlight it for me," I suggested.

Parth sighed. "I think what the knights are doing in regards to the werewolves is wrong. They are not respecting your true nature. I trust your geas and your own true nature will keep you from taking life unnecessarily. And Sig cares for you, and I am in her debt, as you well know."

Sig cared for me.

"You are," I agreed, my throat unexpectedly tight. Parth had violated the rules of hospitality when he attacked me, and Sig was the one he had been obligated to.

"We can't work with this guy," Paul objected. I understood the impulse. He couldn't smell Parth, didn't know Parth, and was trained to maintain operational security.

"There's no point trying to keep Parth out of our business. He's already up in it, so deal with that reality," I told Paul. "And the main thing here is passing along information to the knights, which Parth will do one way or the other. The only real question is whether or not he'll limit that information.

Even if he doesn't, the knights' geas will compel them to go after the Apraxins no matter what we do."

Paul was still thinking that through when I unfolded the paper and held up the credit card and ordering information to the laptop's cam.

"Why aren't you just handling this yourself?" Parth asked casually while he scanned the material. "Why involve the knights at all?"

Because part of my job was to get rid of the knights in Abalmar. Two birds. One bullet. But there was no need to spell that out.

"The house has some serious magical protections," I said. "The knights won't be affected by them. My people would be."

"*Your* people?" It wasn't a question so much as a comment, and I let it pass. Parth added: "Interesting. Since Greg Apraxin is still alive, can I assume he's not working alone?"

"It's a big house," I said. "And there are a lot of people staying there."

Parth laughed darkly. He was kind of scary for a professed pacifist. "I see. You want the knights to draw fire."

"Something like that," I said. "Will you help lay out some bread crumbs for the knights to follow?"

"I already am," he said absently. "Would you like me to copy and send you Greg Apraxin's e-mails or would you like me translate them first? They're in Russian."

"You might as well send them now," I said. "Since you're in Carl's computer anyhow."

We sat there in silence for a minute while Parth continued to work his own brand of magic.

I had to ask. Maybe I sounded casual. "So, how is everyone?"

"Choo is in contact with his ex-wife again. I don't know if that is good or bad." Parth still sounded preoccupied. "Molly is fasting for some reason, and I don't know if that is good or bad, either. Cahill has become a dhampir."

Cahill was a half-human, half-vampire? "How is he handling that?"

"He has left his wife and his job and moved to New York."

Parth stopped there. The smug bastard was enjoying this.

"And Sig?" I asked after a noticeable hesitation.

"She is upset," Parth said nonchalantly.

I was going to kill him. No, I'd skin him first, make boots out of his hide, put my foot up his peeled ass while wearing those boots, and then kill him. Very conscious of the two clan members listening in, I asked, "Why?"

"She developed feelings for Cahill."

I didn't say anything. Sig and I were over, and there wasn't even an "it" to be over. A few kisses. Some lust smells and some common ground. Shared danger. Together for a few weeks, separated for months. Sig had told me she didn't want to be with me.

"Can you still hear me, John?" Parth asked blandly. "I didn't expect you to be so apathetic."

I was plenty pathetic, thanks.

"You seem to be under the impression that I'm a safe person to mess with." My voice was shaved ice. "I'm trying to figure out how you got that idea."

Parth relented. "Sig is upset because she's the one who made Cahill leave."

"What?" Even while I said it, I knew I was being slow. Sig was a weak spot. She made me do things I knew were stupid. She made it hard for me to concentrate. Made me act like someone other than I was, or made me act like someone other than the person I was pretending to be. I still didn't have a handle on that one.

Well, maybe she didn't make me, but I did that stuff anyway.

"Cahill is a newly turned dhampir," Parth reminded me patiently. "He has powerful hypnotic capabilities. And he's been in love with Sig for a long time."

Now my fists were clenching for an entirely different reason. Something went through me. I won't call it fury, because it went deeper than that. I won't call it a bolt, because it hung around.

"When Sig realized that she was suddenly in love with Ted, she broke his neck." It was as if Parth were talking about seeing someone at the grocery store. "And the feelings suddenly went away. Of course, dhampirs heal fast, but Sig told him that if he didn't leave Clayburg, she was going to end him no matter how she felt about it. He believed her too. That is what really hurt him, I think."

My soul unclenched. "He tried to trance her."

"I don't know if he tried or not," Parth admitted. "He swore he did it without knowing he was doing it, and he *was* newly turned. On the other hand, Ted always was a bit of a shit about women."

Yes, he was. "But Sig's feelings suddenly stopped when he left?"

"Well, not all of them. Ted *was* her friend," Parth reminded me. "That's why she's upset. And it wasn't exactly good timing."

"Her friend. What he tried was rape." There was something in my expression, or maybe something missing in my expression, that made Parth stop playing around.

"It really might have been an accident," he said quietly. "And Sig handled it."

I was still processing that when Parth asked, "Would you like me to pass a message on to her?"

Yeah, her and the whole clan, while I was at it. There wasn't any doubt where Paul's loyalty lay, even if mine was torn. I was still having trouble letting Sig—or my fantasy of her—go, but I wasn't free and had no prospect of being free in any foreseeable future. Having my paw die in the forest reserve had changed things. My paw's death…Mayte's death…had opened up a lot of the old wounds and feelings of guilt that Sig had helped me start to deal with. Their deaths really weren't my fault in this case, probably, but I was used to feeling that way.

The knights were only bound to leave Sig alone as long as she wasn't acting against their interests. And even if none of that were true, I had other people whose lives were depending on me being focused, competent, and logical now. All of the things Sig made me forget how to be.

And she was better off without me.

Or maybe I was just tired of hurting every time I thought about her.

"No," I said.

～35～

SHIT, MEET FAN. FAN, MEET SHIT.

I feel like I'm in one of those submarine movies," Tula whispered. "The ones where everyone is staying quiet so ships won't drop bombs on them."

Nobody said anything. Matthew's claw had a problem with Tula being a female, and Gabriel was the only one of our claw here besides me, and Gabriel didn't talk just to talk. I thought she had a point, though. Twelve of us were crammed together in a small basement with thick walls and no windows. The man who lived in the house was recently divorced and currently in rehab.

"They're called depth charges," I supplied.

Tula stuck her tongue out at me.

"I feel like I'm in a cow pen," Brett grumbled. He hadn't spoken to me directly since I'd broken his neck. I don't know what the big deal was. He and his wife had been much bigger pains in my neck than any temporary discomfort I'd caused in his.

We were one of three teams scattered around the neighborhood, viewing events through laptops via a system of carefully concealed cams with long-distance lenses. Virgil was leading one of the other teams, and Paul the third. About half a mile from the Apraxin house, the residence we were in was as close to the magical hot zone as I dared get. Knights had moved into a house two doors down from the Baba Yaga shortly after we'd sequestered ourselves.

That neighboring house belonged to a Miss Hanley, an old widow. Two knights, a man and a woman, had greeted Miss Hanley loudly and cheerily as if they were family when they ushered her back inside her home after she opened her front door. But they were knights. I knew it for sure when four more people snuck out of their van and went into the house later that night.

If all went well, Miss Hanley would probably wake up after the raid filled to the gills with a drug that wiped out short-term memory. If she even went to the hospital, most people would probably attribute her loss of memory to old age or a small stroke.

One of the knight's team, the woman, had walked a dog around the neighborhood several times. A hound that was trained to smell werewolf, I'm sure, but we had been dropped off at our own hiding hole in freshly bleached clothes, and it had been raining off and on for weeks.

Another clan member grumbled, "When are they going to move?"

Matthew smiled but didn't say anything. We weren't supposed to be using any weapons without suppressors, but he had a sawed-off shotgun slung over his back and a gleam in his eye. He was finally in his element.

"Tonight," I said. "It's supposed to stop raining soon, and the knights won't want to lose the cover."

And they didn't.

∽∾

"What the hell are they doing?" This from the youngest member of Matthew's personal claw, Boone, who I kind of liked.

Boone was one of the three different people staring at three different laptops, though visibility wasn't good.

Pairs of knights had suddenly appeared out of nowhere, glimpses of shadows moving through backyards in the dark and the rain, carrying air tanks. They were inserting hoses into house vents and cracked windows, occasionally restocking from two panel vans that were moving through the neighborhood with their lights off. It was two thirty in the morning.

"They're gassing people in their homes," I said. "Relax. It would take them way too long to work this far out."

"What is that stuff?" Matthew sounded worried for the first time. "Are we talking chemical warfare?"

Matthew had served in the army during Desert Storm.

I kept my voice soothing. "It's just a little something to make sure people will sleep through anything. It probably wouldn't affect us the way it does normal people even if they did get this far."

"They do this a lot?" Boone sounded indignant. It was probably some kind of leftover citizen's rights instinct from his previous existence as a human being.

"Not usually on this scale," I said. "They'll do this in rural areas sometimes when there aren't this many houses. They must not be expecting tonight to go smoothly."

Matthew liked that. He smacked Boone on the shoulder. "Fuckin'-A, boys. We got 'em running scared."

Tula was less optimistic. "Do they look like they're running to you? There must be forty of them out there."

"This 'Go big or go home' approach isn't usually how they do things," I said. "Either they suspect we're here, or they're planning on turning the Apraxin house into their base of operations when they're done."

"Holy shit," Matthew breathed. "That makes sense, don't it?"

It did. The knights could turn the house into a fortified camp with the Baba Yaga's wards hiding them. They could take their efforts in Abalmar up to a whole new level.

"We can have more people drive in if we have to," I reminded him quietly. "But if nothing else, we can just record as many images as we can and stay put."

"I didn't spend two days stewing in my juice just to stay put," Brett growled, and several of Matthew's claw rumbled in agreement.

"I'm not starting a firefight in the middle of a neighborhood." Those were the actual words I used. The tone I used said *moron*. Brett bristled, and I gave him a look that added *and maybe a dead moron if you keep this up*. "If it looks like we can contain this to the Apraxin hot zone, we'll go in as wolves, low and fast. The rain will cover us."

"Why did we bring all this firepower if we're not going to use it?" Brett protested.

"To have options. Right now, the fewer of us that are tossing lead around, the better," I insisted. "I don't want little Timmy two lanes over catching a stray bullet while he's asleep in his race car bed."

I gestured at the laptops. "Besides. We didn't even know the knights had this many people in Abalmar. That knowledge alone was worth this even if it's the only thing we get."

"How do they get away with this kind of thing?" Boone was still staring at the shadows who were gassing homes on the laptop screen and shaking his head. "Somebody must see them sometimes."

"It happens," I said. "You ever heard of phantom gassers?"

He shook his head. "Sounds like a fart joke."

"Urban legends," I said. "Just more crackpot ravings buried in the Internet."

༄

The knights charged into an ambush that must have been days in the preparing.

Crows attacked them out of the sky as soon as they crossed over into the hot zone. Black and unnaturally silent, hidden by night and rain, they came hurtling out of the air with claws dipped in contact poison. Not thousands, but hundreds of them, who must have been gathering on the Apraxin house's roof and going through their windows eight or ten at a time, rotating out so their sheer numbers wouldn't be noticed while their talons were being coated.

The knights were covered from head to foot in Kevlar weave, but the crows sank claws into their masks and helmets and gloves and cuffs, tugging, baring patches of skin, obscuring the knights' vision and fouling their aim and buffeting them, hurtling into their bodies.

The knights attacking from the side slope—crossing into the hot zone through backyards and avoiding the lit streets—suddenly found themselves in quicksand, the mud beneath their feet sucking at them hungrily, pulling them down into the ground like a hungry mouth.

A squad moving through the scraggly patch of woods behind the house was buffeted by thorny tree limbs. Those limbs were covered in broken branch stubs that had been trimmed into sharp points. A knight would dance out of one tree's range only to discover that the trees had been arranged to cover each other's perimeters. Those knights that avoided branches were ensnared by thick tree roots shooting out of the ground, wrapping around their throats and choking them beneath their bulletproof padding.

One group of knights gave up its dream of concealment and rushed down the paved street, but some fell to armor-piercing explosive rounds from a far-off rooftop, the work of the Night Horseman.

Others found themselves confronted by a short humanoid figure made entirely of flame, burning so intensely that rain evaporated before it struck him and ground ignited beneath his feet. Bullets whipped through the thing without effect. The Sun Horseman.

A wild-haired old woman who I didn't see clearly until later stepped onto the roof with a staff made of gnarled glass in her hands. She was naked except for oddly shaped metal charms hanging parallel on her breasts and limbs, directing lightning from the sky. Blinding bolts cracked and forked down into knights with a deafening impact that tossed them through the air like straw and left them smoking corpses with stopped hearts. Knights fired upon her, but bullets apparently swerved and curved around her. It had to be those metal charms. They were magnets, and somehow she had found some means of harnessing and amplifying polarities through sympathetic magic. I had never seen a charm or ward like it.

The battle was not all one-sided. After the initial devastating attacks, the surviving knights adapted quickly. That's what we do. I mean...they...do. At some point, a knight triggered a sonic device too high for human hearing that helped disorient the crows, and men killed the birds with knives and bullets and bare hands by the dozens.

The sniper fire stopped, presumably because a knight on rearguard duty had located the Night Horseman where he was lying on some distant roof with a high-powered rifle and showed him what a trained killer really moved like.

A sniper I never saw managed to shoot the young fair-haired witch while she was just a silhouette in a window. Whatever her part in the attack was supposed to be, it never materialized.

One of the Russian olive trees in the grove was ignited by a flamethrower, and I imagine it was the source of a reedy scream emerging from some hollow place. From the tracks I found later, this created an opening in the killing field that several knights managed to make their way through.

The woman on the roof was felled by a quick-thinking crossbowman who cut the metal tip from a fiberglass quarrel and sank the jagged shaft into her soft abdomen. She fell to her knees and brought lightning down upon the man who had just doomed her.

We were already outside the house and running by that point. Almost everyone except my claw were in wolf form. Tula and Gabriel and Paul had gone looking for the knight sniper who was firing uselessly at the Sun Horseman. I think they must have found him pretty quickly too. Nobody put a bullet through my skull, at any rate.

The wolves were faster than my human form, and they swarmed over the knights on the periphery of the hot zone. The wolves weren't immune to the effects of the ward, but no magic is strong enough to override survival instinct entirely, and they could focus on the remaining enemy that was turning to fire on them. And they did. The fighting was all but over by the time I got there, only the Sun Horseman still left, circled by snarling wolves.

I ignored all of that and darted around the flaming specter in the middle of the street, feeling the heat of the Sun Horseman on my skin like a tangible thing, a wall or a wave if either of those things burn microlayers of your skin off even while they give before you.

It had to be a domovik, this Sun Horseman, a fiery guardian spirit, though God knows what the Baba Yaga had done to make this one so aggressive. It had to be a domovik, because if it was some kind of djinn, we were all dead.

A knight had tried to drive one of the panel vans up to the house and through the front door, but the lawn had turned to quicksand beneath it. The van was almost completely submerged into the front yard, only the tops of its windows visible while it lay on or in some tangle of pipes. Bullets were thudding uselessly into the armored roof as knights trapped in the van tried to free themselves from below. I jumped from a sidewalk to the top of the van and then to the front porch of the house, running leaps that covered fifteen feet at a time. Greg Apraxin, the Day Horseman, was actually trying to close the door that had been left open when the Sun Horseman went outside, and I shoulder-charged it and knocked Greg Apraxin off of his feet.

There was only one practical way to kill the domovik.

A short hall led straight to the kitchen, and I saw a large pot on a counter there, so I barely paused to shoot Greg Apraxin in the head before stumbling and running on. I did pause then. There was a long mirror in the hallway, and I saw a beautiful black-haired woman with pale skin in it even though I couldn't smell or hear her. Mila Apraxin. She was wearing a cloak made of dark feathers, and when she began to make a sudden sweeping gesture with her arms, I instinctively grabbed the handle of a bathroom door next to me and threw it open, hiding behind it. Shards of glass exploded outward from the mirror and engulfed the hallway. Some of it was pulverized against the door in front of me, and some of the fragments came at an angle and sank into the door like knives.

If the glass was the kind treated with a film of silver nitrate, and I suspected that it was, it would have killed me.

I didn't have time to think about that, though. Mila Apraxin was gone when I threw the door flat against the wall and charged into the kitchen. There were actually several large pots on the stove, all of them full of grass and mud and some other things I couldn't identify by smell. The mixture was bubbling. I think it was the source of the quicksand magic.

I never found out. I just grabbed a pot and ran around a corner into a dining room, then into a large den where the fireplace was located. Flames were roaring in that hearth. I had never actually seen the house when smoke wasn't pouring out of the chimney, but October was cold in Wisconsin and I had never wondered at it. Now I knew the real reason.

Domoviks are spirits that are summoned and placed into live flames. They are usually ancestors of the summoner, and once they are brought to our plane, the fire that houses them has to be constantly fed. If the family moves, they have to transport flames from the original fire by lamp or torch or firepot, or the domovik is lost.

Which is why I dumped the pot of mud into the fireplace. There was actually another, smaller pot suspended over the fire, and I tipped it over for good measure. It was a foolish gesture. I only did it because my adrenaline was up, and I was fortunate that I didn't cause an explosion or poisonous fumes or send acid trickling over my feet. Instead, boiling water full of dead, plucked crows with stitched bellies cascaded over what was left of the fire.

I actually saw the domovik wink out of existence through a window, its last few flaming footsteps still sizzling in the rain behind it.

There was no time to gawk. I began to search the house for

the third vedma, the woman in the feathered cloak who I had seen watching me through a mirror. Mila Apraxin.

I never found her.

I think I know how the remaining Baba Yaga got away, though. I don't think those birds were just summoned. I think they were led. I think before the battle even began, before her husband died, before her sisters were killed, before whatever dark dreams she had dreamed were destroyed, Mila Apraxin transformed herself into a crow and flew away.

∾36∾

NOT A BEATLES REFERENCE

Paul was dead.

∾37∾

IF YOU WANT TO CLEAN UP, YOU HAVE TO GET YOUR HANDS DIRTY

The sun was coming up and I was starving, but I was standing on the stairs of the Apraxins' porch, and I wasn't eating or drinking anything that came from that damned house. A Heckler and Koch USP Tactical Compact pistol that I'd taken off of a dead knight was holstered by my side. There were only eight bullets in its magazine, but they were all silver. I was afraid that I was going to need every single one of them.

Kneeling or lying in the yard in front of the porch were nine bound and gagged knights whose lives we had been able to salvage. Some of them were burned or broken or listless after being heart-started, although I know that's not a real phrase.

One of the knights was a woman. A woman in full combat gear. I couldn't see much of her—a werewolf had undone her braids while searching for needles and picks, and her shoulder-length black hair hid everything except high, chiseled cheekbones and angry hazel eyes—but she must have been fierce in spirit to have made it to that yard among those men. It was a sign of how desperate things must be getting for the knights if they were willing to overcome their insistence on women being good little knight-breeding factories.

Behind the knights stood twenty-five werewolves facing me. We had lost eleven of our number during the raid. Brett, Matthew's second-in-command, was not one of them.

"What are we waiting for?" he said belligerently.

"Your wife," I said.

He thought I was saying that the same way I might have said "Your mom," but I was actually watching Virgil pull up into the hot zone in a large U-Haul. Barbara Ann, Stacy, and Carl were all crammed into the wide front seat with him.

We were going to trank the knights and send them to Bernard in that U-Haul, but I wanted them as witnesses first.

Barbara Ann made her way to Brett's side. She tried to take his hand, and he moved it away before settling his fingers next to his sidearm again. *Not my gun hand, woman.* Maybe he was smarter than he looked.

"This is the part where I'm supposed to tell you that we won a victory today," I addressed the small crowd. "But we didn't. Someone warned the Apraxins that an attack was coming, and the real Butcher of Abalmar got away."

The werewolves rumbled at that. The backs of those knights with intact spines stiffened, and their eyes rose up to look at me. Brett opened his mouth but Barbara Ann dug her nails into his forearm.

I held up a small envelope with my left hand and they quieted down. I hadn't had to search very hard for it. "The letter that went with this envelope is gone, but this was mailed to the Apraxins' house two days ago. They didn't bother to burn it or hide it because they're not used to thinking like wolves."

I took a deep whiff of the envelope. This was pure theatrics, but it made my point. "Do you want to tell me exactly what you had to say to a bunch of child-sacrificing witches, Brett? Barbara Ann?"

Matthew turned slowly and alertly toward Brett as if he'd just heard a snake rattle. "Brett?"

Brett moved suddenly, and I shot over a kneeling knight and put a bullet in Brett's forehead. Just because we were both werewolves didn't mean we were equally fast any more than all humans are equally fast.

If the wards around the Apraxin house could divert people's attention away from all the noise we'd made last night, I wasn't going to worry about my handgun.

"Everybody chill!" Matthew screamed, but the wiry blond kid from Mathew's claw ignored him and also rushed for his gun. The kid was fumbling and panicking, though, and he lost the pistol while it was clearing his holster, actually tossing it into the air in front of him. It took three shots before I put a bullet in his brain, just because he was jumping around so much while people were running about trying to get out of the firing zone.

I didn't shoot the three other werewolves who tried to draw on me, though. Two of them were killed by Gabriel and Tula, firing from the second-story windows of the house. If the two werewolves were part of a conspiracy, they really should have established where the rest of my claw was before trying anything. If they were just reacting to the sudden violence by drawing on me, they really should have stayed out of it.

The third one was shot by Matthew, who walked up calmly and shot the man point-blank in the head while he was trying to train a Magnum on the second-floor windows. "I SAID CHILL!"

Barbara Ann screamed and started to raise her hand to point at me, but perhaps from Gabriel's vantage point, all he saw was her arm coming up. He shot her through the side of her temple, at any rate.

It took a minute for everyone to quiet down after the last bullet was fired. The crowd was no longer a throng but people spread out all over the yard, some out on the street, crouching behind whatever cover they could find or huddled or lying on the ground.

"LISTEN TO ME!" Matthew yelled, still holding his gun, though it was down at his side. "THERE HAS GOT TO BE A LINE! AND NO CLAN OF MINE IS STANDING BEHIND PEOPLE WHO KILL CHILDREN!"

He looked around. "Anybody else want to join this debate?"

No one did.

Matthew addressed me then. "You got anything else you wanted to tell us, John?"

I wanted to say that it was a pleasure to meet him, but I didn't. "That about covers it," I said.

After a moment, he nodded.

PART THE FOURTH

Old School

∾38∾

A SIGNIFICANT DEVELOPMENT

Tula and I were in the Apraxins' cellar, packing, cleaning, and destroying the laboratory there. It was foul work. I was the most powerful werewolf in Abalmar, at least temporarily, but I was also the only one protected against curses, and there was some ungodly stuff in that basement. We found disturbing illustrations and organic-looking things in glass jars that we didn't want to identify and notes written in a language I didn't recognize. Looking at the words made my mind itch as if spiders were crawling over it, and the writing seemed to move while I stared.

There was also a small chance that the surviving Baba Yaga would come back for something she had left behind. If she did return, I either wanted to be there or make sure she didn't find anything she valued.

"Phoenix will want these," Tula commented, holding two notebooks up.

"Put them in the bonfire pile," I said shortly. "This place is a poison tree. I'm not going apple-picking."

"I'm not arguing." Tula shivered. "But Phoenix won't be happy, and he has a lot of pull with Bernard these days."

"Well, I'll make sure to blame it on you," I promised. "How do you think I made it to upper management?"

Tula rolled her eyes.

The front door of the house opened and Stacy's voice sounded down the stairs. "HEY, JOHN, THE EXORCIST IS HERE!"

I yelled back. "YOU REALLY THINK YOU'RE GOING TO GET RID OF ME THAT EASILY?!?"

"Ha-ha," Stacy said when she realized how close I was. "You'd better get up here, because I'm not going down there."

That was probably wise, and I did want to check out the exorcist. Someone had to take a good, hard look at those Russian olive trees. I had been tempted to just burn them, but if there were souls or spirits trapped in those things, I wanted to make sure we sent them on their way properly.

Her scent reached me a second before I made it to the first floor, sex and butter pecan, but my brain didn't accept what my nose was telling it. My feet kept walking mechanically.

Sig was standing in the kitchen.

"Hello, John," Sig said quietly. The long blond hair was braided, something she usually only did when she was going into combat, and she was wearing a blue overcoat, probably to cover whatever weapons she was carrying. Her body looked the same but its language was different. Her movements were smaller and her blue eyes were shadowed, and not with makeup. She looked like she'd been through hell.

I think Stacy might have been in the kitchen too. I'm not really sure.

"What are you doing here?" I asked stupidly.

Apprehension and irritation went off behind Sig's eyes like flash powder and burned out, quickly replaced by confusion. "You asked for my help."

I cocked my head the way a dog does when it's waiting for things to start making sense. *I know some of those words you're speaking*, my expression said. *But somehow, they have no meaning.*

Comprehension made Sig's eyes go wide and popped her mouth open. "Parth."

Ohhhhhhhhhh.

"You thought I would try to contact you through Parth." I tasted the words in my mouth. They weren't sweet.

"You might if you were desperate," Sig said. "He told me he'd been in touch with you, and it's not like him to lie outright."

"Parth hacked into the system of a computer guy here." I shot Stacy a dirty look that was completely unfair. Oh, yeah, I guess she was there. "Carl and Parth must still be talking."

"Oh," Sig said.

"Let's start over," I said. "What are you doing here?!?"

Now Sig looked at me like I was the one not making sense. "I think I just explained that?"

"You're violating the agreement!" Why was I getting louder?

"What agreement?" Sig's voice, on the other hand, was becoming dangerously low.

I pulled it down to a muted snarl. "The agreement where I turned myself in to the knights if they promised not to harm you or the others."

Sig clenched her teeth. "I know. I just wanted to hear you admit it. You lied to me."

"I did not," I informed her testily. "I told you I was going to do something you wouldn't like. And I had an escape plan! I was almost out of there when the werewolves you sent butted in! Now I'm in the middle of a war! Thanks for bailing me out of trouble, genius!"

"Yeah, I heard all about your brilliant plan from Awesome Sauce!" Sig said sarcastically. "It really sounds like you had everything under control."

She was giving *me* attitude? "Who or what the hell is Awesome Sauce?"

"HE'S THE SPRITE YOU SWALLOWED, YOU MORON!" Sig yelled. "YOU DIDN'T EVEN LEARN HIS NAME?!?"

"WELL, IF YOU'RE ON SUCH GOOD TERMS WITH THE LITTLE BASTARD, WHERE IS HE?" I demanded. "I'D KIND OF LIKE TO HAVE A WORD WITH HIM RIGHT NOW MYSELF!"

"HE'S PROBABLY AFRAID YOU'LL SHOVE HIM UP YOUR ASS NEXT TIME!" Sig shot back.

"NO, I'M GOING TO SHOVE HIM UP *YOUR* ASS NEXT TIME!"

"Uhum?" Stacy cleared her throat from where she was still hanging back in the opening between the hallway and the kitchen. "We're surrounded by werewolves, you know. Everybody within a mile can hear you."

Sig and I both glowered at her.

"I get it now," Tula said from behind me.

Dammit! People only sneak up on me when Sig's around. I turned and saw Tula standing at the top of the cellar stairs with her arms crossed. She was wearing a small smile.

"Get what?" I demanded.

Tula ignored me and addressed Sig. "John and I were in a house together for three days while we were staking this place out. He never hit on me once. I just thought he and Carl were involved."

Sig tried to keep the same expression on her face, but something shifted under it. It was like watching ice crack.

"It's because I'm your claw leader, Tula," I said, irritated. "To hell with both of you. I've been having sex all over the place."

Tula scrunched her face up. "Gross."

Sig suddenly moved away from the counter she was leaning against and examined it critically. "Oh my God, what about here? You haven't had sex all over here, have you?"

"Give me a minute!" I snapped.

Sig's mouth twitched. "It's good to see you, John."

"Don't you go getting mature on me," I warned. "I'm pissed."

"I'll go if you really don't want me here." Sig adjusted her purse strap. Since when did Sig carry a purse around? I guess I'd never seen her when she wasn't actively hunting something.

I swallowed an angry comment about always wanting her there. Holy shit, John. Bipolar much? "Dammit, Sig."

"What, John?" She folded her arms. "What are you really upset about? Help me out here."

I rubbed my hands over my face as if trying to wipe it clear like an Etch A Sketch. "You said in that letter that I'm always in the middle of chaos."

Sig leaned back against the counter again and held her hands out, indicating the kitchen, the house, the Clan, Wisconsin, the world.

"I'm not arguing the point," I said quietly. "It's just, the one thing I've been getting any comfort from with all this craziness is the fact that you were out of it."

Sig began to unbutton her coat. "I get what you're saying. I really do. Do you know why I've never thanked you for giving yourself over to the knights for me?"

"Yes," I said.

Sig took me at my word. "Then do you know what I

discovered about myself while I was creating a safe, chaos-free environment?"

"No," I said.

"I don't handle safe, chaos-free environments well," Sig said. "It's nice to take a break, but I need something to take a break from."

I didn't know whether to smile or be sad.

"Seriously, John. Do you think I'm ever really going to live safely?"

"I . . . no," I admitted.

Sig moved so that she could drape her coat over a chair. She was wearing a fuzzy white sweater and an old-fashioned holster, one that held her firearm under her right armpit. "I came because I wanted to, John. And if I wasn't here, I'd be in some other messed-up place where messed-up things were going on."

I was a step closer to her. "You wanted to come here."

Sig tried to toss her hair with a head flick. I guess she forgot it was braided. Her heart was going pitter-pat. "That letter wasn't really fair. I mean, it was, because I needed time to work some things out. But it wasn't."

"So, have you worked things out?" I took another step.

"God, no." Sig was watching me carefully. "I'm more messed up than ever. Don't kiss me."

"I can't promise that." I stopped.

Sig stood there looking at me, not quite smiling, not quite frowning, and then she stepped into my arms. She was stiff and awkward for a moment, but when she relaxed into me, it was all at once. Her hands went to the small of my back and pulled me in. Our heads rested on each other's shoulders as if we were puzzle pieces that had just come together.

I pressed my lips against the side of her neck. Her skin was silk and warm and her pulse was thrumming beneath her skin.

She shivered, and her hands smoothed out between my shoulder blades and pulled me in closer.

∽∾

"This is just creepy," Sig observed. "I feel like I'm in a fishbowl, except I'm the one watching the people outside it."

We were walking along the boundary of the hot zone. A crowd had gathered to gawk while police and FBI combed the neighborhood. A neighborhood homeowner had found blood and shell casings outside the hot zone despite our best efforts to clean up. With the media frenzy on the recent serial killings still in high gear, reporters who were already in Abalmar anyhow were talking into cameras. Bloggers were on site too, speaking into cell phones while they held them up to record images. Some old-fashioned types were actually talking to each other. But nobody was actually looking at the Apraxin house, and somehow recording devices were always angled away so that we weren't in the background. A clear line was delineated where people had just stopped without thinking about it, their backs pressed against the edge of the hot zone as if against a stone wall. They were facing away from us, and none of them seemed to hear as we walked behind them.

"The hot zone is the only reason I haven't burned the house down yet," I said. "We need its cover to clean this mess up."

I waved to Marty, a short wedge of muscle who was standing next to the Apraxins' mailbox, thought about introducing him to Sig, and then let it go. I wasn't sure if the Clan wanted to know Sig or vice versa.

"What's he doing?" Sig asked, barely glancing Marty's way.

"He's there to help werewolves across the ward," I said. "Even though they know it's there, they still wind up milling around. It's kind of funny to watch from this side, actually. They'll get close to the field and then get distracted by something and then forget why they're here. Or they'll stand right there with their backs to the thing and look north, east, west, and then start over without ever looking south over their shoulder. But if they stand near the mailbox, Marty can reach across and pull them over. "

"That's... disturbing," Sig said quietly.

"It's one of the most powerful wards I've ever seen," I confirmed. "I think it actually taps directly into the Pax Arcana and channels it, like someone stealing power from their neighbor. The Baba Yaga who escaped... she's not just twisted; she's crazy powerful, Sig."

We reached our destination, a portly man in a big, puffy blue coat and a cap with ear flaps, standing in the back of the crowd taking pictures with a professional-looking camera.

"At least the crowds mean we don't have to worry about the knights sending out a strike team for some kind of massive retaliation anytime soon," I continued. "They just have a few spies who aren't affected by the ward out in the crowd. Like this rocket scientist. He keeps turning his camera lens into the sun to take pictures of us. He might as well be flashing mirror signals."

The man tried to pretend that he didn't hear me, but his pulse was pounding. I put my hand on the back of his coat and yanked him into the hot zone with us.

He was of the bloodline, and he'd had training at some point before washing out. Probably as a page. It had been long enough ago that he'd let himself get out of shape anyway, and he was only in his early twenties. He was making a weird sound that wasn't crying and wasn't screaming but was somewhere in between. It definitely wasn't a battle cry, though he was using the hand holding the camera to try to backhand me.

I caught his wrist easily and twisted, leaning down on his elbow so that he could either drop or get his arm broken. He went down to a knee, then tried to go lower and use the slack to hook his ankle behind mine, but I came down on his back like a ton of bricks and pounded him down into the ground.

By the time he got his cool back, I had my knife between his legs.

No one in the crowd I'd yanked him out of turned around to watch or paid any attention to his yells.

I removed a silver steel knife, a can of mace that smelled like wolfsbane, a space-age-looking Taser of some kind, and an asthma inhaler that judging from his breathing was just an asthma inhaler. Less interesting was his wallet, a cell phone, and a small semiautomatic. "Tell the Order that the blonde didn't come here to fight."

He didn't say anything, just kind of blubbered, and I smacked his head against the pavement to get his attention. "Tell the order that the blonde didn't come here to fight. She's not taking sides. She's just here to exorcise the grove that killed a lot of knights."

"All right!" he gasped.

"We've been taking your picture too. Now, get any family you have and leave Wisconsin," I said.

I rose and lifted him up bodily with one hand just to make a point, then kicked him back into the crowd. Several people protested as he stumbled through them, but he didn't apologize. He didn't look back at all. He ran.

"Do you really think that's going to make a difference?" Sig asked.

"No," I said shortly. "But I'm like the ant with a rubber tree plant."

She just looked at me.

"High hopes," I said. The reference was probably before her time. "Let's go ahead and get your sword and spear out of your car."

"How do you know I brought them?" she asked.

I gave her a look. "Please. This might be the first time I've ever seen you when you didn't have all kinds of pointy steel edges sticking out. You're like the human version of a Swiss Army knife."

She laughed and punched me in the shoulder. Is it sick that I'd missed that?

"You seem more solid somehow," she remarked as we walked toward her car. "Being yourself around people has been good for you."

"You seem more unsettled," I told her.

"I'm just not putting up as much of a front." Sig was looking at her feet while she walked. "I was pretty unsettled when you met me."

"I didn't say it looked bad on you."

She punched me in the shoulder again, more gently this time.

⁂

"You should probably get everybody out of the hot zone," I told Matthew. It's possible that I didn't have to phrase it as a suggestion. Matthew seemed a lot more thoughtful and humble since discovering that Brett and his wife were making major decisions and moves without Matthew's okay. The way some of Matthew's own crew had obeyed Brett rather than him had been a bit of a wake-up call too. Matthew hadn't just lost his best friend; he was dealing with the idea that he'd never had one.

"Why do you want us out?" Matthew asked. Not arguing.

"The wards don't just keep normal people out," I explained. "I think they keep the magic of this place in, and Sig is about to release some pissed-off spirits."

There were five of us standing on the Apraxins' back porch, watching Sig walk down toward the grove with her sword on her back and her spear in her hand.

"Let me guess." Tula might have sounded slightly wry. "You're staying behind with her."

I crossed my arms over my chest. "I can't be possessed."

"Yes," Tula said. "That must be it."

Stacy shook her head. Her mouth was a sardonic line. "A blonde. A six-foot blonde."

"She's a Valkyrie." I felt obscurely defensive; I'm not sure if was on my behalf or Sig's. "I think it kind of comes with the package."

It's not as if Sig looked like a runway model. Her shoulders were broad. Her frame was sinewy and sturdy. Her hips and bottom were a thing of beauty, but nobody would ever call her willowy.

"That's some package," Matthew reflected. He was looking at Sig as if he were watching a unicorn.

Stacy smacked Matthew on the back of the head.

Matthew laughed and rubbed the back of his skull. "I wasn't disrespecting John's woman. I was just saying, is all."

What the hell? People will surprise you, but...what the hell? Apparently, Matthew and Stacy had found time to have a serious heart-to-heart while I wasn't around to hear it.

"Sure, why not?" Stacy muttered as she walked off. "Witches. Werewolves. Why not Brunhilde?"

"She's not clan," Gabriel said from the back doorway. "And she never will be."

I moved to follow Sig. "I know."

∽39∾

FOILED CURSES AGAIN

Sig put her sword away as soon as she walked into the edge of the wooded patch. She didn't just sheathe it between her shoulder blades; she set it on the ground. She was looking around at something I couldn't see, and I heard her whisper. "Oh, you poor things."

I sat down on the ground then, watching while she stood at the edge of the grove, sometimes listening, sometimes asking the air questions about times and places and names. There was a compassion in her voice that was palpable, a raw goodness. This was the same woman I had seen decapitate vampires.

I won't lie; it wasn't some feel-good inspiring kind of new age scene. If we had been in a movie, there wouldn't have been an uplifting classical score in the background, or building choral music. It was one of those rare days when there wasn't much of a wind, and the only music I heard was the occasional rustling of branches that shouldn't be moving. My bones seemed to be vibrating slightly. At one point, Sig turned around and told me to go get a shovel, and I did.

When I got back, Sig was deeper into the wooded patch,

kneeling. I had no inclination to interrupt. Suddenly there was a ripple, a seismic line cracking the earth and spreading out from the base of a tree, and then several large tree roots erupted from the soil in front of her. They thrashed around like octopus tentacles while Sig whispered to someone, and then they settled on the ground in front of her.

The tip of some of the roots were tied together in a kind of intricate knot. I could actually see the strands occasionally twitching and tugging at each other as if trying to break free. Sig dug her fingers into that mess, still making soothing sounds, and then began to undo the binding, sometimes easing tendrils out of each other's reach, sometimes breaking a strand loose with a sharp, dry snap.

"The first case," she whispered. Then later, "Fate."

I suddenly realized that there wasn't an animal sound within miles. My own breathing was loud in my ears

Snap. "The power within."

Rustle. "Intensity."

A long, sinuous rasp. "Direction."

The air seemed more concentrated now. There was a pressure on my lungs that had nothing to do with gravity or temperature. A vacuum, perhaps, but I didn't know what kind.

"Revival," Sig hissed, tearing something loose with a violent yank. Then, more softly, "Return."

A breeze blew through the grove then, but I couldn't say where it came from. The high grass beyond the tree line wasn't rustling.

"Not hers," Sig chanted. "Not mine. Yours. Yours alone."

Suddenly, the roots came free in Sig's hands, separate strands falling limply to the ground.

"No guilt," she whispered. "Be free."

Some twenty feet away from Sig, a tree began to slowly

topple backward to the ground, tearing gnarled roots and clumps of soil out of the earth as it fell. A skeleton was partially pulled out of the soil, enmeshed in the roots.

I guess that's what the shovel was for.

Sig had to do that seven more times. Somewhere in the middle, I went back to my car and got sandwich fixings and water out of my trunk, but we didn't talk. Sig ate the food without tasting it, looking at something I couldn't see, listening to voices I couldn't hear. I was almost glad that the knights had set some of the trees on fire. By the end, tears were running down Sig's face, but she didn't convulse with sobs or move to wipe them away. She knelt where she was, drained.

I rose and moved to her then, sat behind her and rubbed her back, kneaded her shoulders. When she leaned back into me, I wrapped my arms around her, and she finally started shaking.

৵৹

"I'm going to kill her," Sig promised, her tears dried on my forearms. "That witch dies by my hand."

I didn't say anything. I was still holding her, and Sig reached her hand up to my forearm and squeezed it. "The spirits told me something. I don't want you to jump to any conclusions, though. The dead aren't great communicators."

I rested my chin on her shoulder. "What?"

"I'm serious, John. Sometimes the dead are vague. Sometimes they talk in riddles. Sometimes they tell malicious partial truths that might as well be lies."

I held her tighter. "Just tell me."

Sig exhaled. "The last time she was here, the head witch said something to the others about leaving. Something about following a firebird. She made some joke about a big bad wolf."

I released her and scooted away as if her back had just grown a giant mouth and fangs.

Sig turned so that she could look at me and hugged her knees closer to her body. "It doesn't have to be about your clan."

I didn't say anything, just held a palm up like a traffic cop telling someone to stop. Sig ignored it. "There are all kinds of Russian stories about following a firebird, right?"

"It doesn't have to be the Russian firebird just because she's Russian," I told her shortly, standing up. "Our clan leader has a cunning man named Phoenix."

Sig's attention suddenly went from concerned to predatory. "Oh?"

I started to walk, I'm not sure where. I didn't even go in circles. I paced back and forth in sudden, jerky halts and reversals, my mind and heart racing.

Something else occurred to me, and I came to a dead stop. "Bernard B. Wright."

"Is that your leader?" Sig was struggling to sound neutral. Part of me appreciated the effort.

"Bernard B. Wright," I repeated. "B.B.W."

Sig got it immediately. "Big Bad Wolf."

I sat down again, a puppet whose strings had been cut.

Sig moved and scooted across from me. Her hand stroked my ankle. "What, you think he's the original evil werewolf from the stories?"

I waved that off. "There was never just one, any more than there was just one *Prince Charming*. But if those initials are his idea of a private joke, it says something about him." And it did. The Big Bad Wolf is always a deceiver in the old stories; he's always pretending to be a concerned neighbor, a loving relative, a wolf in sheep's clothing. At least until his fangs come out. And part of that is a reference to lycanthropes, to wolves who look like men, but it is also a metaphor for a certain type of evil that is very human: the smiling sociopath hiding a monster within.

"Is it possible this Bernard made a deal with the Baba Yaga?" Sig was still trying to sound objective and detached.

"It's possible." My voice was bitter. I knew. Tumblers were clicking into place. "He's obsessed with magic for some reason. He's got Phoenix researching something big, but he won't say what it is. And Gabriel! Shit!"

"Gabriel's the Native American I saw this morning?"

I nodded impatiently. "Gabriel's sister is Bernard's mate. And Gabriel is keeping an eye on me for Bernard's enforcer. That's two ways that Bernard could have found out that the Butcher of Abalmar was a powerful witch."

Sig let go of my ankle and straightened. "So you're think-ing this Phoenix character was like, *Hey Bernard, I'm having trouble making this Ring of Power* or whatever? And then the Baba Yaga came along?"

Actually, I was thinking other things. It was as if Sig's words had untied another kind of knot. My mind was unspooling. I sank and let the back of my head hit the cold, hard ground.

But as the only one here who grew up as a conquered people? Personally, I'd rather be on the winning side than the right one this time. Gabriel's words. Agreeing with Barbara Ann at the meeting. Gabriel, who had shot Barbara Ann in the head with a silver bullet. I had thought it was because he couldn't see that her hand was empty from his elevation and angle, but what if it had been to keep her from talking?

The Baba Yaga had destroyed or kept whatever letter was sent to her...what if Barbara Ann or Brett hadn't been acting on their own? What if they'd been passing on an offer from Bernard?

Was it possible? Of course it was possible. But was it likely? I had never really warmed to Bernard. He was the opposite of Sig. My brain had given me all kinds of reasons not to trust Sig, and I always had, even when I kept trying to tell myself I didn't. With Bernard, there were all kinds of reasons to believe in him. Hell, he always made it in my own interest to believe him. He always said the right things, and people that I liked trusted him completely, but I never had, not really.

I remembered Tula's words while I was destroying black-magical research just that morning. *Phoenix won't be happy, and he has a lot of pull with Bernard these days.*

"John?" Sig scooted forward again and rubbed her palm over my chest. I took Sig's hand, and I don't know if I was trying to stop it from distracting me or clutching at it. My head felt like a whirlpool.

No clan of mine will stand beside killers of children, Matt had said. What if that had gotten back to Bernard too?

"If your clan is sheltering that witch, I won't let it go." Sig sounded regretful. "But I really hope they're not."

"I understand," I said quietly, and I did. She needed to finish what she'd started.

And she wasn't the only one.

∾40∾

PUTTING THE HELL IN HELLO

I take it back," Sig said. "There's no way I'd be in another situation as screwed up as this one if I hadn't come to see you. You have a real gift."

I didn't respond. God knows, I get gallows humor. I can joke in a lot of situations where I probably shouldn't, but right then I wasn't in the mood. Grief had turned to anger, and I was wearing that anger like armor. We were walking back up past the Apraxin house, the bodies of dead knights still lying in the ground beneath our feet. They might not have been good men, but they were men, and they had been swallowed like bitter pills or passing bugs. Swallowed like truths that no one wanted to say or hear.

I needed to talk to Gabriel.

"You're not going to do something stupid, are you?" Sig kept her tone conversational. She was so full of it, talking to me about acting stupid. Her sword was sheathed between her shoulders and she was carrying her spear at her side one-handed, and she was walking beside me when she should have been running as fast and as far as she could in the other direction.

It was kind of the way I'd been around her in Clayburg, come to think of it.

"The smart thing to do is nothing," I answered bitterly.

Sig mulled that over. "Okay. So, how stupid are we talking here?"

"I haven't worked that out yet," I responded. "But if you're going to do something wrong, you might as well do it right."

Sig touched my arm, not punching it for once. "I'm serious. I'm letting you take the lead here because this is your turf and you know the players, but you need to cool down."

We had reached the street. "What the hell?"

Sig looked around warily. "What?"

Nikolai was waiting for me outside the hot zone, him and Gabriel and maybe a whole claw I'd never seen before. The crowd had thinned out a little over the last few hours, but not much, and I could smell werewolves in the air. Virgil should have been back by now, but there was no sign of him or Stacy or Tula or Carl or Matthew or Boone.

Nikolai and Gabriel were standing beside the Apraxins' mailbox, and I moved behind them, staring at the backs of their skulls from less than a foot away. I might as well have been on another continent.

"She could call me with a burner phone," Gabriel was saying.

"Talk about this later," Nikolai commanded tersely.

Nikolai hadn't been around Gabriel for a while; maybe he'd forgotten that when Gabriel wanted to say something, he said something. "I don't care who hears this. You can't keep me from talking to my sister."

"The knights have hit squads all over Milwaukee right now. If they can't hurt Bernard, they'll go after his mate," Nikolai growled. "Catherine is incommunicado."

"Then take me to her," Gabriel said.

"That's what I'm trying to tell you," Nikolai said impatiently. "She's on the move and not telling anyone where she is for the next few days, not even me. It's the only way to keep her safe."

Sig interrupted my eavesdropping. "What's going on?"

"Keep yourself between these guys and the house," I directed, motioning her next to me. "That's where the effects of the ward are strongest."

Sig followed my lead and repeated, "What's going on?"

"This big guy is Nikolai Sokolov." I nodded at Nikolai absently, still half listening to him argue with Gabriel about the importance of keeping Catherine's location completely secret. "He's Bernard's troubleshooter, and he's brought some extra muscle along."

Sig moved beside me. "I still can't get used to these people not hearing us. Why is he just waiting out here?"

"They hear us, but it's like we're the background hum of an air conditioner," I said. "And nobody's standing here to help them across. Or maybe Nikolai is taking my warning about spirits being set loose seriously."

Sig nodded at that. "I would."

"Yeah, but you have a lot of personal experience," I agreed. "I wonder if Nikolai does."

Sig bared her teeth. It was wolflike. "Maybe your friend Nikolai is taking evil spirits seriously because he knows exactly what a scary bitch this Mila Apraxin is."

"Maybe," I said. "The real question is why he's here at all. Where are all the locals and the rest of my claw? Why isn't Virgil back yet?"

Sig didn't like where that was leading. "He's isolating you."

Nikolai rubbed the back of his neck where I was staring at it. I wondered if the two things were connected. He and Gabriel had lapsed into a sullen silence.

"Possibility One," I speculated. "There's been some kind of emergency. Bernard is dead, or there's been a major knight attack or something, and Nikolai couldn't reach me by phone because we've been in the hot zone for hours. So he came here personally."

Sig frowned. "You said he brought help."

I began to walk down the line where people were gathered against the ward, pointing my index finger at werewolves as I went. "I can't really think of an emergency that would explain this, though. Let's say Bernard has been assassinated. Nikolai would just call a local werewolf who wasn't in the hot zone and have them send for me. He wouldn't spend hours in a car to come get me. I'm just not that important. He sure as hell wouldn't stand around waiting with a full claw doing nothing in the middle of a crisis. Same with a knight attack, or some monster popping up that the Clan wants me to handle."

Sig took her spear in both hands and held it like a bo staff.

"If this was a real emergency, he wouldn't be standing here waiting," I continued. "And if it weren't, he wouldn't have come personally. The only thing that kind of makes sense is if some local thing has come up that Nikolai wants to handle personally, and he wants my help with it."

Sig examined Nikolai and Gabriel critically. "So what's Possibility Two?"

She already knew.

"My time in Abalmar is almost up," I said. "Maybe Mila Apraxin really is helping Phoenix with his magical research now, and Nikolai knows me well enough to know that I won't sit still for that. He knows about my geas too. He knows I won't stop looking for the bitch."

"Don't forget Mila Apraxin might have some say in it," Sig reminded me. "You killed some of her Baba Yaga personally, right?"

"I shot the Day Horseman while she watched through a mirror," I said. "He might have even really been her husband. I killed the Sun Horseman too."

"If she's really working for this Bernard now, your death might be her price," Sig guessed.

My mind stopped working for a few seconds. For some reason, the idea that the Clan would sell me out to an outsider was more upsetting than the idea that they might kill me as a matter of clan policy. Wolf instincts again? I worked my teeth silently, baring and gnashing them.

Sig pulled me back. "If any of this is true, this Nikolai doesn't know you suspect them yet."

I agreed. "This whole pack instinct thing has been messing with my head. I'm only suspicious now because of what you just told me, and I still don't want to believe it."

Sig focused on Nikolai. "Or you could just be paranoid because of the mind-set I put you in. We don't have any proof."

I shrugged, though I really wasn't feeling all that nonchalant. "Nikolai does Bernard's dirty work. Sending everyone else away makes sense if I'm the problem he's here to deal with. Nikolai has always thought I was dangerous. He wouldn't trust anyone else to handle me."

"What would you be doing right now if I hadn't shown up?" Sig still hadn't taken her eyes off Nikolai. In fact, she was staring at the place between his shoulder blades where his heart would line up, sighting on it in a way that made me want to adjust his life insurance premiums. "If you were still clueless, I mean."

"I'd be bringing Nikolai over here to talk," I admitted. "My first instinct would be to worry that something seriously bad had happened."

"So you'd be alone with him and six other werewolves," Sig

said. "In a magically warded place where none of the people who have grown to care about you could see or hear what they did."

My voice went down a few octaves. It was coming from deep in my chest, almost choking in my throat. "Yes."

"So what are we…" Sig paused as I removed the USP Tactical Compact pistol. It was a good gun, and I was getting used to it.

"Do you trust me?" I asked.

"Yes?"

I shot Nikolai in the back of the head.

My left hand was reaching for his collar even while my right hand pulled the trigger, and I yanked Nikolai across the ward as he started to collapse.

Gabriel began to turn. He had caught Nikolai's movement, but when he moved to track it…Where had Nikolai…Was that blood on that guy's…

I shot Gabriel in the back of the head too, and yanked his body into the hot zone an instant later.

Sig stared at the two men lying on the street. She was the only person who was. The sound of the gun had originated on my side of the wards. "Does that gun have silver bullets?"

"No, I put a regular clip in it," I assured her as I walked down to the next clan member in line. "They'll wake up when their brain tissue heals and pushes the bullets back out."

The fourth and fifth ones were also easy. The sixth one was farther into the crowd, and I had to walk past the hot zone to get him.

"Come on." I motioned to him. "Nikolai wants me to help you across the ward, since it doesn't affect me."

The sixth werewolf was burly and bearded and young, and he looked around wildly. "Where…"

I sighed and pointed straight at the Apraxin house. "Over there. He's waving at you to hurry up."

He squinted as if that would help. He thought he was turning his neck far enough to see the house, but he wasn't. "I can't…"

"Is something wrong?" I looked at him suspiciously.

"Nothing's wrong," he assured me hastily. "Magic just freaks me out. What do I have to do?"

I led him to the line and got behind him. "I just have to push you across. Ready?"

"I…"

I shoved him over the ward with my right hand, hard, stepping behind him and shooting him in the back of the head with my left while he was still regaining his balance. The last claw member, a young up-and-comer named Shane, wandered over to the edge of the hot zone to see where we'd gone. His hand was on a gun butt somewhere under his coat.

A moment later, he was lying across his friend and I was checking the bullets in their magazine clips. They were silver. An entire claw armed with werewolf-killing weapons.

Sig surveyed the bodies. "That was easier than I was expecting."

"It's about to get a lot harder," I said reluctantly. "And you're going to have to let me handle the next part alone, Sig. This is clan business."

～41～

A TERRIBLE PLAN

Nikolai woke up to a nightmare. He was in the grove where Sig had cleansed the Russian olive trees, the clearing where the vedma had done whatever it is that vedma do in forests at night. The headless bodies of two of his claw members were lying on the edges of the clearing. Three others were sprawled within his sight, visible bullet wounds in two of their foreheads. The other was lying facedown in a huge blood stain, his heart next to his body.

Gabriel was impaled on a small broken tree stump like a letter on one of those old-fashioned note spikes.

I was fifteen feet away from him, methodically thumbing silver bullets out of the magazine of my new pistol.

Nikolai didn't say anything. He rose to his knees and I slammed the magazine back into the H&K compact and pointed it directly at him. "Don't rush me, Nikolai. I still have three silver bullets in this thing."

"Where's your bitch?" he growled.

He could have asked why I'd killed his clan mates. He could have cursed me or screamed or pretended not to know what was going on. But Nikolai zeroed straight in on what and where his threats were.

"I sent her back home," I said. "This is clan business."

Nikolai's eyes widened at that. "You still think you're clan? What the motherless fuck is wrong with you?"

"It's your fault," I said sadly. "You either shouldn't have sent me after Mila Apraxin, or you shouldn't have taken her in. I warned you, and you triggered my geas anyway, you dumb shit." His face went unreadable. People think that means they're not revealing anything, but that's not true. It meant that Nikolai knew exactly what I was talking about. If he didn't, his face would have been showing all kinds of things.

"I don't want to do this, Nikolai," I told him. "I don't want to go on a clan killing spree. I don't want to take Bernard's head off. I don't want to tell the knights everything I've learned about the Clan and how they operate."

Nikolai's heartbeat was steady. The man was stone-cold. "Then don't."

I sobbed and punched my forehead with my left fist. The gun in my right hand didn't waver. "I'm trying. You have to help me. You have to kill me, Nikolai."

"My pleasure," he assured me. "Just put down the gun."

"I'm trying," I repeated. "You have to stop me, Nikolai. I think you're the only one who can."

"We're your people, John," Nikolai told me. "You can't let those punks kill us."

"You came here to kill me," I said.

He didn't deny it. "If I had to, yes. We do what we have to do for the good of the pack. It's what makes us better."

I took a deep breath. "We've got one chance at this, Nikolai. I think I can make myself throw the gun away, but I can't commit suicide. You're going to have to kill me."

"You throw that gun away and I'll see what I can do," he promised.

I screamed and flung the gun down as if it were red-hot. "JUST DO IT!"

Nikolai was already up and across the clearing before the gun finished moving. I kicked a clump of dirt in front me like I was punting a football, and it went spraying upward toward his face. I tried to step on his ankle but his footwork was surprisingly light for such a big man, and his body was centered on mine so that I couldn't get a good side angle. His right jab kept me back while he glided effortlessly and blinked the grit out.

He knocked my eye strikes away with his forearms and turned the blocks into punches and jabs. He kept pace with me effortlessly despite his heavier mass, and he hunched in his shoulder and chin to limit my target areas. I couldn't find a good opportunity to take his feet out from under him, either.

When I attempted to break his arm by trapping one of his punches, he anticipated my turn and freed himself while I was still trying to bring my weight around. Instead of bearing down on a hyperextended elbow, I found myself catching an elbow with my chin. It was all the break in my concentration Nikolai needed.

As fast as he'd been moving, Nikolai had been holding back on his speed a fraction. Suddenly, his fists weren't where my body thought they should be when my reflexes took over to block them. He was inside my guard, and his punches were brutal and devastating. He broke, ruptured, and fractured me, my jaw, my ribs, my teeth, my nose. I lost my air, blood got in my eyes, and he didn't stop when I fell down. His foot came down on my right knee with all of his weight and broke it. I screamed and reached a hand up to stop him, reflexively, and he grabbed it and snapped my wrist using his forearm as a lever.

Then he backed off. There was no need to risk bringing his groin or throat or eyes or thoracic cavity into reaching distance by dropping down on me. I was done. I could barely see him, could barely breathe. One of my eyes was blind again. I think impact had turned it to insensate jelly.

"Just tell me it was worth it," I gasped, though my words weren't as articulate as their spelling might suggest. They came out more like "Juh teh me it wuh wuth id."

Nikolai didn't have any trouble understanding me, though. He spoke Broken. "What?"

"Juh teh me it wuh wuth id," I bubbled through blood and saliva. "Teh me yuh nah evil."

"By your standards, we probably are evil." He walked over to pick up the pistol I'd flung away. "Remember you and Bernard's little argument in the cave? Bernard's real last name is Gandillon."

Oh, shit.

Even as messed up as my face was, he saw something in it. "We are going to change the world, Charming. Take that with you."

"The widj," I gasped. I tried to raise myself up, but some fracture or crack in my breastbone was keeping me from propping myself up on my elbows. I wound up pushing myself backward awkwardly with one leg, making a furrow on the forest floor in a pathetic attempt to get away from him. "Chile killuh."

"She's going to become Bernard's queen." Nikolai raised his hand and leveled the gun. "She won't have to do messed-up shit after that. None of us will."

The gun jammed. This was because there was a piece of

gum wedging the third bullet from the bottom of the magazine up, the angle preventing it from entering the chamber.

The gun that I pulled from the leaves behind me, on the other hand, worked fine. Nikolai and his claw had brought six pistols with silver bullets in them, and they were strategically hidden all over the clearing.

He avoided a killing shot the first three times, turned and caught one in the side, an arm, but the one he caught in his neck slowed him down and made him pivot and expose his torso, and I fired three more into his face.

I didn't try to say anything witty. My jaw hurt too much and I wasn't in the mood.

It seemed to take forever for Sig to make her way to the clearing even though I could hear her running. She'd had to conceal herself a long way off to avoid Nikolai's senses. The profusion of trees hadn't offered her one clear shot while we'd moved around, and she couldn't scramble around to keep following us without him hearing her. She hadn't liked that at all, but the clearing was a little like a boxing ring, and I'd needed Nikolai to feel confident.

Then she was looking over me, reaching and then pulling her hands away as if afraid to touch me. My face was bloody, one cheekbone crushed, jaw broken, teeth shattered, and I couldn't even close my mouth so that I wouldn't look like such a freak show. "My God, John."

"It wuhked," I said.

And no, the werewolves in the clearing weren't really dead. It was all theater.

The werewolves with the bullets in their foreheads hadn't really been shot by silver bullets. The headless bodies were two of the werewolves we'd executed earlier; we were still disposing of bodies, the freshest last, and it had been easy enough to dress those two in other werewolves' clothes and position them downwind to help conceal their scent. The heart next to the overturned werewolf wasn't his.

Gabriel was going to hurt like a son of a bitch when he woke up, but being impaled on that tree wouldn't kill him.

Sig kissed my forehead. It was about the only part of my face that she could. "This was a terrible plan."

"He dahked," I said. I meant *He talked*.

And if I was right, mine wasn't the only terrible plan.

❧42❧

JUST SO YOU KNOW

I'm not going to talk much about how much pain I was in, because nobody likes a whiner. I'm not going to describe the new nightmares that experience gave me, or how violated I felt, or list all of the revenge fantasies I entertained about going back in time and meeting Nikolai again under different circumstances.

And I'm not claiming that I really could have beaten Nikolai, not on those terms. I would never have willingly entered into any kind of physical contest with Nikolai where the conditions so closely resembled a boxing match if I wanted to kill him. I would have used a weapon, or an environment with cover, or I would have executed him from a distance.

What I am saying is that putting myself in a position to be injured isn't easy just because I know I'll heal. Try it sometime. Go place the side of your face on a hot oven grill or stick fishhooks through your skin and pull on them. It won't kill you.

Go ahead. I'll wait.

Yeah, I didn't think so.

Or if you did do something like that...what the hell is wrong with you?

❧43❧

TAKE YOUR MEDICINE

We're calling Stacy." Sig's voice didn't have any give in it, and I wasn't in a great position to argue. Literally. Sig was carrying me. I had a broken knee, and I couldn't even drape an arm over her shoulder because some of my ribs were broken. Finally, she got impatient and slung me over her shoulder. My hero. Or heroine. Or heroin.

"Sig…" I slurred through broken teeth. Have you ever had that dream where your teeth are being pushed out of your gums by some inexplicable pressure? That was happening to me for real as new teeth emerged through my gums to push the old ones out of their way.

"No," she said. "Now we do this my way. You know, the way that doesn't involve one of us looking like a truck ran us over and then backed up?"

"Bud…"

"We can't do this alone," she said. "We have six tranked werewolves to deal with one way or the other and you need a place to heal and I don't know this area."

"Ah can…"

"Shut up."

"Dammid, puh me down."

She did. I managed to land on my relatively good foot, but I didn't have a chance to make my case. Pain tore into my side and Sig tore into me. "This isn't just about you, John. Other people have a stake in this! Those were good people I met this morning, and it's their clan too! They deserve to know what's going on."

Sig did know people. It was part of the whole Valkyrie thing. They don't just talk to dead people; they evaluate souls. Or at least souls not protected from such things by a geas.

"Buh..." I drooled.

She shook my shoulders and I almost screamed.

"Look at me, John. Do you trust me?"

I had wanted her to put me down so I could talk better, but I was in a lot of pain and my body really wanted to pass out so it could reserve resources for healing. I swayed there and the words wouldn't come.

"Yesh?" I said.

∿∽

It turned out Stacy had a safe house, though she probably would have called it something else. It was one of those surprises that don't really surprise you. I was in a basement den that looked like it had been decorated on the cheap from thrift stores—a mishmash of styles whose only common themes were "old" and "comfortable-looking." Propped up on a couch with a homemade palanquin of pillows, I still wasn't in a position to argue. My jaw was realigned enough that I could eat, and I was forcing soup and pudding one-handed down my throat as fast as people could bring them to me. There was currently a huge pot of vegetable stew on the coffee table next to me. To a mending werewolf, food is like coal being dumped into the furnace of an old-fashioned train engine, and I was shoveling it in.

Virgil, Tula, Matthew, Stacy, and Carl were all seated in folding chairs around the couch while Sig sat on the end of it. Bizarrely, an open laptop with Parth's face prominent on the screen was upright on Carl's lap. The real guest of honor, though, was sitting in the room's lone armchair: Ben Lafontaine, a full-blooded Anishinaabe and leader of a large Native American werewolf pack. I'd never met Ben before, but he seemed like five feet ten inches of badassed gravitas in a green polo shirt. He was unusually weathered-looking for a werewolf, wide, hard, and scarred. The man who had informally adopted Gabriel's sister but not Gabriel.

Gabriel was slumped in the center of us. We had gotten our hands on a lot of knight equipment when we cleaned out their vans and hiding places, and Gabriel was bound in silver steel restraints. One of the shock collars the knights had used to limit me to human form was also around his neck. He was awake but not talking.

"What the hell is a Gandillon?" Virgil wanted to know. Of everyone in the room, he looked the unhappiest. With the exception of Gabriel and Ben Lafontaine, he had been in the Clan longer than any of us. "And what does it have to do with Bernard wanting you dead?"

"They were a whole family of really twisted cunning folk four hundred years ago." My new teeth weren't entirely finished growing in yet, but I had worked out how to form consonant sounds again, though my face still hurt when I moved it too much. "The Gandillons were into all kinds of nasty-ass stuff. Cannibalism. Human sacrifice. Devil worship..."

"The usual," Carl deadpanned.

"Yeah," I agreed. "What made them famous is that they figured out how to re-create the spell that made the first were-
beings. They had some kind of ointment they rubbed into their
skin. It set off a hundred years of werewolf trials and inquisitions in France."

"And Nikolai told you Bernard is claiming to be one of
them," Virgil said skeptically.

"Right." I slurped down the rest of the vegetable soup in my
bowl and held it out to Sig.

She leaned over and didn't bother with a ladle, just scooped
the bowl through the pot on the table and licked her fingers
after handing it back to me. She was very tactile about food.
I still couldn't decide if it was mildly disgusting or insanely
hot.

"So what?" Matthew brought me back to my version of
reality. "Some people hunted down some werewolves. Big
surprise."

My wrist had gone from broken to sprained, and I held my
hands up side by side. "On one hand, we've got Bernard des-
perately trying to discover or re-create some kind of magical
formula. On the other, we've got Bernard claiming to come
from a family famous for discovering a magical potion to make
werewolves from scratch. Am I really reaching here?"

"You think Bernard is trying to re-create his family's discovery?" Parth didn't sound alarmed. He sounded intrigued, which
is why I hadn't wanted to include him. To a naga, forbidden
knowledge is like crack. Sig had insisted, though. According
to her, Parth possessing a secret wasn't dangerous, and he had
lots of them to prove it. It was keeping a secret from him that
was risky.

"I do," I said. "Herbs and chemicals that were part of the
first werewolf rituals affect werewolves normally, and Bernard

got really excited when a bakaak's paralyzing poison worked on werewolves. He wanted to isolate its ingredients bad."

I could actually hear Parth clap his hands as if delighted. "He can identify the elements of the compound through trial and error by finding out what other natural elements affect werewolves normally!"

"Yeah."

Stacy frowned. "But why?"

I frowned back. "Nikolai said that the Clan was going to change the world."

"I don't get it," Matthew complained. "We already know how to change people into werewolves. We just bite them. Why all the fuss about some magic potion?"

He made air quotes around "magic potion."

"That's the million-dollar question, isn't it?" I mumbled around a mouthful of soup. "What can you do with a werewolf potion that you can't do with a werewolf bite? How would it change the world?"

Sig hadn't been saying much, maybe respecting the fact that she wasn't clan. But she spoke up now. "It has to be about dissemination. You can't weaponize a werewolf bite."

The kind of too-silent silence that follows a thunderclap fell over the room. People looked around with their eyes only, reluctant to make any sudden rustles or shifts.

"You're talking what, exactly?" Virgil said eventually. "Turning this potion into a gas?"

"Or putting it into water supplies," I suggested. "Making chemical dispersal bombs out of it. Some kind of mass-effect terrorist weapon."

"This is insane," Stacy muttered.

"Why?" Gabriel blurted suddenly. "Even if all this is true, why are you all acting like it's so bad?"

I don't know if he had hopes of convincing the others to turn on Sig and me or if he had doubts that he wanted the others to help him beat down.

"The change to werewolf kills most people, Gabriel," Stacy said angrily.

"Says who?!?" he scoffed. "The knights? Have you ever actually counted how many people die from the change and figured out an average?"

"As a matter of fact, I have!" Stacy snapped. "Who do you think deals with the people who get bitten by werewolves around here? Would you like to see my records?"

That confused him for a moment, but then Gabriel shifted tactics. "Everybody dies anyway, sooner or later. Do you know what overpopulation is doing to this planet?"

"And killing people like trimming off excess fat is the solution?"

"It worked for the men who gave my people blankets infected with smallpox," Gabriel said grimly. "And what kind of life do most humans have, anyway? If everyone became werewolves, the things that make life hell wouldn't matter anymore. No more disease. No more old age. Everyone would be the same…"

"We'd still be human in every way that mattered, Gabriel," I told him. "Humans always find stupid reasons to hate each other."

"Exactly!" Gabriel said. He wasn't a very polished arguer.

"Exactly what?" I asked.

"The Pax can't last forever!" he snarled. "What do you think is going to happen when the spell gets broken and humanity realizes werewolves are real? We're all going to wind up in concentration camps or reservations if we don't do something while we have the chance! This is about survival."

Virgil stood up abruptly. "Oh, hell. This is real."

"What do you mean?" Tula asked.

Virgil leveled an index finger at Gabriel. "I've known this man for six years, and he's no philosopher. Those aren't his words coming out of his mouth. Somebody else has been preaching this trash to him."

"Come on, Virgil," Gabriel urged.

Virgil bent down so he could look Gabriel in the eyes. "John had me when he said Bernard was protecting a child murderer, you dumb son of a bitch."

Werewolves don't use that phrase lightly.

"Tula?!?" Gabriel pleaded. "You came here to fight knights."

I found it interesting that Gabriel wasn't talking to Ben Lafontaine, hadn't even looked at him, though Ben had barely taken his eyes off Gabriel since sitting down.

"I came here because I have a three-year-old daughter in Finland who is better off without me." Tula's voice was flat. "And you want to kill her."

That shut Gabriel up for a moment. I didn't know anything about a daughter. I don't think anyone in the Clan did.

"You want to kill my mom too," Carl added levelly. "I guess she's not right for your new werewolf master race, huh?"

Sig squeezed my ankle and I glanced over at her. She mouthed the word *See?*

Ben spoke up for the first time. "Tell Gabriel what you told me about Catherine."

"What?" Gabriel's head shot up.

"Nikolai also said that Bernard is making Mila Apraxin his new queen," I said. "Have you talked to Catherine lately?"

Gabriel tried to stay angry, but something uncertain and vulnerable came into his eyes. For a second, he looked like the little brother who had clung to a big sister in that Catholic orphanage he'd mentioned. "Bernard wouldn't…"

"Which Bernard?" Ben asked. "The one who's willing to kill four out of every five people for his vision? The one who offers shelter to a child killer?"

Ben indicated me. "The Bernard who sent Nikolai to kill this man who had served Bernard faithfully? The Bernard who's proud of coming from a family of witches? Which one of these men wouldn't get rid of your sister, Gabriel?"

Gabriel tried to talk, but his mind was busy going over conversations that I'd never heard, clues I'd never seen, excuses for Catherine's disappearance. "Everybody loves Catherine; Bernard would never get away with it even if he wanted…"

"He already is getting away with it," Ben said. "He tells me that he has information that the knights are after Catherine to get leverage over him… that a claw is keeping her on the move and that even he won't know where she is from hour to hour for the next few days. Sometime soon, Catherine's body is going to be discovered with a silver bullet in the head, and Bernard will say, 'I told you so.' He will use her death as a symbol to rally the Clan around whatever plans he proposes."

Gabriel began to thrash around in his chains then.

"Compose yourself!" Ben snapped.

And Gabriel did.

"Bernard knows you would never let that happen." Gabriel's voice was ragged. "He knows you love Catherine even if you never liked me."

"Bernard doesn't care if I believe him or not," Ben replied sadly. "He doesn't need our tribe any longer, and some of my own people listen to Bernard more than they do me now, young men like you who think the old ways are weak ways and don't listen to our stories."

"Your stories are the same as any other religion!" Gabriel yelled. "You just use them to keep people from wanting to change anything! You want to pretend we're proud while we're living in slums!"

"This man is right," Ben said calmly, pointing a thumb at Virgil. "You open your mouth, and another man's words come out."

Gabriel's mouth tightened.

"You are such a rebel, Gabriel Flores." Ben's voice was level. "Such a daring young man. Turning against your own people because of the sweet lies of a white man. That's different."

"ALL RIGHT!" Gabriel yelled. "ALL RIGHT!"

We waited.

"All right, what?" I finally asked.

"I'll help you find out what happened to Catherine," he said sullenly.

Matthew laughed bitterly then. He was the only person who did. "Time for a reality check there, Gabriel! They aren't asking for your help. They're trying to figure out whether or not to kill you."

"Ben would never let you do that." Gabriel shot Ben a hot glare full of frustration. "He wants to take me to a shaking tent or some bullshit like that."

I stopped eating long enough to address Ben then. "I can't tell if he loves you or hates you."

Ben still hadn't taken his eyes off Gabriel. "It's complicated."

Matthew stretched and looked around. "Well, this episode of *As the Wigwam Turns* has been great and all, but why am I here? If you guys want to go against Bernard, I'll keep my mouth shut. But if you want me to help, I want hard proof that any of this is real."

I guess expecting Matthew to become a completely different person was unrealistic. Then I saw him slide a sideways glance toward Carl, and it suddenly occurred to me that Matthew was showing off.

Huh.

Come to think of it, Matthew ruled a bunch of macho alpha male types, and he didn't have a female mate. Could it be that he was overcompensating?

"If we had proof, we wouldn't be having a secret meeting," Stacy snapped. "We'd be leading a mob."

"So, most of the Clan really doesn't know about any of this?" I asked. "I wasn't walking around with a big sign on my back that said DON'T TELL THE KNIGHT ABOUT THE BIG WEREWOLF PLAN?"

"We're not monsters, John," Carl said irritably, then paused and laughed bitterly. "Well..."

"Most of us have families and friends and ex-lovers who aren't werewolves," Stacy said. "I'm dating a normal human right now."

I was ashamed.

Matthew cleared his throat. "Proof, remember?"

Ben looked over at Virgil. "You have Bernard's number on your cell phone, yes?" he asked.

"I've got one of them," he said dourly. "He left a few messages on it before I pulled the battery out."

"Put the battery back in," Ben told him.

⚬44⚬

MY, GRANDMA! WHAT A BIG ASSHOLE YOU ARE!

Where the hell have you been?" Bernard's voice demanded. Virgil didn't have the phone on speaker, but he didn't need to. We were all werewolves except for Sig.

"I've been moving bodies out of the hot zone," Virgil said. "Nikolai is dead and John isn't much better."

There was a long pause before Bernard asked, "How?"

Virgil exhaled heavily. "All I know is, Tula comes by and tells me that Nikolai and Gabriel are fighting because Gabriel wants to talk to his sister and things are getting a little out of hand. So I go to the hot zone, but nobody is outside it anymore. So I follow my GPS until it goes fuckways and close my eyes and stomp on the accelerator and next thing I know, Tula and I are in the zone and I still don't see anybody."

Bernard didn't interrupt.

"So we go down to that weird wooded patch," Virgil continued. "And it's crazy. There's a whole claw down there in chains and drugged. Gabriel has got a tree going through him. Nikolai is dead. And John looks like he's been hit by a truck. I mean, he's broken, man. Shattered. You know John can pick pockets, right? It looks to me like Nikolai was beating the shit out of him when John got his hands on Nikolai's gun."

Virgil paused but Bernard still didn't say anything.

"So maybe *you* should tell *me* what happened," Virgil finished.

"I have no idea," Bernard said gravely. "What did John say?"

"John couldn't say anything even if he was awake. His body is taking its time pulling itself back together."

"I sent Nikolai to get John because John took it on himself to execute four werewolves and wasn't telling Phoenix what he was finding at the Apraxin house," Bernard asserted. "John hasn't been returning my phone calls, either. I thought we needed to talk. That's it."

"Nikolai had a claw with him," Virgil noted.

"They were there to replace you guys in Abalmar when you leave," Bernard said. "The knights just lost a lot of people, and they don't handle that kind of thing well. I'm worried about how they're going to retaliate."

"Yeah," Virgil sighed.

"Where's John now?" Bernard asked. "What did you do with the others? I've got locals looking all over for you."

"That's why I've been busy," Virgil explained. "Tula and me have got them all tranked and in chains because I don't know what's going on. We've moved them to John's safe house."

Another pause before Bernard clarified. "John's safe house?"

Virgil made a confused face even though Bernard couldn't see it. He was a good actor. "Yeah. His safe house."

"What the hell, Virgil."

"Hey, man," Virgil said, "I thought you knew."

"I know Nikolai and John hated each other." Bernard's voice was earnest. "I know John's been acting erratic ever since you raided that house. And I know Nikolai is dead. That's all I know. Is it possible these evil spirits you were all talking about this morning brought out the worst in them?"

"John said ghosts couldn't get inside his head," Virgil said slowly. "I don't know about Nikolai."

"Well, what does this exorcist you hired say?"

"I never saw her," Virgil explained. "She had lit out by the time I got there."

"Well, maybe we'd better find her." There was no maybe in his voice.

"What do you want me to do in the meantime?" Virgil asked.

"Get the claw that came with Nikolai back on their feet. You and Tula help them bring John to me. We need to get to the bottom of this."

"Where are you?" Virgil asked.

"Not over the phone," Bernard said. "Just tell Shane to take over for Nikolai and bring John back to the place they came from. Tell him to call me. You can follow them."

"All right," Virgil said. "It might take a bit to get them back on their feet. Do you want me to tell the locals any of this?"

"No," Bernard said. "I think your instincts were good there. We don't know what's going on yet. Don't tell anyone anything that might start a panic."

"All right," Virgil repeated.

"And, Virgil?"

"Yeah?"

"It might be that Nikolai finally decided to kill John for the good of the Clan without my approval. Or it might be that those two finally got in a pissing contest that went too far. Or it might be that the knights are manipulating this somehow. Or maybe John has an agenda I don't know about. Or maybe some evil spirit really did make Nikolai go crazy. Until we know for sure, you keep John drugged, all right?"

"Yeah."

"I mean it, Virgil. I know you've been working with John a lot. I like him too. But he's too dangerous to take chances with. Even to talk to. That's an order."

"I understand."

"And, Virgil?"

"Yeah."

"Did you say Gabriel wasn't chained like the others?"

" . . . "

"Virgil?"

"No," Virgil said. "He was impaled on a broken tree."

"Why wasn't he in chains like the others? Is it possible he and this exorcist helped John take down Nikolai's claw, and Nikolai got free of it?"

Virgil frowned. "I don't know."

"Maybe you'd better keep Gabriel drugged and in chains too. Until we figure this out."

Virgil sighed. "All right."

"I know this is bad business, Virgil. I'm grateful you're there."

" . . . "

"And, Virgil?"

"Yeah?"

"Keep your cell phone on. I'm worried."

The phone went dead.

Gabriel cursed, and Virgil stared at the phone as if someone had just shit in his hand.

"That sounded reasonable." Matthew was thoughtful.

"Bernard always sounds reasonable," Ben said dryly.

"Yeah." Apparently, that was Virgil's new favorite word. "It all made sense."

"What I want to know, though, is if Bernard has locals looking for John, how come this is the first I've heard of it?" Matthew looked at Stacy inquiringly.

"I haven't heard anything, either," Stacy informed him.

"It's because you publically stated that you wouldn't work with Mila Apraxin this morning," I told Matthew. "Bernard wants you out of the picture. I think he was counting on me killing you when he sent me here."

Matthew sighed. "Maybe. I know that Shane and his claw didn't come here to take anybody's place. They're one of Nikolai's kill crews. He calls them waste disposal units."

"How do you know this?" Stacy asked him.

"Nikolai's got...I mean...had people who specialize in making problems disappear. I'm pretty sure he got rid of Ray Morgan."

"The guy that you replaced?" I asked Matthew.

"Yes," Stacy said tightly. "Ray was a good man. I always wondered if Matthew killed him."

That would explain a lot of their dysfunction.

"It's a virus," Gabriel said suddenly.

We all shut up.

"What's a virus, Gabriel?" Ben asked gently.

"That science geek working with Phoenix? He used to work for the government making manmade bio-plagues or something. Bernard says that the thing that changes us to werewolves is a virus, and the potion is the virus in a bottle...that it seeps into our skin and gets in our bloodstream. Bernard wants to make it an airborne disease. Like that flu that killed millions of people."

"Swine flu?" I asked. The swine flu killed somewhere around a hundred million people at the turn of the twentieth century, hundreds of thousands on American soil. It was before my time, but people were still talking about it when I was born. And it's threatened to break out a few more times since.

"Yeah," Gabriel said.

"Bernard wants to make a werewolf flu?" Virgil demanded.

"Yes," Gabriel snarled. "There's more to it. Chants and stuff that have to be said. But if people were already infected, Bernard could drive cars through cities playing the chants on loudspeakers, or broadcast them on radios and televisions, or send them out on prerecorded cell phone messages, or put them on Internet sites. It would trigger hundreds of thousands of people on the first full moon, and then we'd have werewolf outbreaks all over the place."

Holy shit. Bernard never wanted peace with the knights. He just wanted to get them off his back long enough to lay the groundwork for a werewolf plague. He used me to distract them. Again.

I looked at Mathew. "Is that enough proof for you?"

Matthew's jaw tightened. "It'll do."

∽45∽

ARE WE THERE YET?

I woke up bound and gagged in the trunk of a car, silver steel chains locking my hands and feet into a fetal position and one of the knight's shock collars around my neck. The back of my head was covered with dried blood. The trunk was only separated from the main body of the car by vinyl, some stuffing, and a thin layer of cardboard covered in fabric, and my eyes had mutated to see in infrared. I could see two warm glows where bodies were pressed against the backseat. Virgil was talking to Shane from the passenger's side of the front, commenting on some crazy-looking woman who was driving past them, and there was music playing low on the car's radio. Kelly Clarkson, actually, singing some song I recognized but couldn't name. I don't know why that seemed bizarre.

Everything was going according to plan.

They'd had to sedate me. Shane and his claw had werewolf senses, and just pretending to be asleep wasn't going to cut it. I know something about meditation and have integrated skills from a lot of different martial arts too, but putting myself in some kind of trance that resembles suspended animation or hibernation is beyond me. So my friends had sedated me, but they'd sedated me lightly. The dried blood was from where I'd made a shallow slice in my scalp in a place that would bleed profusely. We'd wanted to make it look like Virgil had shot me in the back of the head with a lead bullet just to play it safe.

Shane and his claw were taking me to Bernard's hideaway.

There was a key hidden in the spare tire, and it wasn't hard to work my way loose. The werewolves in the car had enhanced hearing, but between the music, Virgil, and the degraded state of Wisconsin's highways, I had a lot of background noise to cover me. I was rattling around in the trunk like a castanet, and I timed my biggest movements and clicks with passing trucks, of which there were many.

Gabriel was similarly bound in the other car.

The next hour passed like a kidney stone. I didn't take off all of my chains. I just freed my limbs enough that I could reach out and verify that there was a sawed-off shotgun lying under a nearby blanket. The sedation the knights used on werewolves still gave me a bad case of cottonmouth, and my muscles were stiff and cramped. I would have sacrificed a pinky or a small toe just to be able to stretch.

Virgil kept up a steady stream of background noise, chatting as if unaware of how tense the other werewolves in the car were. He fiddled with the radio, found pretexts to call Tula, who was in the car behind us with two other werewolves, and kept up a running commentary on the cars we passed, the people driving them, the weather, the time of year, and the background music. The only thing I really paid any attention to was the description of the places we were passing. The car was headed for Milwaukee.

The amazing thing is, Virgil wasn't annoying. I could feel the atmosphere decompress a little all the way from the trunk as the other passengers gradually relaxed, lulled by the banality and repetition of Virgil's words over time and the complete ease with which he spoke them. You never would have guessed that Virgil thought they were planning to kill him.

Eventually, the density of traffic sounds and the quality of the roads changed. The car headed to some secluded rural place, first traveling over gravel roads and then dirt ones on the way there. Everything was still going to plan—not that it was much of a plan—until I heard Virgil ask, "Why are you messing with the GPS?"

There was an awkward pause. A werewolf's sense of direction is about as close to infallible as anything contained in mere flesh can get, and Shane obviously hadn't anticipated this question. It was a werewolf in the backseat who answered. "This place is real hush-hush. We've never been here before."

I couldn't make out his heartbeat over all the other background hums and thumps, but I didn't have to do so to know he was lying.

"Yeah." Shane sounded a little too grateful for the intervention. He was tough, six feet of coiled, curly-haired, hard-eyed muscle, but Shane was no actor.

That's when I realized that we'd forgotten something. Something critical.

Using a GPS was one of the ways we'd worked out for getting past the hot zone back in Abalmar. Shane had probably turned on his GPS for the same reason that Bernard had stopped calling every half an hour or so. Mila Apraxin was waiting at our destination, and she had set up another hot zone. The problem with that was, Parth was remotely tracking us by hacking into the cars' online GPS systems and sending the coordinates to Sig and Matthew and Ben Lafontaine. If the hideaway was behind one of Mila's magical barriers, all of that would go offline and our reinforcements wouldn't be able to follow us in.

Screw that.

I was already letting Shane's claw drive me God knew where into God knew what surrounded by God knew how many guards while I was shut up in a lunchbox; I wasn't doing it without backup. Risk I can handle. Even insane risk if the stakes are high enough. But I wasn't committing outright suicide.

And with the GPS coordinates, I didn't need Shane's claw to show me where Bernard's hideout was any longer, anyhow.

Change of plan.

We were on a gravel road, not going very fast, and I couldn't hear any other cars except for the claw members following us. I grabbed the shotgun, pointed it at one of the warm red glows where the werewolves in the backseat were showing up on my infravision, and pulled one trigger, then moved the barrel slightly to the left and unloaded the other barrel.

The shotgun's shells were a mix of lead pellets and small silver beads, and the blasts tore through the backseat and ripped into the werewolves while they were still shifting at the sound of my activity behind them.

I wished I'd remembered to bring earplugs.

The backseat of the car was filled with blood and feathery down and viscera as the car abruptly braked. I was hurled forward through the hole I'd made of the backseat, into the corpses of two werewolves and against the front seats where Virgil and Shane were wrestling. I fumbled through the chaos until I found a gun still holstered at the side of one of the dead werewolves.

Shane hadn't managed to get his seat belt off, and his movements were hampered while Virgil managed to get him in a headlock. From there, it was over. Virgil used his greater body weight and leverage to snap Shane's neck.

My body was still stiff, and being hurled through the car hadn't helped. My leg circulation was impaired, and I still had chains tangled around me, and I actually fell out of the backseat while trying to fumble my way out of it. We were on some kind of rural road curving around a mountainside, and the car behind us had screeched to a halt in the middle of it. Gabriel had taken his cue and unloaded his own shotgun from the trunk, but Tula had not managed to subdue her driver. He was a large werewolf who looked like a linebacker.

One of my chains had snagged on something, and I lay on the road and tried to train my gun on the big head of Tula's attacker. He and Tula were thrashing around frantically. Cursing, I lurched to my feet and wriggled out of my bonds and my legs buckled and dropped me to my hands and knees. There was a shot behind me, and then Virgil slammed a car door and walked past me. Part of his left ear was missing and the top of his left shoulder was ragged and bloody.

Tula was helpfully digging her thumbs into the large werewolf's throat and pushing his head up above the dashboard when Virgil threw open the driver's side door and shot him.

I didn't give them much time to think or process. "You two need to go up opposite sides of the road and keep any cars from passing through while I get my circulation back," I gasped. "Tell them there's been an accident and the police are waiting for a tow truck."

Virgil said something that I couldn't hear through ruptured eardrums, but I could tell he saw the sense of what I'd said. The cars were a mess. Literally. So much so that it was kind of surreal. All around us, a thin layer of frost coated the trees on one side of the road and the embankment leading to a creek on the other. The air was heavy and still and sad and solemn. It was as if I were standing in the middle of an unintentionally somber Christmas card.

We hadn't brought a lot of water or industrial-strength cleaners or rags, which was probably another oversight.

By the time Sig and Matthew and Ben pulled their vehicles up and parked as far to the side of the road as they could to join us, Gabriel and I were on our feet and moving down to the creek, taking shirts we'd removed from our victims to soak into the water.

Sig was driving a Honda Fit by herself, and Matthew was driving a Firebird with three werewolves that he still trusted in it. Ben was driving a moving van whose storage area was full of Anishinaabe warriors.

One of the werewolves Matthew had brought along took one whiff of the inside of the cars, saw what I was doing, and vomited. I briefly explained why the plan had gotten yanked sideways.

"How far away do you think we are?" Sig was looking around nervously.

"If there's a hot zone, we're about twenty miles away from it, according to the GPS."

But Sig wasn't nervous about being near Bernard's lair. My forearms began to break into gooseflesh and my neck tensed. The temperature around us was dropping and wisps of mist were beginning to gather in response as hot and cold air currents collided. My heart was beginning to pump blood faster in a fight-or-flight response.

Ghosts were in the air.

∾46∾

DEAD AHEAD

Sig?"

She came up next to me and squeezed my forearm. I followed her eyes and saw that fog was condensing thicker and faster out in the woods to our left, roiling into a ground cloud. A silhouette of a large wolf came stepping gingerly to the edges of visibility. Then another.

More wolves were beginning to manifest as the mist continued to thicken, a rolling bank of it emerging from the woods and flowing over us. A wolf, or at least something with a wolf's general outline, walked past us down the road. Then another.

I whispered to Sig, "And you say weird shit happens around *me*?"

Were Valkyries some kind of ghost magnets or something?

She squeezed my arm again. "People keep saying the Pax is breaking down. Maybe it's true."

Ben was murmuring something in Anishinaabe, and I realized that he was talking to the men in the back of the moving van.

When a wolf with no scent passed near Gabriel, it growled. Gabriel backed away hurriedly, his eyes wide and terrified.

Several more ghost wolves passed. Some kept walking, but some halted, turned, and waited. They seemed to want us to follow.

Ben moved to the back of the moving van and opened it. Then he began taking off his clothes as members of his pack jumped out on the ground. They soon followed Ben's suit. Or followed his un-suit. Or something.

Apparently, the Anishinaabe attitude toward spirits is much different from mine.

"What about your weapons?" I asked.

"They want us to join them as wolves," Ben said simply.

"Ben," I said. "They're ghosts. That doesn't make them smarter or nicer. It just makes them dead."

He ignored me.

I tried again. "We can't leave our vehicles here like this!"

Ben smiled tightly. "This is what happens when you ask a bunch of injuns to play the cavalry."

I just stared at him.

"This is our story, John," Ben told me simply. "You're just a side character."

And Ben changed into a wolf. He transformed seamlessly and ran down the road, after the ghost wolves. His followers... followed.

I heard Virgil yelling as they passed around the bend, but I just stared and listened until I couldn't hear them anymore.

I turned to Sig. "Fucking ghosts. No wonder you have a drinking problem."

Sig didn't smile, but she wasn't offended either, thank God. There's a thin line between a smart-ass and a dumb-ass, and I think I might have crossed it there. I was rattled.

"A lot of werewolves have died around here, John," Sig said somberly. "And died badly. Things like that don't just happen."

"A lot of wolves have," Gabriel offered miserably, and we looked at him.

"I know where we are." Gabriel seemed crushed and empty, the human version of a beer can that had been tossed aside. The ghost wolves hadn't wanted him along.

"What is it, Gabriel?" I walked around and turned the car on while I talked to him. He watched as I pressed the button that made all the windows go down. It would be easier than trying to wipe them off, and ghosts appearing didn't mean we had more time. Hell, it meant we had less.

Gabriel cleared his throat. "We're going to the school."

Matthew directed his friends back to the creek to soak more clothes for rags, and Sig began removing seat covers. Nobody wanted to get in the backseats, but we draped blankets from the trunk over the ruined vinyl and concentrated on cleaning off the parts of the cars that were visible through the remaining windows, while Gabriel talked.

"It used to be one of those old-fashioned schoolhouses back in the fifties," Gabriel said. "The kind in the middle of nowhere. Bernard sends werewolves who can't control themselves there. They get hard-core."

"Define hard-core." I was applying elbow grease to the dashboard by this point.

"Whips. Electric shock. Waterboarding. Bernard said it was a last chance to save werewolves who had gone over the line. Teach them some control. Catherine said..." Gabriel hesitated.

"Catherine said what?" Matthew's voice was quiet as he joined Gabriel.

"She called it Bernard's obedience school," Gabriel said reluctantly. "She was starting to worry that Bernard was using it to get rid of people who were causing him other kinds of problems."

"Yeah, Gabriel," I said. "Just fill the world up with werewolves and it will be a utopia. All the stupid things we fight about will just melt away."

Gabriel shot me a ferocious look. "Can we just get my sister?"

"Hold on," I said, and went to the trunk and fished out more of the gear we'd hidden, including some fresh clothes and a machete. It was no katana, but it was better than using harsh language. "Matthew, I think we've done enough to keep anybody from calling the cops on sight. Can you and your crew stay behind to get rid of this mess and tell Parth and Carl what's going on?"

He could.

What was left of my claw started to pile into Sig's car, and I indicated that Sig should get behind the steering wheel.

"Shouldn't you drive?" she wondered. Sig was used to being the leader of her own team. She had handled me calling the shots for my claw fairly gracefully, but it was still an adjustment. "You're the only one here who won't be affected by the ward."

"They'll have at least one sentry hiding behind the ward wherever your GPS blinks out," I said.

"You're going to use me as bait," Sig said pensively.

"As a distraction," I admitted. "You're good at it."

Her face suddenly broke into a warm smile. "You're not trying to protect me."

I guess if she was sane, she wouldn't have anything to do with me.

~47~

THE ROAD LESS GRAVELED

Two roads diverged in a frosted wood,
One more of an extended driveway
Protected by a strong spell that stood
Ward against any stranger who should
Wander off Route 52 that day.

A sentry guarded the hot zone there,
Watching from the trees behind the edge
Of that dark spell's sway, and in the air
He aimed a rifle at just the spot where
The trail formed a tunnel through the hedge.

He was distracted by yells and screams
From the trees around him, from the school
Where wolves had raced through woods to end the schemes
Of a man, no true wolf he, whose dark dreams
Had led so many of us to play the fool.

But the guard stayed to his lonely end,

DARING

And aimed his gun at my companion,
Sig, caught by the spell at that road's bend.
But I had scouted a path downwind,
And that made all the difference.

Because I shoved a silver steel knife through his fucking ear
  canal before he was finished turning around.

ᔏ48ᔐ

GETTING SCHOOLED

There was perhaps a twenty-foot-long area where it still wasn't clear if we were in the winding path that was a driveway or in the clearing surrounding the old schoolhouse, a limbo where the trees lining the trail thinned and the high, hanging branches overhead opened up to the Wisconsin sky.

Fall had stripped branches of their leaves, and I could see patchwork glimpses of the schoolhouse where Sig had stopped the car. It was a brick building, two stories tall, and according to Gabriel each story was four large classrooms, two on each side separated by a large hall. It was an old building, the brick faded but sturdy-looking, the wood doors and window frames patched and peeling. Only the roof looked new.

I came out of the trees from where I had been scouting the sides of the trail ahead of them, and Virgil emerged from the other side. Sig made the front windows come down so that we could talk.

"Last chance to save your underpants," I said.

Gabriel and Tula were in Sig's Fit. The sounds of gunfire and yells and roars were all around us, but they weren't coming from the school. They were coming from the surrounding woods.

Tula snorted and got out of the passenger side. She was carrying her sniper rifle, and she walked past me. "I'm going to set up at the edge of the tree line."

"What's going on?" Sig circled her finger to indicate the sounds around us.

"I think that schoolhouse is the piece of cheese in a very large trap," I said. "And Ben and his people sprang it."

Sig nodded at the schoolhouse. "So that's wide open now?"

"Gabriel and I have to go. The rest of you don't."

It was true. Gabriel was driven to find his sister, and I was driven by a geas. I hadn't felt its effects full-force in some time, but even the possibility that Bernard was planning to set off some kind of werewolf plague had caused it to kick in with a vengeance. I could practically feel it vibrating in my teeth. No matter what happened, Bernard wasn't going to use the schoolhouse as a secret base anymore after today, and there was no way I was going to let him just disappear without at least trying to run him to ground right here, right now.

"I love cheese," Virgil said. "Why do you think I live in Wisconsin?"

Sig seemed bored. "Get in the car."

I climbed in the passenger side while Virgil got in the back. "Let's go in from the side."

Sig made a comment about me teaching my grandmother to suck something. It wasn't eggs. She stomped down on the accelerator.

As soon as we emerged into the clearing, Sig swerved sharply off the driveway, plowing over the high grass toward the right of the schoolhouse. There was a flash from the attic level of the building, and our windshield and the rear left window shattered as a bullet passed over Sig's left shoulder at an angle. I'm pretty sure the next sound I heard was Tula's TRG-42 from the edge of the woods, taking out the sniper who'd fired at us from the school's attic, or at least distracting him pretty effectively.

Two hybrid wolf-men in full battle frenzy leaped out of first-floor windows in our direction as we neared the building, traveling at least fifteen feet through the air, and Sig swerved toward them. One of them practically bounced off the ground as he leaped out of the way, but the other had to take a few steps as he landed on the uneven surface, and the car rammed him right above the knees before he could clear the hood. Instead of flipping over the car, his hips were carried backward and he went down beneath us.

The jolting impact triggered the airbags and I never saw the other werewolf again. I'm guessing Tula took him out. The car didn't stop and neither did I. I stabbed my knife into the air-bags so that Sig wouldn't have to keep driving from memory, and we cleared the corner of the school. She pulled the car up so that it was parked directly beneath a first-story window.

A man inside that first classroom came running up to the window and started to aim an assault rifle down at us, but I shot him from the passenger seat, firing my sawed-off shotgun through the open space that used to be our windshield. The man went flying backward in a maelstrom of splintered wood and shattered glass, blown out like a birthday candle.

I peeled an airbag off of me and climbed out through the windshield space, got to my feet quickly, and stood on the hood of the car while Sig and Virgil and Gabriel poured out through the doors. I had a clear view into the room and didn't see anyone else, so I grabbed on to the remains of the window frame with one hand, gripped my shotgun in the other, and stepped onto the ledge, pulling myself into the building.

I was in a closed room. There were lab tables set against the west side, not old-fashioned wooden ones with exotic-looking curved glass tubes and pestles like you'd expect to see in a cunning folk's study, but matte black tables with stainless steel cases and a variety of empty beakers and vials and scales that were covered in the blood of the werewolf I had just ended. What was left of him lay on the floor without twitching.

Cages lined the east wall, not jail cells and not pet cages, but animal cages like you would see in a zoo, thick-barred and navel-high. There were werewolves in them, some in wolf form and some naked and human, but werewolves like I had never seen. They were burned and scarred and maimed and covered in patches where neither flesh nor hair had grown back, missing limbs or staring blindly through chemically ravaged faces.

Some were barely standing as the sounds of fighting echoed and some were lying down and some were dead or so close that it made no difference. Some were huddled in a fetal position whimpering and some were pressed against the back of their cages, growling weakly.

Understanding hit me like a tidal wave. Like Parth had said, if the ingredients from the spell that made the first werewolves affected werewolves normally, then one way to discover what those ingredients were would be to expose werewolves to them. You could test werewolves' reactions to a wide variety of plants and minerals and chemicals and compounds and see which ones affected werewolves the same way they would any other human.

Bernard was using werewolves like lab animals.

Virgil came through the window behind me, and I wordlessly handed him the shotgun and indicated the closed door with a headshake. For the first time in a long, long time, my hand was shaking while holding a weapon, and not from fear. Virgil took the shotgun and nodded, training it on the door while Sig and Gabriel climbed through after him.

One wolf seemed fairly unharmed, a female, and she came to the edge of her cage, and Gabriel ran to her, yelling, "Cat!"

I hadn't intended to pause, even for a few seconds, but something happened then that completely took me offline for a moment. The wolf, Catherine, changed to human form, but it wasn't anybody named Catherine I saw.

It was Mayte Reyes.

❧49❧

UNREADY, UPSET, FIRE

Mayte didn't seem physically injured, but she had apparently ingested or been injected with something. She seemed disoriented and sluggish.

We didn't have time for this. Virgil was still training the shotgun on the room's only obvious entry point, and Sig was pulling some keys from what was left of the werewolf I'd killed, probably intending to release at least one of the werewolves so that it could free others.

But I wasted a second anyhow. "Mayte is your sister, Catherine? Bernard's mate?"

"Bernard wanted you to form a bond with someone in your paw," Gabriel said tersely, pulling Mayte out of the cage. "He had Cat pretend to be a newbie to make sure that you did."

Okay, so it was an unconventional marriage. Move on, move on. There was no time. But I stayed rooted there anyway.

"And the fire?" My voice sounded like someone who had been lost in a desert.

"Bernard sent me away before it happened," Mayte gasped.

"Like maybe he knew that it was going to happen. I started asking questions."

And wound up here.

Sig was in the corner of the room, fiddling with a key ring in front of a cage where another wolf had gotten to its feet. "John?"

Oh. I hadn't talked to Sig about Mayte. Something else there wasn't time for. As if to emphasize that point, there was an explosion and the door to the room flew off of its hinges, its outer side in flames.

Virgil fired the shotgun, but the door came straight at him and absorbed most of the silver shot before hitting him. A stream of fire followed while Virgil was knocking the door aside, and Virgil ignited.

Phoenix came charging into the room, wild-eyed and hopped-up on whatever drug or drugs he took, and his black staff was burning. He swiped it through the air and another trail of fire lashed out at Gabriel, but Gabriel managed to pick the door up where Virgil had deflected it and propped it up, hiding behind it while flames traveled over its surface.

I had grabbed a fire extinguisher off the wall by this point, intending to use it on Virgil, but Phoenix was orienting my way and I didn't have time to do anything but run forward and swing the extinguisher like a weapon to intercept Phoenix's staff. Wood and metal collided in a small explosion of flame, the black thorns in Phoenix's weapon actually puncturing the thin metal of the red canister and sending dry foam hissing between us.

I yanked the fire extinguisher back while Phoenix's staff was still caught in it and ripped his weapon out of his hands, flinging the still-burning staff behind me. He took a wild swing at me then, his face contorted, eyes not even seeming to recognize me while thick ropes of saliva clung to his beard. He missed, overbalanced, and I swung the fire extinguisher again, catching Phoenix on the side of the temple and knocking him backward into the next werewolf who was coming into the doorway. I was still reaching for the USP pistol at my side when Sig's spear went through Phoenix's chest and out the other side of the werewolf he had stumbled against.

She does things like that.

They tottered there in the doorway, stuck to each other, a wolf kebab, unwilling Siamese twins, neither of them dead and neither of them completely functioning. I tossed the spouting fire extinguisher on top of Virgil where he was rolling and screaming on the floor, and stepped forward with my pistol drawn. Got up close, one shot, two shots, putting silver bullets square in both their heads, and then I stepped over them when they fell.

The main hallway of the schoolhouse was deserted except for Mila Apraxin.

∽50∾

A MURDER OF CROWS

I was facing the landing of a wide wooden stairway traveling upward. Well, I guess it could have been traveling downward because stairs are like that, but screw it. There wasn't much sound coming from that upper floor, but it was the kind of charged silence people make when they're listening. If you've never heard, or not heard, that type of silence, I don't know how to describe it to you.

Wolf smell was all over the place. There were only two reasons I could see that I wasn't being swarmed en masse. Either the werewolves upstairs had some seriously good fortifications, or they had been told to stay up there because the bottom floor was a trap and they might become collateral damage when I sprang it. I was betting on the latter.

The Baba Yaga was standing at the opposite end of the hall.

Mila was pale and dark-haired, her red lips standing out like a bloody wound against that marble skin. She wore two red sashes of some kind of gauzy material, one loosely wrapped around her breasts and one looped over her waist. A metal charm hung beneath her throat, and draped over her back was a cloak made of living crows. Their wings fluttered intermittently, their caws soft as they rustled against her too-flawless skin. Her hands were empty, though I don't know that I would call her unarmed. Her fingernails were long and painted yellow and glistened with something that probably wasn't nail polish, or at least not any kind that you could buy from a store.

She started to say something about me being someone who had killed someone or other, but I cut her off by firing my gun at her. The only thing she had to say that I wanted to hear was a death scream.

Unfortunately, Mila was protected by the same kind of magnetic charm that had protected the old vedma from metal attacks back in Abalmar, and I could hear my bullets smacking high into the wall to the right and left of her, see the little puffs of plaster and rock dust they made.

I started to cautiously step forward, but Sig's voice from the doorway halted me. "Hold it. It's a trap."

Well, I knew that. "How?"

"There's a ghost tethered in the walls," Sig said tonelessly. "Just give me a moment."

But Mila Apraxin wasn't inclined to wait once she realized that we weren't charging forward. She gestured, and a line of fire began sparking along the wall, the outline of a wire pressing against paint and plaster like a tendon straining against flesh. Plaster shattered and a sparking wire burst free and writhed in the air before us like a long black snake, then hurtled toward Sig, its sparking tip its fangs.

I grabbed the wire out of midair, caught it by the insulated surface beneath its exposed wires, then whirled and managed to wrap it around my forearm several times while its body thrashed. Dancing back, I extended it tight and yanked hard and down with all of my body weight, snapping the wire off from the wall at a point some twenty feet away from us.

Boards in the floor began shooting upward into the air then, in a straight line moving away from Mila, as if they were keys on a piano and a giant invisible hand was running over them, coming toward me. Sig jumped past me and drove a spear that was still covered with the blood of two men into the floor, yelling something in some Scandinavian language that I was going to have to learn if we survived. The boards stopped moving when they reached the point of that spear, as if something underground had run into a large rock.

Just for the record, I don't know how she did that.

"It's all right, little soul," Sig said softly, pulling her spear from the ground and whirling it so that she could heft it backward. The wooden end was sharpened into a point for vampire staking.

Mila threw a fireball then, and I don't think it was magic at all but some cunning folk trick, some mixture of tar and phosphorous and fertilizer. Sig's spear shattered it into flaming pieces at any rate, the wooden point bursting through the blazing sphere in midair and catching fire as it passed. Mila disappeared in a blinding flurry of black feathers and outraged caws as the crows encasing her took flight.

When the maelstrom of carrion birds rose higher, it became clear that Mila was no longer standing there. Sig's spear was embedded in the far wall, quivering. It wasn't until I saw the red sashes and the metal charm lying on the floor that I fully understood.

"She's become a crow!" I shouted, emptying my pistol into that dark cloud and throwing it aside as fluttering wings and glistening claws engulfed Sig. Then my machete was out and we were both inside that murder of crows. I don't know how many of the birds there were to begin with...I never counted. Twenty, maybe? But Sig and I were both wearing layered clothing and wielding edged weapons at speeds that no human could have matched. A talon scratched the back of my hand and left a burning trail there, another took a small piece of my neck with it and left blazing agony in its wake, but the poison wasn't wolfsbane—I don't know if Bernard didn't trust Mila enough to let her arm a small flying army with werewolf poison, or if it had only been a day and Mila had been busy negotiating terms and setting up a new ward. The immune system of my kind is formidable in any case, and I kept moving.

We burst through the other side of that cloud and there were perhaps six crows still alive and no longer interested in attacking us. They were flying toward the stairway that we'd just left behind. Sig took her gun out of her holster, and somehow she picked Mila Apraxin out of those birds, though she must have fired half a dozen shots in rapid succession before she hit her. I don't know if that was some kind of psychic thing, or if Sig somehow figured out which crow was Mila by its position, or if it was just luck. All I know is, there was an explosion of feathers and blood, and then Mila's body fell to the floor.

So did Sig's. The only thing holding her up had been willpower.

I dropped down beside Sig. Her face was covered in scratches. Poisoned scratches, the slight wounds already reddening and turning to rashes as her body fought the effects. Sig is tougher than a normal human, and her bones and muscles are hard, but her immune system doesn't bounce back as fast as mine does. I regenerate. Sig endures.

In a kinder world, I would have had time to drag Sig to a sink and hold her face under running water, but someone upstairs had seen Mila's body at the base of the stairway, and wolves came hurtling down the stairs then, more than half a dozen of them. Gabriel came charging out of the doorway of the lab in wolf form, howling a challenge and meeting them at the base of the stairs, but he didn't have a chance.

He bought me a few seconds. That was all.

I had to leave Sig there. She had a chance of surviving if left alone. She had a chance of dying too. But Sig had no chance at all if those wolves reached her while she was defenseless.

I went a little insane then. Maybe more than a little.

∾51∾

KARMA'S A BITCH

Gabriel was dead by the time I made it down the hall with my machete in one hand and my silver steel knife in the other, wolves pouring around Gabriel and the two corpses he had killed. If they surrounded me, I was dead, and I couldn't back into a corner without exposing Sig.

I swung the machete just to force the first wolf back on its rear legs, then drove the silver steel knife into its left eye socket and spun away, which was all good, except that the wolf's dying body weight tore the knife out of my hands.

I gripped the machete two-handed and pretended to swing low at the next wolf, but when the wolf tried to leap over the blade I was ready for it, whirling crazily and swinging the machete upward with all of my weight and unnatural strength behind it.

The wolf's head came off, and so did the handle of the machete. The tang of the blade flew off violently, and another wolf came at me from above by leaping over the stair rail. I came up from under the wolf's jawline, grabbed it by the throat and threw it into the side of the doorway even while its claws scored my upper arms. Somewhere between its momentum and the force I'd used and its weight distribution and the unnatural angle of the impact, the werewolf's spine broke.

I had a few seconds then, and I used them to throw a side kick into the thick wooden spindles of the stairway railing, breaking one and grabbing it before another wolf came at me from around the landing. I swung the spindle like a baseball bat and shattered the wolf's teeth, knocking it sideways and bringing the spindle down again while its legs were scrambling for footing on the blood-slick floor, driving the broken end of the spindle through the top of its skull and into its brain like a spear.

It wasn't dead, but it wasn't attacking anyone else anytime soon.

A hybrid came at me then, a half-wolf half-man, and it tore the hell out of my left forearm with its talons when I blocked its swing, but I headbutted its front fangs out of its mouth when it lunged forward. It reeled back in shock and I punched my hand through its thoracic cavity, got a grip on its heart, and ripped it out of its chest like we were in a kung fu movie.

And then I was standing alone. The hybrid's teeth hadn't bitten into my head, but skin had still torn. I shook my head like trying to fling water out of my hair and wiped a forearm over my eyes. When I could see again, I was facing Bernard.

He was on the stairs, naked except for the big-bored double-barreled shotgun that he was holding. Bernard had moved down under the cover of the noise his followers and I had been making, and he was pointing the shotgun at me over the railing.

He pulled both triggers.

There was a deafening explosion, and then silver shot swerved violently and tore into the walls on either side of me.

I was wearing Mila Apraxin's magnetic charm.

What, I was just going to leave a defensive weapon like that lying on the floor? It was the reason my knife and machete had flown out of my hands. I'd barely been able to hold on to them *before* they started impacting with muscle and bone. It was also the reason I hadn't taken Sig's gun with me. Like an idiot, I had put the magnetic charm on first, and Sig's handgun had skidded away from me when I tried to grab it afterward, and there hadn't been time to negotiate matters any further.

Bernard stared at me as I stood there, the barrels of his shotgun still smoking. "Well. This is awkward."

"I don't think I ever saw this situation covered in a Miss Manners column," I agreed, rubbing blood out of my eyes again. "Why don't you come down here and we'll figure out the proper way to handle it."

I was swaying on my feet.

The bastard actually laughed. "What's the matter, John? Is it poison or fatigue?"

"We're not going to do that whole speech thing, are we?" I asked. "Because I'll be honest, Bernard; I've heard of enough of your bullshit."

"Fair enough," he agreed, tossing the shotgun behind him. "But can I say one thing before we start? I've been wanting to tell you ever since I met you."

"Sure," I said, wiping my forehead before blood could spill over my eyebrows yet again.

He smiled then, and I saw the real Bernard for the first time. It was a cruel, sadistic, vicious smile. I would call it something other than a smile, actually, if I could think of another word for expressions that show satisfaction by exposing teeth and pulling the corners of the mouth up. "The wolves who bit your mother? The ones who did it so your dying father would know that she wouldn't survive childbirth? Did it so that his last thought was that his child was being turned into an abomination inside his wife's womb while he lay there bleeding out? I was leading them. That was my idea."

It might have even been true.

I nodded. "Can I say one last thing to you?"

Fur began to emerge through Bernard's skin and he continued smiling, more to allow fangs to jut outward from his extending jaw than because he was happy. He remained mostly human, though, and he spoke, something I'd never heard a hybrid do, though his voice vibrated so much that it was a little hard to understand. "Of course."

I stepped casually to the side as if walking toward the stair landing, and Mayte…I mean, Catherine…I mean, Cat… fired four shots from Virgil's handgun from where she was lying on the floor in the classroom behind me. The bullets were hollow-points with silver tips, and after the first one hit Bernard's chest, he didn't have the power to do anything except fall backward against the wall.

Catherine kept firing, and one of the bullets hit his face while the rest tore hell and plaster out of the stairway wall.

"Fuck off," I told Bernard's corpse after the firing had stopped. He was human again, if you can call him that. I guess you'd have to. No other animal could be that cruel.

I could hear Catherine slowly pulling herself up to her feet behind me. Whatever they'd injected her with was still messing with her.

I called out, "You going to be all right?"

She emerged into the hall, bracing herself against the frame of the doorway. She was still holding Virgil's gun in one hand, not that I blamed her. "No."

I pointed toward the two wolves I had crippled. Their

whimpering had helped disguise the click when Bernard's mate had cocked Virgil's gun. I'd barely heard it myself. "Would you mind shooting them?"

"Not at all," she said, and proved it.

"So," I said while vibrations from the gunshots still made the air seem charged. "Catherine Flores, huh? I think I liked Mayte Reyes better."

She sighed. "It's Cat. And so did I."

I began shuffling down the hallway toward the woman who hadn't lied to me. "So, what was the deal? Bernard wanted you to seduce me?"

"Remember how he and the others met you in the woods after you ran away from me? He was supposed to interrupt us after I started something."

I didn't look back. "What about the second time?"

"That was my idea. I don't know if I wanted to see if he'd get jealous, or if I just liked you. He and I didn't have a passionate marriage." Catherine...I mean...I guess I'd better start calling her Cat...hadn't moved.

A werewolf named Cat. That sounded like something a brother would come up with, and Gabriel was lying in shreds at Cat's feet. Maybe the drugs in her system weren't the only reason she was so pale and out of it.

"I was Bernard's believer, not his beloved," Cat said tonelessly.

That sounded like a line she'd used before. Maybe it was something she'd told herself a lot.

"Bernard slept with anything that moved," Cat added. "I think he had something going with Nikolai."

I didn't look back, but only because I was still wearing Mila's charm. If she tried to kill me, she was in for a surprise. "And the knight raid on the paws? You really think he arranged that?"

"He admitted it after I was his prisoner." Her voice trembled. "He sacrificed our paw because he was counting on it turning you against the knights for good. He needed you to teach us how to fight them."

"It worked," I said, and I knelt down and smoothed Sig's hair out of the way so I could check her pulse. It was fast, but it was strong. "You worked. I really liked you."

"I really cared about you too." Her voice trembled. "It wasn't hard, pretending. You made it easy."

I slumped down against the wall, next to Sig. "Glad I could help."

"Bernard had a way of getting you to do things you never thought you'd do," Cat said. "A little step at a time. He could make anything sound reasonable."

"I know," I admitted.

I pulled Sig's head onto my lap. She wasn't dead. She was just sleeping. I know fairy tales are bullshit; believe me, I know it better than anyone. But I kissed her then. You know. Just in case.

"Right." Cat shuffled away. Maybe Gabriel had told her that Ben Lafontaine and his tribe were out there somewhere, clearing the woods of Bernard's most fanatical followers, the keepers of his secrets. Maybe not. Whatever. Tula didn't shoot Cat when she walked out of the building.

And Sig didn't die.

～52～

A DARK PLACE

You'd better go downstairs." Ben Lafontaine smelled like gasoline and was covered with blood and clothes he'd taken off of a dead man.

I looked up. I was making burritos in the kitchen at the back of the school. There were a lot of werewolves doing a lot of healing who needed fuel, and Sig was hand-feeding Virgil food as fast as I could make it.

"I can take over here," Ben said. He was tired. He'd been doing a lot of healing himself.

"You're putting off gasoline fumes," I reminded him. Ben was supposed to be soaking the school down with every flammable substance he could find. He wanted to burn the place down to cinders, and I didn't have any argument.

"Oh. Yes." Ben called for someone named Henry over his shoulder.

"What's this about?"

Ben sighed heavily. He really didn't want to talk about it. "There's a reason the basement is soundproofed. It's full of human women."

My stomach muscles tightened involuntarily. I'd smelled the smells, but I'd assumed they belonged to former humans... scents of people who had recently been killed or were dead.

"Why?"

Somehow, Ben managed to look even more tired and worn-down. "All the women come from knight's blood. A lot of them are pregnant."

For a few seconds I stood there, wishing as hard as I'd ever wished anything that Bernard was alive again so I could... take deep breaths. "Then maybe I should get Sig or Tula to go down there."

Ben shook his head. "This is knight business."

I stared at him grimly. "I'm no knight."

He didn't blink. "Whatever you are, it will have to be enough."

ᐁᐃ

The female knight I'd seen at Abalmar greeted me at the foot of the stairs. Her left arm had been broken and crudely splinted with a broken board and strips made from torn clothing. She wasn't putting weight on her right ankle. Her face was heavily bruised and swollen. I brought her a stack of some relatively clean clothes and a case of water bottles.

She was armed with a piece of pipe and covered only by ripped-out lengths of insulation wire wrapped around her chest and forearms and calves to make crude bracers. I couldn't see any women...it sounded like they were huddled in the southeast corner of the room...but I could see several plain mattresses on the stone floor. No sheets. No pillows.

"We should be leaving in an hour or so," I said. It had taken a while to hike outside the range of the ward and arrange transportation. We hadn't anticipated having a lot of sick werewolves to move, because werewolves don't get sick. "We're letting you go when we do."

She made no move toward the items I set on the stairs. Her eyes were unblinking and patient and savage. "You really are John Charming."

"Yeah," I said. "Bernard is dead."

She saw me looking at the mattresses. "You're not going to hold us hostage?"

"No," I said.

"He's been trying to make more werewolves like you." Her voice was a monotone. "Artificially inseminating those of us who weren't already pregnant. Waiting for us to near term so he could bite us and infect our human fetuses right before delivery."

I didn't respond. Bernard had been talking about looking for ways around the fact that werewolves couldn't reproduce, and that was before I knew he was planning to start mass-producing werewolves.

"You're really letting us go?" Her voice cracked momentarily.

"Yes."

"I heard you make that fine speech in Abalmar." Her voice had become a razor. "And then you turned me over to *him*."

Emil had started this ball rolling when he threatened people I cared about. I had made the best decisions I could with what I knew. But I didn't defend myself. I *had* turned her over to Bernard. And a lot of these women had probably been captured when I was identifying probable knight support networks in Milwaukee. Nothing I said was going to change that.

"If I bring you food and water, will you take them?" I asked.

"If we're leaving in an hour or so?" I could almost hear her forehead hum with calculations and considerations. "No."

"How many women do you need to transport?"

She hesitated. "Fifteen."

"How many of them can drive?"

She didn't hesitate. "If they have to? All of them."

I thought about it. "How about this? When we leave, I'll leave you a working car and a cell phone and the GPS coordinates to this place. You or somebody else can drive out of the spell range and call the knights."

Her face hardened. "So that we can lure them into another trap for you?"

I walked back up the stairs without taking my eyes off her. Armed or not, armored or not, injured or not, this was not someone to take lightly. "All right. I'll find you three vehicles somehow."

∽53∽

CHANGING THE RULES

We were in the center of a crowded university dining room. I won't say which university, but it was a state school, and the room was large and warm-colored. Our tables and chairs were made out of wood and cushioned in soft but scratchy fabric the same color as the carpeting, a shade caught somewhere between yellow and tan and red. Perhaps someone who was really into nail polish or painting could have identified the hue. I couldn't.

Emil and one of the pregnant women we'd freed from the schoolhouse were seated on one side of our table. Ben Lafontaine and I were on the other. The food actually looked pretty good, but I was eating pizza just to be safe. It was a college cafeteria, after all, and it's pretty hard to make inedible pizza.

"Are you sure you wouldn't rather do this outside?" Emil asked, his expression as blank and serene as always.

The building we were in was made of white stone, and there was a large walkway with wrought-iron tables visible through the large windows on the side of the dining hall. It was cold and gray outside, and the tables were empty.

Ben shrugged. "I'm good."

He looked good. Ben wore being the new most powerful werewolf in the Midwest well. He also wore a cowboy hat well, though I'm not sure if it was ironic or what. I was still figuring Ben out.

Emil made an acquiescent gesture with his palm. "How many were-beings do you have hidden in this crowd?"

Ben shrugged. "None. We don't need them."

"How many knights do you have on this campus right now?" I asked.

Emil smiled politely. "None. We don't need them."

I smiled back, even if it was a little tight. I liked Emil in spite of myself. At least he was up-front about being a bastard.

"Do you have it?" the woman interrupted. I'd never gotten her name. She had some kind of multi-ethnic thing going on. Brown hair, amber eyes, high cheekbones, almost at full term. I could smell werewolf coming off her, though she must not have had her first full moon. When it came, she would die. Her geas would kill her if the change didn't. No wonder her heart was racing.

Seeing her next to Emil…she had the same coloring, the same cheeks, the same eyes…even the same smell in some weird way.

"You two are related." It came out sounding like an accusation.

Emil nodded. "Tess is the niece I told you about. I thought she was dead. Hoped she was, honestly."

Tess flushed. Why had Emil brought her along? What kind of game or angle was he playing now?

"Do you have it?" Emil reiterated.

"We do." Ben removed a small gift-wrapped parcel from his coat and pushed it across the table.

"And this is…" Emil trailed off.

"A working werewolf potion," I said. "Bernard did it. He was still trying to figure out two things. A way to turn it into an airborne virus, and a way for werewolf children to survive pregnancy."

Emil's niece got upset then. I could see her shoulders tense from how tightly her hand was clenching beneath the table, and her body was dumping a complex cocktail of pheromones.

"And you're not giving us the secret to this potion." Emil wasn't smiling any longer. "You're giving us a sample so that we can verify that you have it."

"You'll never kill everyone fast enough to keep this a secret, Emil," I said. "There are system commands that will publish the information on the Internet if the files aren't updated. There are sprites who have hidden the information who aren't even on this plane anymore. They're oath-bound to check in every couple of months or years to make sure that the knights haven't tried to wipe us out."

"It's true." Ben shrugged again. "The only way to keep this under control is to keep us reasonable, peace-loving werewolves around. Not kill us or hold us so that who knows who will do who knows what when the information comes out."

"I don't believe you." Emil was looking at me. "John would never risk something like that. The geas wouldn't let him."

My shrug wasn't as good as Ben's but it was pretty casual. "You're right."

Ben cleared his throat. "It wasn't John's idea. He had nothing to do with setting up any of this." Also true. Sig and Ben and Parth had set the plan into motion before telling me. It was sort of the supernatural version of a nuclear deterrent.

We all paused while a young man in tie-dye and a padded jean jacket came close to the table as he threaded his way through the dining hall. He asked us to excuse him and we did.

"It's true," I promised. "I'm not much happier about this than you are, really."

Emil looked at Ben then. "What do you want?"

"Peace," Ben said simply.

The woman gave me a sharp, measuring stare. "And what do you want?"

"Peace," I echoed.

Emil tapped his fingers on the table. I really hoped it wasn't some signal to some knights somewhere to do something messed up. He addressed Ben. "Suppose we agreed to leave your . . . what are you calling your new order, anyhow?"

"We haven't decided yet," Ben admitted easily. "Some of us want to call ourselves a tribe. Some of us want to be a confederacy or a league. I like the idea of being a round table."

I looked at him narrowly. This was the first I'd heard of it. Ben had a strange sense of whimsy. He might be serious. He might be referring to a practice I vaguely recalled reading about where some Native American tribes liked to meet at round tables. He might be tweaking Emil in some odd way because Emil represented an order of knights and, you know, a bunch of werewolves calling themselves the round table? Hell, for all I knew he was making fun of the Algonquin Round Table.

He smiled. "I admit, it's not a very popular suggestion."

Emil cut through the banter. "Suppose we agreed to peace with your tribe, but you had to hand over Charming. Right now. No questions asked."

Ben stopped being amused. "Whatever happens, my people aren't for sale. None of us. Ever."

Emil lapsed into silence.

"Why do you have such a hard-on for me, Emil?" I asked. "I still don't really get that."

He shook his head. "It's nothing personal. You're another crack in the dam."

"What do you mean?" I asked.

"I tried to explain this to you before. The geas doesn't tell us that knights can't kill other knights, John," Emil said. "It doesn't tell us that we have to stay together. It doesn't tell us that we can't experiment with dark arts, or intermingle with the monsters we're supposed to police. We drill that into our children's heads as soon as they start learning to talk and tell them it's part of the geas, but it's not true. The geas is a compulsion to preserve the Pax Arcana, not a sophisticated set of rules."

I stared at him. "I know that."

"Of course you know that!" Emil said impatiently. "You're living proof of it! But most knights don't."

Oh, shit.

"We already have so many factions that it's affecting our ability to function together," Emil muttered glumly. "The Rat Runners hate the Swords of Solomon, and the Swords of Solomon hate the Crusaders and the Pajama Party hates the Warhounds, and the Warhounds hate the Bug Huggers, and the Crusaders hate everyone except the Warhounds. The only thing keeping us together is the idea that we have to stay together for the good of the Pax."

"And because they believe it's a part of the geas, it is part of the geas," I said slowly.

"Most people never question the core beliefs they grow up with," Emil confirmed. "You can look back on any culture five hundred years later and wonder how they could have ever believed some of the contradictory or flat-out insane things they accepted as law or common sense."

"And I'm a constant reminder that knights can question whatever they want," I said.

"Yes." Emil leaned forward and spoke urgently. "You are a loose thread that can cause the whole tapestry to unravel."

I laughed disbelievingly. "Are you trying to make me believe that committing suicide is the best way for me to preserve the Pax so that my geas will start pressing me to do it?"

He settled back in his chair then, his face expressionless again. "Maybe."

"Why don't you write all that down on sandpaper, roll it into a tube, and shove it up your ass?" I invited.

The woman flushed. I don't think it was my unsophisticated crudity...I think it was the fact that I was talking to her grandmaster that way.

"I don't care how dangerous the truth is, Emil," I said. "It's gotten to the point where you're doing worse and worse things to keep your lie going. You can tell yourself that it's to preserve the Pax, but you're just afraid of change."

Emil suddenly looked old though I couldn't say what changed. It wasn't his body posture or his expression, at least not overtly. "I thought you'd say that."

"So what's your contingency plan?" I asked cautiously.

"Knights know you made the sword of truth blaze," he said. "And we have the example of the Kresniks and Benandanti to prove that men can work with werewolves to preserve the Pax. And you did kill Bernard. I can tell people you were my double agent among the wolves all along. Between that and the leverage this...discovery...gets you...I might be able to arrange that armed truce you want."

"He killed those knights in Abalmar," Emil's niece protested.

"No," Emil corrected gently. "He persuaded the werewolves to keep our knights alive after they fell into Bernard's trap. He didn't know what Bernard was going to do with them, and when he found out, he killed Bernard and set them free. And now John's going to continue to be my double agent inside this new, more manageable clan that Ben Lafontaine is trying to start. I need him to spy on Ben and guide events so that this never happens again."

Ben looked at me. "You bastard."

I shrugged. I was waiting for the "But."

"But I have three conditions if you two really want peace," he said. "More than that, actually, but three that aren't negotiable."

"What are they?" Ben sounded indifferent.

"First, you're going to have to let me send you knights to train some of your werewolves to hunt monsters," Emil said. "And you're going to have to send us werewolves that we can use for tracking purposes. That's how I'll have to pitch it. The vampire war weakened us, and you weakened us even more. All-out war with you will destroy both of us. This is the only way to turn werewolves into an asset instead of a liability. To make us stronger than before instead of weaker."

"But the knights will have to think it was your idea," I guessed. "That's why you want to act like you're calling the shots and manipulating the dumb werewolves."

Emil looked at me narrowly. "I'll tell some of them that, yes. Some kind of exchange program where we get to know each other over time is the only way this is going to work. If it's going to work. It probably won't. There's a lot of bloody water under the bridge."

Ben growled. "We'll be your partners but not your dogs. What's the second condition?"

Emil indicated me. "John works for me. Secretly, but with no more games between us. I'm going to need someone capable who can't be traced back to me easily."

"I'll listen if you need a troubleshooter," I said. "But like Ben said, I won't be your slave. What's the third condition?"

Emil put his hand on Tess's forearm. "You both agree to be godfathers to my niece's child."

Okay, that one came out of nowhere.

The woman began to cry. "I'm...getting a C-section tomorrow. I want my baby to live."

I didn't say anything. There was at least some chance that the baby's geas and the baby's curse would find some middle ground while the child was at the most adaptable, instinctive, unquestioning state it would ever be in.

"I don't understand," Ben said slowly. "Why would you want me to be your child's godfather, young lady?"

Her face filled with sudden loathing. Somehow, she managed to get farther away from us without moving. "I don't want any of this."

"This is my condition." Emil sounded exhausted. "We are possibly the only three men on this planet who can and will protect my brother's grandchild, no matter what the consequences. And if you two make a promise to a dying mother to protect her child, you will honor it, even if you don't know her."

"And if I don't promise?" My voice sounded strained.

"Then we destroy each other." Emil's pretense of detachment was gone now. His expression was fire and iron. "Or do you think my will is weaker than yours?"

I didn't, actually.

"You have no idea how hard the thing you are asking for will become. We will bind each other like kings," Emil said. "You protect my blood. I will protect yours. It is the only tie that will hold."

Gabriel had said that the loss of a child drove Ben in ways that were deep and unfathomable. He had said that Ben had adopted Cat out of a need to replace a daughter figure. Ben had moved heaven and earth to save Cat even though she had, in many ways, betrayed him. How shrewd was Emil? I had thought we held all the cards, but now I wondered if he wasn't directing us still. Something was moving inside of Ben Lafontaine. I could feel the currents from two feet away.

"I agree," Ben said.

It was just a kid. A kid with a knight's blood and a werewolf's curse who didn't deserve any of the world of shit that was about to come down on it.

God help that child. God help me.

"I agree," I said hoarsely.

~54~

MY BIG FAT SAPPY ENDING

Sig was living in a town house complex, if you can call that living. Not my kind of place, and I wondered if it was hers or if this was just an easy way to exist while she got her head together. There was a lot I didn't know about her. The thought kept me out there in the snowy parking lot in the dark for a moment while I gathered my courage, listening to some alt-rock Christmas carol coming through Sig's door while one of her neighbors talked about some exercise called "body step" on a phone and another watched some kind of police procedural and a couple across the street argued over which one of them was being condescending.

Oh, yeah. That's why I didn't like places like this.

I knocked on the door and hid the red rose I was holding behind my back.

In a few seconds, Molly Newman, probably Sig's best friend, stuck her head out the door. Her eyes were about level with my chest, big and solemn behind thick, round glasses. She was wearing a fuzzy pink bathrobe over sweatpants and big square SpongeBob slippers.

"Hey, Molls," I greeted.

I could hear Sig running a sink somewhere upstairs, and Molly lunged out of the door and gave me a hug. "John! It's so good to see you!"

"What's with the Christmas music?" I asked.

"It's winter," she reminded me.

"Exactly. Shouldn't you be listening to…I don't know… beach music or something?"

The first time I'd met Molly, she had been listening to Christmas music in April.

"Ha." She adjusted her glasses and held up a palm so that I could see a cross tattooed on it. "What do you think of this?"

Molly was a little random. Smart. Brave. A wide-open soul. But she had been traumatized during an exorcism, and she did this thing where she dealt with stress by going with whatever verbal impulse came her way. She was also one of the most powerful priests I'd ever seen. When she displayed a cross, unholy things couldn't even stand to rotate in her direction.

"Nice," I approved. "Are you going to let me in?"

"It's not my house," she said reasonably. "And you called me Molls. You need to stay out here in the cold and contemplate your sins."

"Priestly," I commented.

"Exactly."

I leaned down and kissed her on the forehead. "It's good to see you too."

"That's sweet. Hold on." Molly turned around and yelled up the stairs. "Sig! John's here! And he's hiding a gift behind his back!"

"Thanks," I said sourly.

She grinned. "Call me Molls again. See what happens."

Sig opened a door and started to come down the stairs fast,

then remembered her dignity. I couldn't see her because Molly was still cracking the door, and I couldn't smell her, not fresh anyhow, because the wind was coming in behind me, but I listened to every step.

Molly stepped back and Sig opened the doorway. She was wearing a pair of blue shorts and a white T-shirt, largely impervious to the cold. Her face was impassive but her heart was beating fast. "So, what's this gift?"

I avoided the question. "What are you two doing? Is this like your version of a pajama party or something?"

"YES!" Molly yelled from the background. "WE'RE PILLOW-FIGHTING AND DOING OUR NAILS!"

"We're about to make fudge," Sig said. "Molly says she can't make fudge unless she's comfortable. Would you like to join us?"

"Somebody probably should," I said, and Sig glowered at me. She's not much of a cook.

"I MAKE GREAT FUDGE, THANK YOU VERY MUCH!" Molly yelled.

I pulled the red rose out from behind my back. "Actually, I've had a long drive, and I still have to go to a storage shed and then find a place to stay for the night. But I wanted to ask you out on a date."

She scrutinized me carefully. "You're going to go get your katana, aren't you?"

"I've missed her," I admitted. "But I did come to see you first."

Sig took the rose from my hand and smelled it. "This is a hothouse flower."

"Yes," I said, then removed a cell phone from my pocket and held it up, absurdly proud. "And this is a cell phone. Well, it's a burner."

She smiled then, and her blue eyes warmed. "And it has a number you can give me and everything?"

"It does," I said, and I proved it.

"This date." She pronounced the word experimentally. "Where do you want to go?"

"I have plane tickets to Italy."

"Really?"

"No," I conceded. "But there is a place in Floyd I like that plays live music."

Her smile turned into a grin. "You realize that if you pursue this, you're going to get punched a lot."

"I'll heal," I said.

She leaned forward and kissed me briefly on the lips. "Yes, you will."

I was still standing there when she said, "I'll see you Friday," and shut the door.

I stared at the door for a little while longer, still feeling the warmth of that kiss on my lips, wanting more.

All right, then.

ACKNOWLEDGMENTS

I don't know if this is the proper format, but I would like to give a shout-out to the good people at the Black Friar Theater and the American Shakespeare Center in Staunton, Virginia. They are keeping language a lot richer than mine alive in a world of tweets and texts and Instagrams. The most sassy yet classy fun live theater around, and the live music rocks.

extras

orbit

meet the author

An army brat and gypsy scholar, ELLIOTT JAMES is currently living in the Blue Ridge mountains of southwest Virginia. An avid reader since the age of three (or that's what his family swears anyhow), he has an abiding interest in mythology, martial arts, live music, hiking, and used bookstores. Irrationally convinced that cell phone technology was inserted into human culture by aliens who want to turn us into easily tracked herd beasts, Elliott has one anyhow but keeps it in a locked tinfoil-covered box, which he will sometimes sit and stare at mistrustfully for hours. Okay, that was a lie. Elliott lies a lot; in fact, he decided to become a writer so that he could get paid for it.

introducing

If you enjoyed
DARING,
look out for

FEARLESS

Pax Arcana: Book 3

by Elliott James

*When your last name is Charming, rescuing virgins
comes with the territory, even when the virgin in
question is a nineteen-year-old college boy.*

*Someone, somewhere, has declared war on Kevin Kichida,
and that someone has a long list of magical predators on their
Rolodex. The good news is that Kevin lives in a town where
Ted Cahill is the new sheriff and old ally of John Charming.*

*The attacks on Kevin seem to be a pattern, and the more John and
his new team follow that thread, the deeper they find themselves
in a maze of supernatural threats, family secrets, and age-old
betrayals. The more John learns, the more convinced he becomes
that Kevin Kichida isn't just a victim, he's a sacrifice waiting to
happen. And that thread John's following? It's really a fuse...*

CHAPTER ONE

Cahill bared his teeth. His fangs were showing, just slightly. "So, this hunt wasn't just an excuse to separate me and Sig or get me out here for some he-man ass-kicking contest?"

"I don't need to protect Sig from you, Cahill," I said bluntly. "She already did that."

Those words hit him harder than the whole sea horse thing.

"What do you fucking know?" he hissed. "You're a man who got turned into something else, just like me. You had people chasing after you, and you put Sig right in the danger zone! How is that any better than my feelings getting out of control by accident? And you've done all kinds of fucked-up things; any cop could tell that just looking at you."

"What do you want me to say, Cahill? That I deserve her?" I asked quietly. "I don't. You want me to say that life isn't fair? What was your first clue?"

It didn't take enhanced senses to hear his teeth grinding.

I took my sling bag off of my shoulders. Might as well use the time wisely, since we were stopping anyway. "The question is, are you going to man up and deal with it or not?"

"You're not sleeping with her," Cahill said. "I'd be able to smell it if you were."

It was true. I was courting Sig, and she was setting a slow pace. And it wasn't any of Cahill's business.

"I left Sig alone when she said that's what she needed," I said evenly. "And she came and found me again. I don't know why. To be honest, I thought she was smarter than that. But she did."

Cahill let out a long, harsh breath. It sounded like some of his soul came out with it. "If I leave her alone, I don't think she's going to come looking for me."

I pulled out a sledgehammer that was rolled up in my sling bag. The sledgehammer was already smeared with mud, which was good. I'd gotten it from a room in the stables while Sig was talking to the student in charge of morning cleaning. "So grow a pair, or freak out and attack me, or shut up while you decide which. I'm about out of bullshit."

"Fuck you," Cahill said, but his heart wasn't in it. Maybe because he didn't have one.

Next, I pulled a bottle out of the sling bag. I usually carried the bottle and a few other things around in a specially made guitar case, but I was in Tatum as an expert tracker, and that would have looked awkward. Cahill watched me pour a small amount of liquid over the metal head of the sledgehammer. Then he watched some more while I removed a matchbook from my pocket and struck a match, causing the top of the sledgehammer to flame briefly.

Finally, he gave in to curiosity. His voice wasn't apologetic, but it wasn't angry either. "What the hell is that stuff?"

"Absinthe," I said. "Distilled down to the point where it's basically jet fuel. Absinthe is made from wormwood, and wormwood is potent against water elementals."

"Why?"

I sighed. One second, he was griping about me giving explanations; the next, he was asking for them. "My best guess? There's a prophecy in the Bible about a fallen star called Wormwood poisoning large bodies of water at the end of time. It may be that so many have read and repeated that verse over the centuries, believing it, that it became a kind of crude magical ceremony, and now wormwood has taken on symbolic properties. Magic works that way sometimes."

"Do you even hear yourself talk?" Cahill's voice was flat, all of the emotion drained out of it.

"Here's the other piece," I held up the weapon while the flames burned out and left a scorched patina behind. "I just combined fire with the earth that makes up this sledgehammer. When I swing this thing fast and cause it to whistle through the wind, I'll be combining air too. That's earth, fire, and air. Three natural elements against the truce this thing made with water to move around our home."

"What am I supposed to do?" Cahill's tone was showing some small signs of becoming normal again.

I sealed the bottle of absinthe and handed it over. It was shaped like a World War II Nazi hand grenade, though a little bigger. "Break this over the Each Uisge and light it on fire. Then grab the biggest branch or rock you can find and go at it."

I removed my jacket and rolled it up in the sling bag and zipped the latter up, careful not to knock the katana inside to an odd angle.

"I don't like you very much," Cahill pointed out, as if that were directly relevant.

"So ignore my friend request on Facebook." I stood and shifted the sling bag back over my chest and shoulders. "Are we going to do this or what?"

He didn't answer, which meant that he sort of did. I started walking again and he followed. We were almost at the lake when Cahill spoke again. "Do you even have a Facebook page?"

"No," I answered tersely, and we emerged from the woods at the edge of a large lake. The Kincaid University material I'd printed off said that the name of the lake was Contemplation, but that sounded like something the university founders had come up with. As opposed to Lake Intoxication or Lake Procreation or whatever the students actually got up to around those waters. But if I'd known we would be dealing with a water elemental, I would have looked up the lake's original name. True names are important.

Hell, I would have brought some rotisserie chickens from the local grocery store too. Back in ye olde days, knights used to lure Each Uisge out of their watery bolt-holes with roasted meat while the creatures still had the taste of flesh in their mouth. But you can never prepare for everything.

"Here's what I don't quite get," Cahill ventured. "This thing just wants to leave? Why don't we let it?"

"Because it broke the rules and killed someone from our home." I didn't take my eyes off the lake. I didn't know much about this Lindsey Williams. I knew she had a passion for horses. I knew she had people who cared about her. And I knew she'd deserved a chance to fuck her life up and learn and love and try to figure out what she wanted to leave behind. And some thing had taken that from her. It wasn't right.

Cahill grunted, so I gave him an answer he could be happier with.

"Besides, it's easier for cunning folk to summon creatures that they are already familiar with," I said. "Letting this thing live so that the person we're really after can summon it again would be like leaving a loaded gun lying around."

He nodded but still didn't look convinced. Fuck him.

I yelled out over the water: "SCIO ENIM QUIA HOC! VENITE CERTAMEN! ET FERTE PRESIDIUM! VENE-NUM EFFUNDAM EN LECTO! ET MATREM TUAM TERPIS!"

Nothing happened.

"What was that?" Cahill wanted to know.

"Latin."

He snorted. "No shit. What did you say?"

"I challenged and insulted it." The sledgehammer was balanced casually on my shoulder, my feet comfortably apart and my left hip angled towards the lake. The terms of the Pax Arcana—the magical truce that ended the war between mankind and magickind that we now call the Dark Ages—actually keeps me from attacking supernatural creatures unless they have done something to make their presence known to the world at large, but if I let a creature smell werewolf and give them a little attitude, they usually attack me.

We waited a while longer. Cahill started to say something but I interrupted. "All right, we're going to have to pull out some juju. Take your badge out and hold it toward the lake. You're the closest thing we have to a symbol of local authority."

He did so, cautiously, as if the badge might catch fire.

"Now stand on one leg—that symbolizes meeting someone halfway between worlds—and hop widdershins…That means in the same direction as the sun travels because it's our earth. Hop in a circle to symbolize the rotation of the earth, and yell *Ego sum stultus* three times."

He started to argue and I cut him off again. "Magic rituals are meant to look stupid. It's one of the ways cunning folk keep random people from messing around with them. Just do it."

Gritting his teeth, Cahill held out his badge, stood on one leg, and hopped in a circle yelling "EGO SUM STULTUS! EGO SUM STULTUS! EGO SUM STULTUS![1]

Still nothing.

"Your ritual didn't work," Cahill's jaw was clenched. It sounded like every bodily opening he had was clenched.

"That's because I made all that up," I admitted. "I just wanted to see if I could get you to do it."

"You ass—" Cahill started, and the Each Uisge erupted out of the water.

---

[1] I to be foolish, I to be foolish, I to be foolish"

introducing

If you enjoyed
DARING,
look out for

DIRTY MAGIC

Prospero's War: Book 1

by Jaye Wells

MAGIC IS A DRUG. CAREFUL HOW YOU USE IT.

*The Magical Enforcement Agency keeps dirty magic off the streets,
but there's a new blend out there that's as deadly as it is elusive.
When patrol cop Kate Prospero shoots the lead snitch in this
crucial case, she's brought in to explain herself. But the
more she learns about the investigation, the more she realizes
she must secure a spot on the MEA task force.*

*Especially when she discovers that their lead suspect is the man she
walked away from ten years earlier—on the same day she swore
she'd given up dirty magic for good. Kate Prospero's about to learn
the hard way that crossing a wizard will always get you burned
and that when it comes to magic, you should never say never.*

CHAPTER ONE

It was just another fucked-up night in the Cauldron. Potion junkies huddled in shadowy corners with their ampules and pipes and needles. The occasional flick of a lighter's flame illuminated their dirty, desperate faces, and the air sizzled with the ozone scent of spent magic.

I considered stopping to harass them. Arrest them for loitering and possession of illegal arcane substances. But they'd just be back on the street in a couple of days or be replaced by another dirty, desperate face looking to escape the Mundane world.

Besides, these hard cases weren't my real targets. To make a dent, you had to go after the runners and stash boys, the potion cookers—the money men. The way I figured, better to hunt the vipers instead of the 'hood rats who craved the bite of their fangs. But for the last couple of weeks, the corner thugs had been laying low, staying off the streets after dark. My instincts were tingling, though, so I kept walking the beat, hoping to find a prize.

Near Canal Street, growls rolled out of a pitch-black alley. I stilled and listened with my hand on my hawthorn-wood nightstick. The sounds were like a feral dog protecting a particularly juicy bone. The hairs on the back of my neck prickled, and my nostrils twitched from the coppery bite of blood.

Approaching slowly, I removed the flashlight from my belt.

The light illuminated about ten feet into the alley's dark throat. On the nearest wall, a graffiti-ed dragon marked the spot as Sanguinarian Coven's turf. But I already knew the east side of town belonged to the Sangs. That's one of the reasons I'd requested it for patrol. I didn't dare show my face on the Votary's west-side territory.

Something moved in the shadows, just outside of the light's halo. A loud slurping sound. A wet moan.

"Babylon PD!" I called, taking a few cautious steps forward. The stink of blood intensified. "Come out with your hands up!"

The scuttling sound of feet against trash. Another growl, but no response to my order.

Three more steps expanded my field of vision. The light flared on the source of the horrible sounds and the unsettling scents.

A gaunt figure huddled over the prone form of a woman. Wet, stringy hair shielded her face, and every inch of her exposed skin glistened red with blood. My gun was in my hand faster than I could yell, "Freeze!"

Still partially in shadow, the attacker—male, judging from the size—swung around. I had the impression of glinty yellow eyes and shaggy hair matted with blood.

"Step away with your hands up," I commanded, my voice projected to make it a demand instead of a suggestion.

"Fuck you, bitch," the male barked. And then he bolted.

"Shit!" I ran to the woman and felt for a pulse. I shouldn't have been relieved not to find one, but it meant I was free to pursue the asshole who'd killed her.

My leg muscles burned and my heart raced. Through the radio on my shoulder, I called Dispatch.

"Go ahead, Officer Prospero," the dispatcher's voice crackled through the radio.

"Be advised I need an ambulance sent to the alley off Canal and Elm. Interrupted a code 27. Victim had no pulse. I'm pursuing the perp on foot bearing east on Canal."

"Ambulance is on its way. Backup unit will be there in five minutes. Keep us advised of your 20."

"10-4." I took my finger off the comm button. "Shit, he's fast." I dug in, my air coming out in puffs of vapor in the cool night air.

He was definitely freaking—a strength or speed potion, probably. But that type of magic wouldn't explain why he mauled that woman in the alley—or those yellow predator's eyes. I tucked that away for the moment and focused on keeping up.

The perp loped through the maze of dark alleys and streets like he knew the Cauldron well. But no one knew it better than me, and I planned to be right behind him when he finally made a mistake.

As I ran, my lead cuffs clanked heavily against the wood of my nightstick. The rhythm matched the thumping beats of my heart and the puffs of air rasping from my lungs. I had a Glock at my side, but when perps are jacked-up on potions, they're almost unstoppable with Mundane weaponry unless you deliver a fatal shot. Killing him wasn't my goal—I wanted the notch on my arrest stats.

"Stop or I'll salt you!" I pulled the salt flare from my left side. The best way to incapacitate a hexhead was a little of the old sodium chloride.

A loud snarling grunt echoed back over his shoulder. He picked up the pace, but he wasn't running blind. No, he was headed someplace specific.

"Prospero," Dispatch called through the walkie. "Backup is on its way."

"Copy. The vic?"

"Ambulance arrived and confirmed death. ME is on his way to make it official."

I looked around to get my bearings. He veered right on Mercury Street. "The suspect appears to be headed for the Arteries," I spoke into the communicator. "I'm pursuing."

"Copy that, Officer Prospero. Be advised you are required to wait for backup before entering the tunnels." She told me their coordinates.

I cursed under my breath. They were still five blocks away and on foot.

A block or so up, I could see one of the boarded-up gates that led down into the old subway tunnels. The system had been abandoned fifty years earlier before the project was anywhere close to completion. Now the tunnels served as a rabbit warren for potion addicts wanting to chase the black dragon in the rat-infested, shit-stench darkness.

In front of the gate, a large wooden sign announced the site as the "Future Home of the Cauldron Community Center." Under those words was the logo for Volos Real Estate Development, which did nothing to improve my mood.

If Speedy made it through that gate, we'd never find him. The tunnels would swallow him in one gulp. My conscience suddenly sounded a lot like Captain Eldritch in my head. *Don't be an idiot, Kate. Wait for backup.*

I hadn't run halfway through the Cauldron only to lose the bastard to the darkness. But I knew better than to enter the tunnels alone. The captain had laid down that policy after a rookie ended up rat food five years earlier. So I wasn't going to follow him down there, but I could still slow him down a little. Buy some time for backup to arrive.

The salt flare's thick double barrel was preloaded with two rock salt shells. A bite from one of those puppies was rarely lethal, but it was enough to dilute the effects of most potions as well as cause enough pain to convince perps to lie down and play dead. The only catch was, you had to be within twenty feet for the salt to interrupt the magic. The closer the better if you want the bonus of severe skin abrasions.

The runner was maybe fifteen feet from me and a mere ten from the gate that represented his freedom. Time to make the move. I stopped running and took aim.

Exhale. Squeeze. Boom!

Rock salt exploded from the gun in a starburst. Some of the rocks pinged off the gate's boards and metal fittings. The rest embedded in the perp's shirtless back like shrapnel. Small red pockmarks covered the dirty bare skin not covered with tufts of dark hair. He stumbled, but he didn't stay down.

Instead, he leaped from the ground with a snarl. His hands grasped the top edge of the gate. A narrow opening between the gate and the upper concrete stood between him and freedom.

"Shit!" Frustration and indecision made my muscles yearn for action. My only choice was to take him down.

Speedy already had his head and an arm through the opening at the top of the gate. I surged up and grabbed his ankles. Lifted my feet to help gravity do its job. We slammed to the ground and rolled all asses and elbows through the dirt and grass and broken potion vials.

The impact momentarily stunned us both. My arm stung where the glass shards had done their worst, but the pain barely registered through the heady rush of adrenaline.

Speedy leaped off the ground with a growl. I jumped after him, my grip tight on the salt flare. I still had one shell left, not that I expected it to do much good after seeing the first one had barely fazed him. In my other hand, I held a small canister of S&P spray. "BPD! You're under arrest!"

The beast barely looked human. His hair was long and matted in some patches, which alternated with visible wide swaths of pink scalp—like he'd been infected with mange. The lower half of his face was covered in a shaggy beard. The pale skin around his yellow eyes and mouth was red and raw. His teeth were crooked and sharp. Too large for his mouth to corral. Hairy shoulders almost touched his ears, like a dog with his hackles up.

If he understood my command, he didn't show it. That intense yellow gaze focused on my left forearm, where a large gash oozed blood. His too-red lips curled back into a snarl.

I aimed the canister of salt-and-pepper spray. The burning mixture of saline and capsicum hit him between the eyes. He blinked, sneezed. Wiped a casual hand across his face. No screaming. No red, watery eyes or swollen mucus glands.

His nostrils flared and he lowered his face to sniff the air closer to me. His yellow eyes stayed focused on my wound. An eager red tongue caressed those sharp teeth in anticipation.

For the first time, actual fear crept like ice tendrils up the back of my neck. What kind of fucked-up potion was this guy on?

I don't remember removing the Glock from my belt. I don't remember pointing it at the perp's snarling face. But I remember shouting, "Stop or I'll shoot!"

One second, the world was still except for the pounding of my heart and the cold fear clawing my gut. The next, his wrecking-ball weight punched my body to the ground. My legs flew up and my back crashed into the metal gate. Hot breath escaped my panicked lungs. His body pinned me to the metal bars.

Acrid breath on my face. Body odor and unwashed skin everywhere. An erect penis pressed into my hip. But my attacker wasn't interested in sex. He was aroused by something else altogether—blood. My blood.

My fear.

The next instant, his teeth clamped over the bleeding wound. Pain blasted up my arm like lightning. Sickening sucking sounds filled the night air. Fear burst like a blinding light in my brain. "Fuck!"

The perp pulled me toward the ground and pinned me. The impact knocked the weapon from my hand, but it lay only a couple feet away. I reached for it with my left hand. But fingers can only stretch so far, no matter how much you yearn and curse and pray.

The pain was like needles stabbing my vein. My vision swam. If I didn't stop him soon, I'd pass out. If that happened, he'd drag me into those tunnels and no one would see me again.

Fortunately, elbows make excellent motivators. Especially when they're rammed into soft temples. At least, they are usually. In this case, my bloodthirsty opponent was too busy feasting on my flesh and blood to react. Finally, in a desperate move, I bucked my hips like a wild thing. He lost contact with my arm just long enough for me to roll a few centimeters closer to my target.

I reared up, grabbed the gun, and pivoted.

The pistol's mouth kissed his cheek a split second before it removed his face.

Backup arrived thirty seconds too late.

CHAPTER TWO

I limped into the precinct a couple hours later. A huge white bandage glared from my right forearm and a black eye throbbed on my face. My blood-soaked uniform had been confiscated by the team that arrived shortly after my tardy backup to investigate the shooting. They'd also taken my service weapon, salt flare, S&P spray canister, and shoes. Which left me feeling naked despite the blue scrubs I'd been issued by the wizard medics.

After sewing up my arm in the back of an ambulance while I'd answered the shoot team's questions, the wizard had slammed a syringe full of saline and antibiotics into my ass. The shoot team had waited until they'd gotten a good eyeful of my rear bumper before they declared me free to go. I knew better than to believe I wouldn't be hearing from them again. Especially after they'd warned me to stay within Babylon city limits.

I'd just dropped by the precinct to grab my things before heading home. I'd called my neighbor, Baba, from the ambulance to let her know I'd be later than usual. She'd said it was no problem staying late to keep an eye on Danny. Luckily, she'd been too wrapped up in the show she'd been watching to question me about the reason for the overtime. If I were even luckier neither she nor my brother would notice the bandage on my arm when they saw me, but it would take a miracle to miss the black eye.

My feet felt like they were encased in lead boots instead of flip-flops as I made my way toward the locker room. I caught my reflection in the glass of one of the interrogation rooms and cringed. My one good eye looked unnaturally blue next to its swollen purple twin. I'd managed to get all the smears off my face, but my brunette hair was still matted in spots with Speedy's blood. I needed a hot shower and a stiff drink—preferably at the same time. But first—

"Prospero, get your ass in here!" Captain Eldritch yelled from his doorway. The entire squad room went silent as cops paused to gape at the unfolding drama.

With a heavy sigh, I dropped my duffel bag at my desk and performed the walk of shame. My colleagues didn't bother to cover their curious stares and smirks. For the next few hours, this scene would be replayed and analyzed around the water-cooler along with the leaked details of the shooting. Cops were worse than housewives when it came to gossip.

"Sit down." Stress lines permanently bracketed Eldritch's mouth. His bald pate glowed dully under the harsh fluorescent lights. The desk hid a paunch that betrayed a lifelong love affair with fried dough, but one would be unwise to mistake his generous midsection for a sign of weakness. He'd maneuvered his way up from patrolman to captain in a criminal justice system rife with political intrigue and bureaucratic red tape. For his efforts, he was rumored to be next in line for chief of the entire BPD. In other words, he was not a man to piss off.

"I won't bother asking if you're all right because I can see you are. Instead, I'll begin by asking what the fuck you thought you were doing?"

"Sir, I—"

He slashed a hand through the air. "Don't bother. You weren't thinking. Not a damned thing. That's the only explanation that makes any sense. Because I know you were trained better than to enter a dangerous confrontation with a hexed-out suspect without backup."

"If I'd waited for backup that bastard would be running free through the Arteries."

"Thanks to you he's not going to be running anywhere ever again."

I leaned forward, my hands up in a pleading gesture. "It was a clean kill, sir." If you could call blowing someone's face off "clean."

He sat back and crossed his arms over his gut. He hit me with his best cop glare—the same one I used on suspects until they broke under the oppressive weight of silence. But I wasn't a criminal—not anymore, anyway—and I knew I'd done the right thing. In fact, if I had to do it over again I would have made the same call.

"Even if I'd waited for backup the outcome would have been the same." I looked right in his eyes. "He was immune to every defensive charm I tried. There was no stopping him without lethal force."

The captain scrubbed a hand over his face and sat up. His chair creaked in protest. "Christ, Prospero. Damned if I wouldn't have done the same thing." I opened my mouth to ask why I was getting the riot act if that was the case, but he held up a hand to stall my arguments. "Be that as it may, since this case involved deadly force, the rules dictate that I put you on suspension pending an investigation of the incident."

My mouth dropped open. "But—"

"There's not a damned thing I can do about it, so don't waste your breath. We got bigger issues to discuss."

I shook my head at him. Forcing a cop to take leave after the use of deadly force was standard procedure, but I wasn't about to sit on the sidelines with a new lethal potion on the streets.

Still, the look in his eyes told me arguing would only prolong the suspension.

"The ME identified your perp." The lightning-fast change in topic nearly gave me whiplash.

"And?" I frowned.

"His name was Ferris Harkins." The female voice surprised me from the doorway.

I swiveled to see a tall woman in a smart navy pantsuit. Her brown hair was cut in a no-nonsense bob. The lines between her brows told me they were used to frowning, and the steel in her gaze hinted at a razor-blade tongue. She wore her watch on her right wrist and her briefcase was clutched in that same hand. Whoever she was, she was definitely a lefty—just like me.

I glanced back at Eldritch. He didn't look surprised by the new arrival so much as resigned to it. He pasted his best politician smile on his lips and rose to shake her hand. "I was about to inform Officer Prospero of your interest in the case."

"That's a diplomatic way to phrase it, Captain." She turned to me. "Special Agent Miranda Gardner."

I frowned at her. "Which agency?"

She smiled tightly. "MEA."

Something heavy bounced off the base of my stomach. If the Magic Enforcement Agency was involved, things were about to get...complicated.

After a moment's hesitation, I rose and offered her my left hand. I usually offered my right to Mundanes to avoid awkwardness, but she offered me her left, which confirmed she was an Adept.

Her handclasp was brief but firm enough to tell me she meant business. When I looked down at our hands, I noticed a cabochon ring on her middle finger.

"Nice ring," I said. "Tigereye?"

She nodded and pulled her hand away. "The stone of truth and logic."

And she wore it on her Saturn finger—the finger of responsibility and security—which meant she wanted a boost in those areas. Interesting.

She tipped her chin at my wrist. "And your tattoo—Ouroboros?"

I placed my right hand over my wrist, as if the snake might jump off my skin otherwise. "A youthful transgression," I said in a flippant tone that disguised the massive understatement it really was.

Eldritch cleared his throat. I looked up to see Gardner watching me with a too-wise gaze. Either she already knew the snake swallowing its own tail was the emblem of the Votary Coven or she merely smelled the lie on me. Time to change the subject.

"Why is the MEA interested in Ferris Harkins?" I glanced at Eldritch, but he looked away.

"What your captain was about to tell you before I interrupted," Gardner said, "is that the man you killed tonight was an MEA informant."

I closed my eyes. "Fuck. Me."

"Funny, that's exactly what I said when his name popped up on ACD two hours ago as deceased."

ACD stood for the Arcane Crime Database, a federal clearinghouse of all magic-related criminal activity in the country. Actually, that's not entirely true. ACD just kept track of the illegal dirty magic. The corporate labs that produced legal, "clean" magical products, aka Big Magic, bought their legitimacy through lobbyist bribes and the generous tax revenue they generated for Uncle Sam.

I opened my eyes. "Were you aware when you recruited him that he was a hexhead with a hard-on for murder?"

"He wasn't a hexhead when we recruited him." She handed over a picture of a male. Midtwenties, scruffy with a hardness to his gaze that hinted at life on the street, but no noticeable signs of magic use—dilated pupils, scabs, etc. A far cry from the gaunt, savage creature I'd killed. A scribbled date at the bottom told me the picture had been taken a week earlier.

"Are you sure we're talking about the same guy?"

"Positive. I've just come from IDing the body."

Usually potions took several months—sometimes years—of heavy use to transform normal people into freaks and monsters. "You expect me to believe a potion turned this guy"—I held up the picture—"into the beast I shot in less than a week?"

She removed her cell from her briefcase and flashed another picture. This one was taken at the morgue. There wasn't enough face left to compare so it was impossible to use that to verify whether the identity matched the first shot. But then Gardner tapped the image to indicate a tattoo of a skull with the words *Et in Arcadia ego* underneath on the dead man's left wrist.

Frowning, I lifted the old picture again. Sure enough, the same tattoo was on Ferris Harkins's "before" picture. "The tattoo's the same. But that's hardly conclusive."

"True. However, as you'll see in the file, the identity was also confirmed through fingerprints."

I blew out a deep sigh. "Okay, so how did this guy"—I held up the first shot—"end up like this?" I held up a screen shot from the file that had been taken from my vest cam. In it Harkins looked like something from hell: a wild-eyed hellhound with bloodstained teeth.

"Four days ago, we sent Harkins to do a buy," explained Gardner. "He was supposed to meet up with one of my agents an hour later but never showed. We've been looking for him since. At first we figured he ran off with the buy money, but then this." She motioned vaguely at me as if I was the *this* in question.

My mouth fell open. "You gave a CI cash and then set him loose in the Cauldron? What the fuck did you think was going to happen?"

"Prospero," Eldritch warned.

"Sorry," I grumbled. "But what was the MEA doing setting up a buy in the Cauldron to begin with? And why didn't we know about it?"

"Forgive me, Officer," Gardner said, laughing. "I wasn't aware the federal government had to ask your permission to run investigations in Babylon."

I crossed my arms and sucked at my teeth to prevent more expletives from escaping. Eldritch wouldn't meet my eyes at all—so much for support from that quarter.

"Your actions tonight have complicated the shit out of my case," Gardner continued.

"Seems like you complicated it yourself when you lost your snitch, Special Agent."

Her eyes narrowed, but she didn't rise to the bait. "A few weeks ago, one of our agents working undercover in Canada reported that an illegal shipment of antimony was being sent to Babylon."

Antimony is a common metalloid used in everything from cosmetics to the treatment of constipation to the manufacturing of ceramics. Gardner's mention of a shipment was notable, however, because the element was also used in a lot of potions. In fact, it was so commonly used in alchemy that the government had started regulating its sale a decade earlier to try to limit street wizes' access to it.

"I don't suppose they gave you a delivery address?" I asked in a dry tone.

Gardner's lips pressed together. Guess she wasn't a fan of sarcasm. "No, but we got our team in place shortly after and have been watching things since. About a week ago, Captain Eldritch called to tell us there had been a couple of unusual assaults."

"Nothing like what happened tonight, but pretty violent," Eldritch said. "The victims had each been bitten multiple times."

"Why didn't you put it in the debriefing reports?" I demanded.

His face hardened at my challenge. "I didn't want to alarm anyone unnecessarily."

I swallowed my retort. If I had to bet, Eldritch hadn't made the report official because then his precinct would have gotten some unwanted attention from the chief and the mayor, who was up for reelection. "So you told the MEA instead?"

"Ever since Abraxas went to Crowley, the MEA has been keeping an eye on Babylon," Eldritch offered, "waiting to see who would step up to fill the power vacuum."

I snorted. "No one would be dumb enough to do that while Uncle Abe's still alive." As I spoke I kept a careful eye on Gardner to see her reaction to my casually claiming Abraxas Prospero as kin. She didn't even blink, which meant she'd known who I was before she walked into that room. Part of me was relieved not to have to explain the connection or how I'd walked away from Uncle Abe and his coven a decade earlier. In fact, the last time I'd seen him was when I watched his trial on TV with the rest of the city. During the testimony, he'd smiled at the camera like he'd been savoring a juicy secret. I shivered, shaking off the memory.

"So you figure whoever ordered that antimony is trying at least to consolidate the Votaries." I crossed my arms and tried to sort through all the angles.

Votary is another name for wizards who specialize in an alchemical form of dirty magic. In the dirty magic food chain, Votaries are at the top, followed by the Os, who specialize in sex magic, and the Sanguinarians, who deal in dirty blood potions.

"That's one of our theories." Gardner was watching me carefully now that she knew I had criminal blood in my veins.

It had been five years since Abe earned his all-expenses-paid trip to Crowley Penitentiary. Before his downfall, he'd been the grand wizard of the Votary Coven and the godfather who'd kept all the other covens in line. Once he was behind bars, no one had the balls to come forward and declare themselves the new kings of the Cauldron, so the covens splintered, which resulted in lots of turf battles. If Eldritch and Gardner were right about someone's trying to make a power play, we were looking at a lot more dead bodies piling up before this was all said and done. But that was a pretty huge *if.*

"Antimony has lots of uses besides alchemy, Special Agent."

She crossed her arms and smirked at me. "That's true, I suppose. But we've checked the official shipment manifests of every freighter that's come into Babylon in the last month. No shipments of antimony showed up. That means whoever received it was trying to keep it off the record."

"Look, even if you're right and the antimony was used in the potion Harkins was on," I countered, "it doesn't mean we're looking at consolidation of power. It could just be a new wiz who wants to make his mark."

"You could be right." She nodded. "That's one of the reasons we sent Harkins to make a buy. We were hoping that once we knew who was dealing the potion we could convince them to flip on the distributor."

"But he got hooked before he could report back to you," I said.

She nodded.

"What's the potion called?"

Gardner exchanged a tense glance with Eldritch, who'd remained tellingly silent during the exchange. No doubt about it. Special Agent Gardner was in charge. "The street name is Gray Wolf."

"Clever," I said.

"Why?" Eldritch asked. He'd worked the Arcane beat for years, but he was still a Mundane. Sometimes the intricacies of the craft eluded him.

"The gray wolf is the alchemical symbol for antimony," Gardner explained.

"Shit," I said. "If this stuff takes off, we're toast." From what I'd seen, Gray Wolf created both immunity to defensive magic and a ravenous craving for human flesh. Plus it acted incredibly fast on the user's body chemistry.

"And now that Harkins is dead, we're back at square one," Gardner said.

My stomach dipped. I didn't regret killing Harkins, but I was sorry my actions made getting the potion off the streets more difficult. "How can I help?"